D1040763

Only *Time* Will *Tell*

Sherry Lewis

JOVE BOOKS, NEW YORK

TIME PASSAGES is a registered trademark of The Berkley Publishing Corporation.

ONLY TIME WILL TELL

A Jove Book / published by arrangement with the author

PRINTING HISTORY
Jove edition / April 2003

For information address: The Berkley Publishing Group, a division of Penguin Putnam Inc., 375 Hudson Street, New York, New York 10014.

ISBN: 0-515-13366-3

A JOVE BOOK®
Jove Books are published by The Berkley Publishing Group, a division of Penguin Putnam Inc., 375 Hudson Street, New York, New York 10014. JOVE and the "J" design are trademarks belonging to Penguin Putnam Inc.

PRINTED IN THE UNITED STATES OF AMERICA

10 9 8 7 6 5 4 3 2 1

With grateful thanks to my Father above,
who guided me through the many pitfalls
I encountered in writing this book
and gently pulled me back each time I ran from it.

And to my editor, Gail Fortune,
who patiently waited as I found my way
and encouraged me to keep going.

Chapter 1

COURTNEY MOSS PUSHED open the door to her grandmother's attic and stared at the jumble of boxes, trunks, and cartons waiting for her attention. Heavy heat, trapped inside during the long summer, poured through the open door, and beads of sweat immediately formed on her nose and upper lip. Her heart sank as she took in the layer of dust on every surface—dust so thick it was clearly visible in the dim light seeping in through windows covered with years of grime.

Lowering the bucket of cleaning supplies she'd lugged up three flights of stairs, Courtney shuddered at webs of uncertain origin hanging from corners, dangling from ceiling beams, and draped across the walls. She knew it sounded horrible to complain about having to sort through her grandmother's possessions, but the timing truly couldn't have been worse.

She was due in New York on the first of October—just a little over six weeks away. She should have been in Denver putting the finishing touches on the collection of sketches that she hoped would land her the job creating cover art at Hendrickson Publishing. Instead, she was back in Montana, dealing with yet another crisis brought on by someone else's neglect, taking care of things that should have been handled months ago.

She sagged against the door frame and glanced over her shoulder at Ryan Dennehy, her best friend since second grade and the one person in her life who'd never let her down. "I should have looked up here when I was in town for Grandmother's funeral," she admitted with a sinking heart. "At least I'd have known what to expect. We'll never get all this sorted before we have to vacate."

Ryan's dark eyes gleamed behind his horn-rimmed glasses, and his narrow chin quivered with excitement. He'd come dressed to work in a pair of old jeans and the Aerosmith T-shirt he'd been wearing since high school. "Sure we will." He nudged his glasses a little higher onto his nose. "This place is amazing. I'll bet your grandmother kept everything she ever owned."

"That's not good news just now." Courtney wiped her sweaty palms on the seat of her jeans and nudged a box out of her way with her shin. Unfortunately, that dislodged several inches of dust, and that made her sneeze—not just once or twice, but half a dozen times at least. When she could speak again, she glowered over her shoulder. "Have I mentioned lately how much I resent Leslie for leaving all this for me to do?"

Ryan had covered his mouth and nose with the hem of his shirt to avoid choking on the cloud she'd created. Now he lowered it again and stepped onto the landing beside her. "Not within the last thirty seconds, but I don't know why you're surprised."

Frankly, neither did she. At twenty-seven she should have been old enough to let go of the childhood fantasies in which the woman who'd given birth to her finally began acting like a responsible human being. It wasn't ever going to happen.

Just thinking about Leslie turned Courtney's mood sour. "If I can't pull a decent presentation together because of this . . ."

Ryan waved off her concerns. "Hey! Don't worry. You brought your sketchbook, didn't you?"

"Yes, but most of my work is back home."

"So we'll do as much as we can up here during the day, and you'll work on your sketches at night, and you'll throw it all together when you get home." As if that had settled the question to everyone's satisfaction, he swept his gaze across the room and grinned. "I can't wait to find out what your grandmother was hiding away up here."

Courtney reminded herself how grateful she was for Ryan's help. She hadn't seen him since her grandmother's funeral six months earlier. Before that, it had been eight long years. He had no reason to put his own life on hold to help her, and yet he had. He hadn't changed much from the nerdy second grader who'd come to her rescue on her first day of school in a scary new place. He was still coming to her rescue—and he was still the only man alive she'd *let* rescue her.

"I'd love to let you wallow in it," she said with a grimace. "But we don't have time to go through all this junk piece by piece."

Ryan gasped and his hand flew to his chest. "Junk? I can't *believe* you just said that."

Courtney reached for her bucket again. "Value is in the heart of the owner, and I can assure you there's nothing *I* consider valuable anywhere in this house."

"That's only because you insist on holding a grudge." Ryan sidled past her and stepped over several boxes to stand in the center of the room. "If you'd learn how to forgive your mother and grandmother, you'd feel differently."

Courtney sent him a look of irritation that even the perpetually optimistic Ryan couldn't fail to understand. She'd refused to use the word *mother* since the first time Leslie dropped her on her grandmother's doorstep twenty years earlier, and she resented anyone bestowing the undeserved honor on her now.

"I'm not angry with my grandmother," she said for what surely must have been the millionth time since she'd known him. "I'm hurt. There's a big difference. And that's never going to change because she's gone." She pulled a bandanna from her back pocket and tied it over her hair. "As for forgiving Leslie, don't hold your breath. She didn't even bother to come to Grandmother's funeral. She hasn't called or written, and she won't, either. Not unless Loser Number Twelve walks out on her."

Ryan shrugged casually. "Maybe she's afraid to call you."

Courtney's sudden, sharp-edged laugh echoed through the attic. "Afraid? No, Ryan. That would mean she cared. Besides, what would she have to be afraid of?"

Ryan gave his glasses another nudge. "Gee, I don't know. . . . Your reaction, maybe?"

"If she cared about my reaction," Courtney said firmly, "she wouldn't have dumped me on Grandmother's doorstep every time she found a new boyfriend. She would have acknowledged the fact that Grandmother died in February and that she's now my only living relative. She *might* even have sent me more than three birthday cards in twenty-seven years. The only thing *she's* afraid of is not having a man in her life. I doubt Number Twelve even knows that I exist."

Just talking about Leslie made Courtney's stomach knot. Leslie had never loved her. Her grandmother had taken her in each time the need arose, but she'd made her displeasure felt. In fact, Courtney had grown up feeling like an irritant— a pebble in someone's shoe—and she'd lain awake nights as a girl, envying friends who knew they were loved and wanted, treasured members of close-knit families like Ryan's.

She'd put all that longing behind her a long time ago, but she couldn't help resenting having to put aside her own life now because Leslie couldn't even be bothered to sort through her own mother's effects. She had the very strong feeling that opening these boxes would rip apart defenses she'd struggled to put in place, and she wasn't ready or willing to do that.

Ryan turned, saw the look on her face, and scowled gently. "Hey, you okay?"

Courtney waved off his question and stepped around a leaning stack of boxes to stand beside him.

Ryan was the kindest man she'd ever known. He knew when to offer an opinion and when to shut up and listen. When to push and when to back off. He didn't suffer from that annoying need to fix everything that plagued so many men or the disgusting habit of ogling other women, which had been her last boyfriend's trademark. If Ryan had been even *slightly* interested in women, Courtney might have made a play for him. Then again, if he'd been interested in women, he wouldn't have been Ryan, and she wouldn't have felt the same way about him.

A web caught on the hem of her jeans and sent another shudder rippling through her. "I'm fine," she said, trying to dislodge the filmy strings without actually touching them. "It's not as if Grandmother and I were close."

"I know. But she was still your grandmother."

"Can we stop talking about my so-called family and just sort through this crap?" Courtney tossed a roll of garbage bags at him and peeled one from the roll she'd kept for herself. "I'll appreciate this junk a whole lot more when it's loaded on a truck and heading for the dump."

Ryan caught the garbage bags in one hand. "That's almost sacrilegious."

"No, that's honest." She lay her roll of bags aside and took another long look at the mess in front of her, hoping to get a handle on the task that lay ahead. "Why don't we take these boxes down to the trash first?" she said, motioning toward a tilting stack near the door. "That will clear some room so we can maneuver the rest of this stuff out of here." Without waiting for an answer, she hefted a box and started toward the door.

"You're really not going to look at what's inside?"

She didn't miss the quick flash of disapproval on Ryan's face, and that only made her mood worse. Even Ryan didn't know how deeply Elizabeth's disapproval had cut or how far into her heart the tendrils of Leslie's disinterest reached. "It's not as if Grandmother wanted me to have this stuff," she pointed out reasonably. "It's mine by default. So if you don't mind, let's just haul it out as fast as we can and be done with it."

"Fine," Ryan said with an elaborate shrug. "If you don't mind throwing out pieces of the past that can *never* be regained, it shouldn't bother me."

Courtney turned her back on him. "Quit trying to manipulate me."

"I'm not manipulating," Ryan said firmly. "I'm stating facts. We don't have to sort every single piece of paper, but we should at least open the boxes and see what's inside. If it looks like we've found something valuable and you don't want to deal with it, let me take it home. I'll send you a check for everything I sell."

Courtney rolled her eyes again, but Ryan had aimed straight at her Achilles' heel—and scored a hit. Money and financial security. She'd lived from paycheck to paycheck her whole life and worn other people's cast-off clothing until she was eighteen—and those were the times when she'd felt well off. In the middle of her senior year in high school, when Leslie had been living in Arizona with Loser Number Eight and Elizabeth was being unnecessarily tight with money, Courtney had had an honest-to-God Scarlett O'Hara moment. On her knees in the back garden, fist to the sky, she'd vowed that she'd never be poor again, and she'd meant it.

But she wasn't about to let Ryan know he'd scored a bull's-eye. "Whatever," she said with a casual shrug and tore open a box just to show him what a waste of time it was. She rifled through the contents and smiled with satisfaction at what she found. Dragging out a thick file folder, she wagged it in front of Ryan's face. "Tax returns from the 1960s. What do you think? Worth saving for posterity?"

Ryan held up a handful of papers from the box he'd been digging through. "Dance programs from the early twenties," he countered. "Two *very* old silk fans in *fantastic* condition, and a bundle of letters postmarked during World War II. I'll bet there's stuff from at least three different centuries in this attic."

Courtney tossed the tax returns back into the box and dragged it toward the door. "Whatever," she said again. "Just make sure you keep your treasures away from my garbage.

I'm not responsible for keeping it all straight."

Ryan laughed and went to work, and other than an occasional murmur or grunt, they didn't speak again until Ryan let out a whoop nearly two hours later. When Courtney turned to see what all the fuss was about, he held up a thick bundle of pink silk. "Look at this, Court. It looks like an old-fashioned ball gown."

Courtney spared it a brief glance and turned away. "Fascinating."

Ryan scrambled to his feet and shoved the thing at her. Smudges decorated his nose and chin, and one lens of his glasses sported a fingerprint in the center, "Hold it up, okay? Let me get a good look at it."

She sidestepped him easily. "Come on, Ryan. We don't have time to play with everything we find."

"We've been working for hours, and this is the first thing I've done more than glance at. Indulge me."

He was right, but it wasn't in Courtney's nature to lose arguments graciously. Sighing pointedly, she found the shoulders of the gown and held them up in front of her, letting yards and yards of skirt sweep to the floor.

Ryan cleaned his glasses with the hem of his shirt and let out a low whistle. "That," he whispered, "is one spectacular dress."

Deep inside, Courtney agreed with him. The rich silk shimmered, even in the low artificial light of the attic. The tiny stitches had obviously been taken by hand instead of machine, and the intricate beadwork on the low-cut bodice took her breath away, but she still wasn't willing to show signs of weakening.

She shrugged nonchalantly and started to set the gown aside. "It's probably just one of the gowns Grandmother had made for the Victorian Ball. You know how much she liked going."

Ryan eyed the fabric and Courtney with equal doubt. "You could be right, but it's not a dress *I* ever saw her wear." He touched the cloth reverently and leaned in for a closer look. "You know what? I don't think this *is* a reproduction. Judging from the style, it *could* even be a gown somebody saved from that very first ball."

"Back in eighteen sixty-four?" Courtney carefully spread the gown across the tops of several boxes she'd dusted earlier. "But it can't be. If it were authentic, it would be almost a hundred and fifty years old." She stepped back and gave the gown a lingering once-over. "Maybe it was Leslie's. It looks too big for Grandmother."

"I thought one of Elizabeth's big complaints was that Leslie never went to the ball with her."

"That doesn't mean she never had a gown made. Leslie *was* her only child, after all." Courtney shoved a hand through the air, dismissing the gown and her family along with it. "You might as well take the dress with you. I don't want it."

Ryan beamed with delight and dug around for something to store it in. "Actually, the gown looks about your size. You should try it on for fun."

"For fun?" Courtney stepped away from the gown firmly. "You have a twisted idea of 'fun,' Ryan. Knock yourself out with it. I'm getting back to work."

Ryan stood and turned halfway back. He looked as if he planned to say something more, but the gown slipped from the boxes toward the dusty floor and froze the words in his throat.

Acting purely on instinct, Courtney caught the dress in her arms. Without warning, the attic faded and an image of herself wearing the gown replaced it. She'd worn her hair short and spiky since her eighteenth birthday, but this version of herself had long hair with thick dark ringlets dancing on her bare shoulders. The room darkened, and she could have sworn that candlelight flickered on the walls. The soft strains of a waltz filled the air along with the stench of cigar smoke and wind.

She gasped, trying to fill her lungs and shake off the trance. Someone moved on the edge of her vision and she turned eagerly, hoping that seeing Ryan would help.

A man she didn't recognize stepped out of the shadows and took her hand in his. She couldn't see his face clearly, but he looked at her with eyes as clear blue as a summer sky, grinned broadly, and evaporated into the shadows again.

The instant he disappeared, air rushed back into Courtney's lungs. She felt the gown slip from her arms and the rest of the vision faded. She was back in the attic with Ryan . . . and he was staring at her as if she'd suddenly grown a third arm.

Laughing uneasily, Courtney backed away from the dress. "Is it hot in here, or is it just me?"

"It's warm," Ryan said uncertainly. "Are you okay?"

"I'm not sure. Did you see anything odd?"

"Just the look on your face. What happened?"

She shook her head and rubbed her temples with her fingertips. "I'm not sure," she said again. "It was the weirdest thing." She glanced at the gown and realized how foolish she'd sound if she admitted the delusion aloud. Anyway, she was probably just overheated and hungry. "I saw my life flash in front of my eyes," she said with a tight laugh. "I think that means we need to eat before we do anything else."

Ryan gathered the yards of material and began folding the dress carefully. "I thought you'd never be ready for a break. What sounds good to you?"

Courtney headed for the door. "Steak and potatoes. A hot roast beef sandwich and fries." She started down the stairs and called back over her shoulder, "Anything as long as it's substantial."

"You know what I think you should do?" Ryan asked as he trudged down the stairs behind her. "You should wear this gown to the Victorian Ball this weekend."

"I don't think so. Pink is *not* my signature color." She stopped on the third-floor landing, where the air was a whole lot cooler and substantially fresher. "Besides, I'm not going to the ball this year."

Ryan stopped just behind her. "You're kidding, right?"

"Actually, I'm not."

"But the Victorian Ball is a tradition, and you're here for the first time in forever. You *have* to go."

"I don't *have* to do anything," she said sharply, then tempered her voice with a smile. "I went when I lived here because Grandmother made me, not because I enjoyed it. One of the best parts of moving away was that I didn't have to dress up in some froufrou dress and play 'let's pretend' all night."

"It's once a year, not every week."

"That's still once a year too often."

Ryan's smile faded and disappointment clouded his eyes. He wore Courtney's least favorite expression—hurt and betrayal mixed with a dash of self-righteous indignation. "You're too good for us, is that it?"

Courtney growled in frustration. "That's not what I said. The ball's just not my cup of tea. You *know* that."

Still holding the bundle of silk, Ryan pushed past her and headed down the stairs to the second-floor landing.

She had to grab the railing and take the stairs two at a time to keep up with him. "Come on, Ryan. Don't act like that."

"Like what?"

"Like I just broke your favorite toy."

He didn't break stride as he headed toward the main floor. "Why would I be upset just because you suddenly want to change a tradition we've followed our entire lives?"

"One we've followed under protest."

"*I* happen to enjoy the ball. I thought you did, too."

"I *hated* going. The only reason I did was to keep Grandmother happy."

Ryan strode into the foyer and laid the gown over one of Elizabeth's wing-back chairs. "So go to make *me* happy this year. Who knows when we'll get another chance to go together?"

Courtney sagged onto the bottom step and hugged her knees, scowling petulantly even though she knew her reaction was a bit childish. Ryan had taken vacation time from work to help her. She really couldn't say no.

"You're right," she said, forcing a smile. "And I'm sorry. If it'll make you happy, I'll go to the ball."

Ryan's petulant look matched her own. "Don't do it just to placate me."

Courtney gripped the banisters and pulled herself to her

feet again. "But I *am* doing it to placate you, silly. And that's exactly what you want me to do. I'm also agreeing because I'm starving to death. I'm afraid that if I *don't* agree, I'll waste away to nothing before we get out the front door."

Ryan grinned victoriously. "Does that mean you'll wear the dress?"

She rolled her eyes in exasperation. "Just say we can eat lunch sometime today, and I'll wear anything you want me to." She checked her pockets for money and keys and waved him toward the door. "Can we go now, please?"

Still grinning, Ryan slipped out the door. Courtney followed, reaching behind her at the last minute to turn out the light. Something brushed her fingers as she pushed the switch, and in that instant before the light died and shadows filled the foyer, she could have sworn she saw the man from the attic bending over her hand. Adding to the delusion, a breeze from somewhere felt almost like the soft caress of lips on her fingers.

She jerked her hand away and slammed the door on the shadowy figure. But she couldn't shake the uneasy feeling that followed her as she hurried toward her Accord in the driveway. Maybe her grandmother's death had affected her more than she'd thought. Or maybe the dust had gotten to her brain. Or maybe she'd been right all along. There was a Pandora's box in the attic . . . and Ryan had opened it.

On Saturday night Courtney stood at the back of the overcrowded city gym, holding a glass of punch in one hand and the skirt of her pink gown in the other. Red, white, and blue banners draped between gigantic pine and flower wreaths on the walls, one of which kept catching the phony ringlets Ryan's sister Dee had pinned to the back of Courtney's hair that afternoon. She looked ridiculous and she felt terribly self-conscious, but tonight wasn't about her. Tonight was for Ryan.

She sipped from the cup she held, made a face at the sweet punch, and set the cup aside. Her head throbbed, her back ached, and the corset she'd been forced to wear so the dress would fit had her afraid of throwing up if she moved too fast. On the dance floor men and women whirled and swayed to the Virginia reel, and the sound of countless feet sliding and thudding on the floor kicked the ache in her head up another notch.

She'd been fighting a headache ever since that first day in the attic. She didn't know if she might be fighting her first migraine or just feeling the results of stress, but nothing seemed to make it feel better. Maybe she should take advantage of this quiet moment to slip outside before Ryan finished dancing with his sister and came looking to Courtney for another waltz.

She maneuvered through the crowd and ducked outside, dragging twenty yards of silk through doors that had been propped open with cinder blocks. After the heavy press of people inside, the cool summer night felt like heaven on her skin. She stepped into the shadows and wrapped her arms around herself, turning slowly and taking in the town and the sage-stubbled sweep of surrounding hillsides glowing beneath the moon and stars.

She'd grown up in this town—as close as she'd come to growing up anywhere—and she would probably always feel some kind of attachment to it. But she'd never truly belonged here, and she probably wouldn't come back now that Elizabeth was gone. Ryan was the only thing she'd miss about this place.

She walked slowly, grimacing when a pebble poked through the thin-soled pink dancing slippers she'd found in the attic, and wondering what the first Grand Ball—held smack in the middle of the gold rush and the Civil War—had been like.

The citizens of Virginia City did their best to copy that night every year, but she was sure that a population of sixty, plus tourists, couldn't even come close to re-creating the energy and noise of ten thousand miners, thieves, and prostitutes.

Smiling ruefully, she rounded another corner and the music faded even further, eventually giving way to gentle cricket songs and the sounds of gunfire from some cop or cowboy show on a nearby TV. She thought of her grandmother and wished, as she often did, that things could have been different between them.

If it had only been earlier in the day, she might have walked to her favorite spot along Alder Creek to think. But in this gown and slippers, she'd never make it. As she turned back toward the gym, she caught the beam of a strange light coming from an old storage shed in the empty field behind the gym.

Curious, she turned toward it. As she watched, the light spread from the floor to the ceiling, and within seconds the entire door glowed in an almost fluorescent purple light in the darkened sky.

How odd.

She started across the uneven ground toward the shed, and realized that the light was pulsing. Brighter, darker, brighter, darker, it seemed to change with every step she took. But that was silly. It must seem that way because she was moving.

Unless it wasn't light at all, but fire.

That possibility got her moving faster. A person couldn't spend even part of a lifetime in a town where the past is so carefully and painstakingly preserved, and not take the threat of fire seriously. One careless blaze could wipe out years of history and spell disaster for the whole city.

It took only a few seconds to reach the shed. She touched the door cautiously, just the way she'd been taught in school, to check for heat. The plank door was cool to the touch, which meant if there *was* a fire inside, it wasn't raging out of control. It might even be something she could put out with a fire extinguisher.

She checked the knob next, found it cool as well, and jerked open the door, shielding her face with one arm just in case. But there was no fire inside, only a brilliant white light that pulsed like a special effect from a movie and a gentle force that exerted a tug, as if someone or something was trying to pull her inside.

She resisted, of course. She wasn't about to walk into the shed like a bad actress in a cheap horror movie. But the more she resisted, the more forceful the pressure became. One minute it felt as if someone was pulling her toward the light; the next, as if someone was pushing from behind. She glanced over her shoulder, hoping to find that Ryan had come looking for her, but the narrow strip of field was empty and she couldn't see anyone on the street, either.

The light seemed to be coming from every direction now. Above her. Behind. Even shining up from beneath her feet. She was surrounded by its rays, caressed by a warm breeze. She tried backing up, but the force grew even stronger. She stepped forward, trying to break its hold, but she couldn't feel the floor beneath her feet.

Everything seemed to have disappeared—everything, that is, but the light. She shielded her eyes, but she still couldn't see. She called out for help, but the most complete silence she'd ever heard swallowed the sound. The only thing she heard was the door slamming shut behind her.

Courtney would have been lying if she'd said that she wasn't nervous. No, nervous wasn't nearly strong enough. She was terrified. With the door closed, the pressure ceased and the blinding light faded, but the sudden eerie darkness was absolute and ominous.

She whipped around and groped for the doorknob, but she couldn't find it. She couldn't feel *anything* on the door. No hinges. No knob. Only splinters as her fingers ran along the weathered wood.

This was not funny.

She tried to keep her sudden panic under control as she pounded on the door and shouted for help, but the strange silence swallowed every sound she made even before she could hear it. Images danced in front of her eyes, forming and fading in rhythm with her pulse.

The man from the attic swirled in front of her, followed by an image of herself in the gown, people she'd never seen before, and people who looked vaguely familiar. Her heart hammered and the only sound she could hear was a deep electrical pulse that kept time with her heartbeat.

She could feel the walls closing in on her, the floor rising up toward her, but she tried desperately not to panic. "Open the door!" she cried out. "*Please?* If anyone is out there, could you please help me? I'm stuck and I'm getting claustrophobic."

Silence was her only answer.

She pounded on the door with the flat of her palm, then her fist. The sensation of being suffocated was so intense, she threw herself into the door, kicking with all her might and screaming as loud as she could. But nothing happened and no one answered.

Unbelievable as it seemed, she was stuck inside until someone came along to rescue her.

Chapter 2

VIRGINIA CITY, MONTANA TERRITORY
AUGUST 1864

THE EERIE SOUND *of baying hounds echoed, then faded to nothing. A man, the quarry, raced like the wind toward a tree. Thundering hooves kept time with the beating of his heart.*

He was on the ground, then, in a blink, high overhead in the branches of a tree; the only part of him visible was a pair of wide, dark eyes. Frightened and angry, he searched the ground. He waited, not even daring to breathe, while the first of the hounds streaked past. Relief flashed through him, so strong he nearly lost his grip on the branch, but the relief lasted only a second before the hounds circled and came to rest beneath him. Baying. Baying.

On the ground the hunter dismounted and swaggered toward the hounds. The journey seemed to take forever, and with every step the pounding heartbeat grew louder. Slowly, slowly, the hunter lifted his gaze and met the wide, frightened eyes of the man above his head. . . .

With a gasp, Heath Sullivan bolted upright and stared at his surroundings. His entire body shook and sweat ran in rivulets down his chest. It took a second or two for him to fully comprehend that he was safe.

The hangover hit in the next breath, the second he registered that he wasn't in the dream tree or standing beneath it. The instant he realized that dingy white curtains fluttered at an open window above his head, not moss threading through the branches of ancient live oak trees. That the scent of newly cut lumber and old whiskey filled his nostrils instead of the distinctive smell of the swamp.

He buried his face in his hands, hating the hangover, hating the dream . . . hating himself most of all. His head throbbed as the baying of hounds receded and the lazy buzz of black flies replaced it. His labored breathing slowed as he glanced around and remembered the room bit by tawdry bit. Now if he could just remember the woman who'd come with it.

He lay back on the mattress and squinted at the narrow sagging bed, the lone rickety chair in front of a makeshift dressing table covered with a faded scarf, one gown on a peg near the door. He rubbed his eyes and vaguely remembered stumbling up the stairs of the Pink Parasol behind Sloe-Eyed Sally.

He'd been nearly too drunk to stand but not so drunk that he could escape the memories that had caught him unaware earlier that afternoon. In his diminished capacity, trying to lose himself in a woman's softness had actually seemed like a good idea. He should have known that once the memories came back, nothing could kill them except time.

Sally was already gone, thank God. But the pounding in his head was not. In fact, it got worse every minute he was awake. He swore under his breath, tried swallowing around his swollen, cotton-dry tongue, and dragged himself upright to sit on the edge of the bed.

Keeping his eyes partially closed, he felt along the small table beside him for the bottle he could have sworn he'd left there. A little hair of the dog . . . the best cure he knew.

After several minutes his fingers curled around the bottle. He lifted it. Realized that it was empty. Tossed it onto the bed with another curse.

Either he'd polished off the whiskey without remembering or Sally had helped herself—and he'd bet on the latter. He'd been in town only a few days, but it had taken only a few minutes to discover what a greed-soaked place it was. Folks would do or say anything if they thought it might put a speck of gold dust into their pouch. Hell, half of 'em practically refused to breathe unless someone tossed gold dust into the air first.

Considering how much Heath despised greed and those who allowed it to rule their lives, he couldn't have found a more despicable place if he'd tried for a hundred years. He couldn't wait to get the hell out of here.

Sounds roared in through chinks in the wood and gaps around the window. Tinny music from a dozen different saloons clashed unharmoniously, and shouts of jubilant prospectors mingled with exclamations of angry ones to form the harmony.

Trying to ignore the grit in his eyes and the drum inside his head, Heath searched the floor for his trousers. He found them at the foot of the bed, checked the pockets for the change Red Will had shoved at him across the bar a few hours earlier, and scowled when he encountered nothing but lint.

Damn Sally, anyway.

Working unsteadily, he pulled on his trousers and boots, slipped into his shirt, and settled his hat low over his eyes. Five minutes later he clattered down the stairs and found Sally sitting with Fat Nell at a table near the bar. It was well after midnight on a Sunday morning, and though business would usually have been brisk at this hour, most folks were high-stepping at the Grand Ball across town and the saloon was nearly empty.

Both ladies wore wrappers over their undergarments, but they were so sheer they qualified as clothes in name only. Nell's gaped open to reveal a set of lightly freckled breasts so full and ripe even the most cynical of men couldn't doubt God's mercy. But the Lord's bounty stopped at her neck. Pale hair hung in tired curls to her shoulders, and even thick face paint didn't make her attractive.

Sally didn't look much better. There'd been a time just before Heath had passed out when he'd made the mistake of looking into her eyes, and he'd glimpsed a young woman beneath the rouge and powder. Now that girl had disappeared again, and the years sat heavily on the woman's shoulders.

Strands of thin red hair fell from the bun she wore high on her head, and her face looked pale and drawn. Like Nell, Sally's charms weren't in her face. She'd been blessed with a set of curves and dips and swells that ran from head to toe, far more generous than most women would ever know and most men could ever hope for.

Heath tugged the brim of his hat down further over his eyes and started toward their table. Sally looked up at him with supreme disinterest and shared an annoyed glance with Nell. "Well, well, well. If it ain't Bonnie Prince Charming."

"Ladies." Heath tugged on his hat and forced a smile. He hated the nickname Sally had christened him with, but he wasn't going to waste time arguing about it. He had bigger fish to fry. "You want to return the two dollars you helped yourself to last night?"

Sally didn't even bother to look guilty. "Why should I? You owed it to me."

"Did I?" Heath scratched above one ear as if she'd confused him. "You'll have to help me out here. I remember paying you before we even went upstairs."

"Oh, you paid me all right." Sally gave her limp curls a toss and shared another smile with Nell. "And you paid well enough I suppose, considering the performance you gave— or should I say *didn't* give."

Heath resisted the mild urge to defend his honor. Judging from the way he felt, his performance probably hadn't been inspiring.

"Not that I'm disappointed," Sally went on. "I don't expect much when it comes to that. But I warned you that I don't let men stay in my bed all night long, and you've been up there for nearly four hours. You cost me business, Charming. I took the two dollars to pay for it."

Heath smiled sheepishly and checked his pocket watch.

"Looks like you have a point, ma'am. I must have been more tired than I thought."

She raked her gaze the length of him and curled her lip. "Not from anything you did with *me*. But, then, if you'd gotten your money's worth on *that* score, you'd owe me more than two measly dollars."

Heath chuckled, somewhat relieved to learn that he'd at least had class enough to pass out before consummating his mistake. "I hope you'll accept my sincere apology, ma'am. And if you'll give me enough to buy a shot of whiskey for the road, I'll be more than happy to call it even."

Sally's mouth pursed and she shook her head. "Nothing doing, Charming. Two dollars is little enough as it is."

"Maybe, but it's all I have with me."

"Yeah?" Sally flapped a hand at him. "Well, it's mine now. I need it a whole lot more'n you need whiskey."

"No doubt you're right about that, as well." Heath tugged off his hat, straddled a chair, and worked up his most winning smile. It wasn't as if he was destitute, after all. He still had most of the cash he'd been paid to come to Virginia City, but that money was hidden beneath a floorboard in the cabin he'd been using since his arrival, and he wanted to spare himself the long trek back through town to get it. "I'm appealing to your woman's heart. I'm asking you to have mercy on an ailing man."

Nell snorted a laugh and leaned back in her chair. "We've seen men like you in action, Charming. If you have one shot, you'll want another. Two, and you'll need four. Before you know it, the whole two dollars'll be gone and Sally'll have nothing at all—not even a memory."

"Ladies! I beg you not to condemn me for what others have done. My need is purely medicinal. I wouldn't ask otherwise."

"Your need is pure hangover," Sally said with a harsh laugh. "Why don't you go home? You look like hell, Charming, and *that's* the truth. Will's bringing in some new girls in a few days. Maybe you can convince one of them to let you slide."

Heath might have laughed, but a sudden, sharp pain exploded in his head, sending a bolt of lightning from the back of his neck to the tips of his toes. He wrapped his arms around the chair's back and rested his chin on his hands. "You wound me, Sally. But we're straying from the point."

"If you want tea and sympathy," Nell snarled, "go somewhere else. We need to make a living here." She turned sideways on her chair, a clear sign that she thought Sally should stop listening.

Sally folded her arms high across her chest. "Nell's right. You should go . . . unless you want me to tell Olaf that you're bothering us."

Heath's head might be filled with cotton, but he hadn't lost all sense. The last thing he needed was trouble from the huge, bald-headed bouncer who'd already started glowering at him from across the room.

He stood unsteadily, tipped his hat to the ladies, and shoved his hands into his pockets, then sauntered outside before Olaf decided to use his poor, aching head as a battering ram. The night air cleared away some of the cobwebs, but the cacophony of discordant sound that seemed to be so much a part of this city made him ache all over.

If he hadn't needed to wait until morning to get Warrior from the livery, he'd have ridden out now and slept under a tree somewhere along the trail. It wouldn't have been the first time, and it wouldn't be the last. For the past five years he'd been wandering the West without purpose, landing wherever the wind blew him, hiring himself out for whatever jobs were available—as long as they didn't threaten to tie him down. He'd stay for a few days in some towns, a few weeks in others, but he avoided anyplace that might lure him to stay.

Most of the time a bottle and a bed were the only things he cared about, but lately the hankering to settle down, to find a place to call home, had been cropping up at the most unexpected times.

Like now.

He shrugged off the urge as he always did, though it was getting harder and harder to simply ignore it. Maybe he'd settle down some day. Some far distant day when he was an old man and the pain of his youth had faded enough to let him stop running. But it was for damn sure he wouldn't land here. Not in this sad collection of tents and cabins, this wallow of dirt and mud, this accumulation of lost souls, bed of iniquity, den of thieves.

Fourteen miles of heartache and greed lay along Alder Gulch, with Virginia City the largest of all the towns that bled one into another. No sir, Fourteen-Mile City, as many called it, was the *last* place Heath would consider settling down—if he was going to consider it at all.

Which he wasn't.

He wound through the city, past tented communities and new construction, to the squat cabin that had once belonged to Ellis Bailey. Inside, he resisted the urge to collapse on the bed, lit a lantern, and pried up the floorboard instead. If he went back to bed now, he'd just dream again. He didn't want that. In fact, if he was smart, he'd take everything with him and kill the hours until the livery opened at a poker table. It would save time in the long run.

Within minutes he was back on the street carrying everything he owned in his hands or his pockets. He stuffed the watch he'd been sent here to retrieve for Ellis Bailey's widow into the deep pocket of his coat and whistled softly as he walked. Just a few more hours and this godforsaken place would be nothing but a memory.

He'd only gone a few blocks when the usual sounds of music, laughter, and gunfire were sliced open by angry shouting. He could have ignored that, but the next noise he heard sent icy water through his veins. He'd have known the crack of a whip anywhere. Even after all these years it still made him nauseated.

Shivering slightly, he turned away from the sound and told himself that it could have been anything. Someone trying to convince a mule or an ox to move. Someone showing off his ability to snap a twig at forty paces. He almost had himself convinced when a cry of pain rent the air and told him the gut-wrenching truth.

This time he couldn't pretend he hadn't heard it. He turned back toward the sound and broke into a run. Within seconds his heartbeat matched the one from his dream. His throat burned and his stomach heaved with the effort of breathing and keeping his fear in check at the same time.

Images he'd been trying to forget floated in front of his eyes as he ran. A humid night. A set of dark hands tied to a tree. The keening of heartbroken women—one of whom had been as close to Heath as his own mother. Closer, even, if he told God's honest truth.

Bile rose in his throat and threatened to choke him, but he didn't let himself stop running until he saw a knot of four or five people surrounding someone or something in the center of their circle. The ugly sound of cruel laughter lashed with as much venom as the whip.

Heath tossed aside his bag and ground to a halt as the overhead clouds parted and the moonlight glinted off of the whip raised for another assault. He didn't even stop to think. He couldn't. Bursting forward, he caught the lash in his hand and jerked with all his might.

The element of surprise worked in his favor, and the whip's handle sailed out of the hand of a tall, ugly-faced, and foul-spirited man. Heath let go of the lash and gripped the handle tightly as those nearest him slowly realized that someone had interrupted their fun. Two of the men edged into the shadows. The two remaining stepped aside to let their ringleader through.

The jackass took a long, slow look at the whip and spat a stream of tobacco onto the ground near Heath's foot. "You got a problem, mister?"

Heath spotted their target then—a grizzled little miner with a skiff of white beard across his chin and a shock of matching hair on his head. By the light of a lantern someone in the crowd held aloft, Heath could see that the man's clothes were torn and full of holes, the soles of his boots worn through. The old guy cowered with his arms over his face, as if he hadn't yet realized that his torment had stopped.

"Touch him again," Heath warned, "and you'll get a taste of your own medicine."

"Is that right?" A vile sneer stretched across the ringleader's face as the foul man sauntered toward him. "You think you're big enough to take on all five of us?"

"Count again," Heath suggested. "I think I can handle three."

"Do ye?" The man shared a look with his two cohorts and laughed. "You really think you're man enough to square off against Tyree Caine and his boys?"

"If I have to be."

The old man chose that moment to look up, and the expression in his eyes sent a shock of recognition through Heath. He'd seen that look a hundred times in his dreams over the past five years. No amount of whiskey had taken it away. No amount of running had dulled it.

But letting himself be distracted, even for a minute, was a big mistake. He heard the footstep behind him a split-second too late. The instant the sound registered, something connected with the back of his head, light exploded in front of his eyes, and the world went black as he felt himself crumple to the ground.

Heath regained consciousness with agonizing slowness. He could feel himself waking up, but he couldn't seem to make his eyes open or his arms and legs move for what felt like forever. When he finally pried one eye open, pain lanced through his head and shot down his neck, and he immediately wished for oblivion again.

He closed the eye and lay there, breathing dust, until he had to admit that he was awake for good. But the hammering in his head and the sour taste in his mouth made him nostalgic for the hangover he'd been cursing just a short time earlier.

Moving with agonizing deliberation, he inched one hand and then the other beneath his chest, then pushed to his knees. That, of course, made the agony worse, and he had to cradle his head in his hands for a long time before he could finally get to his feet.

He staggered a bit, then found a wall to lean against while he took inventory. He touched the back of his skull, winced, and brought his hand away. Hell would have probably felt better than his head did at that moment, but at least he wasn't bleeding. He checked his breast pocket next and discovered the three cigars he'd tucked there earlier, which gave him courage enough to slip his hand into the pockets of his trousers.

The *empty* pockets of his trousers.

Stunned with disbelief, he tried again, but his pockets were still empty. He checked his coat pockets quickly, but everything was gone. His money. Ellis Bailey's watch. Everything.

He cursed aloud, kicked a rock, and cursed again when pain shot through his foot and up his leg. And when he realized that the bag containing his clothes had disappeared along with everything else, he let out a roar of frustration and anger. The only thing he had to his name were the clothes on his back and three cigars in his breast pocket. He didn't even have enough money to get Warrior out of the livery stable so he could leave.

Still swearing under his breath, he pulled one of the cigars from his pocket and lit it. That pause was just enough to make him realize that the pounding he could hear wasn't all in his head. He even thought he heard a muffled shout from somewhere nearby.

He stopped and listened, told himself he'd only imagined the voice, and reminded himself what came of playing Good Samaritan. He turned to walk in the other direction, but the shout came again, and this time he realized that the voice belonged to a woman. Heath drew to a stop again, struck a Lucifer, and held it aloft. He spied a small shed deep in the shadows just as another volley of frantic-sounding bangs erupted followed by, "Dammit! This isn't funny. Would someone *please* let me out?"

Heath moved a little closer to the shed, still arguing with himself about the wisdom of attempting another rescue. "Who's in there?"

The pounding stopped and the voice inside changed from frantic to excited. "You can hear me? Oh, thank God. Please. The latch is stuck and I can't get out. I'm terrified of small places. Please *help* me."

Heath wondered if it was a trick, then reminded himself that he had nothing but his life and three cigars left to lose.

Slowly he lifted the latch, then gave a sharp tug. He expected resistance, but the latch lifted easily, and before he could so much as take a step backward, the door swung open and a bundle of perfume and silk tumbled out of the door and straight into his arms.

He stumbled under the unexpected weight, and the woman's flailing arms hit his as she landed against him. His burning cigar flew out of his hand and into the tinder dry weeds at his feet. Without thinking, he shoved the woman aside and scoured the dry grass for the smoldering fire.

She landed with an *oomph* just as he spied the burning end of his cigar, and she swore at him as he ground out the fire with the heel of his boot. He ignored her and kicked dirt over the embers to make sure the whole city wouldn't go up in flames.

Finally satisfied, he turned toward the woman, expecting a warm thank you. Instead, he found her glowering at him from beneath a tumbled mass of dark curls that had slipped to one side of her head and all but obscured her eyes. Her knees were bent, her skirts in disarray and showing a healthy expanse of trim ankle and even a bit of shapely leg.

But it was the anger burning in her eyes that held Heath's attention because it seemed, unbelievably, to be directed at him.

After everything else he'd been through already? After he'd risked life and limb to save her? *This* was the thanks he got? Unbelievable. Absolutely un-be-damn-lievable. Some days it just didn't pay to wake up.

Shaking with fear, anger, and frustration, Courtney glared up at the man who'd let her out of the shed and then tossed her to the ground like a sack of potatoes. If there was anything wrong with her, he'd pay the doctor bills. Not that he looked like he *could* pay.

He was a large man with the broad shoulders, sturdy chest, and solid thighs of an athlete . . . and the wardrobe of a Wild West derelict. Dark blond hair curled wildly from beneath a dusty black cowboy hat and brushed the worn collar of his dirty jacket. A thick beard covered his cheeks and chin, and she detected the unmistakable odor of alcohol on his breath.

Lovely.

Fate had finally gotten around to assigning her a knight in shining armor, and *this* is what it sent her. Not that she'd expected anything else. She'd watched a dozen Boy Wonders swagger into and out of Leslie's life in the past two decades, and she knew the drill. They acted like superheroes at first, full of big ideas and lots of talk about how they were going to make life better. That lasted a week or two and then their real colors started to show. It hadn't taken Courtney long to catch on. Leslie still hadn't.

"Well," she said in a voice dripping with sarcasm. "*That* was fun. Thanks a lot."

The man looked her over and had the nerve to look equally unimpressed with what he saw. "You're quite welcome."

"I was being sarcastic." She tried to stand, but the wide bell of her skirts knocked her back into the dirt. Growling in frustration, she stuck her legs out in front of her and slapped down the skirt with both hands. "Why in the hell did you throw me on the ground?"

He seemed to finally realize that she needed help and offered a hand that looked roughly the size of a baseball mitt. "Because I dropped my cigar when you fell on me. I didn't want to be responsible for setting the city on fire."

"Oh. Well, I guess that's all right, then." She slid her free hand into his, and he pulled her to stand in front of him. The top of her head barely skimmed the bottom of his nose, which left her feeling smaller and even more vulnerable than she had before.

His gaze swept across her face, dropped to her neckline as her breasts settled back into place, and then lifted to her hair, which probably looked as if someone had run it through a food processor. He dragged his gaze away from her and scowled at the dark interior of the shed. "Do you mind telling me what you were doing inside there?"

"I'm not sure," Courtney admitted. "I saw a weird light and decided to investigate. The door shut behind me and I couldn't get out." She gave another annoyed push at the curls

Dee had pinned to her head and forced a smile at her rescuer. "I suppose I should thank you."

The man shrugged and patted the pockets of his old-fashioned jacket gently. "In that case, I suppose I should say that you're welcome . . . again." He stopped patting and glanced around the field with a frown. "Are you out here alone?"

"Yes, but my friend Ryan is inside waiting for me."

"Inside?" He took another look around. "Inside where?"

"He's at the ball." Courtney gestured toward the city gym and noticed for the first time that the gym wasn't there. Certain that she'd gotten turned around, she pivoted to look behind her, but all she saw was an empty field and the shed she'd just fallen out of. "What's going on here?"

His brows knit. "You don't remember?"

"I remember being at the Victorian Ball and stepping outside for some fresh air. I remember seeing what I thought was a fire in the shed and getting locked in. What I *don't* understand is what happened to the city gym."

"You do remember that you're in Virginia City?"

"Am I? Well, that's a relief."

"Far as I know, this town doesn't have a city gym."

"Well, it does. Trust me. But it should be right there." Courtney turned slowly, looking for something familiar and wondering if she could possibly have fallen through a trapdoor without realizing it. "What street is this?"

"I wouldn't know."

"That's helpful." Courtney rubbed her temples and took a long look at the street behind her. Slowly she began to make out the shape of a small, familiar house on the opposite corner of the narrow street and a sense of uneasiness began to overshadow everything else. "That's Merk House, isn't it?"

"I don't know."

"No. It is. I recognize it. But that means that Wallace Street should be over there, and the city gym should be *right here*." Her headache kicked up again and she rubbed her temples a little harder. "And the Methodist church should be there. But it's not." She scowled into the star-filled sky. "Why is it so dark? It's hard to see."

"Ah!" Her rescuer grinned broadly. "*Finally* a question I can answer. I *believe* it's dark because it's nearly two o'clock in the morning."

"That's not what I mean," Courtney snapped. Her uneasiness grew and she took a step backward. "Who are you, anyway?"

The man tipped his hat. "Heath Sullivan. And you are . . . ?"

"Courtney Moss."

"A pleasure, Miss Moss."

"Courtney," she corrected automatically, and turned slowly in her tracks. "Okay. I must be tired. That's the only answer. I'm stressed out. There's the interview in New York and sorting through grandmother's things. I'm just seeing things—or *not* seeing things. But it's stress. I know it is. So if you'll just tell me how to find my way back to the ball, I'll let you get back to what you were doing."

"I thought you wanted to find your friend."

"I do. But his Suburban was parked right there and now it's gone, which means he's either home already or he's at my grandmother's house looking for me." The thought of walking across town in the middle of the night made her a little sick, so she decided to take a chance she might not otherwise have taken. "I don't suppose you'd be willing to give me a ride home? It's not far, but that little stint in the shed wore me out."

Heath pushed back the brim of his hat and eyed her thoughtfully. "I don't know if you've noticed, ma'am, but I'm on foot myself."

"You don't have a car?"

He shook his head slowly. "Or a buckboard, or a carriage, or a buggy."

Courtney forced a tight smile. "Cute. So I guess that means you don't have a white steed, either? What kind of knight in shining armor *are* you?"

Heath stared at her, uncomprehending, for a moment. Then, "I'm not a knight in shining armor, ma'am. I'm just a man who opened the door to a shed and let you out."

Great. A knight with no sense of humor. "Fine. Well, it's

been a real kick meeting you, but I'm tired, and if you won't give me a lift, I'm out of here." She headed toward Wallace Street where the faint glow of light gave her some hope that she'd find someone who could give her a ride.

For some reason, Heath decided to trail after her, but he looked more curious than threatening, so she didn't let him bother her. But once she reached Virginia City's main street, Heath slipped way down on her list of things to worry about.

Wallace Street was as unrecognizable as everything else she'd seen since she fell out of that shed. The paved road was gone and a long stretch of dirt reached from one end of town to the other. Empty lots gaped in places where buildings should have been, and the skeletons of new structures reached toward the night sky on the very lots where historical buildings had existed for longer even than her grandmother had been around.

It might have been two o'clock in the morning, but the streets teemed with activity—and not the usual summer swarm of tourists, either. Horses and wagons traveled along the dirt road, and every soul in sight wore a period costume similar to Heath's.

There wasn't a single car or SUV anywhere. Not a pair of sandals or hairy white legs in sight. No video or digital cameras. No soda cans, empty cigarette packages, or gum wrappers. No country music or hip-hop playing from someone's car stereo, just the scrape of fiddle and the plink of piano music from saloons that had long ago been converted into other businesses.

No electric lights or the blue glow of televisions, just the glow of oil lamps and the flare of campfires dotting the hills covered by a city of white tents and temporary structures that seemed to fill every inch of land.

Courtney tried to swallow, but her throat was tight and swollen. A strange numbing spread from her fingers up her arms and into her shoulders. She glanced back at Heath, who lounged against the wall of a very new-looking Wells Fargo office and didn't seem to notice anything out of the ordinary.

The entire town had changed in the blink of an eye. It looked different, sounded different, even *smelled* different.

She tried to convince herself that this was a dream, but there was nothing dreamlike about it. She told herself it was an elaborate joke at her expense, but no one could have pulled this off, and no one had a reason to. But that left . . .

No! That was not an option. It wasn't even possible. Forget all the strange things that had been happening since Ryan unearthed this dress. Forget the floating images and her overactive imagination. People did *not* travel through time. Especially not in rickety old sheds.

Determined to prove it, she dodged a pair of staggering prospectors and moved closer to Heath. "Can I ask you a question?"

"If you'd like."

"What is the date today?"

His glance traveled to a poster, a corner of which she could see flapping in the evening breeze. "If you were at the ball, it has to be Saturday."

"The date," she pressed. "What is the *date*?"

Heath's eyes narrowed slightly. "I believe it's the twentieth . . . of August."

Courtney yanked the poster from the wall. She'd seen hundreds of similar advertisements over the years. The wording on every one was identical. Hostilities would be set aside for the evening. Insults, fighting, and profanity would not be tolerated. Weapons, other than swords, would be held at the door. There was absolutely nothing to set this announcement apart . . . except one small detail.

The Grand Ball of Virginia City, it said, would be held on Saturday, August 20th . . . *1864.*

Chapter 3

NOISE ROARED IN Courtney's ears and her blood seemed to thicken and move slowly through her body. She crumpled the poster in her fist and tossed it away. "You have *got* to be kidding."

Heath stared at her in confused silence, which didn't help.

She grabbed him by the collar and shook him, as if she might be able to jar his pickled brain into working, so she could get an explanation that made sense. "Tell me this is a joke. Somebody's cruel idea of a practical joke. Who's doing this? Is it Ryan? I want to know *right now*."

Heath covered her hands with his and unknotted her fingers from his shirt. "Maybe you should tell me what's upset you."

"Isn't it *obvious*?"

"Not to me."

Courtney searched his eyes for proof that he was part of a hoax. His gaze remained steady and unblinking, so either he didn't know anything about the joke or booze had erased his memory. But to be honest, practical jokes weren't Ryan's style.

She moved a few steps away and gulped air to clear her head. Desperately afraid that she might faint, she looked around for a park bench. But the amenities that the Preservation Society would one day install for tourists didn't exist yet.

With nowhere else to go and knees that refused to work, she felt herself folding onto the boardwalk. Just before she hit the rough planks, Heath caught her beneath both arms and hauled her to her feet again. "Maybe you should tell me where you live so I can see you home."

Courtney ignored the whiskey fumes and leaned against him, more grateful than disgusted for the moment. The idea of being in the past should have been laughable. Obviously, there'd been some sort of mistake in the Universe. Sooner or later the mistake would be rectified. Courtney had to believe that. She just had to hang on until whoever was in charge realized there was a problem and set everything right again. And she had to pray that it would happen soon.

If only she hadn't let Ryan talk her into going to the ball in the first place . . . if he'd just let her throw the boxes away instead of digging through them . . . if she hadn't opened the door to that stupid shed, none of this would have happened.

All at once her hands stilled and a bud of excitement blossomed in her chest. Of course! *The shed!* Why hadn't she thought of that before? If she *hadn't* opened the door to the shed, she would probably still be in her own time. So what if she went *back* inside? Would the mistake reverse itself?

It seemed almost too simple to work, but it was worth a try. At this point she'd try anything.

Jerking away from Heath, she hoisted her skirts and headed back toward the field. She wasn't used to maneuvering around twenty yards of silk and layers of petticoats, or to walking fast with a steel band cutting off her breath, so it didn't take much effort for Heath to catch her.

"Do you mind telling me where you're going?"

"Back to the shed."

"For God's sake, why?"

"Because someone has made a horrible mistake, and I intend to fix it." She lost her grip on her skirt and the hoop swung out wildly, brushing a nearby post and almost knocking her off balance.

Heath caught her arm and pulled her back around to face him. Night shadowed his face, but moonlight made it possible to see his scowl. "What kind of mistake?"

Courtney wondered what he'd do if she told him. He'd probably think she was crazy—or drunk. "It's difficult to explain," she said. "Just trust me, I'm not supposed to be here."

"I see. And how will going back to the shed rectify the error?"

Courtney tried to pull her arm away, but his grip was too strong. "It's complicated. You wouldn't understand."

"No doubt it would boggle my simple mind, but perhaps you'd be good enough to satisfy my curiosity anyway."

"Sorry. I can't."

"I see." Heath rocked onto the balls of his feet and back down again. "Would it change your mind if I told you that I've just been through one helluva night and I'm running a little short of patience?"

Courtney gave that some thought, but shook her head. If this poor jerk thought he'd had a bad night until now, just imagine how he'd feel if she told him the truth.

"Well," he said with a sigh of resignation, "my mother did teach me that a lady is entitled to her mysteries, so I suppose the gentlemanly thing to do is to leave yours unsolved."

Courtney made a mental note to say a prayer for his mother's soul and darted past him again into the darkened field. She could hear him moving through the weeds behind her and wondered what he'd do when she disappeared almost in front of his eyes.

But she couldn't worry about that. Judging from the fumes he emitted, he'd probably just write it off as the result of too much alcohol, anyway. When she reached the shed, she paused with one hand on the door and turned back to him for what she hoped was the last time. "Thank you, Mr. Sullivan. It's been interesting meeting you."

"Likewise." He glanced at the leaning walls behind her. "Am I to assume that you plan to go back inside?"

"You are."

"And you'll be shutting the door?"

"I'll have to or it won't work."

"Now you have me at a disadvantage. *What* won't work?"

"Like I said before, it's complicated."

"Of course." He pulled off his hat and held it against his chest. Lazy curls drooped in every direction, and a lock fell across his forehead. "Would you like me to stay here in case you get stuck again?"

"Thank you, but I'm sure I'll be fine."

Skepticism narrowed his eyes, but he nodded as if he believed her and shooed her toward the door with his hat. "All right, then. In you go."

Courtney gulped one deep breath of fresh air, stepped into the tiny enclosure, and closed her eyes. "You can shut the door."

"You're sure about this?"

"Absolutely."

The door clicked and she experienced a brief flash of claustrophobia. Edging open her eyes, she waited for the light, the warm caressing breeze, the gentle tug that had pulled her into the shed in the first place. But no beam relieved the darkness and no breeze stirred the still, close air.

She waited for anything else that might mean the Universe was setting itself straight, but the only thing she heard was Heath's muffled voice. "Are you okay in there?"

"I'm fine."

"Do you want me to let you out?"

"No. Thank you."

"You'll let me know if you do?"

She took another deep breath and tried not to sound annoyed. "Actually, Mr. Sullivan, I think it might help if you stopped talking."

Silence. Then, "Sorry." Something scraped against the side of the shed, a footstep scuffed in the dirt, and the noises that followed made her pretty sure Heath was sitting, leaning against the shed, settling in to wait.

Courtney leaned her forehead against the wall. "Are you touching the shed?"

Silence. More rustling. More scuffing. "No."

"Good."

"How long are you going to stay in there?"

"Hopefully only about two seconds after you *stop talking*." She knew her irritation was showing, but now *her* patience was growing thin. When more noises filtered through the boards, followed by the undeniable stench of a cigar, she lost her composure completely. "For hell's sake, what's wrong with you? Don't you understand that you're upsetting a very delicate balance here?"

"I am?"

"You are. Now put that damn thing out." When she was reasonably certain that he'd complied, Courtney took another calming breath, closed her eyes again, and waited. Gunfire erupted too close for comfort, followed by roaring laughter and angry shouts. The scents of horse manure and dirt filtered inside and tickled her nose, but she refused to let herself sneeze.

She didn't know how long she stood in the dark. It felt like eternity, but it was probably only a few minutes later when the rustling noise sounded again and Heath's voice drifted in through the boards. "Would you mind telling me what we're waiting for?"

A ball of helplessness opened in Courtney's middle and spread outward, quickly, like a black hole enveloping her. She sagged against the rough plank wall and tried not to cry. It had been a long time since she'd felt so defenseless, so alone, so *abandoned*. Not since the day Leslie dumped her on Grandmother's doorstep for the first time and drove away with her truck-driving, beer-swilling, toothpick-chewing boyfriend.

The intervening years might never have been, and all the hard work Courtney had done trying to turn herself into an emotionally healthy woman could have been a figment of her imagination. She felt seven again. Lost and alone. Frightened and insecure and utterly at someone else's mercy—and she hated the feeling now as much as she ever had.

Courtney remained silent for so long, Heath began to wonder if something had happened to her. She was a strange one, that was for sure. Addled, maybe. Or, as Sukey used to say, "touched." He wished Sukey were standing beside him now. She'd know what to do. She might have been a slave in his father's eyes, but she'd been Blue's grandmother, and she'd spent more time with Heath than his own mother had.

She'd know what to do with the strange young woman he suddenly found himself saddled with. She'd have taken Courtney under her wing, coddled her until the world came right again, fed her and clothed her and clucked over her as long as there was need. Heath certainly couldn't do *that*. Nor did he want to.

He didn't have much experience caring for other people— and the few chances that had come his way had been miserable failures. But he had to do something. He couldn't just leave her wandering the streets of this miserable town by herself. She had people somewhere. All he had to do was find out where, and then deliver her to them safely. It should be an easy task, and he might even wrangle a small reward for his trouble. Enough, he hoped, so he could put this sorry excuse for a town behind him for good.

Without warning the shed door banged open and came damn close to hitting him in the head. He scrambled to his feet as Courtney came outside, eyes red-rimmed and puffy, curls askew. One shoulder of her gown hung limply down her arm, making her look off-balance, and she gave a loud unladylike sniff as she slammed the door.

Thank God she'd stopped crying. Heath hated tears. They left him feeling huge and inept and clumsy, and he wasn't up to dealing with tears tonight.

Courtney sniffed again and gave the door a vicious kick that made the curls slip another couple of inches onto the side of her head. Heath watched the door bounce shut and spring open again, and the whole night combined into one ludicrous picture that tore a wry smile from him. "Does this mean you're disappointed?"

Courtney glared at him, but there was a flicker of fear in her eyes now. "That I'm stuck here? What makes you think that?"

"A wild guess." Heath brushed dirt from his sleeve and wondered what she'd expected to happen. He shook off the idle curiosity and glanced up the street. "I hate to rush you, but it's late. We should find your friend."

"There's no reason to hurry," she said, her voice strangely flat. "He's not here."

"Well, then, I'll escort you wherever you want to go. Just name the place."

"Thanks, I don't have anyplace *to* go."

Heath took in the silk gown, the hooped skirt, and the pearls at her neck with a snort of disbelief. "Let me guess. You had a disagreement with your husband?"

She curled her lip in disgust. "*No.* I'm not married. Thank God. Nor will I ever be."

"With your father, then."

The curls slid another few inches and settled just above her ear. She yanked them off and tossed them into the weeds. "Wrong again. Look, I really hate asking people for help, but I think I'm going to have to make an exception, here. I think I'm in trouble."

Heath's smile froze. "Oh?"

"I'm completely alone. I don't have a cent to my name. I have nowhere to go, no place to sleep, no food, and no clothes except the ones I'm wearing." She turned back to face him and a thin smile edged with fear curved her lips. "And you're the only person I know. I realize that you have no reason to help me. All you did was open the door and let me out of that shed. You really didn't ask for this much trouble." She stopped talking and her lip began to quiver.

Heath held up both hands to stop her. "Don't cry. Whatever you do, *don't cry.* But, lady, I can't help you. I couldn't help you if I wanted to. A gang of ruffians stole everything I own about an hour ago, so that description you just gave could be of me."

Her eyes grew wild. "Are you *kidding*?"

"You want to look at the bump on the back of my head and see what you think?"

"Okay. I mean—No! I—" She paced nervously in front of him, twisting her hands together. "Surely there's someplace in town where a woman with no money can spend the night for free? A homeless shelter or a YWCA?"

Heath glanced toward the campfires flickering on the hill-side. "Not in this town. You could probably find a miner who'd be willing to give you a bed and a meal, but you'd pay a hefty price for both."

Her gaze shot to his. "There's no kind-hearted woman who runs a boardinghouse? No minister with a respectable wife who might have a spare bed?" She whirled to face him eagerly. "What about *your* wife? Do you think she'd be willing to let me stay?"

Heath refused to let the hope in her eyes get to him. "I don't have a wife. Marriage and I do not see eye-to-eye. And I wouldn't know about the rest. I told you before, I've only been in town a few days, and I have no intention of staying any longer than I have to. If you're smart, you'll catch the first stage out of here."

"And pay for it how?" She pivoted away before he could answer and shot another volley of questions at him. "Where are you staying? In one of the hotels? Do you think the proprietor would let me work for lodging?"

Heath shook his head slowly. "Money's more plentiful than beds around here. Folks are sleeping three and four to one mattress in the hotels, and if *you* can't pay for what you want, there are a thousand other people who will gladly take your place. Besides which, folks in these parts aren't much interested in the next person's problems."

"Well, I have to do *something*," she snapped. "I can't stay *here* all night." She began to pace with quick nervous steps that took her from one end of the clearing to the other. She didn't seem to notice the weeds clawing at her skirt or the rocks beneath her feet.

Heath watched her until a solution popped into his head, and argued silently with himself afterward. Letting her stay in Ellis Bailey's cabin, with a community of vagrants and prospectors all around it, was no solution at all. The kindest thing he could do would be to bid her good night and wish her luck, turn his back, and walk away. She *wasn't* his responsibility.

He fought to ignore the obvious signs of dwindling hope, of despair and hopelessness on her face, but he'd been there himself, many times. He tried to remember what she'd said about what a poor knight in shining armor he made, but he still couldn't turn away.

"Maybe I *can* offer some help," he heard himself saying in spite of all the reasons he shouldn't. "It so happens that I have the use of a cabin while I'm in town. You're welcome to stay there for the night."

Distrust suddenly replaced everything else. "With you?"

"Not in the way you're thinking," Heath assured her. "There's only one bed, but that would, naturally, be yours."

"And what would you do?"

"I can sleep outside. It wouldn't be the first time."

She eyed him warily, but he thought the suspicion looked a little less brittle. "I can't leave you without a bed. That wouldn't be right."

Thinking about the cabin made Heath realize how tired he was. Maybe even tired enough to sleep without dreaming. He stifled a yawn and waved her toward the street. "Well, you can't make yourself a target for every vile creature in the city by staying here. I won't have that on my conscience. So please just say yes. I have few opportunities these days to behave like a gentleman, and I'm not entirely sure I remember how. The least you can do is let me try." He held out his arm and waited until she reluctantly took it, then started toward the cabin he'd expected never to see again.

Courtney smiled and he felt the stirring of satisfaction at being able to wipe the worry from her eyes, if only for a moment. Somewhere deep inside, a voice whispered caution. He'd worked hard to avoid entanglements since the day he rode away from Bonne Chance five years earlier, and it would be a mistake to let down his guard now. But their arrangements were only for one night. First thing tomorrow he'd help Courtney get back to where she belonged, and that, he promised himself firmly, would be the end of his involvement.

Still not sure what she was doing or why, Courtney followed Heath through streets she barely recognized, away from the city, past several squat cabins and fields of dirty tents until he finally turned up a narrow path and stopped in front of a cabin that looked roughly the size of her grandmother's front parlor. Unless Courtney had gotten hopelessly turned around during their travels, they were standing shockingly close to the spot where her grandmother's house would be built in about sixty years.

She studied the tiny cabin and vacillated between relief and apprehension about what she'd gotten herself into. How could she spend even one night in such close quarters with a perfect stranger? She knew nothing about Heath Sullivan, and what she knew of the city's early inhabitants didn't make her feel any safer.

She could have asked him for some family background— assuming he'd tell the truth—but that would just open the door on questions about herself. Courtney had never been good at keeping stories straight, and she had no reason to believe that traveling through the centuries had changed that. So she'd be smart to keep her big mouth shut. No stories about herself, her family, or her past.

When she realized that Heath was watching her, waiting for her reaction to his very unimpressive cabin, she forced a smile. "So, this is it?"

"It is."

"It looks . . ." *Small. Cramped. And way too intimate to share with a complete stranger.* She forced her lips to hold their smile and did her best to look sincere. "It looks very nice."

To her surprise, Heath contradicted her. "It looks like what it is—a very small, very ugly cabin in the middle of hell."

Courtney smiled in spite of the exhaustion creeping into her bones. "It is a little smaller than I expected, but I'm very grateful that you're letting me stay." Her eyes burned and she battled a huge yawn, and she had to concentrate to keep from leaning against the wall and falling asleep right there.

She focused on the questions that had been dancing out of reach while she solved her most immediate problem. Had Ryan noticed yet that she was missing? What did he think had happened to her? Was he looking for her? Or did he think that she'd grown tired of the ball and slipped away?

She couldn't even let herself think about the biggest question of all—how was she going to get back home again? She'd be better able to puzzle through this whole unbelievable mess in the morning.

She needed all her concentration to focus on the here and now. Never in her life had she followed a complete stranger into such an isolated place, and she was more than a little nervous. Leslie probably would have thought this was a perfect way to meet a new man. Elizabeth would have been horrified and would have spent the night standing in front of the shed. Her stern face would have been enough to keep her safe.

Courtney had spent her whole life being buffeted between their opinions, and, frankly, she didn't know what to think. She'd never have done something like this under normal circumstances. But the world she knew had evaporated while she was inside that shed, and she was utterly lost in the one she'd tumbled into. If she had a safer or better choice, she didn't know what it was.

She followed Heath up two rickety steps and nearly ran into him when he stopped to open the door. She stood in the doorway and tried to look brave and confident while he fumbled with an old-fashioned oil lamp on the table, but when the lamp flared to life and she could finally see the room, all her efforts to look brave flew out the window.

She blinked rapidly and let her gaze travel from the rock-faced fireplace on one wall to the narrow bed across the room. Slabs of cured meat swayed gently from the room's low rafters, and metal pots, pans, traps, lanterns, horseshoes, and other pieces of equipment she couldn't identify hung on nails in the walls.

Besides the bed, the only other furniture in the room were several crates along the walls, a pine box at the foot of the bed, and a crudely fashioned table flanked by two equally crude chairs beneath one high, narrow window.

This was no dream. It wasn't even good enough to qualify as a nightmare.

She glanced uncertainly at Heath, and the idea of bolting crossed her mind. But it wasn't as if she'd find anything better if she ran away. She might be able to improve her situation tomorrow—if she was even here tomorrow. To-night, she'd be smart to buck up and soldier through.

"What about sleeping arrangements?"

"What about them? I told you I'd sleep outside."

Courtney glanced out the door and tried to calculate how many prospectors might be out there—and how long it had been since any of them had seen a woman. "I'm not sure I want you to leave," she said, hating herself for sounding so much like Leslie but too frightened not to. "I don't think I want to be here alone."

Heath grinned slowly. "Then you want me to stay?"

"Yes, but not—not *that* way."

His grin widened, but his eyes actually seemed kind. "Re-lax. I may have forgotten most of what I once knew about gentlemanly behavior, but I've never taken advantage of a woman in need. Besides," he said with a wink, "I like my women a little plumper and a whole lot more willing."

Surprisingly, his teasing relaxed something inside of her, and she sank onto the foot of the bed. "Don't get me wrong, I appreciate everything you're doing, and I'm really grateful that you're not planning to take advantage of me. But I'm con-fused about why you're helping me. If you don't want . . . me—and thank God you don't—then what *do* you want? What's in it for you?"

Heath tossed his hat onto the table. "Does there have to be something in it for me? Can't a fella just be nice?"

"Well, yes, but—"

"But you don't believe I'm capable of being nice?"

"I didn't mean that," Courtney assured him quickly. "It's just that most people don't do things for somebody else with-out expecting something in return."

"And you want to know what my motives are before we finalize our arrangements."

"Exactly."

His smile faded, but the kindness in his eyes grew warmer. "Well, Miss Moss, it may surprise you to learn that I don't want anything other than the peace of mind that comes from knowing that you're not going to be harmed by some drunken miner and that you won't take sick because you've been left without a roof over your head. And maybe one night of self-respect—a commodity which has been in short supply lately."

"Courtney," she corrected again. She watched his face as he talked—what little of it she could see beneath the thick coating of whiskers. His body language all clearly said that he had no interest in her, and his eyes were dull with disinterest whenever he looked at her. But there was something else in his expression that piqued her curiosity. It was the ever-so-slight clenching of his jaw and the merest shadow that passed behind his eyes, and it was enough to convince her that there was more to Heath Sullivan than met the eye.

Chapter 4

THE BAYING OF *the hounds and thundering of horses' hooves echoed across the landscape as the quarry watched the hunter walk toward him. The sound of his own rapidly beating heart filled his senses.*

It was the sound of fear. Fear so strong he could taste it on his tongue and smell it all around him. He looked out on his pursuers and watched the hunter's eyes lift and then lock on his own.

Something flashed in the hunter's eyes, but the quarry knew. He knew. The hunter spoke, but the quarry could make out only the final two words. Trust me. The words echoed through the swamp, growing louder with each repetition until they overtook the sound of the quarry's heartbeat and drowned out the hunter's voice.

Trust me.

Though the quarry knew it would mean the end, he slowly, hesitantly, began his descent from the tree. And still the hunter's voice echoed. Trust me.

Trust me . . .

Arms flailing, Heath sat up and heard the echo of his own cry of dismay fading away. Reality returned quickly as he registered the steady, rhythmic sound of work crews hammering on buildings being constructed somewhere nearby. One of the miners in the camp across the way sang off-key. Someone else bellowed like a bull moose as he came rushing out of his tent.

Heath leaned against the cabin wall, scrubbed his face with his palms, and waited for the impact of the dream to fade. Twice in as many days, and this time it had progressed further than ever before. He didn't know whether being set upon by thieves the night before had triggered the dream again, or whether he'd simply run out of places to hide from it.

Trust me.

The words brushed past his ear on the early morning breeze, and he shuddered. It had been a long time since he'd last uttered those words. Longer still since he'd had the right to say them.

He pulled his hands away and tried again to shake off the effects of the dream. His shoulder hurt and his back was stiff from sleeping on the ground. It might be August, but this far north the earth grew cold when the sun went down, and he felt the night cool in every joint.

Moving slowly, he stretched out his legs in front of him. He'd lost the feeling in one, and tiny needle-sharp points pulsed from ankle to hip as sensation returned. Look at him. Only thirty years old and already creaking like an old man. Maybe nature would make him pay for the excesses of the past few years, after all.

Smiling coldly, he got to his feet and tested his weight on each leg before he walked around to the outhouse behind the cabin. When he emerged, the sun was just beginning to come up on the eastern horizon, a splinter of silver against golden hills bathed in dew.

He couldn't remember the last time he'd seen a sunrise, but he couldn't see this one without thinking about those days long ago when he and Blue had stolen away from Bonne Chance to fish. Back then, Heath's father had found their antics amusing, and he'd showered affection on both boys as if he'd genuinely cared about them both. But those days were long gone. Everything had changed, but Heath hadn't noticed it happening until too late, and the price for his inattention had been too high.

With the ease of long practice, he shut down the memories and jammed his hat on his head. Blue had been the best friend a man could have. But he was gone, and no amount of longing would bring him back.

Stuffing his hands into his pockets, Heath pivoted toward town. Courtney would be wanting breakfast, and the food stores inside the cabin were pitifully depleted. He had no idea how he'd add to them, but moving made him feel better. Maybe he'd find Tyree Caine and his boys, pay them back for the crack on his head, and take back the cash they'd relieved him of the night before—along with Ellis Bailey's watch.

But that would take good luck. Heath wasn't going to hold his breath.

The sights and sounds and scents of life surrounded him as he walked. The sour aroma of fermented grains coming from the brewery mingled with the bitter scent of burning wood and strong lye soap waiting for laundry. Somehow, the wholesome scent of baking bread topped everything else and reminded him again that dinner wasn't the first meal most people ate in a day.

Obligation weighed heavily on his shoulders, and he resented it being there after the work he'd done to rid himself of liability. He'd spent the first twenty-five years of his life bound by duty, defined by responsibility, controlled by obligations. He'd spent the past five years removing that yoke splinter by splinter, and he wasn't about to let Courtney Moss—or anyone else, for that matter—lock it around his neck again.

Agitation spurred his pace and he reached town in only a few minutes. There, he stood with his hands on his hips and glared at the shops on both sides of the street, as if they were somehow responsible for the fix he found himself in. Lost in thought, he didn't hear the horse and rider until they were almost upon him. The rider jerked his reins at the last minute, sent up a cloud of dust for Heath to choke on, and tossed down a vicious oath from the saddle as he swept past.

Heath threw back an apology, quick-stepped to the side of the street, and hopped onto the boardwalk. Here he was, up at the crack of dawn and nearly getting himself killed trying to take care of someone else when he should have been on his way back to Kansas City and the other half of his fee.

He wasn't going to make a habit of this rescue business, that was for damn sure.

Glowering at the world in general and his damn fool self in particular, he made his way along the boardwalk through rapidly growing crowds as the day got underway. Outside the Alder Gulch Hotel, he had to move quickly to avoid plowing into a dark-haired man who came outside stretching as he walked. Heath deepened his scowl and started past, but the man tipped his hat and grinned.

"Morning, friend."

Heath glanced at the man who looked roughly Heath's age and very nearly Heath's size. "Morning."

"And a fine morning it is, too. Don't you think?"

Heath didn't think anything of the sort, but he didn't want to get caught up in a debate about it. He muttered something noncommittal under his breath and tried again to get past.

The man flashed another smile and went on as if Heath had looked interested in conversation. "If the good Lord made a finer place or a more beautiful day than this, I'd like to know where he put them."

Heath looked into the poor fool's eyes. "You might want to rethink that. It's a fine day, all right. But hell's a better place than this, make no mistake about it." He started away again, and the man fell into step along with him.

"Roderick Dennehy's the name. Those who know me call me Derry." That grin flashed again. "Those who love me call me things I can't repeat in polite society."

Heath wasn't in the market for friends, but the man's wide open smile and easy manner were hard to resist. "Heath Sullivan," he said.

"And have ye been here long?"

"A few days. I'll be leaving again before nightfall."

"Why so soon?"

Heath slanted a glance at him and stepped out around a

couple of old men arguing on the boardwalk. "Like I said earlier, hell's a finer place than this."

"Too bad. You're not a prospector, then?"

"Nope." Heath took another quick look at him, decided he didn't look destined for the gold mines, and decided to prove himself right. "You?"

Derry shook his head and squinted into the rising sun. "Digging one thing out of the dirt is the same as digging another. I left Ireland to escape a life in the coal mines, so it wouldn't make much sense to grub for gold now that I'm here."

They reached the corner and Heath stepped off the board-walk onto the dirt road. "If that's the case, why are you here?"

Derry hopped down beside him and tugged down his hat brim against the glare of the sun. "I never said I wasn't interested in making me fortune, just that I wasn't going to crawl in the dirt to do it."

"You're a gambler, then?"

"Some might say that, I suppose. I prefer to think of myself as a man of opportunity." At the opposite side of the street, he stuck out a hand and smiled again. "I'm sorry you won't be around, Heath Sullivan. You've an honest look about you, and I like that. And who knows, perhaps we'll meet again some day."

"Perhaps," Heath said as he extended a hand of his own. A minute later he watched Derry stride away along the boardwalk and shook his head in wonder. The world was full of strange people, he told himself as he turned toward the Mercantile. And he'd met two of 'em in less than twenty-four hours.

Now that he was finally on his own again, he gave himself a sharp reminder about why he was out and about so early and began his search in earnest. After walking past several shops, he found a small, sparse man with an even sparser head of hair unloading a buckboard at the back of the Mercantile and decided to take his chances. "Hey! You there. Need some help?"

The man stopped working just long enough to shoot a

dagger-sharp glare over his shoulder and shake his head. "No, and even if I did, I ain't gonna hire you. I don't believe in hiring transients."

In spite of his mood, Heath smiled. "No transients? Is there anything else in this town?"

Wrong question. The man straightened and turned to face Heath, glaring as if Heath had called his baby ugly. "There's a few of us who'd like to see this place become a real town. Unlike some others."

"Well, I wouldn't count on that happening for a while," Heath warned. "Not until the gold's gone, anyway. But I didn't stop by to debate the merits of the city. I'm just looking for work. Just enough to earn money for one meal. You wouldn't even have to pay me in cash. Food would do just as well."

"Don't give handouts, neither."

Heath removed his hat and held it in front of his chest. "Perhaps you didn't hear me when I said I'll be glad to work for whatever I get."

"And perhaps *you* didn't hear *me* when I said I ain't got no work. 'Specially not for the likes of *you*. The quicker your sort gets out of Virginia City, the better for everyone."

Heath should have been used to folks judging and finding him wanting, but it stung more without the veil of alcohol to shield him. "That's a pretty sweeping statement, friend."

"I ain't your friend."

"A figure of speech," Heath assured him. He'd always hated his father's attitude toward those he'd called the lesser-born, but it still galled him that this squirrel of a man had the nerve to look down his nose. "Would it make a difference if I told you there was another person involved? A lady?"

The rodent stopped working and slid a glance across Heath's face. "One of the girls from down the road?"

"Not at all. A lady you would undoubtedly approve of."

"And she's with you?"

"Temporarily." Heath propped one foot on the back of the buckboard and offered a hand to shake. "Heath Sullivan's the name."

The rat eyes narrowed speculatively. "What's she doin' with *you*?"

Since that was a question he'd been asking himself all morning, Heath ignored the insult. "It seems that she's lost touch with her family and finds herself in reduced circumstances. I offered a place to stay the night, and I plan to provide breakfast, as well. Maybe you know her or her family. If not, maybe you know someone of good repute who'd be willing to help her find her way home."

The ferret stuck out a paw. "Gunther Schmidt," he said belatedly. "What's her name?"

"Courtney Moss."

Schmidt squinted into the sun as it rose above the rooftops across the street. "Moss? That's her family name?"

"That's what she told me."

Schmidt sat on the side of the wagon and gave that some thought, but after only a few seconds he shook his head. "Never heard of 'em. Not around here, anyway."

That was *not* the answer Heath wanted. "Are you sure?" he prodded. "She would have been at the ball last night—at least for a little while."

"Sure as I can be without taking a census." Schmidt's lip curled, but Heath couldn't tell if he was smiling or getting ready to bite.

He forced an answering smile in spite of his rapidly sinking spirits. "Take your time. Think about it. Maybe they're new in town. Maybe I got the name wrong. Maybe—"

"Maybe *you* should get your foot off my wagon and leave it be." Schmidt watched, pointedly, while Heath removed the offending foot and then, flush with victory, relented a little. "Tell you what I'll do. You go inside and tell Bessie to give you enough food for breakfast. You bring your lady in afterward and let me take a look at her. If she's from around here, I'll know her."

"I'm more than willing to work," Heath reminded him.

"And you will . . . next time."

Elated, Heath tossed a thank you over his shoulder and hurried toward the front of the store. It looked as if last night's bad luck was a thing of the past. In an hour or two

Courtney would be safely delivered to Gunther Schmidt, and
Heath would be free to look after himself. Whether or not
he found Ellis Bailey's watch, he'd be out of Virginia City
before the sun set.

That was a promise.

Groaning in protest, Courtney turned away from the glare of
sunlight in her tightly closed eyes. She rolled onto her side,
hoping she could drift back to sleep for a while longer. Exhaustion still dragged at her limbs and made her bones heavy.
It didn't even matter that her old bed at Grandmother's
seemed lumpier than she remembered, she was *not* ready to
wake up yet.

Without opening her eyes, she bunched the pillow beneath
her and pulled the sheet over her head. She lay that way for
several minutes, listening to the sounds drifting in from outside. Hammering echoed from somewhere not far away, and
the unlikely rattle and clop of a horse-drawn wagon passed
outside her window. Driven by someone who was still in the
spirit of Heritage Weekend, no doubt.

Masculine voices deep in conversation drifted inside so
clearly, she wondered if she'd opened her window in the
night without remembering. Annoyed, both with herself and
with everyone else, she slapped the sheet away from her face
and ran her fingers through her hair while her eyes adjusted
to the sunlight. Very slowly a log wall beside the bed came
into focus.

She blinked. Rubbed her eyes, and checked again. But the
view hadn't changed. She wasn't looking at her grandmother's sedate wallpaper. She *was* looking at mud daubed
between chinks in a log wall—just like in the cabin she'd
dreamed about.

Clutching the sheet in front of her, she sat up and looked
around nervously. The overpowering scent of horse manure
mingled with the bitter scent of campfires and stung her nose,
bringing her even more fully awake.

It wasn't a dream!

It wasn't a dream?

But how could that be?

An uneasy laugh lodged in her throat and a sense of unreality flowed through her veins. She pinched her arm, half convinced that she was in the middle of a nightmare. This *couldn't* be real, that's all there was to it.

When the pinch didn't change anything, she shot out of bed and raced to one of the narrow windows, dragging the sheet behind her. Wagons rolled past on the rutted dirt road, and men of all shapes and sizes hunkered down in front of fires or paraded in front of their tents, snapping suspenders into place and covering dirty union suits with equally filthy shirts and pants.

Down the street, empty lots gaped and a new building was going up in the same spot where one of Virginia City's most famous historical landmarks should have been.

Another burst of laughter punctuated the morning, and a horse paused to relieve itself directly in front of the cabin. A man wearing a heavy brown coat and a set of whiskers that brushed the top of his chest stepped around the newly created puddle; the lanky young man behind him stepped right in the center of it, shook off his boot, and kept walking.

If she remembered right from the night before, more tents filled the space behind the cabin. She sank against the wall and trailed her gaze toward the hills where the temporary community of white tents scrabbled up the hillsides, and every spare patch of earth had been turned over in a mad search for gold.

Not a dream.

Apprehension made the hair on her neck stand up. She really *was* in 1864. Penniless and alone. Her knees turned to mush and her hands began to tremble. Dread pumped through her with every heartbeat. What was she going to do?

What *could* she do?

She didn't belong here. She barely belonged in the present-day Virginia City.

When she realized that the panic was taking over, she gulped air and tried to calm herself. But questions pelted her mind endlessly. Could she get home again, or was she at the mercy of whatever whim of fate had brought her here? She hadn't been able to get back last night, but maybe that was because Heath was with her.

Heath. Was *he* real? He must have been, or she wouldn't be in this cabin. But where had he gone? Would he come back for her, or was she on her own? On her own in a town full of prospectors, prostitutes, and gamblers.

Before she could find a single answer, the questions looped and began again. But becoming hysterical wouldn't solve anything. She had to think.

Think!

She needed a blueprint for getting home again and a survival plan just in case she couldn't.

Crossing to the bed again, she sank onto the mattress. The first coherent thought she managed was the realization that she was wearing only her underclothes and that Heath—if he came back at all—could walk in on her at any moment. Forget the fact that her underwear wasn't exactly provocative or skimpy. It would be to Heath, and she didn't want to give him any ideas.

She lunged for the hoop skirt, petticoats, and corset that lay in a heap on a chair near the fireplace, along with the pink gown that was probably to blame for everything. She'd have given almost anything for the chance to trade them in for a pair of jeans and a T-shirt.

Even that little bit of exertion made her lungs pinch and cut off most of her air. Either she was dangerously close to hysteria, or traveling through more than a century in the blink of an eye had weakened her.

She lowered the dress to her side and lectured herself sternly. She would *not* panic. She would not *allow* herself to panic. She was smarter than this. Stronger than this. Braver than this.

She was a woman of the new millennium, and that meant she was capable and efficient. Capable enough to survive Leslie's muddled mothering skills. Resilient enough to bounce back from Elizabeth's lackluster grandmothering. Efficient enough to make her mark at the Denver-based magazine she'd worked at for six years, and competent enough to earn a shot at an even better job in New York.

A job she was *not* going to lose just because she'd taken an unplanned detour into the nineteenth century.

She slipped the dress over her head, pointedly ignoring the hoop skirt and corset. But it only took a few minutes to realize that she couldn't fasten the dress without the corset, and that twenty yards of fabric dragged on the ground without the hoop to fill it out.

Swearing softly, she pulled the gown off again, picked up the corset, and made a face at it. Ryan's sister had laced her into the stupid thing the day before, but Courtney had no one to help her today. And no matter how enthusiastic her pep talk, it was pretty hard to maintain a confident attitude when she couldn't even get dressed without help.

Glaring at the mound of pink silk, she lifted her chin defiantly. If the dress wouldn't fit without the corset, she'd find a way to get the damn thing on. It was just whalebone and canvas, for Pete's sake. An inanimate object. Surely, she could outwit it if she concentrated hard enough.

She worked until sweat beaded on her nose and forehead and trickles of perspiration snaked down her back, but no matter what she did or how she twisted and reached, she couldn't lace herself into the corset. And no matter how hard she wished, she couldn't create the extra two inches of fabric she needed to make the dress fit without it.

Seething with helplessness, she threw the corset across the room and kicked the leg of the chair, then dropped onto the foot of the bed and held a pillow in front of her face to muffle her scream of frustration. She was so deep in her misery, she didn't hear the door open until a strong hand pulled the pillow away and Heath's face swam into focus.

Blond hair curled lazily across his forehead and out from beneath the brim of his hat. His eyes, an intense, shocking blue, made a long, slow journey from the tips of her toes to the top of her head. "Something wrong?"

Heat flamed in her cheeks, not only because she was quite sure he'd witnessed her temper tantrum, but because she was so pathetically grateful to see him. She told herself to stay cool and not let him know how afraid she'd been, but the instant she opened her mouth all the neediness she'd been battling poured out in five desperately spineless words. "I thought you'd left me."

After its long journey along her torso, his gaze jumped to the corset on the floor, then settled on her face. "Do you always kick furniture and toss clothing when you're worried?"

"Of course not." She turned away to break eye contact. "Where were you?"

Heath bent to retrieve the corset and motioned for her to turn around. Her first instinct was to refuse, but that would only mean that she would spend the whole day in her underclothes, and that hardly seemed intelligent. When she complied, he leaned in close to slide the corset around her.

His arms wrapped her waist for the briefest of moments, but it was long enough to send a shiver along her spine. Every cell in her body pricked with the awareness that she was alone and helpless in a strange place . . . and that a man—who could have been anything from vagrant to hired gun—was lacing up her underwear.

"I slept outside," he said at last. "Believe me, you had the better accommodations."

Courtney lowered her head and closed her eyes, struggling to concentrate on anything but the strong feel of his hands and the warmth of his body. It seemed to take forever, but Heath finally finished, stepped away from her, and leaned against the wall. He watched while she fumbled with the sash on her hoop and swam through countless yards of silk for the third time in less than an hour.

To her surprise, Heath was watching as her head emerged. The instant her gaze locked onto his, he glanced away and crossed to the door. "Now that you're presentable," he said as he hauled a bag inside, "we can concentrate on having breakfast and then getting you back where you belong. I assume you're hungry?"

"Ravenous," Courtney admitted. "Are there restaurants around here?"

"There are. But I thought we'd eat here." He lowered the bag to the table and stepped back. "There's nothing fancy in here, but there's nothing fancy anywhere in this town, so you're not losing out on much. A batch of biscuits and gravy would satisfy me."

It took a second or two for his meaning to sink in. When it did, Courtney gaped at him. "You want *me* to cook?" He had *no* idea what he was asking.

Cooking for one seemed like an incredible waste of effort, so she usually ate out or ordered in. She couldn't remember the last time she'd heated anything without a microwave, and she'd never even tried cooking more than a hot dog over an open fire.

Heath tossed his hat onto the bed and shrugged off his vest. "I thought you might. Cooking isn't one of my greatest skills."

"Or mine." She caught the quick scowl of disapproval and realized how ungrateful she must sound. "Look, I know I probably owe you breakfast for letting me stay here, but it would be *much* smarter to eat someone else's cooking." She loosened the drawstring and glanced into the bag. "There's nothing fresh here, so it's not as if anything's going to spoil if it doesn't get used right away."

Heath slowly untucked his shirttail. "You don't know how to cook?"

"Not like this."

He nodded once and turned away. "Then I'd say we have a bit of a problem. I have no money, and neither do you. So either we eat this, or we eat nothing. I groveled to get the food. The way I figure it, doing something to make it edible is your responsibility."

Courtney resented his attitude, but a healthy dose of reality kept her from arguing. She didn't have a whole lot of bargaining power. "I see. Well, if that's what you want, then I guess I'll try. But don't blame me if we both die from food poisoning."

Heath smiled and turned away. Courtney chewed on her thumbnail and tried to remember if she'd ever read a recipe anywhere for biscuits or gravy or anything else, for that matter. But if she had, the memory of them was back in 2003 . . .

along with Ryan, her job, her entire portfolio of work, and anything else that qualified as her life.

She really had to get out of here . . . and the sooner, the better.

Chapter 5

WISHING SHE HAD the courage to tell Heath just *why* having her cook was such a bad idea, Courtney dug into the burlap bag and brought out a smaller cloth bag filled with something that felt like marbles. "What's this?"

Heath hunkered down in front of the pine box by the bed and began digging through it. He spared the bag an annoyed glance and tossed a one-word answer. "Peas."

"*Peas?*" Courtney hated the slimy things under any circumstances, and she had *no idea* how to make these little bits of gravel edible. "You want *peas* for breakfast?"

Heath lifted one shoulder and tugged a worn quilt from the box. "I thought you might. I already told you, biscuits and gravy are fine for me."

"Okay. I don't suppose you've noticed a cookbook around here somewhere?"

"Sorry. But from what I've been able to gather, Ellis Bailey wasn't the kind of man who'd have such a thing. But there's no need to get fancy. All we need is something in our stomachs. After that, we'll get you back where you belong, I'll leave town, and we'll both be happy."

"Yeah? Well, I'd like to *see* you get me back where I belong." She kneaded the bag of peas with her fingers. "I'd *really* like to see you do that."

Heath stopped working and suspicion turned his eyes blue as ice. "Oh?"

"I told you last night, I don't have anywhere *to* go. Not here, anyway."

"Oh? What about the friend who was waiting for you at the ball?" He stood to face her and she realized again how tall he was. "What about the grandmother you mentioned?"

The room suddenly seemed too warm and *way* too small, and Courtney's brain felt like mush. What could she tell him? What *should* she tell him? "I didn't lie," she said. She slid a glance toward the window and wondered if she should take her chances out there. Just then a barrel of a man staggered out of his tent, scratched enthusiastically, and relieved himself in full view of anyone who might be watching.

"My friend doesn't actually live here," she said, looking away quickly. "I was . . . confused last night. I know you can't take care of me forever, and I don't want you to. I hate taking help from anybody. But if I agree to cook and clean for you, will you let me stay for a couple of days—just until I can find a job and a place of my own to stay?" *Or, God willing, get back home where I belong?*

"Sorry. I'm leaving town the minute I turn you over to your family."

"But that's the point. I don't *have* a family."

"Your friends, then."

"I don't have any friends, either."

Heath's eyes roamed her face for what felt like a century or more. His mouth drew into a tight, pinched line beneath the covering of whiskers. "You were at the ball last night alone?"

"Yes."

"And your things? Your clothes and jewelry and such? Where are they?"

"I don't have anything else." Courtney's heart slammed against her chest and her head began to pound again.

"Indeed?" One eyebrow arched over an ice-blue eye. "You are so destitute that a ball gown of fine silk and dancing slippers to match are your only possessions?"

"I know it sounds unusual. Unlikely, even. But it's true."

At his smirk of disbelief, Courtney's fear began to fade and irritation took its place. Her voice seemed to echo inside her head. She closed her eyes and rubbed her forehead, wondering if she was getting a migraine or something even worse. "All I need is a day," she bargained. "Maybe two. If I can't find my way home by then, I'll find someplace else to stay."

The ensuing silence brought her eyes open again to find Heath regarding her warily. "If you can't find your way home? What do you mean by that?"

"Just what I said." Lights flashed in front of Courtney's eyes, and her stomach churned. Her heart hammered in her ears so loudly she wasn't sure that she was actually speaking. "I don't know how to get home again."

Heath's eyes narrowed to mere slits in his tanned face. "Now you're telling me that you don't remember where you live?"

The lights grew brighter and the pitching of her stomach more insistent. Cold beads of sweat dotted her forehead, and she dropped into a chair so she could use her hands to keep her head up. She felt so utterly lousy, keeping the truth hidden suddenly seemed far less important than just surviving the moment. "That would be mild compared to what I'm asking you to believe," she said between the pitches and rolls her stomach was taking. "The problem isn't *where* I live, it's *when*."

"I don't understand."

How could he *be* so irritating? Couldn't he see that she was sick? Suffering? About to pass out? Didn't he *care*? No wonder she hated men sometimes.

Anger with Losers Number One through Twelve mingled with irritation at Heath and the relentless pitching of her stomach. The lights flashing in front of her eyes took away the last of her self-control, and she lashed out with the truth even though she knew it was a bad idea the second she opened her mouth.

"I mean, hotshot, that I don't belong in eighteen sixty-four, or even nineteen sixty-four. I'm from so far in the future, my great-grandmother probably hasn't even been born yet."

Heath blinked once. Twice. Pulled back a step and ran a hand across his beard. He started to talk, clamped his mouth shut, shook his head, and started over. "Say that again."

Courtney lowered her head to the table and closed her eyes. The pounding in her head grew a little less insistent, and some of the queasiness abated. "I know this sounds impossible. I *know* it does. But I swear to God I'm not crazy and I'm not making this up. When I stepped into that shed last night, it was August of two-thousand-three and I was at a reenactment ball with my friend, Ryan."

She eased open one eye and tried to keep her stomach calm. "I found this gown and these slippers in my grandmother's attic a few days ago. Don't ask me how they got there, because I don't know. Don't ask me how *I* got *here*, because I don't know." She lifted her head an inch or two. "I don't, in fact, know anything at all except that I'm here and, apparently, stuck—at least for the time being."

"I see."

But he didn't see anything. Any fool could hear that in his voice. Courtney sat up straight. "I'm between a rock and a hard place, here. More than anything in the world, I hate asking for help, but I don't know how to live in your world. If you make me leave, I don't know what will happen to me."

"That's not my problem."

"I know, but that doesn't alter the facts."

His expression tightened. "You're not listening. I don't want or need someone underfoot. I don't plan on staying in this dreary place a minute longer than I have to. And *you* need to see a doctor, lady, because you're plumb *loco*."

Courtney ground her teeth and tried not to lose her temper a second time. She wouldn't make anything better with another outburst. "I know it probably seems that way, but I'm as sane as you are."

Heath's lips curved, but she wouldn't have called what they did a smile. "That's not saying much." He planted his fists on his hips and gave her another long look. "I don't want the responsibility for another person, lady. I'm no good with that kind of responsibility."

"And yet here I am. If you kick me out and something bad happens to me, won't *that* be your responsibility? Which one would be worse?"

She didn't really expect the question to shut him up, but that's exactly what it did. He moved to stand by the fireplace and stared at the hearth for a long time without speaking. When he finally turned back, his expression was hidden beneath shadow and whiskers. "And if I let you stay?"

Courtney let out a breath heavy with incredulity and edged with relief. "You believe me?"

"I didn't say that. I asked what you expect if I let you stay."

"Nothing. I just need a place to be safe while I either figure out how to get home again or find a way to earn some money so I can take care of myself."

Heath smiled as if she'd said something amusing. "What kind of work will you get?"

"I don't know, but I'm sure I can find something."

"In a place like this, there are only two things men want from a woman—the creature comforts of home or the other kind of comfort. You say you can't offer the one, and I gather you're not interested in offering the other."

"No, I'm not," she said firmly. "I refuse to believe that Fate brought me all this way to turn me into a . . . a strumpet." She paced a few feet away and kneaded her temples again. "But it *has* stuck me here, and I *am* going to survive."

"Of that," Heath said with a smile, "I have absolutely no doubt."

"Then you'll let me stay?"

"Until we find somewhere else for you to go."

She turned to say something, but the sunlight through the window hit him just-so, and what she saw stopped her cold. It was the tilt of his head, the look in his eye, the curve of his lips that brought back the image she'd seen in her grandmother's attic. Blond hair. Blue eyes full of mischief and a smile to match. Even the shape of his face was the same.

Did that mean that *Heath* was the man in the attic? Or was she just imagining the similarities because she was half starved, sick to her stomach, and close to fainting?

She didn't know what to think or what to believe. She didn't know how to feel or how to react. Everything she'd once known had been tossed into doubt. Everything she'd believed about life and logic, gone.

If Heath *was* the tall blond man she'd first imagined in Elizabeth's attic, what did that mean?

Courtney took a covert glance at his shaggy hair, his stubble of whiskers, his slightly red eyes. She caught a whiff of last night's whiskey on his breath, and a shudder racked her body. He couldn't be the same man, she told herself as she lay her head down again with a groan. He simply couldn't be.

Because if he was, that would mean that Fate had brought her here . . . to *him*.

He had a crazy woman on his hands, Heath told himself as he watched the emotions play across her face. First relief, then disbelief, then annoyance, and now horror—and all within the space of about a minute.

This is what came from being a Good Samaritan. This was precisely why he'd avoided people for the past five years, and why he *should* have avoided that damn shed last night. In one weak moment brought on by an entire night of bad luck, Heath had dug himself into a hole. Now he'd have to work like hell to get out of it again.

He turned away from her and clapped his hat on his head and headed for the door.

"Where are you going?"

"Out."

"Now? What about breakfast?"

"I'll survive." Heath grabbed his coat from its peg and shoved one arm into a sleeve.

"But—"

"I'll be back," he promised grudgingly. "Don't worry."

Courtney came around the table and stood in front of him. "What am I supposed to do while you're gone?"

If she hadn't been crazy, he might even have found her attractive. All dark eyes and creamy skin, the soft swell of breasts and the gentle swish of silk. He shoved aside the unwelcome memory of standing behind her and lacing that corset, the nip of waist and swell of hip that had made his mouth go dry. "I'm sure you'll think of something."

Courtney moved her hand and Heath jerked backward, knowing that if she touched him right then he'd never be the same. Her eyes widened at his response, but only for an instant. As they narrowed again, a smile curved the corners of her mouth.

He turned away so he wouldn't have to see it. Bad enough that he was reacting to her at all. Even worse that she realized it. But he couldn't bear to see that smile creep into her eyes or the flush of power stain her cheeks. Ladies had a way of twisting men around their little fingers and then dangling them like fish on a hook.

Ladies made promises, then changed their minds. Offered vows of undying devotion, then broke those vows the instant a man failed to live up to their expectations or a better man crossed their paths. Well, Heath couldn't fail to disappoint, and almost any man was a better choice, so he didn't stand a chance.

Not that he wanted one.

He yanked open the door, strode through, and glanced back at her. "Don't wait up."

She probably came back with a response, but Heath slammed the door between them before she could get a word out. He didn't need to hear what she had to say. He knew how ladies' minds worked.

She'd have played upon his unfortunate attraction for her to get what she wanted. Women did that. Used their smiles, their eyes, the softness and curves that men found so fascinating to render a man helpless. Once they had him paralyzed—or near as—they set about taking whatever they wanted while he was too numb to speak.

He'd been there before, and he had no intention of repeating that mistake. No sir. A soiled dove might raid your pockets, rob you blind, and drink the last of your whiskey when you were sleeping, but at least they were honest about it.

Given a choice between a shady lady and a virtuous one,

Heath would choose the shady variety any day of the week.

Unfortunately, he made it only about half a block before Courtney caught up with him, snagged his arm, and jerked him back around to face her. Her eyes flashed fire and her cheeks burned with anger. "You can't seriously intend to leave me in that horrid cabin alone."

Luckily, that moment he'd experienced in the cabin was over, and her touch did nothing to him. Or very little, anyway. "That horrid cabin," he snapped, pulling away just in case, "is a whole lot nicer than some of the other places you could have landed in this town. But if it doesn't suit, feel free to find other accommodations."

Her gaze faltered slightly. "That's not what I meant. But if I stay there all day long pacing the floor, the chances that I'll get home again are pretty slim."

He had no idea what she was playing at, but if it meant getting rid of her, he'd listen. "Does that mean you have an alternative suggestion?"

"Well, yes. Sort of." She raked the fingers of one hand through her hair and brought her hand down to shield her eyes from the early morning sun. Two grimy prospectors rounded the corner and cast a long, lingering glance at her. She gave a violent shudder and inched closer to Heath.

"I have only one goal, and that's to get back home again. I've been thinking about how to do that all morning. The way time travel always works in books and movies is that someone—that would be me—is sent through time because someone else—in this case, probably you—has made a mess of something and needs help fixing it."

Was she joking?

She apparently mistook his stunned silence for acquiescence. "So I think the best way to figure this whole thing out is to start at the beginning. You tell me about yourself, and together we can figure out where you went wrong."

Heath shook his head and turned away. "Find someone else to help, lady. I don't discuss my past."

"But why?"

She darted in front of him again, but he stepped around her and kept going. "Because I don't."

She fell into step beside him and let out a little laugh. "Well! I guess that proves me right, doesn't it?"

He stopped walking abruptly. "How do you figure?"

"That's pretty obvious, isn't it? If you refuse to discuss your past, that must mean you have something hidden back there. And whatever you have hidden is what we have to work on."

"There *is* no 'we,' lady." Heath started walking again, setting a brisk pace in the hopes that he could discourage her from trailing.

She lifted the hem of her skirt and came after him. "Of course there is. I'd be willing to bet that you're the reason I'm here. It's not a coincidence, you know. There *are* no coincidences."

Heath stepped around a man lugging a heavy crate toward a supply wagon and increased his pace, but he still couldn't shake her. She was a dogged little thing, he'd grant her that. "You're saying that you think Fate led me to the shed last night?"

"That's exactly what I'm saying."

"Then it was also Fate that put me in the middle of a robbery and earned me a crack on the head? Fate that took away all my money and my clothes?"

"Probably. If you'd left town, how could we have met?"

Heath plunged from the boardwalk onto the street. "That's an interesting way of looking at things, but I don't believe in Fate."

"Are you kidding? How can you not believe in Fate?" The rapid pace Heath was setting didn't seem to bother her in the slightest.

"It's quite simple, really. I choose instead to believe in common sense. I believe in what I can see, touch, and hear. You'd be wise to do the same."

"So, you're a skeptic."

"I'm a realist."

"You're a cynic."

Frustrated almost beyond his ability to cope, Heath stopped walking again. "Call me what you will, Miss Moss. It still won't convince me to talk about my past."

"Courtney," she corrected. "And you have to talk about it. I *know* there's some reason the two of us have been brought together, and I know you sense it, too. Why else would you have taken me in the way you did?"

Heath had to give up trying to outwalk her, and he was rapidly growing short on hope that he could outreason her. "I have done all that, Miss Moss, because I was raised to be a gentleman. That means I shudder at the thought of turning my back on a woman who has nowhere else to go and no one to care for her—especially when it is abundantly clear that she is incapable of caring for herself. There is absolutely nothing more than that behind my actions."

Her gaze darted to his and locked there. An angry flush stained her cheeks. "*Incapable?* I've got news for you, buddy. I'm not asking you to take care of me. *I* take care of myself. I always have. And call me Courtney, dammit. I *hate* being called Miss Moss."

"Fine. If you're so adept at caring for yourself, then please—go right ahead."

"I would. I *will*. Just as soon as I find work."

"Yeah?" He turned away again, disconcerted by the effect the light in her eyes and the flush in her cheeks were having on him. "Well, good luck with that."

She moved with startling speed and planted herself in front of him. "Have you listened to even one word I've said? I don't *want* to stay here and find work. I *want* to go home again. Like it or not, I need your cooperation to do that."

He mopped his face with one hand and tried to hang on to what little patience he had left. But when he spotted Gunther Schmidt's Mercantile half a block down the street, a different idea occurred to him entirely. "Tell you what," he said, taking her by the hand and dragging her toward his new target. "You cooperate with me, and then, if you're not back where you belong, I'll cooperate with you. How does that sound?"

She glanced up at him uncertainly. "What do you want me to do?"

"I'm taking you to meet someone. If you have people in this town, he'll know them."

The light in her eyes faded and her smile faltered. "You don't believe me, do you?"

"Nope."

"You really do think I'm crazy."

"That's one word for it. I might look like a simple, uneducated man, but I was educated at some very fine institutions of learning, and I've been told that I'm quite bright. I *know* that what you claim is impossible."

"But that's the irony of this whole situation. *I* know that, too. And yet, here I am. I'm an extremely practical person in real life, but I'm standing here with you in the middle of the Virginia City gold rush. I keep expecting to wake up and discover that I'm locked in a dream, but I don't think that's going to happen. I'm supposed to be interviewing for the job of my life in a few weeks, and the only thing I want is to get home again. But that's not going to happen unless you'll trust me."

"I," he said sharply, "don't trust anyone."

"Really? I never would have guessed." Courtney's gaze flickered to their joined hands and the color returned to her cheeks. She snatched her hand away as if she suspected him of trying to steal it. "Then maybe *that's* why I'm here. Maybe I'm supposed to help you learn how to trust other people. Maybe we're supposed to help each other."

"There's one thing wrong with that theory," Heath said, shoving his hands into his pockets to keep from reaching for her again. "I have no interest in trusting anyone else. Trust is a highly overrated commodity."

"Now *that's* cynical." She sighed, shook her head, and started over.

Yep. Dogged.

"All I want is to get back where I belong," she said, enunciating carefully. "Is that so much to ask?"

"I believe that's my opportunity to point out—again—that you're welcome to leave my company whenever you like."

"Then I have to remind you that I *can't do that*." Her voice grew sharper with every word, until the last one hit his ear like a knife point.

"Oh, but I'll bet you can." He snagged her hand again and

tugged her along the boardwalk. Two minutes later he jerked open the door to the Mercantile and held it for her. "It's been an interesting morning, Miss Moss. I hope the rest of your life is very happy."

She started through, eyes straight ahead, chin high, but as she drew even with him, she slowed and smiled. "Don't say good-bye just yet. This guy *isn't* going to know me."

"We'll see."

She shrugged and sailed on through, tossing "And you think *I'm* delusional" at him over her shoulder as she passed.

Heath wasn't about to waste another second arguing with her. Time would prove him right. Let Gunther Schmidt and his wife get one good look at her, and she'd be on her way back to friends or family and out of his hair forever.

He leaned against the counter and crossed one foot over the other to watch her. She looked around the store's dark interior as if she'd never seen it before. But that didn't bother Heath in the slightest. She could have lost all memory of her life, and it still wouldn't matter.

They'd only been there a minute when Gunther Schmidt came into the store from the storage room in back. He gave Heath a jerk of his chin in greeting. "You're back, then."

"I said I would be. This is the young lady I told you about."

Courtney tossed a pointed half-smile at Heath and warmed it up a bit for Gunther. "This gentleman seems to think you know me. Is he right? Have you ever seen me before?"

Heath folded his arms, smiling, as he waited.

Gunther didn't answer immediately, and his hesitation disturbed Heath a little. He hadn't expected it to be a difficult question. Gunther looked from Courtney to Heath a couple of times and then shook his head. "No. Can't say that I have. You sure she's from around here?"

Damn and blast! Heath ignored the gloating smile Courtney sent him and moved closer to Gunther as if that might help him remember. "Are you *sure* you didn't see Miss Moss at the Grand Ball last night?"

Gunther spent another second or two studying Courtney's face. He looked straight into her eyes and even walked partway around her before he shook his head again. "Nope. Not last night. Not before that, either."

"But she was there," Heath argued. "At the ball. At least, she *claims* that she was there."

"Not that I saw, and I would've. But if you want to check with some of the other merchants around, go ahead. Won't hurt my feelings any."

But Hans Grubber from the bakery next door was no help at all. Neither was Roscoe Harper from the meat market across the street or No-Nose McNulty from the assay office. The city didn't have a church yet, or a schoolhouse, but nobody at either bank had heard of anyone named Moss, and neither had any of the folks at the laundry.

An hour later Heath and Courtney stood on the boardwalk without a single lead. Heath wanted to throttle somebody. Courtney wore a very annoying smile, and the gleam of triumph lit her eyes. "Do you believe me now?"

"No."

"Oh, come on. It's Fate. I told you—"

"Don't start," Heath warned, cutting her off before she could go any further. "I don't want to hear it."

"Fine, but you can't change what's true just because you don't want it to be."

Heath matched her look exactly. "Believe me, I know that. If I could, there are a whole slew of things I'd change." Starting with losing Blue and moving right on down the list to Courtney, herself.

"So? Tell me what they are."

"Absolutely not."

She scowled up at him. "You promised."

He frowned right back. "I lied."

Her scowl deepened. "That's not fair."

Heath smiled coldly and stopped in front of Buck's, the only restaurant in town where he stood a chance of getting their breakfast on credit—and those chances were slim. "The first thing you're going to have to learn, Miss—*Courtney,* is that life is rarely fair."

"You think I don't know that? My life hasn't exactly been a bed of roses up until now, you know. I didn't need this any more than you probably did. But at least I'm willing to *try* setting things right. If you have your way, I'll be stuck here forever . . . with *you*. Frankly, I'd rather be dead." And with that, she swept off and left him standing there, holding open the door while three old prospectors tromped into the restaurant.

Heath swore aloud and let the door swing shut behind the last one. He thought about following Courtney, but his patience was worn as thin as the soles of her slippers. He'd tried to help her. God knew, he had. So from here on, she could do as she wanted and he'd make no effort to stop her. If she got herself into trouble, well, she'd just have to find her own way out. Heath didn't owe her a damn thing, and he was tired of her acting as if he did.

Chapter 6

DERRY STEPPED ONTO the boardwalk outside his hotel, stretched, and sucked in a lung full of clean, fresh, early morning air. Another beautiful day and him standing right in the middle of it. A man couldn't get much luckier.

Imagine. Just three years off the boat from Ireland, and here he was smack in the middle of a gold strike. Money lay out there. Money just itching to be scooped up and taken. And in the short time he'd been here, he'd scooped up a bit already.

It wasn't that Derry thought making a fortune would be easy. He wasn't a babe, after all. And nothing came easy to the Dennehy men—with the exception of horse thievery, that is. But he'd made himself a vow to lay off that particular occupation here in America, and so far he'd been able to keep that promise.

He was standing in the land of milk and honey, a land rich with opportunities, where anything was possible if a man just had enough gumption and determination. Derry had both in abundant supply—and a healthy dose of common sense thrown in for good measure.

He took another deep breath and stepped off into the dirt, whistling softly under his breath. He'd spent the night before stitching his life savings into the lining of his coat. His most recent winnings sat heavily in his pocket, reminding him that he had a dozen people or more counting on him to make good. Derry wasn't in the habit of making mistakes, but just knowing that he couldn't afford one, that lives would be ruined and even lost if he failed, weighted his shoulders.

He'd have to be cautious in his choice of companions. No business with those who didn't have an honest look in their eyes. No dallying with the ladies. No excessive use of whiskey—although if it had come right down to it, he'd have had a hard time deciding what was necessary and what was excess.

He'd have to be conservative when it came to doling out the cash, as well. Another trait not usually associated with the family Dennehy. But there was a first time for everything . . . at least, that's what he'd been told.

Still whistling, he stuffed his hands into his pockets and strolled aimlessly through the streets. Somewhere in Virginia City he'd find his golden opportunity. He'd been brought here for a reason. He knew that as surely as he knew his own name. So until he found out why, he'd bide his time.

Patience wasn't a typical Dennehy trait, either, but Derry had been working on his for the past three years. He was a whole lot closer to being a patient man today than he'd been when he left Ireland.

And so he meandered for a while, still trying to get a feel for the city and the folks in it. But it didn't take long in the August heat to work up a thirst, and once the thirst was upon him, Derry saw no reason to ignore it. Sure now, he reasoned, couldn't his Golden Opportunity be inside a saloon as easily as anywhere else? In fact, in a place like Fourteen-Mile City, a saloon might be the most logical place to look.

He pushed through the swinging doors of the very next saloon he came to and wandered to the bar without even paying attention to where he was. He slapped a coin on the counter and ordered a drink, then turned with one elbow resting on the bar's polished wood surface to let his eyes wander around the room.

His gaze landed on the woman almost immediately. That

she was a soiled dove was obvious from the first glance, but it was the look of her that caught Derry's attention and held him spellbound. She was, quite simply, the most remarkable woman he'd ever seen.

There was fire in her dusky eyes and determination lifting her chin, and though his mother would have found his interest in a fallen woman shocking—not to mention proof positive that he was bound for hell alongside his father—her opinion didn't matter to Derry in the least. She was, after all, half a world away, and God above only knew when he'd see her again.

But Derry knew in that instant that he wouldn't rest until he had the woman. Not in his bed—he could have accomplished that with the coins in his pocket. Derry wanted her the way a man wants the woman who'll bear his children and grow old by his side.

There was such a woman back in Ireland, picked out for him by his mother and waiting for him to send for her. But in the space between one heartbeat and another, Derry knew that Mary Margaret O'Toole would have to find someone else to marry. Derry was no longer available.

He lowered his beer to the bar and turned slightly, and he found the bartender—a ruddy man with hair as red as his cheeks—watching him.

The bartender nodded toward his Glorious Creature and ran a rag round and round inside a glass. "Are you interested?"

Derry looked at her again, took another long pull from the watery beer he'd paid too much for, and shook his head. He didn't want to meet her under these circumstances.

"You sure? She's new. Just in from New Orleans. I can call her over if you'd like."

Again Derry shook his head, and this time he forced a smile so the bartender wouldn't guess the full extent of his interest. He nudged the coin he'd left on the bar with one finger. "I'm a little short tonight."

"Ah. Too bad. She's a purty one, isn't she?"

Pretty didn't even begin to describe her, but Derry lifted one shoulder as if he had no opinion at all. "Another time, perhaps." And then, before he could change his mind and ruin everything, he pocketed his change and left the saloon.

Outside, he checked the name of the place and committed it to memory. The Pink Parasol. Sure, and he'd be back. That was a promise.

By Thursday, Courtney was starting to worry. She'd been in the past for nearly a week already, and it was beginning to look as if she would be stuck here a while.

Shortly after Heath strode down the street into town and away from her, she scraped leftovers from yet another disastrous breakfast into the trash pile near the outhouse. How could something that seemed so simple, like biscuits, be so difficult?

Once or twice during the past few days she'd accidentally produced something edible, but she'd never been able to duplicate her efforts for two reasons: one, she had no way to write down what she'd tried; and two, that dreadful pounding in her head still hadn't gone away and she was having trouble remembering much of anything. Sometimes she thought that traveling through time had damaged her in some way. Others, she figured hunger might figure into the equation.

She'd made flat biscuits, soggy lumps of dough, and then something that had closely resembled hockey pucks. This morning's efforts looked like miniature tortillas, but they had the snap and crunch of saltines. And the list of failures when it came to gravy was just as long. And don't even get her started on how many times she'd tried and failed to get back home again.

She let out the breath she'd been holding on a sigh of frustration and gulped another breath through her mouth as she reached for the second plate. It seemed that every day she added a handful of things to the growing list of items she missed from her own life. First on this morning's list—trash collection.

Showers were a high priority item, right up there with her own bed and comfortable clothes. There weren't even words to describe how much she missed antiperspirant—and not just for herself. The entire population of Virginia City could have benefited greatly from a liberal application.

Fast food. Soda. Television. Radio. The video-rental store down the street from her Denver condo. Her favorite bookstore. Any book at *all*, even one she'd read a dozen times already.

She missed her job. Missed the hustle and bustle and feeling as if she mattered to somebody somewhere. She was even starting to miss co-workers she didn't particularly like. She missed Ryan, and she longed for any mode of transportation other than her feet, anything to eat that hadn't been produced by her own hands and wasn't cured pork, venison, or elk.

She'd sponged spots out of the dress nightly in a washbowl and scrubbed the smelliest parts with strong lye soap that felt as if it was eating her hands bit by bit. The once beautiful silk hung limply in some places, puckered with wrinkles in others. The spots she'd scrubbed had lost their sheen and she was beginning to look as if she *belonged* in a cabin with Heath Sullivan. The only thing missing was the horrid stench of whiskey that seemed to float in the air whenever he was around—and there were times when she thought that might have been an improvement.

The hope that Fate would realize its mistake and take her home again was rapidly fading. Apparently she was here to stay—at least for a while. She just hoped she hadn't scrubbed out the dress's magic.

This was their fifth day together—if you could call their brief encounters every morning and evening *together*. Heath barely spoke to her about anything that wasn't a necessity, and every attempt she made to draw him into conversation met with a frown so deep she was sure it must hurt. After an almost silent breakfast, he'd disappear into town and return long after dark to sit across from her and mutely eat whatever disaster she spooned onto his plate.

More than once, she'd heard him leave him late at night and then come stumbling back hours later reeking of whiskey, cigars, and probably women. She could have counted on one hand the number of times he'd broken the silence between them voluntarily, and the longer this went on, the less she wanted him to break it at all. But she was also more convinced than ever that she'd have to find out his story before she could get home again.

True or not, at least that gave her some hope to cling to.

Letting out another heavy sigh, she scraped the last of breakfast into the pile of rotting food and turned back to the cabin. Once she left the stench of garbage behind, she walked slowly, enjoying the feel of sunshine on her face and shoulders, and dreading another day inside that tiny, dark room with its narrow glassless windows, its corners filled with shadow, and air heavy with the scent of burning wood and charred food.

On impulse, she left the plates beside the door and walked to the edge of the street. The more she watched the community of prospectors around her, the less threatening they seemed. If any of them had wanted to harm her, they'd had ample opportunity with Heath gone most of the time.

Far from appearing frightening, they actually seemed friendly—friendlier than Heath, anyway. One old man in particular spent hours every day sitting on a barrel in front of his tent and working on something Courtney couldn't identify from a distance. He owned a dog, or the dog owned him. She couldn't tell which. It was a mangy yellow mutt with a broad plume of tail, and it trailed the old man everywhere he went and lay at his feet while he worked, and Courtney had begun to envy the old man his companion.

They were there now, but the old man was so tightly focused on his task, he hadn't noticed her. Suddenly fed up with Heath, bored to tears with the pattern of her days, and so hungry for conversation she'd even seek out male companionship, Courtney squared her shoulders and started toward the old man's tent.

He looked up as she approached and scrambled to his feet. The dog lumbered up from the ground and wagged its tail warily. Wrinkles of concentration on the old man's face smoothed into a broad smile barely visible beneath his thick white beard. He yanked off his hat and sketched a rusty bow. "Ma'am. Is there something wrong? Something I can help you with?"

Courtney couldn't see anyone else nearby, but she could

feel them watching her. She still felt no threat, just a palpable
curiosity. And it occurred to her that she had more in common with these displaced men than she would ever have
thought. Their reasons for being in the city might be different
from hers, but homesickness didn't seem to be a respecter of
boundaries. If it had been, Courtney might have been able to
avoid longing for a place she'd once hated.

She smiled and shook her head in answer to his question
as she took in the ring of ashes where he built his nightly
fire, the tent that didn't look as if it would last another winter,
the few crates of supplies on the ground nearby. "There's no
trouble. I've just noticed you out here the past few mornings,
and I thought it was time I said hello." She held out her hand
and added, "I'm Courtney Moss."

"Philo Keegan." The old man shook quickly and released,
but his lips curved slightly beneath his whiskers. "Guess I'll
admit that I've noticed you, too." He glanced behind him
and shrugged. "We all have. A lady like you is a welcome
sight in a place like this."

Courtney glanced at her gown and laughed. "Then that's
a sad commentary on what life is usually like."

Philo folded what looked like a newspaper and stuck it
aside, then jerked his head toward the cabin. "That husband
of yours going to object to this visit?"

"Heath?" Courtney scowled deeply. No one had ever cared
that much about what she did, and Heath wasn't likely to be
the first. "He's not my husband," she said. "And even if he
was, it wouldn't matter whether he objected or not. He
doesn't own me."

A knowing look filled Philo's old gray eyes. "I see. Well,
I suppose you won't find many around here who'll pass judgment on your choices. It's hard enough just survivin' in a
place like this. Judging others is a luxury for folks with
nothin' better to do."

"It's not like *that*, either," Courtney assured him quickly.
"Heath's a friend." How was that for an overstatement?
"He's just giving me a place to stay until I can get home
again, that's all. But we're not . . . not . . ." The look in

Philo's old eyes made it hard to get the words out. She finally settled for a lame, "Believe me, we're *not*."

"Well, that's all right, too, I reckon." Philo pulled a grimy handkerchief from his pocket and used it to dust the barrel he'd vacated, then motioned her toward it. "I don't get visitors often, but I haven't forgotten all my manners. Would you like to set a spell? I don't have much, but I can offer you a biscuit and a daub of chokecherry jam."

Courtney made herself reasonably comfortable on the barrel's top. "You *cook*?"

Philo laughed easily. "A fella wouldn't last very long out here if he couldn't." He poured water from a jug over his hands and wiped them carefully on his handkerchief. Squatting near the side of the tent, he moved a rock from the top of a crate and unwrapped a towel that held two golden-brown biscuits cooked to perfection—at least, they *looked* perfect. He busied himself with a jar of ruby-colored jelly and handed her the plate with a flourish that made her laugh.

She bit . . . and for the first time in her life, she understood what it felt like to swoon. That biscuit was the single best thing she'd ever tasted in her life.

She wolfed half and would have licked the jam from her fingers if Philo hadn't been watching her so closely. Remembering that she was *supposed* to be a lady, she lowered her hand to her lap and promised herself to take the second half slower. "It's delicious," she said when her mouth was empty. "How did you learn to cook like this?"

Philo shrugged nonchalantly, but she could tell that the compliment had pleased him. He dragged a crate closer and made himself comfortable. "Had me a partner who taught me when I first started out. His grandfather taught him. Geezer, here"—Philo jerked his head toward the dog—"helps by giving his honest opinion." He leaned forward and scratched between the mutt's ears. "There ain't a better judge of a good biscuit anywhere on earth than this old fella."

Courtney tore a bite from the treasure on her plate and slipped it into her mouth. "Maybe I should ask if I can borrow him, then. I've been trying for days to make an edible biscuit—an edible anything, in fact—and failing miserably."

Philo straightened again and regarded her with interest. "Your mother didn't teach you how to cook?"

"I'm afraid not."

"No grandmother or aunt who could step in and help?"

"My mother was an only child, and my grandmother—" She broke off with a shake of her head. "My grandmother took me in when my mother left, but she really didn't want to be bothered with me."

"Well, now, that's a shame. Things like cookin' are best learned when they're passed down from generation to generation." He slanted a smile at her that made it hard to slip into self-pity. "But that don't mean that's the only way to learn. You want to learn how to make a good biscuit, I can teach you."

For the first time in days, Courtney felt a flicker of hope. She didn't even care if the old man had an angle. She was too hungry to worry about it. "That would be wonderful," she said, "but don't you have other things to do?"

Philo scratched his chin thoughtfully. "Important as it is to whittle a bunch of nothin' and then turn it into kindling, I could probably see my way to giving it up for an hour or two."

Courtney was surprised by how relaxed she felt around the old man. "Why *do* you sit here all day long? Don't you have a claim to work?"

"Did. Did." He nodded and rested one ankle on the opposite knee. "Truth to tell, the Jezebel's not giving up the gold like she should. I left her a couple of weeks back and thought I'd get on with one of the mining companies. But that don't sit well with me, neither. I've been my own boss too long to settle easily under somebody else's thumb now." He popped half a biscuit into his mouth and spoke around it. "Maybe I'm just tired. I'd go home—if I had a home to go to."

"You don't have a family somewhere?"

"Not anymore. Leastwise, nobody who'd be happy to see me if I did go back."

"Sounds like we have something in common." Courtney

took another bite and licked the jam from her lips. "How long have you been doing this?"

"Prospecting?" Philo ran a hand across his beard and squinted one eye. "Verlis and me first set off in 'forty-seven. We had it in mind to make our fortunes and then find ourselves a couple a' wives and settle down. . . ." He winked and added, "One wife apiece, that is. But the fortune never came, and I passed by every woman I met along the way who could a' been a good wife. And now here I am, a lonely old man with no place to go."

Courtney polished off the rest of her biscuit and set the plate aside. "And what about the Jezebel?"

"Got me a friend who's watching her for me until I figure things out. Which I'd better do quick." He scratched his beard and looked out over the camp. "Gang of thugs out there'll take her from me if I don't, and the decision will be made for me."

Courtney resisted the urge to lick the jam she'd left on her plate. "What gang?"

"Tyree Caine and his boys. Worthless bunch of critters. You ever come acrost 'em, steer clear. That's my best advice." He slapped his knees and pushed to his feet. "You want me to show you how to make them biscuits now or later?"

"Now would be great if you really have the time." Courtney stood with him and tried not to let the idea of a gang of outlaws make her nervous. She wondered if Heath knew about them, and if so, how he could leave her alone day after day.

Listen to her, she thought with a silent laugh of derision. How many times did Heath have to tell her he didn't want her around before she started believing it? How many nights did he have to leave her alone in that cabin before she got it through her thick head that he wasn't the man from the attic? And why, after all the times Leslie had shown how easy she was to leave, did she still long for someone who cared enough to stay?

•   •   •

By nightfall Courtney had turned out three batches of mouth-watering biscuits in a row and earned Geezer's unqualified approval in the process. She'd made not just one friend, but half a dozen—men from the camp who'd trailed one-by-one across the street to see what Philo was doing.

One of the youngest, a boy of about eighteen whom the others called Moonshine, had overheard her grumbled complaint about the pink silk ball gown and run off to bring her a pair of almost-new trousers and a spare shirt. Someone else had offered a clean pair of socks and boots that needed only a little stuffing in the toes to make them fit. Much as Courtney hated wearing secondhand clothes, she was almost painfully grateful for these. Just getting out of that dress and the corset made her feel human again for the first time in days.

By the time she heard Heath coming up the walk long after dark, she was happier than she'd been all week and eager to show him what she'd accomplished while he was away. He was either too much of a gentleman or too stubborn to complain about her cooking, but maybe seeing that she was making progress would put him in a better mood.

Something had to.

She waited by the fireplace where the pan of biscuits she'd taken from the coals a few minutes earlier lay cooling. Her heart beat with a strange exhilaration until she realized that she wanted to please him, which made her shudder with dread and quickly renew the vow she'd first made when she was seven years old. She would *not* turn into her mother, no matter what might come her way.

She replaced the smile she'd been wearing with a scowl just as Heath opened the door. He came inside without even so much as a glance, which only made her irritation more biting. Bad enough that she should want to please him, even for a minute. Far worse that she should have such a weak urge when he continually acted as if he wished she weren't alive.

He hung his hat on a peg, draped his vest over the back of his chair, and sat without so much as a word.

After the day she'd had, his sullen silence infuriated her. It wasn't as if she'd *asked* for this, either. She picked up the pan of biscuits and started toward the table, but she hadn't even taken two full steps when searing heat tore through her hand and she lost her grip on the pan.

It clattered to the floor and golden-brown biscuits flew into the air. One landed in Heath's lap, one bounced off the table, a couple skidded under the bed, and the rest took off for parts unknown.

Courtney wasn't sure which was worse—the pain in her hand or the bitter disappointment of failing again. Unbidden, tears of frustration began to blur her vision. She blinked rapidly and turned away, furious with herself and determined to keep Heath from noticing.

An uneasy silence stretched after the pan stopped clattering, and Heath's voice sounded frighteningly close to her ear. "Let me see it."

Clutching her aching hand to her chest, she whipped around to face him. "See what?"

"Your hand, of course." With surprising tenderness, he took her by the wrist and lowered her hand. "Just as I thought," he said, frowning at the red welts on her palm and then lifting his gaze to treat her to his disapproval.

His expression was so reminiscent of the one her grandmother had used to show disfavor, Courtney squirmed uncomfortably and tried to pull her hand away. "I know. I know. I should have used something to protect my hand. You don't need to tell me."

"It might have been a good idea," Heath said, "but I wasn't going to tell you. I figure you're smart enough to know that." He pulled her toward the table and plunged her hand into the bucket of cool water she'd left there. "Keep your hand there so the burning will stop. I'll try to find something we can use as a bandage."

"I don't need a bandage," she said petulantly. "I'm sure it'll be just fine."

Heath ignored her protest and dug through the crates against the wall. "You want to tell me what's going on here?"

"Isn't it obvious? I burned my hand."

He slanted a glance over his shoulder. "That's not what I meant." He jerked his head toward her clothes and turned away again. "I meant the new getup. Where did that come from?"

Courtney pulled her hand from the bucket and reached for the flour-sack towel she should have used in the first place. "I made some new friends today. They each donated something so that I could get out of that dress. I swear, if I'd worn that for another minute, I'd have gone stark, raving mad."

Heath straightened slowly and fixed her with another of those looks that brought her childhood back in a rush. "What new friends?"

She waved her good hand with an airiness she didn't feel. "Just a few of the men who live in the camp across the way."

Heath's expression hardened, then turned to ice. "You made *friends* with the men in camp? Are you crazy?" He apparently gave up trying to find a bandage and strode across the room so he could look mean and foreboding close-up. "Do you have any idea what kind of men they are?"

But Courtney had been glowered at by too many of Leslie's boyfriends to cower. "Very nice men," she said, matching his tone exactly.

"*Nice?*" Heath's question echoed off the walls. "Do you know what could have happened to you?"

"Of course I do. I'm not an idiot." She hated him for bringing back the doubts she'd shed that afternoon and backed a step away to put some distance between them. "But I don't know why *you're* so upset. It's not as if you'd *care* if anything bad happened to me."

"Of course I'd care. Like it or not, you're my responsibility until I can find—"

"Someone to pass me off to?" Courtney finished before he could. "Gee, thanks. You have no idea how special that makes me feel." Restless energy flowed from him in waves and mixed with her own agitation. No matter where she moved, turbulence filled the air around her and pricked at her skin. The pulsing in her hand grew worse by the minute, but pride wouldn't let her admit it aloud.

She pulled her chair away from the table and stood behind it. "You're a jerk, you know that? For five days all you've done is ignore me. You barely speak to me except to yell when you think I've done something wrong, and you've made it abundantly clear that I'm nothing but a thorn in your side. So don't you dare pretend that you care whether I make friends with the prospectors across the way, or that you'd even blink hard if they raped or killed me. *We* aren't friends," she said, waving her hand in the space between them. "You don't get a say in what I do."

Heath's eyes flashed and his nostrils flared slightly. "Are you finished?"

"For the moment."

"Good. Then you can listen." Heath caught her upper arms before she realized he was moving, hauled her to her chair, and planted her firmly on the seat. He loomed over her, one hand on either side, trapping her in place. "You *are* a thorn in my side," he said, his face just inches from hers. "I won't pretend otherwise. If not for you, I'd be long gone from this town and everything in it. But instead of spending my days trying to track down the property that was stolen from me—property I was paid to return to its rightful owner—I've been trying to find somebody in this godforsaken town who knows *you*."

"And you're going to blame that on *me*? I *told* you that you wouldn't find anybody. But did you listen? No!" She tried to duck under one of his arms, but he moved too quickly for her. She lifted her chin and glared back at him, determined not to let him think he'd won even a small victory. "Let's try it again, shall we? I'll speak slowly so you can understand. *I. Am. Not. From. Here*. Can you understand that, or should I use even smaller words?"

"Oh, I understand, all right." He leaned in even closer and his brittle energy surrounded her. "Now let's see if you can understand this: You are *not* from the future. You cannot *be* from the future. So either you're a very sick and confused woman, or you're running some kind of game and using me as the patsy. Which is it, Courtney? Are you sick? Or are you trying to con me?"

"Con you?" Courtney laughed contemptuously. "Out of *what*? A tin of lard? A bag of dried peas? What do you have that I could *possibly* want?"

His gaze stayed riveted on hers and his eyes darkened. For the space of a breath Courtney thought he was actually going to kiss her. It wouldn't have taken much to accomplish the deed. If either of them had moved even slightly, their lips would have brushed against the other's. Courtney told herself that she couldn't imagine anything more foul, but the catch in her breath and the tingle in her belly told a different story.

Did she want to kiss him?

No. Of course not. *Absolutely* not. He was everything wrong. Everything she didn't want. Everything she despised in a man. He was big and brash and dirty and foul and rude. He lived for the moment and cared diddly-squat about the future. He wasn't even *alive* in her world. Kissing a man who was, technically, dead seemed sick and wrong.

Except that he seemed very much alive right now.

Just as she thought Heath *would* kiss her, he pushed away from the table and backed a foot or two away. Casting an angry glance at her, he mopped his face with his hand and strode toward the door, jerking his hat from its peg and slamming outside before Courtney could even catch her breath.

She sank against her chair and put her trembling hands on her overheated cheeks, and she wondered what in the *hell* had gotten into her. She stood uncertainly and moved to the window where she could watch him churn up the distance to the street and hurry toward town. And she almost managed to convince herself that the sinking sensation in her heart was relief, not disappointment.

Chapter 7

HEATH SHOVED THROUGH the doors of the Pink Parasol and signaled for Red Will to bring him a bottle before he even got to the bar. He downed two shots of dust cutter without breathing in between, and scowled at the glossy wood beneath his elbows while he waited for Courtney's image to fade. When it only grew stronger, he tossed back a third shot and curled his fist around the empty glass.

He'd almost kissed her.

Talk about a damn fool thing to do. What had gotten into him? What the hell was he thinking?

He *wasn't* thinking, obviously. If he had been, he wouldn't have taken Courtney to the cabin in the first place. He'd have found somewhere else to sleep himself. He never would have let those deep brown eyes coerce him into staying in the cabin with her. And he'd *never* have let the idea of kissing her cross his mind.

Scowling darkly, he turned the empty glass in his hand and tried to figure out how to extricate himself from the situation he'd created. He couldn't let Courtney stay in that cabin alone and unprotected—not with all these ragamuffin scoundrels running around. But *he* sure as hell wasn't going to spend twenty-four hours a day around her. His mind would conjure even more ridiculous ideas if he did that.

Lost in thought, he didn't even hear Sally come up behind him until one soft arm slithered around his neck and the cushion of breasts pillowed against his arm. "Well, well, well," she purred as she pressed against him. "If it isn't Bonnie Prince Charming." She nuzzled a little closer and pouted up at him. "You're looking mighty dour. Is something wrong?"

Grateful to the center of his bones for the diversion, Heath turned on his stool and wrapped an arm around Sally's waist. "Nothing a few hours, some good company, and a bottle can't fix."

She smiled seductively and snuggled closer, but Heath must still have been too sober to appreciate her charms. Her eyes seemed vague and shadowy, and her smile less than genuine. At least there were no delusions here, Heath told himself as he poured another shot with his free hand. He couldn't pretend that Sally cared about him, but then he'd never wanted to. He was well aware that her enthusiasm wasn't for his company.

But, dammit, that had never mattered to him before, and he wasn't going to let it matter today. And anyway, Courtney hadn't meant what she'd said back at the cabin. She'd been angry and she'd lashed out with the first thing she could think of. So why did he have this empty spot in his chest, and why this strange yearning for someone to *want* his company?

Sally trailed one finger along his jawline and drew his attention back to the moment. "I'm flattered that you came back to see me instead of staying with that other one."

Desperate to put Courtney out of his mind, Heath abandoned his glass and pulled Sally closer still. "What other one?"

"The one I saw you with in town the other day. I never could understand why a man would want to chase the skirts of those proper types. The rewards aren't nearly so sweet, are they?"

What *would* the rewards have been if he'd followed his natural inclination and kissed her? Would she have been cold as ice or would she have responded with fire? Would she have returned his kiss or rewarded him with a sound slap on the cheek?

He didn't care. That was the whole point. *He didn't care.* He was mildly curious, that's all. He sure as hell wasn't going to kiss her just to find out.

To prove his utter lack of curiosity, he nuzzled Sally's neck and trailed his lips to her chin. He wanted what he always wanted. A little comfort, even if it was bought and paid for. A man in his position couldn't afford to be choosy.

A sultry laugh escaped Sally's lips. "You're not gonna start ignoring me now that Will has some new girls, are you?"

Heath shook his head and waited for the desire that had begun stirring back at the cabin to wake up again. But it didn't come, and twenty minutes later he was beginning to wonder if it ever would.

A person would think it was Courtney he wanted, but Heath knew better. It was something more basic than that. But for some reason, she'd sparked the yearning. Well, he resented her for doing it. For the first time in years he couldn't shove aside that yearning to belong.

He wanted a home. Family. Friends. People who sought out his company because of who he was, not because of the gold in his pocket. People who could look beyond the ugliness of his past and forgive the choices that had driven him into the wilderness in the first place.

But that would never happen. Hell, he couldn't even forgive himself.

He reached for the bottle again and caught Red Will's quick, satisfied smile. He was nothing more than an easy buck to the folks here at the Pink Parasol. He knew that. Accepted it. Didn't care. He *wanted* his life to be this way. He'd worked damn hard to get it here. And he wasn't going to make changes now just because some crazy woman had crossed his path. It didn't take Sally long to figure out that she was wasting her time and move on. Business was business, after all. It took a whole lot longer for Heath to stop envisioning a set of bottomless brown eyes and an unruly shock of short dark hair. To stop seeing that hint of red created by the sunlight and the gentle curve of lips just before a full smile claimed them.

In fact, it wasn't until the commotion erupted behind him, a woman staggered into his arms, and an entire shot glass full of dust cutter splashed across his chest, that Courtney left his thoughts at all.

The woman, obviously one of Will's new girls, was dressed in lavender silk. She landed heavily, pinned his back against the bar, and knocked the wind out of him. All he saw was a mass of dark hair and the curve of a breast before she dug one dagger-sharp elbow into his chest and tried to stand.

Knowing that she was going to leave bruises behind, Heath took her by the arms and tried to help her back onto her feet.

She lurched off his lap, ran her hands across the curls on her head, and tossed a glance at him. "Sorry. I didn't mean to fall on you." Her gaze passed across his face, but she didn't really look at him. If she had, she might have recognized him. She might even have felt the same cold fist in the gut Heath felt when he got a good look at her face.

Delilah.

She was exactly as Heath remembered her, but seeing her after all this time—in this place—froze any reaction he might have had. Even if he'd doubted his eyes, his ears would have convinced him. How could anyone forget that summer-night voice? He'd never heard another one like it before or since the summers they'd spent together as children.

Memories came rushing back at once, and the empty hole that had taken the place of a heart for so long puckered and coughed painfully. In that short span of time—no more than the fraction of a second it would have taken a heart to beat— all the pain he'd worked so hard to drown came rushing back. All the memories. All the happiness and all the misery.

As if he were standing on a mountaintop and looking down, he saw three young adults laughing together—two light-skinned and one dark. Two slaves, one master. Heath had been more comfortable with them than he'd ever been with his own family.

He felt the smile Blue had always worn when he saw Delilah and remembered how the adoration had shone in his dark eyes. And for the space of another heartbeat, Heath imagined Blue standing beside him now.

As a boy, Heath hadn't been able to understand what they felt for each other. As a young man, their love had fueled his dreams of finding a woman who would look at him in the same way—and he at her. Now, he felt the pang of regret, both for his part in separating them and because he'd never know a love like the one they'd shared.

Delilah's skin had always been light enough for her to pass as white, and apparently she'd found the chance to do just that. There were too many southern boys in the gold fields around Virginia City, and Will was too much an opportunist to risk offending them and hurting his business by putting a Negro to work in his house. But how had she gone from slave to free, white sporting gal in five short years?

She stood with her back to him, ramrod straight, chin jutting into the air, exactly the same way she'd stood when he and Blue had watched the wagon bearing her away from Bonne Chance and to her new home.

That was the last time Heath had seen her . . . until tonight. Worse, it was the last time Blue had ever seen her. And all because Heath's father had sold her with less regard than he spared for one of his precious horses.

Guilt and regret gut-punched Heath and knocked the breath from his lungs. She hadn't recognized him. He could turn around and walk away and pretend that he hadn't seen her. He *should* do exactly that. Facing her would be too hard. It would require too much of him.

How could he tell her that Blue was dead? What words could he use to explain why? And where would he find the courage to speak aloud for the first time about his own part in the death of a man he'd loved like a brother?

It wasn't surprising that Delilah didn't recognize him. Not only was some poor excuse for humanity grabbing for her, but Heath looked nothing like he had the last time she saw him.

"Come here, ye little tramp—" The heathen grabbed her by the arm and spun her around to face him. He lifted his hand to strike and ground out a threat between tobacco-stained teeth. "See if this teaches you to give a man what he pays for."

It was the man's voice that struck Heath first. The gold watch fob hanging from his waistcoat filled in the blanks for him. Heath was out of his chair before Tyree Caine finished speaking, and he had the pond scum by the scruff of the neck before his hand could fall. He'd have acted to save Delilah alone, but Heath owed another debt to Tyree Caine, as well.

Tyree had all the qualities of humanity that Heath had come to detest. He embodied every piece of white-trash overseer his father had ever hired to drive the slaves, every low-life tracker who'd ever chased another human being down. And Heath would kill this waste of humanity before he'd allow him to touch one of the finest women who'd ever lived.

He squared off against Tyree and put all the hatred he'd been carrying with him since Blue's death into his voice. "Hit her only if you want to die where you stand."

Tyree's surprise lasted less time than an indrawn breath, then he let out a bellow and tried to butt Heath in the stomach with his head. Shouts went up immediately, a few urging calm or trying to smooth things over, the vast majority pressing Heath and Tyree to fight.

Heath threw himself into the fray wholeheartedly. He dealt two good blows to Tyree's midsection before Tyree landed an uppercut to his jaw. Pain shot through his face and rattled his teeth. He shook it off and followed with a right and a left of his own.

Tyree buckled and Heath locked his hands together above the man's neck. Old fury drove him, and the beating he'd suffered at Tyree's hands fueled the fire inside. He yanked Ellis Bailey's watch from Tyree's pocket, but before he could land the blow that would have sent the dungbag sprawling, Red Will fired one shot into the floor at his feet. "Not in my bar, you don't. You want to kill each other, take it outside."

Tyree spat blood to the floor beside the fresh bullet hole. "I only want what I paid for. Tell the wench there to give over, and we'll call it square."

Will turned an angry glare on Delilah. "How many times have I got to tell you, the men pay for you, you give them what they want . . . within reason." He leveled this last at Tyree.

Delilah's eyes narrowed. "I will not go with this one. He's a pig. He may pay for my services, but he doesn't pay for *me*. No man does that."

Grinning coldly, Will took her chin in his hand. "You picked an odd profession for a woman with such a distaste for buying and selling flesh." But then his smile faded and the expression in his eyes sobered. "I've told you before, I'll tell you again: Leave if you don't like it here. I've no time or patience for shrinking violets."

Heath expected Delilah to head for the door, but something doused the fire in her eyes. Her gaze flickered to the floor, she took a shuddering breath, and when she glanced up again she looked like a different person entirely. On the surface her eyes looked dead, but a slow hatred burned below the surface.

Heath had seen that look many times back on Bonne Chance and his blood ran cold at the sight. Delilah's mother, a kitchen slave they'd called Birdie, had turned that look on his own father more times than Heath could remember. It had taken Blue's death and leaving the plantation for Heath to finally understand that it was the look of hatred so deep nothing could expunge it, of hopelessness so overwhelming nothing could relieve it.

Was Delilah going to give in? Would she go with Tyree Caine and give him what he'd paid for?

Heath had been guilty of buying a woman's services in the past, but now bile rose in his throat and the sheer ugliness of it threatened to choke him. "Whatever Caine paid for time with her," he heard himself saying, "I'll give you double."

Will pretended to consider, but his eyes gleamed and Heath knew what his answer would be. When money talked, Will listened.

Sure enough, Will gave Heath the go-ahead with a wave of his hand. He clapped an arm around Tyree Caine's shoulders and urged him to pick out another lovely for his money.

The look in Caine's eyes warned Heath that he didn't plan to forget this. But for some reason, he dropped it now.

The possibility that he'd inadvertently put Courtney in danger crossed Heath's mind, followed quickly by the certain knowledge that he'd made things worse for Delilah. But he'd have to work all that out later. Right now he could only think about what he'd say to Delilah when they were alone.

"A pair of eights, gentlemen. King high." Derry tossed his hand into the center of the table that stood smack in the middle of the Pink Parasol. "Too bad your mothers aren't here to mop up your tears."

He half stood in the smoke-filled room to sweep his winnings toward him and kept a watchful eye on the dusky beauty who'd been walking past him every night for nearly a week without so much as noticing that he drew air into his lungs. He recognized one of the men who'd come to blows over her as his old buddy Heath Sullivan, met and befriended on his very first morning in Fourteen-Mile City. The other one was the one Derry wanted to keep his eye on.

He'd seen the whole thing, from first glance to the moment Red Will called the fight over. If he'd not been watching Delilah with marriage in mind, he might have joined in the fight—and not only for her sake, though that would have been most of it.

Derry liked a good fight as much as the next man. He wasn't known for backing down from them often. But he didn't want Delilah to see him as a scrapper.

Of course, if she kept acting as if he didn't exist, it wouldn't matter, now would it?

He scooped his winnings and drew them across the table, split a grin between his partners at the table, and sat heavily while the Glorious Creature he adored climbed the stairs with Heath Sullivan behind her. She'd be safe enough with Heath, Derry told himself. And a man had to have something more than pipe dreams and promises in hand before he went courting, now didn't he?

Upstairs, in the shabby room that served as both home and place of business to Delilah, Heath felt his revulsion stirring again. It looked exactly like so many rooms he'd visited over the past few years, with its lumpy bed and poorly built furniture. What made Heath's stomach pitch was the realization that this room, horrible as it was, was still nicer than anything Delilah had experienced on Bonne Chance.

He closed the door behind them and waited for Delilah to say something. He tried not to think about what Blue would have said if he'd seen the love of his life selling her body for money. Then again, how different was this from what she'd lived through on Bonne Chance? Maybe now she had *some* control over what happened to her.

She rounded on him the second she heard the latch click into place. Fire spit from her eyes and fury colored her cheeks. "What do you think you're doing?"

Heath backed up a step in surprise. "What?"

"Did you imagine that I'd be *grateful* for your interference?" Her nostrils flared and she waved one hand dramatically in the air. "You *did*, didn't you? I can tell by the look on your face."

Her complete lack of gratitude stunned him. But why should it? It was the second time in a week that he'd protected a woman and then been castigated for it. "Considering who that was downstairs and what he wanted, the possibility *did* cross my mind."

"Well, I'm not grateful. What makes *you* any less despicable than he is?"

Heath pulled off his hat and held it in front of him. "You don't recognize me, do you?"

"Oh, I recognize you, all right." Delilah closed her eyes and shook her head as if she'd never seen anyone so stupid. "Even *with* all that dirt and those ugly whiskers, you're the same Heath you've always been."

"Well, then, why—?"

Delilah growled low in her throat and snatched her dressing gown from a peg behind the door. "Why what? Why don't I throw myself at your feet in gratitude?"

"Of course not," Heath lied. He watched her jam her arms into the gown and tried to understand the jerkiness of her movements as she tied the sash. "Why are you so hostile? I thought we were friends."

"Friends?" She laughed bitterly. "When were *we* ever friends?" When he didn't answer, she switched to a heavy dialect. "I was your *property*, Mastuh Heath. Plain and simple. Your daddy made *that* clear if I ever had the nerve to doubt it."

His daddy. Heath could go a lifetime without discussing that sonofabitch. He sank onto the mattress and sat his hat on the bed beside him. "You don't know how many times I've wished I could undo the things that happened back on Bonne Chance."

"You've wished. How nice. Well, then, you're absolved of all responsibility. Isn't that what you want to hear? Now get out of here."

Heath regretted the shots of dust cutter. It made it so much harder to think straight. "I can't go yet."

"Yes, you can." She wrenched open the door and jerked her head toward it. "It's damn simple, actually. All you have to do is walk through the door and keep going."

He was sorely tempted, but something kept his butt planted on the bed. "I can't, Delilah, any more than you can absolve me of my responsibility for what happened back on Bonne Chance. I was little more than a boy, but I should have tried harder to stop him from selling you."

She slammed the door and hissed at him. When she spoke again, her voice was little more than a whisper, but the fire in her eyes flashed even brighter. "You think that's all I care about? Listen to how easily you say that. Do you even *know* what you're saying?"

"Of course I do."

"Your daddy *sold* me. Like a cow. A horse. Worse. He took me from my mama, from my sisters . . ." Her voice trailed off, and Heath wondered why she didn't mention Blue.

If he'd had an ounce of courage, he'd have seized the opening. But a bitter taste filled his mouth and kept him silent. It was still too hard to think about Blue when he was alone. He couldn't bear to talk about him with Delilah. Not tonight.

Her eyes darkened with sadness and doubt, and with a

history he could never undo. Her lips trembled slightly, but she pressed them together to hide her agitation.

"You *were* my friend," he said. "I guess maybe I'm asking for a chance to prove it."

Delilah's gaze trailed across his face slowly. "I'm a free woman, Heath. You don't own me anymore. No man does. And no one here knows the truth about who I am. They all think I'm white."

"They won't hear differently from me."

Her lips curved, but there was nothing gentle or friendly in her smile. "Then I thank you for that." She lifted her chin defiantly. "You bought and paid for my time tonight, but you can't stay, Heath. I'll get your money back from Will, or I'll find a way to pay you back myself, but you *can't* stay."

Heath shot to his feet. "I don't want to stay. I would never ask that of you. Never." Even if she hadn't been Blue's great love. Even if they hadn't been more like sister and brother than friends. He walked to the door, even though unfinished business still lay between them. He knew it and he suspected that she could sense that there was more left unsaid than either of them had spoken aloud.

His conscience urged him to be a man and tell her. But she hadn't mentioned Blue's name, and Heath wondered if she even cared anymore. He settled his hat on his head and bent toward her, leaning close and intending to kiss her cheek, but she jerked away from him as if he'd raised his hand to strike her. The rejection stung and another bolt of self-loathing tore through him, as painful as the lash, as deadly as the noose.

He was right back where he always landed. His own weakness repulsed him. Made him long for the oblivion that would only come at the bottom of a bottle. But something told him that no amount of whiskey would wipe this moment away.

He clambered down the stairs and out into the night, battling the overpowering need to retch until his guts lay on the ground. But he couldn't even do that. He stood in the shadows for a long time, gulping fresh air and assessing himself without mercy.

No doubt about it, he was one sorry sonofabitch.

Music and laughter filtered out into the night; sounds that usually lured him with promises of quick gratification and forgetfulness. Tonight, they only sounded cheap and unsatisfying.

He didn't want to be one of a hundred in a crowd. He wanted to matter. For the first time in years, he wanted to matter to someone—and the only person he mattered to even slightly was lying in his bed back in the cabin. Other than Courtney, not another living soul cared whether he lived or died—and she only cared because without him she'd be out on the streets with nowhere to go.

Ah, well . . . Heath couldn't afford to be fussy. She would, no doubt, be asleep already, but that was fine with him. He wasn't searching for conversation. Conversation would only lead to questions. And questions would only remind him how few answers he had, even for himself.

Courtney was still trying to get to sleep two hours after Heath left her. Her body was exhausted, but her mind wouldn't stop racing. From her real life to this one. From Grandmother's attic to this shabby cabin. From lunch with Ryan a week earlier to the aborted dinner with Heath that night, her mind wouldn't stop running.

That near-kiss had left her shaken and uncertain, and furious with herself for showing another similarity to Leslie. Courtney would never—*never*—use men the way Leslie had, and she'd never let them use her. She wouldn't allow herself to "fall in love" just so she didn't have to take care of herself.

And yet here she was, nearly a week after landing in the past, cooking and cleaning and playing housewife for some jerk who didn't want anything to do with her. She couldn't have done a better imitation of Leslie if she'd tried for years.

Well, she couldn't keep taking Heath's charity. She simply couldn't. But the prospects of making it in this unfamiliar world alone terrified her. What kind of job could she find? What kind of money could she hope to earn? Even if she found a job, she knew so little about life in this century, she had no idea how she'd survive.

She rolled onto her other side and stared at the light coming in through the window. She *had* to get home again. But how? Was Heath the key? If so, what would unlock the secrets that kept her here?

She'd been lying in bed for what seemed like forever when she heard footsteps outside her door. Heath's warnings about her safety came flooding back, and when the latch began to lift, her heart slammed against her ribs in apprehension. The door creaked open and a huge figure filled the doorway. The scent of cigar smoke and whiskey drifted across the room and shadow curls bobbed beneath his hat brim as he came inside.

Courtney's breath caught and her heart began to race— but this time for a different reason entirely. Afraid of what she was feeling and too tired to have another argument with him, she closed her eyes and pretended to be asleep. Light played against her eyelids for a second or two, then faded as he closed the door softly.

Even with her eyes closed, she was acutely aware of him. Mingled now with the whiskey and smoke, the strong, cloying fragrance of some soiled dove's perfume. Underlying it all, the scent she'd already begun to identify as uniquely his.

With the door closed, the silence seemed overpowering. There was still music and laughter outside, still the occasional gunshot or whinny of a horse, but she could hear the soft intake of each breath he took, and her own breathing instinctively found his rhythm and matched it.

Fabric rustled, and she imagined him pulling off his coat and rolling it into a pillow. Slipping the pouch he used to carry his money into its folds. Folding his waistcoat and laying it on the bureau as he did every night. They rarely spoke, yet his routine was becoming disturbingly familiar.

His boots scuffed softly on the floor as he moved from the door to the bureau and then to the blankets beside the bed. There he paused, just inches away from Courtney's face, as she struggled to keep her eyes closed and prayed he couldn't tell that she was awake. She pictured him scowling slightly as he looked at her, and it was all she could do not to open her eyes and study the look on his face.

And then, without warning, he moved again and the calloused tips of his fingers touched her cheek. The contact was gentle and fleeting, and over so quickly Courtney wasn't sure it had actually happened. She was even less certain what it meant.

She forced herself to keep breathing and to keep the rhythm slow and steady. More than ever, she didn't want him to know that she was awake. Finally she heard him slip between the blankets on the floor, and she was able to relax again.

"You're awake, aren't you?" His voice came softly through the darkness.

She hesitated for a long moment, then forced herself to speak. "No."

"No?"

"I'm sound asleep. Can't you tell?"

"I can now." His voice sounded different somehow. Kinder. Gentler. Almost vulnerable. "Why didn't you say something when I came in?"

"I don't know." She opened her eyes slowly, but the landscape of shadows cast by the furniture hadn't changed. He must still have been lying down. Which was probably a good thing. "I didn't know what to say, and I figured you'd want your privacy." She resisted the urge to lean up so she could see him. "Are you okay?"

The pause before his answer stretched a beat or two longer than normal. "I'm fine. Why?"

"You seem different, I guess. Quieter than usual."

"It's the middle of the night. I expected you to be asleep."

Courtney wondered if she only imagined the slight tensing of his voice. "Are you sure that's the only reason?"

The pause this time was even longer. "I'm sure."

"Oh. Well, okay, then." Courtney wasn't sure whether or not to believe him, but she was too tired tonight to push. Or maybe it was just that pillow talk in the moonlight made the conversation feel more intimate than she was ready for. She punched the pillow beneath her head and rolled onto her other side. "Good night."

Another lengthy pause filled the space between them before Heath murmured, "Good night."

She must have fallen asleep—though just how she did was beyond her—because something jerked her awake a little while later. The room was still bathed in shadow, and she had no idea how long she'd been sleeping or what had woken her. It took a few seconds to process the sounds of labored breathing coming from the floor beside her.

Heath? Was he sick?

She leaned up and tried in vain to see through the inky darkness. She ran her hand along the nightstand for the box of matches she'd seen earlier, fumbled until she had one in her hand, and finally managed to light it after three tries.

Heath was still asleep, but he moved restlessly. Sweat beaded on his nose and forehead, and his cheeks were deeply flushed. His breathing was ragged and harsh, and his eyes flicked rapidly beneath his lids. He was either sick or having one really bad dream.

The match burned down to her fingers. She struck another and lit the lamp, then slid from the bed and knelt beside him on the floor. His head thrashed from side to side, and he kicked aside the blanket. Courtney dodged a kick and reached out tentatively to put her hand on his forehead.

He pulled away sharply, but he didn't wake up. She didn't think he had a fever, but she couldn't be sure. She leaned up a little and touched him again. His skin felt a little clammy, but not overly warm or alarmingly cool. His movements ceased abruptly, and she could feel the tension leaving his body in a rush.

A dream, then. And not a good one.

She pulled her hand away and rested it in her lap as she studied his face. Like most people, he looked young and innocent in sleep, and Courtney felt that strange connection to him stir inside her. She touched her palm to her cheek where his fingers had rested earlier. She was more convinced than ever that he was the reason she'd been brought into the past, but no closer to figuring out why.

He shifted slightly, then curled onto one side. His hand grazed her thigh, and Courtney moved away quickly. She was letting her imagination run away with her. She might not know why Fate had brought her to the past, but she couldn't afford to let herself grow even slightly attached to Heath while she figured it out.

She got back into bed, blew out the lamp, and turned her back on him. Forming an emotional attachment to Heath, or to anyone else for that matter, would be just plain foolish.

And Courtney was no fool.

Chapter 8

HEATH WOKE UP in a far less expansive mood than he'd been in when he went to sleep. The gentleness Courtney had glimpsed the night before had vanished along with the wisps of his nightmare. He was back to his old self again, kind when he wasn't being rude, and more distant than ever. Probably not very likely to spill secrets just for the asking.

When he stepped outside to use the outhouse, she washed quickly and slipped into her clothes. Without cleanser, her face felt dirty. Without moisturizer, her skin felt tight and dry. Without deodorant, she felt sticky and hot, and she would have sold her eye teeth for a toothbrush and toothpaste. Baking soda on her finger just wasn't doing the job.

Personal hygiene: Just one more reason she needed to figure out if there was a reason for her being here—and fast. She'd throw herself off the cabin roof if she wasn't home before her monthly cycle started.

When Heath came back inside, he gave her a quick once-over, and the memory of that one moment of tenderness seemed to fill the space between them. She turned on her best smile and measured flour for a fresh batch of biscuits. "You seem well rested this morning. I'm surprised."

"I suppose I am. Why?"

"You were dreaming last night, and from what I could tell, it wasn't a very pleasant dream."

His eyes shot to her face and the corners of his mouth turned down. "When was this?"

"After you fell asleep, of course." Courtney added another cup of flour and did her best to look like someone he might want to confide in. "Do you remember it?"

"Remember what?"

"The *dream*."

"No."

The word snapped out so quickly, Courtney knew instinctively that he was lying. Even beneath the whiskers, she could see a deep scowl turning down the corners of his mouth, and his eyes . . . well, he didn't exactly look receptive to questioning. But the way he'd touched her cheek the night before left her with hope that he was softening a little.

She smiled and used two knives to cut lard into the flour the way Philo had shown her. "You don't remember? Or you don't want to talk about it?"

Heath caught the corner of his blanket and swept it from the floor, but he made a shambles of folding it. "Why does it matter?"

"Because it disturbed you enough to wake me up. And you know what they say about dreams—they're your sub-conscious mind processing stuff it doesn't get to deal with during the day."

Heath gave her an odd look. "Why are you so interested in a damn dream?"

"Why not? It'll give us something to talk about."

Heath tossed his blanket into the corner. "There are plenty of other subjects we can discuss," he said. "Every one of them more interesting that some nightmare you think I had. We could, for instance, talk about making sure you know how to protect yourself if the need arises."

Courtney frowned slightly. "Protect myself from what?"

"In case you haven't noticed, you're surrounded by low-lifes and reprobates. The list of potential harm is a long one." He pulled a shotgun from beneath the bed and held it up to the light. "Do you know how to shoot?"

Courtney's blood froze at the sight. She'd hated guns ever since Leslie had taken up with Loser Number Four—a long-haired dirtbag who'd hunted for fun and profit, and skinned his prey on their kitchen counter. Twice before Leslie took her back to Grandmother's he'd gotten drunk and started waving his guns around, and once he'd even held a pistol to Leslie's head during an argument.

Courtney shook her head firmly. "No guns. I hate guns. I don't even want that thing in the same room with me." She shivered slightly and tried to go back to their original conversation. "We were talking about your dream. Tell me about where you came from."

A muscle in his jaw twitched. "*You* were talking about my dream. *I* don't talk about my past. And I'm not getting rid of the shotgun. It might be the only thing that stands between you and disaster one of these days. You'd be smart to learn how to use it."

So the dream was about his past. Courtney filed that helpful hint away. "Then I guess I'm not very smart," she said. "And if you won't talk about your home or your past, I might be stuck here forever. If that happens, I'll never forgive you and we'll both be miserable. At least tell me about your family."

His eyes turned the color of slate and his gaze grew ominous. "My family doesn't matter. Being squeamish about guns does. That kind of thinking might be all right back East, but it could get you killed here."

"And waving a gun around like I know what to do with it won't?" She laughed sharply and sent him a look. "Really, Heath. Can we just focus on what's important?"

"Saving your damn hide *is* important," he snarled. "This isn't Charleston. This is Montana Territory. And you won't be waving a gun around, you'll know how to use it because I'll *teach* you."

"No." Courtney turned halfway away and slanted a look back at him. "So you're from Charleston, then?"

His eyes turned to stone. "I never said that."

"Not directly." She smiled and savored her small victory. "Do you ever hear from your family?"

"No. And let's get one thing straight. There are some things I'll never talk about. *Ever*. My family is one of those things. Do you understand?"

The expression on his face shocked her and even frightened her a little. He seemed deadly serious and far more intense than she'd seen him yet. But Courtney wasn't going to let him think he could intimidate her. "I understand perfectly. Do *you* understand that I won't use a gun, no matter what?"

"Fine."

"Fine."

He raked his gaze across her face as if he thought she might be lying. She forced herself to look him in the eye without flinching. "Fine," he said again. He looked as if he intended to put the shotgun back, then changed his mind and slammed out of the cabin with it.

Courtney watched the door bang shut behind him and drew in a shaky breath. Last night's mood had been shattered for good. But if Heath thought he'd squelched her curiosity, he couldn't have been more wrong.

She was more curious about him than ever.

The less time Heath spent around Courtney, the better off he'd be. Could there be a concept any simpler than that? The less time he spent looking into her eyes, listening to her voice, watching her sleep, anticipating her smile, the less likely he was to feel anything for her. And if he didn't feel anything for her . . .

Well, did he have to spell it out for himself?

Apparently, he did.

He looked around for a safe place to leave the shotgun. Somewhere close enough to get it if the need arose, but not so obvious that Courtney would find it.

She was the most exasperating woman he'd ever met, bar none. Only Felice had come close to making him feel so out of control, and she'd only had that effect on him once. Of course that was back when he'd still imagined that he *had* some control. Before he'd learned the truth about his father. Before he'd had to face the cold hard facts about himself.

He'd tried to put Felice behind him along with everything else from Bonne Chance, but every time he turned around, something made him remember. It was almost enough to make a man believe in Fate.

First Courtney, then Delilah. What next?

Scratch that. Forget he'd asked. If Fate did exist, he wasn't fool enough to tempt it.

The smart thing to do would be to ignore this growing— and ridiculous—sense of responsibility he felt for Courtney, to put aside this niggling urge to help Delilah, and to get out of Virginia City before anything else happened to keep him here. He'd gotten Ellis Bailey's watch back the night before. All he needed was to get Warrior from the livery, and he could be on his way. Courtney could live on in the cabin, and her new friends could worry about keeping her safe. Delilah was apparently living the life she wanted; at any rate, she didn't want any interference from Heath.

So what was he waiting for? What perverse part of himself kept him from heading to the livery and using the cash in his pocket to pay his bill? He was some piece of work, wasn't he? Trying to shake off responsibility with one hand, and clinging to it with the other.

For nearly a week the longing for a place to belong had been growing stronger. If he didn't leave now, he wouldn't be able to blame anyone but himself for what happened next, and he might not be able to leave at all. He knew all that, and he still couldn't make himself put one foot in front of the other to walk to the end of town where the livery stable held the key to his freedom.

Like it or not, he was as stuck in Virginia City as Courtney was—and just about as helpless to walk away.

He was in a foul mood when he came back to the cabin two days later. He'd tried all weekend long to approach Delilah, but without success. She wouldn't speak to him. No matter what he said or how hard he tried, she wouldn't say a word, and that look she gave him . . .

Hell.

Finding half a dozen men crowded into the cabin's narrow

yard eating huge slabs of homemade molasses pie on a Monday night didn't help. Young and old, short and tall, fat and thin. Courtney had assembled quite a variety. And she was feeding them a pie that should have been his, if only by virtue of the fact that it was made with *his* molasses.

Not even caring that he sounded like a petulant child, he strode through the open door and glared at Courtney, who was measuring cornmeal into a bowl at the table. A bewhiskered old prospector sat nearby whittling wood shavings onto the floor and giving her directions. A kid with just a few thin cat whiskers on his upper lip sat nearby reading aloud from the newly established *Montana Post*. A dog—probably the *ugliest* dog Heath had ever seen—lay near the fire.

The scene was so cozy, Heath's temper boiled over. "You want to tell me what's going on here?"

Courtney glanced up and the smile slipped from her face. "Heath? What are you doing here?"

Her reaction did nothing to improve his humor. He yanked off his hat and tried hanging it on its peg, but agitation affected his aim. He missed twice and finally nailed it on the third try. "I live here, remember?"

The boy lowered the newspaper. The old fart straightened slowly and regarded Heath through one squinty eye. "There's no call to speak sharply, son."

Heath had spent too much time lately thinking about his father, and the sobriquet landed with a thud on his bruised heart. "I'm not your *son*," he snarled. He peeled off his waistcoat, folded it carefully, and left it on the dresser. When he turned back, he found Courtney lancing him with a look of stern disapproval.

"Don't you dare talk to Philo that way. He's a guest in this house."

"And I'm . . . what?"

"*You're* never here." She thrust a plate bearing a huge triangle of pie at him.

He took it grudgingly and wondered how and when she'd learned to make an edible pastry. "I'm here now."

"Yes. You are." She turned away, dismissing him, his

mood, and his opinions as if she'd slammed the door in his face.

The sway of her hips outlined by the soft drape of her worn shirt caught his eye as she crossed the room. He jerked his gaze away and found himself staring at the soft skin just above her top button, the curve of her chin, the soft slope of her cheek. His heart beat a little faster, though just what he found so alluring about a woman dressed up as an old prospector was beyond him.

He caught the old man's amused expression and turned away, swearing softly under his breath.

"You might as well sit down," she said. "I'll fix you some supper if you want." And then, as if lightning wasn't arcing in the space between them, as if she wasn't making Heath want things he shouldn't want and long for things he couldn't have, "Have you met Philo and Moonshine?"

Heath filled his mouth with pie and shook his head and tried not to let her see that she'd actually managed to impress him with her creation.

"Philo Keegan," the old man said, half-standing and holding out a hand.

The boy followed Philo's lead. "Absalom Warriner . . . but everybody calls me Moonshine."

Heath shook hands as if they were all standing in his mother's parlor. As if either of these men would have been allowed anywhere near his mother's parlor. "Heath Sullivan," he said, though he suspected they knew that already.

It had been too long since he'd engaged in small talk, and he saw no point in conversation for its own sake, so he kept himself busy with the pie while Philo and Moonshine went back to what they were doing.

Courtney sent him a no-nonsense look that left no doubt she expected him to entertain her guests. But what did she expect them to talk about? The weather? Politics? Or did she think that he'd suddenly change his mind about discussing his family with other people around?

Sparing one quick scowl at the crowd through the window, he stacked crates against the wall and perched on a corner of the top one, which left one foot flat and the other dangling a few inches from the floor. "So you gentlemen are prospectors?" Stupid question, but it was the only way he could think of to break the ice.

Moonshine didn't seem to think anything of the question, but the slight narrowing of Philo's old eyes told Heath he understood exactly how stupid it was.

Heath kicked his free leg gently against the crates. "You work on your own, or are you working for one of the mining companies around?"

Moonshine straightened slightly. "On our own. Ain't no money to be made workin' for somebody else."

"That's true enough. You two partners?"

"Naw." Moonshine answered quickly, but he cast a glance at Philo as if there was a possibility the old guy would contradict him. "I wouldn't mind a partner," he said when Philo didn't. "But you gotta be mighty careful in a place like this." He leaned back in his chair and made himself comfortable. "Philo did have a partner until a couple of weeks ago. Didn't you, Philo?"

Philo nodded, but he seemed reluctant to do so. "Me and Verlis was together for a long time. Twenty years or more."

Courtney looked up from what she was doing. "Verlis is the one who taught you to cook?"

"The same."

Her eyes clouded and she glanced uncertainly at Heath. "I didn't realize he'd died so recently." He looked back to Philo with a scowl. "Was he sick for a while, or was it sudden?"

Philo took a while scratching the underside of his chin before he answered, which left the way open for Moonshine. "It was sudden," the boy said with another glance at the old man. "And I know what happened, too—even if Philo don't want to admit it."

Well now, this was getting interesting. Heath shifted forward on his crate chair. "Are you saying there was something suspicious about Verlis's death?"

"Nope." Moonshine leaned back in his chair and cocked one ankle across the opposite knee. "I'm sayin' straight-out that he was murdered."

"We don't know that," Philo grumbled under his breath.

"Near *as*." Moonshine set his foot jiggling. "Tyree Caine's boys came knockin' one day and the very next Verlis was dead." He split a satisfied glance between Heath and Courtney. "You tell *me* what that looks like."

Heath's pulse slowed. "You think Tyree Caine is responsible?"

"You know him?" Moonshine asked.

"We've met." He turned to Courtney and explained, "He's the one who relieved me of my possessions the night we met." But he stopped short of mentioning their run-in at the Pink Parasol.

Courtney stopped stirring and very slowly lowered the bowl to the table. "If he killed Philo's partner," she said with surprising calm, "then it sounds like you got off lightly."

"We don't *know* that he killed Verlis," Philo cautioned.

"No, but him and his boys have been tryin' to get their hands on the Jezebel as long as *I've* been hanging around Philo and them." Moonshine looked from Heath to Courtney again and jiggled his foot a little harder. "Verlis told 'em no. Now he's gone." He lifted his chin, looked Heath square in the eye, and asked again, "What does that sound like to you?"

It sounded like Philo and Verlis had been messing with the wrong person. "It's hard to say, but I think it would be a mistake to underestimate him. You mind telling me your version of what happened to Verlis?"

The old man seemed to know that Heath was asking for more reasons than idle curiosity. "We don't know nothin' for sure. Verlis was an old fool. He took chances sometimes that a man with an actual brain in his head would never have taken." In spite of his harsh words, Philo's voice was filled with a tenderness Heath understood. "We was livin' on the Jezebel at the time. I came down into town after supplies and left him up there alone. When I came back, he was at the base of the hill with his neck broke. Could a' been an accident. Them hills is steep up there."

"Except that Verlis would never have climbed up Widow-maker on his own," Moonshine put in. "You know he wouldn't have."

Courtney wiped her hands on a clean flour sack and

moved, almost trance-like, to sit on a crate next to Heath. But her attention was focused on Philo. "Why didn't you tell me about this before?"

"I didn't see any need to. We don't know what happened to Verlis. Can't do anything about it, anyway."

"No, but we can make sure *you're* safe." She looked to Heath to back her up.

Heath held up a hand to ward off the suggestion he could feel coming. "Maybe Philo was right and Verlis's death was nothing more than an act of carelessness." But what if he was wrong? What if the old prospector had been murdered? "But it doesn't hurt to be cautious. Will you listen to me now about learning to use the shotgun?"

Her eyes narrowed. "No. And I thought you got rid of it."

"Well, I didn't."

"You told me you did."

"I never told you that," Heath pointed out reasonably. "And I can't help if you jump to the wrong conclusions."

"If I jumped to any conclusion, it was because you took the shotgun away after I said I didn't want it around."

"The point is, there are some very bad people around here and you aren't safe."

"I won't be any safer with a gun."

Heath threw his hands into the air in exasperation, then rounded on Philo to beg for help. "Will you tell her, Philo? Tell her what it's like around here. Tell her that she could get herself killed out of sheer stubbornness. Tell her that she's being pigheaded and downright foolish—and all just because she can't stand for me to be right."

Philo peeled a long curl of wood from his stick and let it drop. "I think she heard you, son. She ain't that far away. If she don't want a shotgun around, maybe she's right."

That was the last straw. Heath shot to his feet and let out a roar of frustration. "For the last time, I am *not* your son." He shook a finger at Courtney. "Go ahead. Do it your way. But if you get yourself killed, don't come crying to me." And before anyone could point out the flaws in his argument, he slammed out into the yard and plowed through the miners who were smart enough to give him a wide berth on his way through.

But he didn't even have time to reach the street before he realized that someone was behind him. Furious, he spun back around and found the mangy yellow cur dog on his heels. Its tongue lolled out of its mouth, and its feathery tail waved in the breeze.

Great. Philo and Moonshine got Courtney. Heath got the world's ugliest dog.

Being out in natural light didn't make it look any better. It's long yellow snout was freckled with brown, a scruff of white beard rimmed its chin, and thick white hair sprouted from its ears.

He felt someone watching and looked up to find Philo in the doorway. "Geezer's a good trail dog. Followed me and Verlis when we came here. Knows how to take care of himself, for the most part."

"Uh-huh." Riveting.

"Just needs someone to latch on to, that's all." Philo came down the steps and closed the distance between them. "Someone to dump a few leftovers into a tin at night." He scratched at the whiskers on his chin and added, "Sure seems to like *you*."

"Yeah? Well, dogs like me. People are another thing entirely."

"Dogs are good at judging a man's character. Geezer there thinks you're all right. Might even be thinking of throwing his lot in with yours."

Heath gaped at him. "You're not suggesting—" He broke off and backed away. "Oh, no, you don't. He's *your* dog."

"Geezer? Shucks. He's nobody's dog but his own. He picks and chooses who he wants to stay with, and looks to me like he's pickin' you."

"Funny. But I don't want a dog."

The old man scratched his side lazily and spit a stream of tobacco into the dirt. "Well, that part's up to you, I s'pose. Guess the dog won't die if he's left on his own."

Heath turned away from the huge brown eyes in that ugly

mutt face. "It's your dog," he said again. "Whether it lives or dies isn't my concern."

"He's a purty good hunter . . . although he *is* gettin' older. Trailed after Verlis nigh on to twelve years, close as I can figure. Took up with me just because he didn't have nowhere else to go." He turned his gaze to the sky that was still ripe with summer and sighed heavily. "Don't know how he'll get through the next few months with winter comin'."

As if on cue, a high-pitched whine pierced the air. Heath glared over his shoulder and could've sworn the damn dog smiled right before it buried its snout under one mangy paw.

He turned away again, determined not to let the flea-bitten dog get to him. Determined not to let Philo manipulate him. Determined to remember the one abiding principle in his life—*no entanglements*. He'd already broken the rule for Courtney and again for Delilah. But he drew the line at a dog.

Philo hotfooted after him, only a step slower than the dog itself. "You going to let this poor dog *die*?"

"That dog is hardly at death's door," Heath growled, rounding the corner and trying like hell to get away. "He's probably healthier than I am."

"Not so. He's pining for Verlis, and that's God's truth. The poor thing's been wasting away right in front of my eyes."

For hell's sake. Heath ground to a halt and turned back, dead set on putting an end to this nonsense, once and for all. He wasn't a bit surprised to find that the mutt had managed to keep up quite nicely. Nor was he surprised that it lowered its head and looked positively fragile when he turned around.

If Philo wouldn't listen, maybe he should just work on the dog. He hunkered down in front of the animal and lifted its chin so he could see into its eyes. "Go away."

The dog turned a set of golden-brown eyes on Heath, and his tongue caught Heath's wrist in a wet kiss.

Which didn't affect Heath. At all. "I don't want you."

That great plume of tail began to wag slowly.

Heath made a point of not noticing. "I'm warning you right now, I won't feed you. You want food, stay with Philo."

Another wet slurp slathered his wrist.

"I won't let you inside when it rains," Heath warned. "Won't care if you're outside when snow comes."

The plume swept back and forth, clearing away the dirt and dust from the boardwalk. Another swipe of tongue left a moist patch on Heath's chin. Heath still might have been able to resist if the damn dog hadn't chosen that moment to nudge his arm with its massive white-whiskered head and lance him again with those soft brown eyes.

Ah, hell.

Philo put the final nail in his coffin with a well-timed "Might be good to have Geezer around. He's one helluva watchdog."

Heath's heart sank and he felt another solid weight settling on his shoulders. He stood abruptly and turned his back on the mangy cur. "Do what you want," he snarled over his shoulder. "Follow me or don't, doesn't matter to me."

He started away again, and tried not to notice the pleased grin on Philo Keegan's weathered face or the mangy yellow dog with the ostrich-feather tail trotting happily at his heels.

Chapter 9

THE DOG TRAILED him all the way to town, through the crowded streets, along the boardwalk and off again, and finally to the doors of the Pink Parasol. Heath expected to have to tell him to stay there, but before he could say a word, the mutt curled into a ball beneath one of the windows and rested his chin on his paws.

That wasn't so bad, he supposed. If the ratty thing had to trail after him, that is.

Inside, music and laughter filled the small establishment. Nearly every table was occupied. The bar packed. And on a Sunday, too. Just like back East, folks came to their houses of worship. It's just what they worshiped that was different.

Heath pushed up to the bar between a couple of foul-smelling miners, ordered whiskey, and turned around to watch. He'd rather be in his cabin, having a conversation with Courtney, pretending not to like that molasses pie and biscuits. Instead, he was standing in a smoke-filled tavern trying to ignore the not-so-subtle come-hither looks Sally cast him from the other side of the room.

Well, Heath wasn't in the mood to hither, and especially not with Sally.

He looked around for Delilah, but he couldn't see her anywhere. He did, however, notice a man watching him from a table across the room.

Before he could work up a healthy dose of worry that the man might be one of Tyree Caine's boys, he recognized him as Derry Dennehy. And when Derry motioned him to join him, Heath decided to oblige, if only to avoid Sally.

Derry signaled for a drink apiece and grinned as if they were old friends when Heath drew up a chair into the empty spot at the table. "I thought you were leaving town."

"I was. Change of plans."

Derry jerked his head toward the cards on the table. "You want in?"

"Not tonight." Heath waved smoke from in front of his eyes and glanced around at the others. "Anybody mind if I watch?"

The question earned him three mumbled responses which varied in degrees of enthusiasm, but the bottom line was that nobody seemed to care as long as Heath didn't help Derry cheat, so he straddled the chair and feigned fascination with the game so Sally wouldn't bother him. It was a hard and fast rule at the Parasol. If a man was gambling, the girls were to leave him alone—unless, that is, he seemed about ready to call it a night and needed incentive to stay. That's where the girls came in.

Derry remained silent while the cards were dealt.

Heath caught sight of Sally moving toward the table, languidly wagging a fan in front of her face. The crowded room still bore the traces of that afternoon's heat, but in another hour or two the air outside would cool enough to make the saloon almost comfortable.

Derry picked up his hand, fanned it slowly, and flicked a glance and an almost imperceptible smile at the table itself. Heath figured one of two things: either he didn't know much about playing poker, or he knew how to make his opponents think he had a good hand. Whichever it was, that's the impression the other gentlemen seemed to get, and their bets as they went around the table reflected that.

Derry tossed two cards aside and motioned to the dealer, then turned his attention back to Heath. "I saw you in here couple of nights ago. You were having a disagreement over one of the girls."

Heath would prefer not to discuss the fight with Tyree, but it was hard not to when it had happened in front of so many people. He shrugged casually and glanced around to see if Delilah had returned yet. "It was nothing."

Derry quirked a brow and ran an assessing gaze across Heath's face. "I know people and I know fights. That wasn't nothing." He situated his hand again and waited to speak again until after his turn to bet. "You know the woman?"

For Delilah's sake, Heath didn't want to answer that. "I've seen her."

"And are you interested in her?"

Something in Derry's tone caught Heath's attention. He shifted on his chair to escape another cloud of smoke that billowed toward him from a nearby table and tried to read the expression on Derry's face. But the shutters that should have been in place when he looked at his cards were locked over his eyes now.

Heath settled for a point-blank "How do you mean, interested?"

Derry shrugged and tried to look casual, but his mask slipped and gave Heath a glimpse of something behind his eyes. "I don't mean anything," he said with a ghost of his usual smile. "It's just a question."

One Heath didn't intend to answer until he knew why Derry was asking it. "I haven't seen her around tonight. Is she here?"

Again that fleeting something darted across Derry's expression. "Upstairs."

Heath's stomach tightened uncomfortably. He shouldn't have asked. "How do you know her?"

"I don't."

"Just from here, huh?"

Derry shook his head again. "Not even that." He played out his hand and collected the pot on a pair of eights, then turned toward the stairs, and his expression suddenly became a whole lot easier to understand. His eyes softened and the lines in his face smoothed, and for the space of a breath, his heart lay on the table for anyone who was paying attention to see.

His expression changed again before Heath could even blink, and he turned back to the game with that easy grin Heath remembered from the first time they met. Delilah hadn't noticed, and neither did anyone else, it seemed. But Heath had seen it.

He just didn't know what to think about it.

He was late getting back to the cabin that night, but for some reason it didn't surprise him at all to see light spilling out through the windows and under the door when he got there. Geezer panted happily at his side as he padded toward the cabin. But unlike the way he'd acted in town, he strolled right to the door with Heath and stood there, chin up and ears back, as if he expected to be let inside.

Heath paused with his hand on the latch and scowled down at the dog. There had always been dogs at Bonne Chance, but they'd been working hunters, not family pets. They'd been fed out back behind the kitchens, not on the family hearth. And *they'd* at least been relatively clean.

Not Geezer.

"Don't even think about it," Heath warned. "You're not coming inside."

Geezer cocked his ears and whined.

"I said no. Anything could be crawling in your fur, and I don't want it crawling on me by morning."

Geezer tilted his massive head, gave up on Heath, and scratched at the door with one paw. Of course, Courtney answered before Heath could stop her, and Geezer trotted inside as if he belonged there.

Heath shot a look of frustration at Courtney as he brushed past her and planted himself in front of the dog who was making a beeline for his blanket. "I said no. You're not sleeping on my bed. You're *not* sleeping inside at all." A trill of laughter sounded behind him. He whipped back around, not sure whether he was more pleased or annoyed by it. "You're not helping, you know."

"I'm sorry." She bit her lip and tried to look serious. "It's just that . . . well, you're arguing with the *dog*. I thought *I* was the only one you argued with."

Heath tried to remain annoyed, but the laughter in her eyes and the delight on her face was hard to resist. "Yeah? Well, I *have* to argue with him. He refuses to listen to reason."

Courtney laughed again, and warmth raced up Heath's spine. "Geezer? But he's as reasonable as a dog can be." To prove it, she patted her thigh softly. Geezer shifted direction and padded across the floor toward her. He nudged her with his huge head and treated her to a look of pure adoration.

Heath bit back a smile, pulled his chair away from the table, and straddled it so he could watch Courtney interact with the flea-bitten old thing. "I don't suppose you've noticed that he's filthy."

She hunkered down beside the dog and scratched between its ears. "I know you think I'm crazy, but I have noticed. If water were easier to come by, I'd suggest giving him a bath." She moved her hand to the dog's chin. "But if anybody's getting a bath around here, it's me." She sobered slightly. "Is Philo telling me the truth? Is he really letting you *have* Geezer?"

"It wasn't my idea," he said, just to set the record straight. "And Philo claims it's not his, either. He says the dog chooses."

"That's what he told me, too." She sat on the floor beside the dog and made a face at his matted fur. "I'm worried about him, Heath. Do you really think Verlis was murdered?"

He thought about denying it just so she wouldn't worry. But if Tyree Caine *did* decide to even the score with Heath, she'd be safer if she had her eyes open so she could see trouble coming.

"I think it's possible," he admitted. "I've run up against Tyree Caine twice now. The first time he was whipping an old man. The second, he was trying to force his attentions on a lady who'd made it clear she wasn't interested." He decided to leave out the fact that Tyree had paid for the privilege—or that Delilah was no stranger to accepting money for it. He still had trouble thinking about Delilah in those terms, so he forced her out of his mind and focused on

Courtney's question. "Unfortunately, I think Tyree Caine is capable of almost anything."

"I was afraid of that." She moved slightly and the firelight played across her cheek and hair. "Why are some people so cruel? What makes them that way?"

Heath had been asking himself the same question for years, and it always came back to one thing. "Greed," he said without hesitation. "The insatiable desire for wealth and power. Some people will do anything to get it."

"So what are we going to do about it?"

Heath shot a surprised look at her. "About what?"

"About Philo, of course. We can't just leave him over there. He's a sitting duck."

Again, Heath held his hands to ward off the suggestion. "Oh, no. No, no, no. That old man is not *my* responsibility, and he sure as hell isn't *yours*."

"But what if he's the reason I'm here? What if I'm *supposed* to save him so I can go home again?"

Heath ignored the way the firelight played on her hair, the soft glow of it on her cheek. He ignored the way her breasts strained against the shirt when she moved her arm, and the deep well of her eyes. Even when she didn't speak, they asked too much of him. When she did, the demands were almost painful.

"Saving Philo isn't going to open some magic door and take you away from here," he said. "Nothing is going to open some magic door, Courtney. You're going to have to accept that."

"You don't know that."

"I *do* know that. And if you were thinking logically, you'd know it, too." Geezer's head came up and he fixed Heath with a look that fell just short of menacing. But Heath wasn't going to pretend to believe Courtney's wild tale just to keep the dog happy.

Courtney's smile faded and her movements became shorter and more agitated. "What is it with you and people? Why are you so determined to be unlikable?" When he didn't jump right up with an answer, she rushed on. "You know what? I have the feeling you could be a very nice man—even pleasant—if you'd let yourself be. You *might* even be fun if you didn't work so damn hard to be obnoxious."

Heath glowered at her, but her observations struck a cord deep inside that left him uncomfortable. He used to love to laugh, but that had been a long time ago. After Blue's death, levity had felt like a betrayal, and he'd long since grown out of the habit.

"What is it with *you* and people?" he countered. "Why do you open the door to anyone who wants in and feed anyone who looks hungry? People you know nothing about, by the way."

"I don't know."

"You don't know?"

"Well, I do. But you'll just tell me I'm insane if I tell you what it is, so it seems a whole lot easier just to say I don't know." She patted Geezer's side and hugged her knees to her chest. "I don't know why I want to find out why I'm here. I can't explain why I want to get out of here, either. You'd think I'd *love* staying in this little box of a cabin all day long instead of going to work and watching my pictures make it into magazines and knowing that people's lives are touched by what I do."

She jerked her chin toward the fireplace. "And why would I want to cook something in a microwave in mere seconds when I can have the joy of standing over an open flame all day and singing old songs of the sea to time what's cooking? Why would I want a hot shower every day and clean hair and fresh clothes when I can look and smell like a cross between Geezer and a saloon instead? You know? Now that I think about it, my life back home was . . . well, *boring*. Who'd want that if they could have all *this*?" She finished with a dramatic—if sarcastic—flourish, sweeping her arms wide to take in the room around them.

In spite of her caustic tone, his well-placed defenses, and his generally foul mood, Heath felt a chuckle start low in his throat and rise upward. It startled him so much, he couldn't hold back, and what made it worse was the look in Courtney's eyes that told him she'd heard.

Confused by his reaction, he turned away sharply and stifled the laughter. But the damage was done. If he could call it damage. He didn't know what the hell to call it, or what to think. He hadn't laughed in so long, he could hardly remember what it felt like. The only thing he knew for sure was why he'd stopped laughing in the first place. It still felt like a betrayal of the friendship he'd shared with Blue and a mockery of the death he felt so responsible for.

He wasn't sure that would ever change.

Heath spent the next few days arguing with himself over what to do with Geezer, how to handle Courtney, and what to tell Delilah about Blue's death if she ever did agree to talk to him. He'd never discussed that night with another human being, and he wasn't sure he could talk about it now, even with Delilah. She would hate him if he told her the truth, but she couldn't possibly hate him any more than he hated himself.

He went back and forth for days, one minute convinced he could tell her the partial truth—Blue had died trying to run away—and leave out the damning details. The next minute he'd realize that telling her the cold hard facts would never be enough.

Before he knew it, he'd let almost a week slip by and he still hadn't told her.

He had to tell her before he could help her, and he had to help her. He owed it to Blue. Owed him one helluva lot more than that.

Obviously, his first task was simply to get her to talk to him. But that proved even more difficult than he'd anticipated. On his first try she flatly refused to speak to him. On his second she sent Red Will to his table with a message to leave her alone. The third night Red Will didn't bother with words. He and Olaf the bouncer each took an arm and escorted Heath to the door with a stern warning not to come back until he'd sobered up. How were they to know he'd been stone sober at the time?

Heath considered giving up after that, but a determination he hadn't felt since before Blue's death shored him up. If she wouldn't talk to him inside the Parasol, he'd just find some other way to reach her.

He spent his days working whatever odd jobs he could find while Geezer napped in some shady spot nearby. He spent his evenings ignoring the music of Courtney's laugh and the sun in her smile. And he spent his nights not noticing the soft curves in the bed and the whisper of her breathing while she slept. But a week and a half of that was beginning to take its toll.

When he found a few days' work at the livery stable, he took a perverse pleasure in imagining what Sebastian Sullivan would have said if he could see his only son shoveling horseshit and getting paid for it. It was backbreaking work, but the stable gave him a clear view of the Pink Parasol and a perfect opportunity to catch Delilah if she ever came outside.

It was early in the morning of his third day on the job when his patience was rewarded. Just as the sun crested the hilltops and began to warm the still-cool air, Delilah slipped out of the saloon wearing a faded gingham gown and knitted shawl, sturdy boots, and a bonnet that would have looked right at home in a chapel. He was so anxious to talk with her, he abandoned the shovel without a thought for the job and took off after her with Geezer, of course, at his heels.

She strolled along Warren Street for two blocks, then turned onto a side street and increased her pace. Even from behind, he could tell that she kept her eyes straight again, looking neither left nor right and barely acknowledging the presence of other people along the way.

He kept his distance, waiting until the moment felt right, and running through what he'd say when it did. He'd been following for nearly a mile when without warning, she stopped walking and rounded on him. "What are you doing? Why are you following me?"

Heath fell back a step in surprise, but he recovered quickly. It might not be the encounter he'd been imagining, but he'd take what he could get. "We need to talk, Delilah."

Her expression turned to ice. "I don't want to talk. I want you to leave me alone."

"Don't talk then, just listen." The scent of coffee reached him from somewhere nearby, and the rich aroma of frying bacon made his stomach rumble. If Delilah hadn't been looking at him with murder in her eye he might have suggested they go somewhere to eat. He touched her arm in a gentle appeal.

She jerked away and fire flared in her eyes. "I'm a free woman now," she said, her voice ominously low. "You don't own me. No man does. That means I don't have to listen to you, and I don't have to let you *touch* me, either."

Heath could have pointed out that she'd enslaved herself at the Pink Parasol, but he was pretty sure she wouldn't appreciate the observation. He dropped his hand and clenched his fist to keep from inadvertently reaching for her again. "I'm not trying to force you to do anything," he said quietly. "But there are things we need to talk about. Important things."

Delilah lifted her chin and looked down her nose at him. "No," she said firmly, "there are not."

"Delilah, please—"

She turned away and started walking again, clutching her shawl close against the early morning chill. "Leave me alone, Heath. I mean it. There's nothing you could possibly say to me that I want to hear."

"I don't believe that," he said, falling into step beside her. "You left too many people behind at Bonne Chance. People I know you loved."

She aimed a venomous glance at him. "What do you know about love? What do any of the Sullivans know about it?" She slipped again into her old way of speaking, dropping her voice so that Heath could barely hear her. "They ain't no love for a person like me, massuh. White folks like *you* make sure of that."

"Well, then, we're wrong." Heath almost reached for her again, but caught himself in time. "Look, Delilah, I understand why you're angry and I don't blame you. But I'm begging you to remember that I am not my father."

"No." She tossed one end of her shawl over her shoulder

and raked another dose of poison across his face. "But you're his son."

"Not any longer." He ground the words out between clenched teeth and almost missed the slight change in her pace that told him she'd heard him. "I know I didn't do enough to change his mind about selling you, but I tried. I really did."

Delilah curled her lip and shook off his argument. "I do *not* want to talk about your father."

Heath let out a breath thick with relief. "Neither do I. In fact, there's no one I want to talk about less. I'll probably always feel responsible for what he's done, but I'm not the one who tore you away from your family . . . and from Blue." It took everything he had to open the door by saying his friend's name aloud.

Delilah slammed it shut again with a bitter laugh. "My family? You have the *nerve* to use that word near me?" She moved into a patch of sunlight, but that only showed the deep circles beneath her eyes and the worry lines etched into her forehead. "I have a new life here. One that has nothing to do with the Sullivans or Bonne Chance. I've worked harder than you can imagine to leave all that behind. I don't want to think about it. I don't want to hear about it."

"But I know how much you love your mother. You and Birdie . . . *Surely*—"

"When was the last time you were on Bonne Chance, Heath?"

"Five years ago, but—"

"Before the war started?"

"Yes, but—"

"Then you don't know anything about them, do you? They could be dead. Birdie. Tango. Blue. They could all be dead."

"And you're saying you don't want to know?"

"That's exactly what I'm saying. You tell me, Heath. Is what you have to say going to make *me* feel better? Or do you just have to say whatever it is so that *you'll* feel better?"

The question startled him into silence.

A smile as cool as the morning curved her lips. "That's what I thought. Don't you think I've already lost enough? Memories of the people I love and dreams about them living a better life than mine are all I have left of them. Am I supposed to just let you take those away, too?"

Heath swallowed around the thick lump in his throat and shook his head. "I didn't think of it that way."

An immense sadness filled her eyes and altered her expression. "Go away, Heath. If you ever cared anything about me at all, then *please* . . . leave me be."

This time when she started walking away, Heath let her go.

Maybe she was right. Maybe telling her about Blue's death would be more cruel than kind. Maybe he *was* trying to soothe his own conscience, hoping that Delilah would absolve him of the guilt he carried if she heard the details of that night.

He stuffed his hands into his pockets and turned back toward town. Geezer stood just a few feet away, looking at him with such reproach, Heath wondered if the dog actually understood what had just happened. He shook off the notion and tried to shake off his conversation with Delilah, as well.

He'd run out on the horse dung, and now he'd probably be lucky to salvage the job. Five years ago he'd felt like the golden son of a rich and powerful man. A prince, well on his way toward ascending the throne at Bonne Chance. Now he had to beg to shovel horseshit.

It wasn't that he wanted to go back to the life he'd had, but the life he was living didn't have a whole lot to recommend it, either. He was almost back to the livery when a petite figure in dungarees and a plaid shirt caught his eye. He nearly ignored it, but there was something too familiar in the sway of her hips.

Geezer saw it, too, and took off at a happy trot.

Heath had no idea what she was doing wandering around town on her own, but he intended to find out. He cast one last glance over his shoulder at the livery and set off toward her.

Shoveling dung was a highly overrated occupation, anyway.

He caught up with her just a few feet from the Mercantile and clapped a hand on her shoulder. She swung around to face him, her expression tight and her eyes snapping. But the anger on her face evaporated when she recognized him and a slow smile replaced it.

After the morning he'd had and the stinging rejection from Delilah, that smile touched a place deep inside him that needed a little softness, and he realized how long it had been since anyone but Courtney and Geezer had seemed pleased to see him.

He fully intended to demand an explanation for why she was walking around town on her own, but that smile and the soft skin showing above the buttons of her shirt made his voice come out a whole lot less challenging than he wanted it to. "What are you doing here? I thought we'd agreed that you'd stay in the cabin when I wasn't around."

"We did, but you're never around. I can't sit there twiddling my thumbs all day." She planted her hands on her hips, unwittingly dragging his attention to them. "I'll never get home that way."

Heath swallowed thickly and forced his gaze to her face again—with a short stop at the soft swell of breasts beneath flannel along the way. "There's a murder a day in this town, Courtney. Sometimes more." He caught his voice raising and dropped it again. "You can't wander around on your own. It's not safe."

She started walking again, but she kept talking as if she expected him to follow . . . which he did. "Don't worry about me, okay? I'm used to being on my own, and I know how you feel about having me underfoot. You don't have to pretend to care what happens to me." She waved her hand toward the end of the street. "Just go back to work, okay? I'm going to see if I can figure out some way to get out of your hair."

Maybe her dismissal wouldn't have bothered him if he hadn't just had the disastrous conversation with Delilah. But the past twelve days had dredged up emotions he hadn't let himself feel in years, and that had left him more in tune with other people than he'd been in a long time. She might sound airy and dismissive, but there was a deep hurt underlying her words. A hurt as deep as the one he'd been carrying around.

"I'm not pretending." The words slipped out almost before he formed them consciously.

"Excuse me?"

The skin above her nose creased in confusion, and he had to fight the urge to touch his lips to it. "I said I'm not pretending to care what happens to you. I do care. I don't want you to get hurt."

She laughed uncertainly, but her eyes roamed his face, and he knew she was trying to decide if he was being honest with her. "That's sweet, but—"

"It's not sweet," he said, cutting her off. "*Sweet* is not a word most people associate with me." He took both of her hands in his and pulled her to one side of the boardwalk. "Look, Courtney, we got off to a bad start and I'll admit that it was mainly my fault. I can be difficult. I know that. I can be stubborn and surly and . . . and . . ."

"Rude."

"Yes. Rude." He gave in to the smile she won from him. "On occasion."

"Don't forget snippy. Distrustful. Moody."

Her eyes danced and Heath felt the urge to laugh stronger than ever. "I won't argue with any of that. I don't know about you, but it seems to me that sharing that cabin might be easier if we were friends."

Her gaze narrowed distrustfully. "Friends?"

"You know the word?"

She grinned. "I've heard it. Do you mean friends, as in you believe what I tell you?"

That was a tall order, but the longer he spent around her the harder it was to believe that she was crazy. "I'll try," he compromised. "I'm not sure I can promise more than that."

Some of her skepticism faded. "That's fair enough. If you just try to keep an open mind, I'll be happy." She lifted one hand to shield her eyes from the rising sun. "Does this mean you'll tell me something about yourself?"

His first instinct was to refuse, of course. But finding Delilah again had changed everything. He finally had a chance to do something good for Blue. He just didn't know how to go about it. Maybe Courtney could help him understand how a woman's mind worked and why Delilah refused even to listen to him.

But it still nearly killed him to agree. "Friends," he said. "As in all of that."

Chapter 10

HEATH WATCHED COURTNEY'S lips curve slowly and the expression in her eyes change from teasing to relieved to amazed. "Why the sudden change of heart?"

He took her arm and turned her away from the center of town. "I ran into an old friend."

"Here?"

"Here."

"Someone who knew you in South Carolina?"

"Yes."

The relief in her voice turned to delight. "Who is it? Where is he?"

"Not a he," Heath said as they rounded the corner onto a side street. "It's a woman. Her name is Delilah. She's working at the Pink Parasol."

Courtney's gaze shot to his. "As a . . . ?"

"Sporting gal? Yes."

"I see." Courtney's expression changed subtly. "Is she an old girlfriend?"

"No. It's not like that." He argued with himself about betraying Delilah's confidence. He'd promised to keep silent, but he couldn't ask Courtney for help without giving her at least part of the story—the pertinent part. And for some reason he didn't fully comprehend, he trusted her. As much as he trusted anyone.

He glanced around to make sure no one could hear them and lowered his voice for good measure. "She lived on my parents' plantation in South Carolina. We grew up friends. Inseparable. There were three of us." The words came out unevenly at first and then began to clog his throat. To keep from closing off entirely, he backed away from talking about Blue. "About six months before I left, my father sold her."

Courtney's expression went through another subtle change. "She was a slave?"

"Yes. But she's light enough to pass as white, and that's what she's doing here. I'm trusting you with this, Courtney. No one can know the truth."

"Of course not. It's just that I've never met anyone who actually owned slaves before, or anyone who *was* a slave. I've read about it, of course, but it's always seemed like such an abstract idea. So . . . unthinkable." She stopped walking and touched his arm tentatively. "I don't mean to sound judgmental, but how could you practice slavery? How can you look at someone and decide they're less than human just because of the color of their skin? And how can you say you're friends with someone but you own them at the same time? How can you—"

"Own and sell other human beings?" Heath cut her off, pleased by her reaction but uncomfortable with the issues she was raising. He had to take them one at a time. "I can't. I don't. At least, not anymore."

He started walking again, more out of restlessness than a pressing need to get back to the cabin. "You once asked me why I'm here. The immediate answer to that would be that a man named Ellis Bailey died here in a mine cave-in about three months ago. I happened to be in Kansas City when it happened, and his widow desperately wanted someone to retrieve his personal belongings and bring them back to her. She hired me to do it. It's his cabin we're living in. I have nothing of my own, but that's fine because I want nothing."

Or so he kept telling himself.

He shook off that thought, glanced at her hand that remained on his sleeve, and forced himself to keep going before he lost his courage. "The real answer is that five years ago, I left my family's plantation and turned my back on everything they stood for. I've been wandering ever since."

Questions filled her eyes, but she didn't ask them. Heath could have kissed her for understanding that he had to proceed at his own pace. "I couldn't condone my . . . family's actions any longer. I couldn't live the life they believed in so strongly."

"Do you ever miss it?"

"South Carolina? I don't let myself."

"And your family?"

That was a little harder to answer. He did miss his sisters, but couldn't see them without also seeing his parents. "I don't let myself miss them, either."

"Is it a big family?"

"Not especially. A father. A mother. Three sisters—Annabella, Lorelei, and Cozette. Last time I was home, I had two nieces and two nephews, but only God knows how many I have now."

"And you really don't miss them?"

"No."

Courtney turned to get the sun out of her eyes and brushed up against him. It was a subtle movement, and the momentary contact of soft breast against his arm must have been unintentional. Even so, heat raced up his back and spread through his chest.

The look in her eyes told him that she'd felt something, too. "And this woman? How did she get here?"

"I don't know. She didn't say and I didn't ask. She was too busy telling me to go away." He smiled ruefully. "I owe her a huge debt, Courtney. I need to help her, but I don't know how. She wasn't exactly happy to see me."

"Maybe she just needs time. Seeing you here was probably a shock, and she may be worried that you'll tell someone about her."

"Which I've done."

"Well, yes, but you know I won't tell anyone. You knew

that before or you wouldn't have said anything. You're not exactly the world's biggest gossip."

Heath smiled gratefully. "Your confidence is nice, but I'm not sure I deserve it."

She returned the smile and their eyes met and held. He couldn't move and he couldn't speak and he couldn't look away. "Then you don't plan to go back home again?" she asked. "Not ever?"

"Not in this lifetime." His gaze shifted to her mouth, to the softly parted lips, and then to her throat, where he could see that her breathing had become labored. He inched closer, giving her a chance to stop him if that's what she wanted, and praying at the same time that she wouldn't. It didn't matter that a kiss would change things between them forever, or that it would be harder for him to leave when the time came. Just now, leaving didn't seem nearly as appealing as it had just a few weeks ago.

Heath watched the pulse point in Courtney's neck jump and the urge to cover it with his lips became almost stronger than he could resist. He'd been sharing a cabin with her for less than two weeks, but it was more of a home than anything he'd known in the past five years, and he had the strangest feeling that he would miss it when it was over.

Which only made kissing her the *wrong* thing to do.

Courtney's eyes roamed his face and she swallowed convulsively. "You're going to kiss me, aren't you?"

Her forthright nature pleased him and his smile widened. "I'm considering it. Would you object?"

She shook her head and moved a step closer. "I should, but really I think I'd object if you didn't."

Heath pulled her gently to him and lowered his mouth to hers. The instant their lips touched, her eyelids fluttered shut and searing heat soared through his veins. She melted against him, all curves and softness beneath the denim and plaid, more desirable to him than any woman he'd ever held in his arms. Even the woman he'd once expected to marry.

Her arms slid up his back, found his shoulders, then encircled his neck. Her fingers curled into the back of his hair, and she sighed softly against his mouth. Warning bells sounded in the back of his mind telling him that he was getting in too deep. His life would never be the same after this. But he was in no condition to listen.

For the first time in years he felt as if someone wanted him. Even if it lasted for just one moment, it was too hard to resist.

Too late, Courtney realized that she'd made a huge mistake by kissing Heath. It wasn't that she didn't feel anything. That wasn't the problem at all. The problem was, she felt too much. As if she'd been shriveled and empty inside, her heart and soul began to fill, to warm and expand so quickly it almost hurt.

She told herself to pull away, but she couldn't seem to move. There was something hypnotic about the touch of his lips, the sweep of lashes against his cheek, the feel of his tongue brushing against her mouth and urging her to take the kiss to another level. But if she did that she'd be stuck in the past forever. Courtney knew that as surely as she knew that Heath Sullivan might just be the great love of her life.

She'd never believed in love or in happily-ever-after. Even as a little girl, she'd known that there was more to the fairy tales than what the storybooks told. She'd seen Leslie go through too many "ideal" relationships to believe in love that lasted.

The Prince and Cinderella might have said "I do," but eventually they realized how ill-suited they were for each other. He'd realized that beauty didn't compensate for a lack of breeding. She'd woken up one day to the stark knowledge that her new husband was a snob.

Sleeping Beauty had discovered that the charming stranger who'd awoken her with a kiss was really a control freak who screamed at her children. Prince Charming had found himself tied to a nag until the end of time.

Courtney had seen love die time and again right in front of her eyes, so there was absolutely no question of falling into it herself. And there was no question of tying herself to this century just because she had a fleeting attraction to Heath.

Sooner or later, she'd come back down to earth and realize how badly his socks smelled, boiling his laundry in a kettle would lose its romantic charm, and she'd be stuck in this hellhole with no way out. Maybe he'd shave and she'd see what he *really* looked like. Or he'd start ordering her around the way all of Leslie's losers had.

No, thank you.

She moved stiffly in his embrace, and Heath slowly released her. He obviously sensed the change in her mood because his expression grew quizzical. "Did I do something wrong?"

She put some distance between them and shook her head. She certainly couldn't lay the blame at his feet when she'd been as eager for that kiss as he'd been. "No," she said with an apologetic smile. "It's just that I don't think this is such a good idea, after all."

"Oh?" He made a visible effort to keep his smile from fading. "Do you mind if I ask why not?"

He was still standing too close. She could smell that mixture of cigar smoke, whiskey, and wind that was becoming so familiar. Below that, the male scent that was his alone.

She folded her arms tightly across her chest and put a little more distance between them so she could think clearly. "No, of course not. You have every right to know." When even distance didn't help, she stooped to pet Geezer and hoped a good blast of dog breath would snap some sense into her. She let herself look in Heath's general direction, but she was very careful not to make eye contact again, "I just think that getting involved in any way would be a mistake since we don't know how long I'm going to be here. I could be zapped back home any minute."

"And you might not."

She lifted her gaze slightly and made the mistake of looking at a button just beneath a tuft of golden hair on his chest. Her heart took off at a dead run and her throat grew dry. "But I *might*. I don't know about you, but I've had enough disappointment in my life without purposely adding to it."

Heath lifted her chin so that she had to look at him. "Tell me."

"Tell you what?"

"About your disappointments. I want to know."

He was making it harder, not easier. If she confided in him, if she opened her heart to him in any way, she'd never get it back again. She pulled away from his hand, but she couldn't make herself look away from his eyes. "I can't talk about that, Heath. Not now."

"Why not?"

She laughed sharply, aware that their roles had suddenly reversed. There was no way to explain what she was feeling without stepping over the line she couldn't cross, but she couldn't leave Heath hanging, either. She scratched Geezer between the ears and envied the dog his simple existence. "I can't tell you all my disappointments," she said, trying to sound lighthearted and teasing. "It would take too long."

"Then give me one."

"Why? What possible difference can it make?"

His lips curved slightly. "Maybe you're here so that *I* can help *you*."

"With what?"

"You say that as if you have no problems. And yet you do allude to disappointments. . . . Come on, now. I told you something about my family despite a very firm rule against it. The least you can do is tell me a little about yours."

She didn't want to talk about her family, but then, he hadn't wanted to talk about his and she'd pushed him into it. And talking about Grandmother and Leslie was almost guaranteed to get her feet back on the ground.

"My family is small," she said uncertainly. "There's just my grandmother and me."

"Your parents are dead?" Heath's eyes darkened with such genuine concern, Courtney didn't have the heart to lie.

"No. At least, I don't think they are." She pulled a weed from the ground and tore the stalk into tiny pieces, a nervous habit that had apparently traveled with her. "To understand my family, you have to understand the times I live in. I was born in nineteen seventy-six, the year of the bicentennial celebration."

Heath quirked an eyebrow, but he didn't say anything.

"My mother liked to call herself a free spirit. I have another term for it, but we won't get into that. When she was eighteen, she left home and moved into what's called a commune. She lived with, maybe, two dozen other people, and their style of living was . . . radical, to say the least."

She looked at him to gauge his reaction, but she couldn't see anything but caring, and that made it almost impossible to hold back. "The commune was made up of men and women, and none of them believed in marriage. They all flitted from one partner to the next whenever the whim suited. The result is that I have no idea who my father is. What's even more charming is that neither does my mother. And not one of the men who might be him cared enough to even pretend."

She fought to keep her tone light, but all the old pain made her voice crack, and the ache she'd battled for twenty years began to burn in her heart. She tried so hard not to let this missing piece of her life fill her with self-pity, and she hated when she failed.

Heath digested the news in silence, but he reached for her hand and held it against his chest. It was a simple gesture, but so sweet that her eyes blurred and her throat tightened with emotion. This was *not* the way he was supposed to react. It only made her like him more.

"When I was five," she went on hesitantly, "Leslie decided to leave the commune, but she didn't bother to think ahead. Leslie never thinks ahead. In the commune, everyone shared responsibility so that whatever needed doing got done. Kids pretty much belonged to the community, so she could ignore me and someone else would make sure I was fed and warm. I don't know why she left, but life on the outside wasn't what she wanted. It required her to pay attention. She hated that, and she hated me for being what needed paying attention to."

Heath tilted his head slightly. "And this is in the future?"

"Yeah. A hundred years or more." He nodded as if that made perfect sense, so she went on. "When I was seven Leslie met the first in a long line of really awful boyfriends. He didn't want a kid around, so he gave her an ultimatum.

She jumped at the chance to get rid of me and dumped me on my grandmother's doorstep. She left me there until he got tired of her and left, and then she came and took me home again so she wouldn't have to be alone. But then in a few months she found a new boyfriend and I was in the way, so it was back to Grandmother's."

Courtney forced a smile and tried to look as if thinking about her history didn't feel like nails in her soul. "The last time I saw her was eighteen months ago. I have no idea whether she's still alive or if she's dead. She didn't respond to any of the letters we sent telling her that Grandmother died, so who knows? The only thing I *do* know is that I wish I didn't have that woman's blood pumping through my veins."

The admission slipped out almost before she realized what she was saying, and she felt the heat creeping into her cheeks. She'd never admitted that to herself, much less to anyone else. But there it was, splat on the dirt in front of them, and she couldn't take it back now.

Heath laced his fingers through hers and squeezed her hand gently. "I understand what you're feeling—better than you can possibly imagine."

But Courtney didn't want sympathy, and she didn't want him to pretend to understand. She pulled her hand from his and backed away. "You *can't* understand how I feel. You can't possibly understand." The ugliness she'd been trying to hide from her entire life rose up like a giant shadow and threatened to swallow her.

It didn't matter whether she was in this century or her own. She'd had enough of being left behind, and she couldn't take the chance that Heath would grow tired of her down the road. And besides, there wasn't enough left of her heart to offer even a tiny piece of it to someone else.

Something inside urged her to go back and seek solace in his arms, but she couldn't do that. Her own *mother* hadn't cared enough to stay with her; why should she believe that some stranger would? And she knew only too well how quickly men got bored and moved on.

He took a step toward her, but she backed away, shaking

her head frantically. "Please don't, Heath. I can't be what you want. I can't do what you want." She lifted her gaze to the sky and shouted at whoever might be listening, "It's too much. You can't ask this of me." And before Heath could even try to stop her, she bolted down the street.

Heath stared after Courtney in stunned disbelief. He argued with himself for a full ten minutes about the wisdom of going after her. He'd been right about one thing—kissing her had changed everything between them. The trouble was, he wasn't sure exactly what it had done.

He had no idea where he wanted things to go from here. Now that he'd been spending time around Courtney, life alone seemed empty and cold. But maybe that was just the mood he was in. Maybe finding Delilah again had more to do with his mood than Courtney did. And maybe if he could just get out of Virginia City and get back to the life he loved, he'd feel better.

Except that he couldn't honestly say that he'd loved life alone. He'd been a miserable excuse for a human being for the past five years. Ornery. Bristly. Hell, he couldn't remember the last time he'd laughed. He'd felt more like his old self in the past ten days than he had in years.

So what did he do about it? Did he even have what it would take to build a life with someone else? Could he settle down and stay in one place for more than a few weeks at a time? Maybe buy a little stretch of land and farm it. Or raise horses. Or cattle. Or open a shop in some town somewhere. The possibilities were endless.

But the question remained: could he do it? Could he stay, or would he grow bored with the life of a regular man and start to feel that old urge to wander? And what would happen to Courtney if he did?

Assuming, of course, that it was Courtney he created this fictional life with.

He raked his fingers through his hair and turned his back on the corner where Courtney had disappeared minutes earlier. Geezer stared up at him, his golden-brown eyes full of reproach, his freckled snout curled in disapproval.

"See?" Heath demanded as he started walking away from the cabin and the dreams he'd been toying with. "I can't even make a dog happy. What am I doing thinking about a wife and children?"

Geezer yawned. Whined. Smacked his lips once or twice and fell into step beside him.

"That's the trouble with staying too long in one place," Heath said as they turned back onto Wallace Street. "You're a drifter. You know what I'm talking about, don't you? The only things I need are a horse, a cigar, and a bottle. And occasionally—*very* occasionally—a willing woman."

Geezer sneezed twice and sat back on his haunches to scratch his ear with a hind foot. And Heath told himself that the dog had given him a signal of some sort—a sign that he was thinking the right way for the first time in days.

But the truth was that Geezer didn't look any more convinced than Heath was—and Heath wasn't convinced at all.

Delilah lived for Wednesday mornings.

She spent an entire hellish week selling her body and slipping away to the secret place in her mind where Blue was waiting for her. To that grove of trees beside the river where she'd played as a child when she'd been allowed to play, and where later she and Blue had turned friendship into love.

If it hadn't been for the memory of that place, she couldn't have survived the long days and endless nights in the Pink Parasol. She'd have died during the drunken mauling of foul-breathed miners with filthy hands and pockets full of gold dust. Men willing to shell out good gold for a few minutes of her time. She hated them all. Every last one of them.

But that all faded on Wednesdays.

She lived for those few short hours when she was able to leave the Pink Parasol and steal through town to where NannyBeth lived with the light of her life. To the cabin where the kind old woman cared for Isaac, bathed him when she could, fed him and kept him warm while Delilah did the only thing she *could* do.

Wednesdays.

Some day, please Jesus, this would be over and she and

Isaac could leave this horrible place. Some day, God willing.
Until then she had Wednesdays and the prayers that on many
days she worried fell on deaf ears.

She'd lived on dreams and prayers for a long time. Dreams
that one day Blue would find them and prayers that they'd
some day be a family. But those dreams were gone, and so
was Blue.

All this time she'd told herself that she would know if he
was gone. She'd felt his presence nearby so many times she'd
convinced herself he was still alive and searching for her.
And when he found her, she'd tell him about Isaac, and they
would laugh and sing and dance and praise the Lord for His
mercy. Against all odds, she'd believed it. For hadn't he
promised all those years ago while they held each other in
the grass? Hadn't he sworn on the moon and the stars that
he would never lose her?

She'd clung to her belief and she'd let it sustain her while
she did what she had to do to keep her baby alive. And then,
suddenly, there was Heath, big as brass and just as bold.
She'd seen the truth in his eyes the instant she'd turned
around and recognized him. She'd read the sorrow in his
eyes, and she knew Heath well enough to know that only
one thing could have put it there.

He'd been trying to tell her for well over a week that Blue
was gone. But Delilah couldn't let him say it aloud. Couldn't
bear to hear the words. She wouldn't survive the knowing
of it. The harsh reality of being told that she'd lost forever
the only man in the world she'd ever be allowed to love.

What mattered now was keeping a roof over Isaac's head
and food in his belly. If her nights were long and cold, that
was a small price to pay. Having to pretend that Isaac wasn't
hers . . . now *that* nearly killed her. But just as soon as she'd
saved enough to get out of Virginia City, she would. They'd
leave and keep on going until they found a place where they
could live without anyone passing judgment.

She just hoped a place like that existed this side of heaven,
because she wasn't ready to meet Blue or her daddy at the
Pearly Gates.

On a Wednesday in early September, she cast aside all the

trappings of the Pink Parasol and dressed in her plain clothes. Not for anything would she let Isaac see her in those rags of sin. Not her precious, innocent boy. He could never know what his mother had become in order to provide for him.

Never.

She stepped outside and drew in a greedy breath of fresh air. Clear air. *Free* air. Just knowing that for twenty-four hours no man could touch her was a heady feeling. *No man*.

She curved her fingers around the trinket in her pocket—a carved wooden horse on wheels that she'd bought with the money she'd been saving these past months. She smiled softly, anticipating Isaac's reaction and the eruption of that smile that was so much like his father's.

As she reached the first corner, she noticed a tall, dark-haired man watching her from across the street. She recognized him as the man who'd been watching her inside the Parasol for days now. She expected that. What she didn't expect—and wouldn't tolerate—was this intrusion on these few precious hours that were her own.

She could see his reflection in the windows of the shops as she passed. Him thinking he was sly. Subtle, just like Heath thought he was. Were all men born without the brains God gave a goose? Or did they just think women were stupid?

Just as she'd done with Heath, she led him a merry chase for a few blocks, then turned around without warning and met him head-on. "What's wrong with you?"

He smiled a big friendly smile and twinkled his eyes as if she'd said something amusing. "Absolutely nothing. Unless there's something wrong with a man noticing a beautiful woman out for a stroll and offering to escort her through a dangerous section of town?"

Oh. So that was it. She wagged a hand at him and started walking again. "I don't need your fancy talk, Mr. Man. And I *sure* don't need you to escort me down the street."

"Well, now, who said anything about need?" He grinned again, a big infectious smile that probably got him anything he wanted—from other people. "Roderick Dennehy, ma'am. At your service."

Delilah slid a resentful glance at him. "Maybe it escaped your notice, Mr. Roderick Dennehy, but I'm not working at the moment. So if you'll excuse me . . ."

Mr. Roderick Dennehy fell into step beside her, hands linked behind his back. At least he hadn't tried to touch her. In fact, he seemed to be taking great care not to. She slanted a glance at him and decided he wasn't bad looking, for a white man. But she had no room in her life and no place in her soul for any man—white, black, or otherwise.

She jerked her chin and sent Mr. Roderick Dennehy a look that would have made her mother proud. "Have you heard a word I said?"

"Yes, ma'am."

"Then leave me be. Get on with your business and let me attend to mine."

He shook his head as if she'd asked him to change the world or right some grievous wrong. "That's going to be a little difficult. You see, you *are* my business."

Delilah stopped walking abruptly. What did he know? *How* did he know? Had Heath told someone? No matter what they were to each other, if Heath Sullivan had put her baby at risk, if he'd jeopardized this life she'd just about killed herself to provide, she'd kill him. The world would be a better place without the Sullivan men in it, anyway.

She tried not to look frightened, even though her hands had turned cold and her heart was flopping around in her throat and threatening to choke her on the spot. "What do you mean? How could I possibly be your business?"

Mr. Roderick Dennehy sent her another of those smiles that, under other circumstances, might have been endearing. Before she could react, he caught her hand and lifted it to his lips. "I mean, beautiful Miss Delilah, that I intend to make you my wife if you'll have me. And I'll do it before the new year, if I have any say in the matter."

Delilah gaped at him. The ice in her fingers turned into needle-sharp pricks against her skin. "You're mocking me, aren't you?"

"No, ma'am, I am not."

"I don't find this amusing."

"Neither do I. I fell in love with you the moment I saw you."

"Love?" She snorted an angry laugh and started away. "Well, Mr. Roderick Dennehy, you won't be making me your wife, and you *don't* have any say in the matter." And because that didn't seem quite strong enough to convey everything she felt, she turned and added one more thing. "You can go to the devil . . . and don't bother saying good-bye when you go. I *won't* miss you."

Chapter 11

IT HAD BEEN a week since that kiss. A miserable, lonely week during which Heath and Courtney had changed places without Heath fully understanding how or why. There were times when he thought he saw regret shimmering in her eyes, but he couldn't tell whether it was regret for having run from him that day or for having kissed him in the first place.

She certainly wasn't saying. She wasn't saying much of anything, in fact.

He wasn't having any better luck getting Delilah to talk to him. Maybe he'd been right to find what he wanted in the bottom of a bottle, after all.

It was late in the evening—long after sundown—when he bellied up to the bar at the Pink Parasol with a handful of other dirty miners and downed a shot of red-eye that he already knew wouldn't even begin to touch the longing. After several minutes he tried another, but two shots were enough to let him know he wouldn't be finding release in a bottle. Not today.

He stayed anyway, nursing his memories of Courtney's deep eyes, the gentle arc of her cheek, the softness of her lips, the taste of her kiss. And most of all, the pain he'd glimpsed on her face just before she'd run away from him.

Just after dark Philo Keegan came through the front doors, but Heath was in no mood to hear someone call him "son" or to stand around envying some old codger just because Courtney talked to him. Keeping his face averted, he ducked out the doors and into the night before Philo noticed him. He found Geezer waiting patiently in the shadows beneath one bank of the saloon's windows.

The dog lifted its head, stood, stretched, and yawned, then came toward Heath, claws clicking on the wooden slats of the boardwalk. In spite of himself, Heath smiled at the dog's loyalty. At least someone still liked him.

Knowing he'd regret letting down his guard when it came time to leave, Heath patted his thigh and beckoned the dog closer. The dog responded without question, and Heath's smile grew.

The scents of supper wafted out on the late summer breeze, and Heath's stomach rumbled. He hunkered down to eye level and moved his hand to the space between the dog's ears. They'd been gone from the cabin since before sunrise and other than a few scraps at noon, the dog hadn't eaten all day. "What about it, you old nuisance? Are you hungry?"

Geezer whined softly and released a blast of the worst breath Heath had ever encountered.

Interpreting that as a "yes," Heath glanced up the street, then down, trying to decide where he could find something for the dog to eat. Gohn's Meat Market would have been the perfect choice, but it had been closed for almost an hour. But there was bound to be something Geezer would appreciate at the restaurant across the street. Come to think of it, Heath could use a bite or two himself. A little food in his stomach might clear his head before he had to face Courtney again.

Shoving his hands into his pockets and whistling softly, Heath crossed the dusty street, climbed the boardwalk on the other side. After motioning for Geezer to lie down and wait again, he stepped into the room lit with dozens of oil lamps in sconces on the walls and candles to brighten it even further.

He found an empty table covered with a nearly white cloth near a window overlooking the street, where he could keep

an eye on Geezer and watch the city through the windows.
He placed an order for venison stew with a short, balding
waiter who was as round as he was tall, then sat back with
his fingers laced across his stomach to wait.

Light from several lamps flickered behind him. Two giant
ferns—imported at great cost and with great care from the
East—graced each end of the small restaurant. Signs of civ-
ilization already, and the city just a year old.

He turned toward the window and noticed a shaggy-haired,
dust-covered miner sitting at an outside table. Heath might
not have paid attention if the man hadn't been staring straight
at him. But he was, and that made Heath instantly alert in
case he was one of Tyree Caine's men.

He took the man's measure carefully. The miner stared
back without blinking.

The emaciated, hollow-cheeked, dirt-encrusted scoundrel
seemed a little too interested, and his careful scrutiny—not
to mention the haughty look of disdain in his pale eyes—
annoyed Heath. In fact, the longer the man stared at him, the
more irritated he became.

On the off chance that the prospector might be looking at
someone else, Heath glanced over his shoulder. The other
man turned at the same moment. Heath looked back quickly,
and the miner did the same. He was obviously playing at
something, but Heath was in no mood for whatever it was.
He put his hands on the table ready for a confrontation, and
again his counterpart mimicked him.

Seething, Heath grabbed his hat and jammed it on his
head, only to watch the other man retrieve his own hat and
jam it on his own head—a hat that was identical in every
respect to the one Heath wore.

As if time had slowed to a crawl, Heath realized what was
happening. His stomach lurched and his blood ran cold. He
dropped into his seat again and leaned closer to the glass.
When had his cheeks become so pale and gaunt? When had
his eyes become so deeply shadowed? When had those rims
of red first appeared? He looked dirty. Disgusting. Downright
disreputable. He probably smelled.

No wonder Sally and Nell thought that calling him

"Charming" was such a grand joke. No wonder Delilah wanted nothing to do with him. No wonder Courtney had been so disgusted by his clumsy attempts to kiss her. He could barely tolerate looking at himself. He was damn lucky that Geezer hadn't run howling into next week at the sight of him. He knew for damn sure Sukey would have worn him out with a switch if she'd seen him looking like this.

He traced a finger along his cheek, and remembered that last argument with his father just before he left Bonne Chance forever. Sebastian had called him weak. Pathetic. *Disgusting*. Heath had hated him for that almost as much as he'd hated him for everything else. He'd spent the past five years thinking that he was proving his father wrong; instead, he'd proven the bastard right.

He grimaced and dropped his hand to the table again, and his father's voice filled the caverns of his mind. He heard it all, every word, every accusation, every drop of hatred. A shudder racked his body at the memory, but at the same time a new determination began to grow inside of him.

No more.

He'd been running from his father's influence as hard and far and long as he could, but he'd been carrying Sebastian Sullivan with him every step of the way. He'd wanted so badly to prove that he was twice the man his father was. Instead, he'd turned into a mere fraction.

And by doing that he'd given power to what he detested most. This man couldn't pay the debt he owed to Blue. This man couldn't help Delilah leave the life she was living. He couldn't do much of anything, in fact.

Well, he was through running. He was through proving his father right. Starting here, starting now, he was through letting hurt, anger, and disillusionment turn him into the very thing he didn't want to be. He'd show them all the man he was meant to be. And maybe he'd find that man for himself along the way.

Sweat poured down Courtney's back as she bent over the embers in the fire to check her first batch of corn fritters. Philo sat behind her, elbows on his knees as he whittled and dropped shavings onto the floor. She swiped her sleeve across her forehead and tried to feel some satisfaction in a job well done.

In the past eighteen days she'd learned to make biscuits and corn fritters, molasses pie and venison stew. She'd done laundry over an outdoor fire, and she'd even been thinking about learning to make candles. But keeping this cabin neat and tidy and occasionally having a brief, unsatisfying conversation with Heath wasn't going to get her back home again.

And she still wanted to get home. As much as she ever had. Or nearly, anyway.

She missed the push and drive of the business world, but even more, she missed the challenge that sketching had always provided for her. She missed the creative process she'd been developing bit by bit over the years, and the satisfaction that could only come from turning air into images and emotion.

She had to be honest and admit that she didn't miss the long commutes and traffic jams, or breakfast on the run, or the days when she hadn't found time for breakfast at all. She didn't miss panty hose or heels—not that she'd ever worn either when she didn't have to. And she didn't miss the insistent buzz of her alarm clock in the mornings. She didn't even miss listening to the morning television news as she dressed or watching Letterman as she fell asleep.

What she did miss was feeling as if what she did mattered. The only place in her life where she'd ever managed to capture that feeling was in her work—and now she'd lost even that.

She might be filling Heath's belly and her own—and with increasing frequency, Philo's—but her achievements in the kitchen didn't really matter, not to her and not really to anyone else. Heath barely noticed what she put in front of him, and he practically broke his neck getting out of the cabin afterward. Philo appreciated the food, but corn fritters didn't soothe a troubled soul. Baked apples, though heaven in this dreary place, wouldn't help someone else find their true potential. Boiled laundry would never lift a demoralized housewife out of the doldrums. It was far more likely to put her there.

She turned slightly and realized that Philo was watching her from beneath his bushy gray eyebrows. "Somethin' wrong?"

She started to shake her head, then caught herself and wondered just why she was holding back. At least Philo cared what she was feeling—which was more than anyone in her biological family had ever done. She cast one more glance at her fritters, then sat at the table across from him.

"I don't know how to explain what I'm feeling," she said with a thin smile. "I guess *useless* is the best word. I've always wanted to do something that mattered. Something that made the world a better place. Don't get me wrong, I appreciate everything you've been teaching me. But this just isn't enough."

"What do you want to do?"

"Back home I was an illustrator for a magazine. My sketches appeared along with stories and articles in a women's magazine." She propped her chin in her hand and smiled ruefully. "I like to think I helped people with what I did."

"Well, then, you probably did."

Courtney tried to decide if he was patronizing her, but he didn't seem to be. "I miss it," she admitted.

Philo looked away from his whittling and fixed her with one squinty eye. "You can't draw pictures here?"

Courtney shrugged. "No paper. No pen."

"Well, that can be fixed easy enough. I got paper. Moonshine's got lead pencils. I'll bet he'd give you some. He don't need 'em all."

Courtney grinned slowly and her heart lifted as if someone had taken a rock from it. "Are you serious?"

"Would I lie?"

She laughed and shook her head. "No. I don't think you would."

"Well, then." He brushed wood shavings from his lap and leaned back in his chair. "Draw your pictures. Maybe them fellas down at the *Post* would be interested in seeing 'em."

"The newspaper?"

"We got us one. Not very old, but it's a newspaper. And there's no tellin' what they might want."

She wasn't going to hold her breath, but the thought of being able to draw again, even if only for herself, made her almost delirious.

Philo sniffed and went back to his whittling. "As for the other, I reckon what you're doing matters to Heath. A man likes a clean house, meals on the table, and a purty woman to come home to."

It had been a week since that kiss, but Courtney still wasn't in the mood to talk about Heath—and especially not in this context. "Well, I'm glad. He's done a lot for me."

"And if you get married some day, you'll have to know everything I've learned you."

"That's true. But I'm not going to marry Heath, so it really doesn't matter right now, does it?"

Philo peeled a long, thin piece of wood from the stick in his hand and watched it curl onto the floor. "Who said anything about marrying Heath?"

Courtney flushed and looked away. "I just meant that all this Dolly Domestic stuff might be important if I was planning to get married. To someone. Anyone. Which I'm not. I just used Heath as an example, that's all."

Philo's squinty eye closed a little further. "Does he know?"

"Does he know what?"

"That you want to marry him, of course. Does Heath know?"

Courtney sat up straight. "I *don't* want to marry him. I don't want to marry anyone. I just told you that."

Philo peeled another strip of wood from his stick and watched it drop. "You in love with him?"

"*No.* Aren't you listening to me? He's . . . he's dirty and he's rude and he's everything else I don't want in a man." Even as she spoke, she could hear the lie in her words, but she wanted so desperately for them to be true, she kept adding to it. "He's selfish. He's never here. He doesn't think about the future *at all*, and I don't believe in living for the moment. I've been around someone who does that, and it's horrible."

Philo chuckled and flicked the knife across the wood two or three times. "So you're sayin' he *doesn't* know?"

"There's nothing *to* know."

"If you say so. Too bad love don't always work out logical-like, isn't it?" Philo grinned up at her and dropped another curled shaving onto the floor. "And don't blame me for hearing one thing while you're sayin' another. Your mouth's telling a whole different story than your eyes."

Courtney threw her hands into the air and strode to the window. "Nonsense. My *eyes* aren't saying anything."

"The hell they ain't—if you'll excuse the language. I seen the way a woman looks when she's in love. If you ain't there yet, you're fallin'."

"I am *not* falling," she insisted. The smell of burning fritters drew her back to the fire. "I haven't even known Heath for three weeks yet," she said. "That's not enough time even to become friends, much less fall in love." She wrapped her hand in a flour sack and pulled the pan from the coals. "If there *is* such a thing as love."

Philo's hand stilled and even his good eye squinted. "You don't believe in love?"

"No, I don't." She set the pan aside to cool and planted her hands on her hips. "And don't tell me you do, because I won't believe you. If you believed in it, you wouldn't have passed up every woman who might have made a good wife. You'd have fallen in love and settled down to raise a family instead of searching for gold your whole life."

Philo shook his head slowly. "Believin' and doin' are two different things, little girl. I believe in love, all right. And so do you, way down deep."

Courtney laughed harshly. "How do you know what I believe?"

"Because I'm a smart old coot."

She shook her head in mock despair. "You're dreaming, Philo. I've seen love in action. Love is a word people use to manipulate each other with, that's all. All it does is bring heartache and misery. I should know. I've been on the losing end of it my whole life."

Philo set his knife aside and rested his hands on his knees. "You really believe that?"

"Absolutely."

He considered for a long moment, then slowly reached for his knife again. "Well, then, I feel sorry for you."

"Don't."

"Have to. You don't know the first thing about love, and here you are thinkin' you're some kind of expert."

Courtney raked her fingers through her hair in agitation. "And I suppose you *do* know about love?"

Philo snorted a derisive laugh. "A sight more'n you do. Sometimes, those who watch know more than those who do." He worked his knife on the wood for a few seconds and squinted at her again. "I'll admit there's folks out there who use the word the wrong way. I suppose that's always been and probably always will be. But love ain't ugly, and it ain't mean, and it ain't whatchacallit . . ." He circled the knife in the air as he sought for the word. "It ain't manipulatin' somebody to do what you want 'em to, neither." He jabbed the air with his knifepoint. "And it ain't just what happens between a man and a woman in a private moment—though that's part of it."

Courtney didn't know whether to laugh or cry at the notion of this old prospector trying to teach her about love. She folded her arms and tried to keep her expression neutral. "I'll keep that in mind."

"I *know* about love, missy. I've been loved and I've felt my share of it, too, so don't you take that tone with me. You've gotta know how to love, but you also gotta know how to *be* loved for it to work. And that's where your trouble is. How can folks love you if you keep pushing 'em away?"

"I wouldn't push them away if they didn't always leave."

"Not everybody leaves." He wagged the knife like a finger. "I'll tell you what love is. It's caring as much about another person as you do about yourself, and sometimes more. It ain't flash and it ain't all that stuff that makes your blood sing. It's quiet. It's knowing someone values you, and valuing them right back. It's trusting somebody else with what you think and feel, and being worth trusting with those things your own self. It's putting your hand in somebody else's and knowing that person won't shake you off to save their own sorry hide. Standing on a ledge and knowing they'll be there to catch you if you jump. *That's* what love is, missy. And only a damn fool would shove it away if it were to come his way."

She smiled wistfully. "I think that's the nicest description of love I've ever heard. It's almost enough to make me *want* to believe. But if *you* believe that, why are you alone?"

"Because I'm a damn fool, that's why." Philo sheathed his knife and swept wood shavings onto the floor. "Love'll give you a chance or two, but it won't keep waiting forever. And if you're fool enough to think it matters *one bit* what a person looks like, then you ain't the woman I thought you was." He strode to the door and yanked it open. "Children look at the face. Grown-ups look at the heart."

And with that, before she could defend herself, he was gone.

Courtney glanced at the cooling corn fritters and thought about calling after him, but the conversation had left her uneasy, and she'd rather not continue it. She had no idea what had prompted Philo to be so concerned about *her* love life, and she wasn't sure whether to be offended or touched. Frankly, everything that had happened in the past eighteen days left her confused and uncertain.

Did she love Heath? Maybe as much as it was possible for her to love anyone. Yes, it was unfair and childish to pretend that his looks mattered to her, but the barriers around her heart were growing perilously thin, and she was grasping at anything to keep them in place.

Could she let Heath love her?

That was the most frightening question of all, and the one she had no answer to. But she told herself that Heath hadn't ever said anything about love, so it wasn't a question that needed answering. Not tonight, anyway.

Shaking off Philo's warning, she slid the nearly cool fritters onto a plate, swept up the pile of wood shavings, and cleaned the table thoroughly. She was just finishing with that when the door opened again and footsteps sounded on the floor behind her.

It was still early—far too early for Heath to come staggering in—so she turned, expecting to see that Philo had come back to sample the fritters and tell her what she could do to improve them. Instead, she found herself facing a tall well-dressed man wearing tan trousers and a matching jacket, and an obviously new hat. He was the stuff male models were made of, stunning as a Norse God with short-cropped sun-bleached hair and a strong, firm jaw. The scent of spicy aftershave drifted inside with him.

Who was he? Some relative of Ellis Bailey's who'd come to claim the cabin? Someone who'd lost his way? A stranger in dire need of a corn fritter? Or someone to be wary of, like Tyree Caine?

She dusted her hands on her apron. "Can I help you?"

"Perhaps."

It only took one word for the frisson of recognition to snake up her spine. She inched closer and took another look at the sky blue of his eyes and the unfamiliar crease of a small scar near his lip. "*Heath?*"

"Yes, ma'am."

Her heart slammed against her ribs and her fingers grew numb. How was it *possible* that *this* had been hiding beneath all that dirt and hair? He was watching her, waiting for her to say something more. Heat crept into her cheeks as she fumbled with the corn fritters like a blooming idiot.

He glanced at his jacket and grinned, and her heart somersaulted in her chest. "Didn't recognize me, huh? Well, don't feel bad. I almost don't recognize myself."

She battled a flash of envy for his clean clothes and freshly bathed body. "Does this mean you've had some sort of financial windfall?"

He shrugged casually, hung his hat on its peg, and dropped a bag with his old things beside the bed. "No. A spiritual one, maybe." He took in her appearance with one sweeping glance. "There's enough left for one more hot bath and another set of new clothes. Maybe even two."

Temptation nearly knocked Courtney's legs out from under her, but suspicion kept her standing. What was he up to? Why was he suddenly changing himself and offering her the chance to do the same? He'd barely looked at her since she'd left him standing on the boardwalk after their kiss. Now he was acting as if nothing had ever happened.

On the other hand, he was offering a bath. Did his motives even matter?

"A *real* bath? With hot water and everything?"

"As hot as you can stand." He dangled his money pouch in front of her. "And soap."

She shifted her weight onto one leg and folded her arms. "Why are you doing this?"

"I told you. I've had a reawakening." He sauntered closer and gathered her into his arms before she knew what he was up to. He kissed her as if they stood this way every day and then smiled and brought the sun into the cabin with him. "This is better, then?"

"Better than what?"

"I wasn't exactly the kind of man you'd be proud to be seen with before."

Courtney gaped at him. "Is *that* why you did this?"

"Partly. And partly because you make we want to be the best I can be instead of the worst."

Courtney felt another wall slip away from her heart, but she didn't have the strength to keep it there any longer. In all the men she'd watched wander into Leslie's life and out again, she'd never seen one who'd improved with time.

He dipped his head and kissed her again, and without consciously willing it, another phrase added itself to Philo's description of love. Love, she thought with a tiny frisson of pleasure, was a man who'd spend the last of his gold to buy a lady a bath.

Pride had always kept her from accepting help before, but a different kind of pride was at work now. The kind that wouldn't let her look like some urchin and smell like she'd been born in a stable while Heath walked around town looking as if he'd stepped off the pages of a nineteenth-century fashion magazine.

She told herself not to stand around nuzzling with him. It wouldn't be fair to either of them when she didn't know how she felt or how long she could stay. But the feel of his hands on her arms, his clean spicy scent, and the look in his eyes all combined to keep her right where she was. "I'd feel better if we could consider it a loan instead of a gift."

He smiled gently. "You know that's not necessary. If we have to call it anything, it should be compensation for the work you've been doing around here."

Courtney glanced at the fritters on the table and laughed. "You know what? I don't think I'm even going to argue that point with you. So are you going to tell me about this grand awakening of yours?"

He pretended shock. "My dear, a gentleman never discusses such indelicate matters with a lady."

"But *I'm* not a lady," Courtney reminded him. "Not the bona fide, parlor-bred, fan-fluttering kind."

Heath chuckled and led her toward the door. "I'll let you in on a little secret," he whispered so close to her ear it sent shivers along her spine. "Those kinds of ladies aren't nearly as interesting as you are."

Another thrill raced up her spine, and Courtney didn't even try to fight it.

He reached for his hat and settled it at an angle, and she found herself grinning broadly. Yes, indeed, she thought as she took his arm, he *did* clean up nicely . . . and knowing that he'd done it at least partly for her was probably the nicest compliment she'd ever been given.

Heath dodged Geezer and a hard-hitting round of second thoughts as he paced impatiently outside the barbershop and bathhouse where Courtney was freshening up. He didn't like the idea of her being inside alone. He didn't like it at all. There were too many unsavory characters in this town. Men who'd take advantage of a lady in her situation.

He should have used the money to buy a tub. He'd had enough at one point during the day. Not any longer, though. He was wearing half of it on his back and the other half was inside the bathhouse with Courtney.

He just hoped she'd hurry so he could stop worrying. Caring about somebody else still made him feel like he'd put on a too-small pair of boots or last year's trousers. It didn't feel right. He wondered if it ever would.

He mopped his face with one hand and sat on the edge of the boardwalk. Geezer thumped his tail and thrust his shaggy head under Heath's hand. Heath started to pull away, but the look in those expressive brown eyes stopped him short. He gave the dog a scratch between the ears and then rested his hand on the mutt's matted shoulder. "You could use a bath, too, you know."

As he always did when Heath spoke, Geezer set his tail in motion, and the eager look on his little face touched yet another newly resurrected piece of Heath's heart. He bit back a smile and looked out over the street. Slanted another glance at the dog and lowered his voice in case anyone was paying enough attention to hear the affection he couldn't seem to hide. "You're nothin' but a damn nuisance," he said softly. "That's what old Verlis should have called you."

That gigantic tongue lolled out of the dog's mouth, and he gave Heath's elbow a nudge with his head.

"So what do you think, fella? You think I'm doing the right thing?"

Geezer let out a high-pitched whine and head-butted Heath's shoulder—almost as if he understood what Heath was saying.

Heath pushed back the brim of his hat and studied the dog's earnest expression. "I'll grant that she's beautiful. No argument there. And smart. And spirited. And kind. But there's something odd about her. *You* can't argue with *that*."

And Geezer didn't.

"She can't be what she says she is, but she doesn't seem to be anything else."

The dog let out a belly-deep groan and licked its chops lazily.

Heath sighed and plucked a weed from the ground beside him. "It's those eyes, you know. The way she looks at you with those . . . *eyes*. You've seen 'em. All dark and wide and deep and mysterious. Like she knows something about you she's not telling. Like she thinks you're more than you really are. That's hard to live up to."

Geezer panted in agreement, and Heath rubbed the dog's head absently. "One minute I think she'd be fine if I left here, and the next minute I know she wouldn't be. One minute she's weak and vulnerable, and then I blink and *she's* the one with all the strength. Who is she, Geezer? Where did she come from? Sometimes I think I can't rest until I find out, and sometimes I just don't want to know."

Geezer didn't look even slightly concerned. As long as Courtney fed him, scratched him, and let him sleep at the foot of her bed, he didn't care where she came from. Maybe Heath ought to take a page out of the dog's book. What did her past matter?

Heath patted his pocket and found a cigar. He lit it and leaned back against a post to smoke in peace. "I don't think anything has ever had me more confused," he admitted after a few minutes.

Geezer flopped onto his side, thoroughly bored by Heath's confusion.

Heath laughed softly and scratched the dog's belly. "Fine. Make yourself comfortable, then. God only knows how long we'll be waiting."

They sat that way for several minutes, Heath smoking peacefully and Geezer dozing, until Geezer's eyes opened and a low, menacing growl sounded deep in his throat. He didn't move, but his eyes grew cold, watchful, and wary.

Heath was instantly alert. He'd spent too much time around animals not to take Geezer's sudden shift seriously. Trying to keep his movements unhurried and unconcerned, he dropped his cigar and ground it out with the heel of his boot. He eased his gaze along the street, swept it past the buildings across the way, and tilted back to check the rooftops. But the sun had gone down long ago, and it was hard to see much of anything.

Even so, Heath knew that someone was watching him. The awareness of it pricked at the skin on his shoulders and made his blood slow to a crawl. Voices and laughter faded into the distance as he tuned into the small sounds around him. The groan of wood beneath someone's weight. The brush of an indrawn breath. The hiss of a horse relieving itself into the dirt. No sound was too small to escape his notice.

Geezer lifted his head and growled again, then curled his legs beneath him as he got ready to stand. His hackles rose protectively, and Heath realized he was growing rather fond of the old dog.

He stood beside Geezer, so alert he could almost feel the hair on the back of his neck growing. The clang of metal on metal from somewhere nearby made him swing around to his left; the creak of a door opening brought him back around to his right.

He located the threat at the same time Geezer did and pivoted toward it just in time to see Tyree Caine step through the door of the barbershop with two of his paid goons behind him.

Chapter 12

HEATH WATCHED TYREE and his men move toward him and realized for the first time that he and Tyree were of the same height, but Tyree probably had a good thirty pounds on him—and those thirty pounds looked like solid muscle.

For the second time in just a few hours, Heath realized what a hash he'd made of his life. Until five years ago he'd been in excellent shape, not only from the work he'd done on Bonne Chance, but from the fights he and Blue had staged between themselves where no one but a few trusted slaves could see. He'd had size, shape, and cunning on his side. Now . . .

Well, he'd have to rely on his wit. He had nothing else.

Tyree swaggered toward him, a feral smile curving his thin lips. "Well, well, well. Look what we have here, boys. A regular dandy. And doesn't he look purty?" He reached for Heath's collar, but Heath dodged him easily. Snorting a laugh, Tyree looked at the two imbeciles behind him. "Did you see that? Can't even pay a compliment anymore without somebody getting all uppity about it. Seems our Mr. Sullivan thinks he's too good for us now, boys. What do you think about that?"

An ugly cuss with matted hair, round eyes, and a broad brow took a while to consider that question. "I think maybe he needs to be taught a lesson."

Heath held back the sneer of disgust he could feel threatening and shifted slowly to his right—slowly enough to make Tyree turn with him. He'd left his back exposed the first time he'd met Tyree and his boys. He wouldn't make that mistake again.

"Hell, yeah," Tyree's other buddy said with a cold laugh. "I don't take kindly to folks who think they're better than me. You know what? None of us do."

Heath took another almost imperceptible step, maneuvering himself patiently into position and resisting the urge to toss taunts back at them. The only thing he cared about was making sure Courtney didn't get caught up in something ugly when she came outside.

"You think you're too good for us, Sullivan?" Tyree pulled his whip from the back of his trousers and smacked his palm with the handle just the way Heath had seen countless overseers do when they had a point to make. "I got news for you, fancy man. You ain't no match for Tyree Caine."

Tyree's taunts were so familiar, his threats so predictable, Heath knew there was a real danger of underestimating him, and that could be the quickest way to disaster. He noticed folks steering around the circle they made, obviously anxious to avoid the confrontation. But a small crowd of less squeamish townsfolk had begun to gather across the street.

Obviously aware that he had an audience, Tyree leaned in closer and lowered his voice. "You think I've forgotten how you took that little filly off my hands at the Parasol? You've always been eager to stick your nose where it don't belong, haven't you?"

When Heath didn't answer, Tyree pressed harder. "You think I'm going to let you get away with it?" He leaned in close. "I had a hankerin' for that piece of woman you took from me the other night. A real hankerin'. If you hadn't stepped in, I'd a' had my fill of her by now." He glanced at the windows of the barbershop and his eyes darkened dangerously. "So I been thinkin' that since you don't have a problem taking what ain't yours, maybe *I* should help myself to what *you* got a hankerin' for."

It was bad enough hearing him talk about Delilah that way, but Heath's blood turned to fire at the thought of Tyree Caine anywhere near Courtney. If he'd thought it would protect either woman, he'd have killed Tyree where he stood, but he could protect them a whole lot better if he didn't get himself shot by Tyree's idiot henchmen.

"I seen the way you look at her," Tyree went on. "Don't think I don't. I can see everything goes on in that cabin of yours." He uncoiled the whip with deliberate slowness and began to coil it again the same way. "Gotta admit, you've got taste."

Geezer let out another low growl, but Heath motioned for him to stay. Tyree obviously wanted to provoke a reaction, but Heath wasn't going to give him one. Affecting boredom, he pulled another cigar from his pocket and leaned one shoulder against the wall. He matched Tyree's deliberation as he bit off the end of his cigar, struck a Lucifer, and touched the flame to the tip.

He took his time getting a good draw and then very carefully blew smoke into the air above his head. "Is that all?"

The smirk on Tyree's face slipped, and anger flared in his eyes. "What's the matter, big man? Can't you even defend your woman?"

"From you?" Heath ran his gaze the length of Tyree and looked away again. "Don't make me laugh, Caine. You won't do anything to me. You won't fight anyone who's not smaller and weaker than you are. Everyone knows that."

"Is that right?" Color flooded Tyree's cheeks and his eyes grew even more opaque. "You *tryin'* to piss me off, or are you just too stupid to know better?"

Heath blew a circle of smoke and regarded the burning end of his cigar for a moment. "You know what, Caine? You're not worth the time it would take to crush you."

Tyree lunged but Heath was ready. He tossed aside the cigar and brought his right fist straight up into Tyree's face in one move. Tyree had been moving fast, and his own speed did half of Heath's work for him. Heath followed with a sharp left to the middle, and Tyree's legs buckled an instant before he sagged to his knees on the boardwalk.

Geezer was on his feet before Tyree left his, and his bared teeth and ominous growl kept Tyree's buddies from making a mistake. Luck had been on Heath's side again, but nobody's luck lasted forever. This was three times in a row, and one of these days his luck would turn. It was only a matter of time.

Tyree and his boys were gone by the time Courtney stepped out of the barbershop a few minutes later. Heath took one look at her and decided not to mention the run-in just yet. Her face was alight with joy, and he didn't want to ruin the moment for her.

Her short dark hair curled softly around her face, and the new dungarees and soft cotton shirt they'd picked up at the Mercantile fit her far better than the miners' cast-offs had. They fit a little *too* well, perhaps. The shirt fell in soft folds that accentuated her curves, and the trousers showed off to perfection what the blouse didn't hide.

He swallowed thickly and stood, putting Tyree Caine out of his mind, at least for the time being. He'd have to warn Courtney . . . but there would be time for that later. In the time he'd known her, he'd never seen her smile so easily, and he found himself wanting to keep that smile on her face all the time.

Geezer padded over to her with the absolute certainty of affection that only dogs and small children possess, and Heath battled a brief flash of envy, regretting that he couldn't change places with the mutt, just for a minute.

Thinking that he'd contributed to the look of pure pleasure on her face could easily have made Heath feel a whole lot more important than he really was, and he wondered if this feeling, this momentary delusion that he could conquer anything, was the real reason more men didn't resist falling in love.

Friends, he reminded himself. They'd agreed to be friends. Neither of them was ready to make it more. He stood grinning, turning his hat in his hands, while he tried to get words into his mouth.

Courtney's gaze drifted to his hands, and she watched the hat go round for a minute before a soft smile curved her lips. "What are you doing?"

"I was taught to stand in the presence of a lady." He gestured toward her trousers with his hat and cleared his throat uneasily. "Are you sure these clothes are a wise choice? Don't misunderstand—*I* think you look great, but that could be a problem down the road."

Courtney's smile widened and a sparkle lit the dark pools of her eyes. "Mr. Sullivan, are you jealous?"

He started to shrug, intending to give the impression that it didn't matter, then stopped himself. Following his instincts hadn't gotten him anywhere. Lying to himself hadn't accomplished a thing. He could keep evading the truth and spend the next five years miserable and alone. And the next. And probably the next, as well. Or he could face the truth and admit that he cared a whole lot more than he ever thought he could.

He gave in to that shrug, but it was more sheepish than nonchalant, more uncertain than uncaring. "I wouldn't use the word *jealous*," he said with a slow smile. "Let's just say that I don't relish the idea of having to beat that bunch of louts away from the cabin all day long."

She laughed softly. "You mean Philo and Moonshine?"

"And the rest."

"And that thought bothers you? Why?"

The moment was getting a little serious for both of them, so Heath tried to lighten it. "Because if I hurt my hands, I'm going to have one helluva time shoveling horse manure."

Courtney laughed, and Heath's heart soared. The relief in her eyes was palpable. "For a minute, I thought you were going to get all mushy on me."

"Me?" Heath took her by the arm and led her along the boardwalk. "I care about you, Courtney. You may never understand how hard that is for me to say, but I do." He looked down at her. "And I wouldn't say that if I didn't mean it."

"Thank you."

He waited for her to say something back. To tell him that she cared, to admit to having feelings beyond friendship for him, but she remained silent for so long his hands began to itch. Finally she smiled up at him. "Do we have to go back to the cabin right away? Or can we walk for a while?"

"After dark? This isn't a good time for a lady to be out and about. Besides, won't you be chilly?"

"I don't think so." She lifted her face and took a deep breath, and Heath found it impossible to deny her anything. So they walked in silence for a while, and Heath argued with himself every step of the way about when to mention his encounter with Tyree. Letting her enjoy the moment was one thing, but Tyree had threatened her. He couldn't let her wander around not knowing that.

He was all set to tell her as they rounded a corner onto a side street, but one look at her face told him that she'd been worrying right along with him. But about what? "You're quiet," he said. "Is something wrong?"

"Not really. Sort of. I guess." She smiled apologetically. "It's just that I've been here almost three weeks, and I'm no closer to understanding *why* I'm here than I was the first night."

"So you still believe that you came from the future?"

"I don't *believe* it, Heath. It's true." She slipped her hand beneath his arm and sighed softly. "I just wish I could think of some way to prove it to you so you'd stop thinking I'm insane."

Her stride matched his so that their pace was a comfortable one, and without the huge bell skirt to keep them apart, she fit neatly against his side as if all their parts had been built to connect. "And how would you prove it if you could?"

"I'd tell you something that was going to happen in the future. Like tomorrow. I'd tell you about the modern-day city if I thought that would help." She gazed out at the street and shuddered slightly. "It's nothing at all like this, and yet it's strangely similar. Some of these old buildings are actually still standing, but there are a whole bunch of different ones, too. And the population is only sixty instead of ten thousand."

"Sixty?"

"Sixty year-round. During the summer months, people come from all over to try and relive this experience, if you can believe it." She wagged her hand to encompass the scene in front of them. "They think all this dirt and stench and mud is romantic."

Heath laughed. "Are you serious?"

"Completely. Of course the experience they get is *nothing* like this. Not really. I was completely unprepared for the reality. I *do* know that within a year from now they'll discover gold up north and people will start leaving here to go there. Virginia City will be the Territorial Capital for a while, but before long everything will shift to a city that will be named Helena. But those things won't happen for a long time, and I want to prove that I'm not crazy now."

She'd thought through the details of her story thoroughly. Heath wondered how it was possible to have such a fertile imagination. "And what of the war?" he asked, deciding it wouldn't hurt to indulge her briefly. "What happens with it?"

She brightened visibly, and Heath wondered if he'd been smart to pretend, even for a moment. "It will be over by next year and the slaves are freed."

"Some of them have already been freed," he reminded her.

"Some. Not all. Not yet. The South surrenders, by the way. I hope you're not too upset by that."

"Not in the slightest. But my father will be distraught."

"A lot of people are," she said with a slight smile. "It takes a long time for the country to be stitched back together again, and tempers simmer for a long time. Old hatreds die hard."

"Hatred always does."

She nodded and watched a wagon rattle past. "The world I come from isn't perfect, by any means. There's still too much poverty and bigotry. People still discriminate against each other for stupid reasons like the color of their skin or the religion they choose to believe in. But at least it's illegal to do it, so things are slowly getting better. I wish it could happen faster."

Heath would like to believe that, if he couldn't believe anything else she told him. He liked the light in her eyes when she spoke of her future, and he couldn't resist asking, "What else?"

"There's bad news. President Lincoln is assassinated after the war ends. Shot by an actor named John Wilkes Booth." She sighed softly and clutched his hand. "I wonder what the world would turn out like if that *didn't* happen."

"Are you suggesting that you should stop it?"

"I don't know. There are so many things that could be prevented if I could just warn people. Maybe I could change the world into a better place if I did."

"And maybe not." He took her hand and held it. "Blue's grandmother used to say that everything happens for a reason. She would probably tell you that Mr. Lincoln has to be assassinated so that people will learn something."

"Is that what you believe?"

"I don't think so. It's too cruel." He stared at their joined fingers while he tried to puzzle out what he did think. "I can't believe that God makes horrible things happen just to bring about good."

Courtney's expression grew thoughtful. "*My* grandmother believed that God lets bad things happen because he can't interfere with our right to make choices. Maybe the truth is somewhere in the middle. Maybe people do make choices that cause bad things to happen, and then everyone else gets the choice of letting it turn the world ugly, or of doing something good to make sure it didn't happen in vain."

"I could live with that." Heath led her past the door to a saloon and then onto the next block. "So what good will you make from your misfortune?"

She tilted her head thoughtfully. "Friendships, I think. I got to meet you and Philo and Moonshine. And Geezer, of course. And I think you're all helping me to change some of the attitudes I've had that needed changing. What about you?"

Heath laughed abruptly. "I'm just trying to decide whether I should be offended at being lumped into a category with the dog."

"Geezer's not just any dog."

"No." Heath looked over his shoulder and grinned. "No, he's not."

"So? What good *will* you make from your misfortune?"

He gave that some thought. To answer truthfully meant brushing up against things he'd never talked about. But he couldn't make himself lie, or even hedge. "Redemption," he said after a long moment.

"Redemption?"

Heath felt a momentary urge to shut down, but the need to finally talk about it with someone he could trust was a whole lot stronger. "I grew up on a plantation called Bonne Chance," he said. "It means 'good luck' in French, and until my twenty-fifth year, I thought it was a prophetic name. Everything seemed to go my way. Everything my father touched turned to gold. Everything my mother wanted was hers. Even the rumblings of war didn't seem to affect us the way they did our friends and neighbors."

"I can't even imagine."

"Don't try. It's not everything you might think. My father's family was always wealthy, but my father accumulated even more wealth and power than he inherited. It didn't take him long to become one of the richest and most powerful men in South Carolina. And I . . ." He broke off and shook his head. "I wanted to *be* him. The only thing I ever wanted as a boy was to follow in his footsteps."

Courtney didn't speak, but she tightened her grip on his hand and smiled encouragement.

"My sisters were treated like princesses," he said, forcing himself to keep going. "I was the prince. The son and heir. The golden child. I never wanted. Anything I could have desired was provided for me before I even had a chance to want it. I grew up thinking that normal and natural. I was Sebastian Sullivan's heir, after all. I deserved it. That's what my father told me. That's what my mother let me believe.

"And then I met Blue. Sukey was my mother's favorite and Blue was her grandson. He was a child, like me, but instead of sitting inside the house and being showered with gifts, instead of learning from books and being taught how to live, he was outside running. *Running*. I watched him and

marveled at the power in his legs, at the freedom he had."
He laughed bitterly. "It seems so *wrong* to say that now, but
that's how I felt at the time."

Tears burned his eyes as the image of young Blue raced
away in front of him. "He ran like the wind, and I was fascinated by him. I wanted to spend time with him, and because
I was the little prince, I was allowed to. My father made
quite a show of 'giving' Blue to me, but he never had any
idea that I might start to see Blue as a person. Slaves were
property to my father. Nothing more. And because I had
always wanted to be like him, he never imagined that I might
feel differently about something that he considered so basic."

"So it was Blue who changed your mind about slavery?"

"I guess so. And maybe just growing up and learning to
think for myself. I don't know what might have happened or
what I might have become if not for Blue and Sukey and
Birdie and Delilah. And an old man named Tango. Maybe
I'd have freed them all. Maybe I'd have been just like my
father. But I abhor slavery now, and that's one of the reasons
I'm here. There are some people here in Montana Territory
who have strong feelings about the war and the issues that
led to it, but most of us are just happy to put all that behind
us."

"So Blue is the third person you mentioned the other day?
You, Delilah, and Blue?"

Heath's pleasure that she'd paid attention and remembered
made it easier to keep going. "We were friends, yes. *Brothers*
is probably a better word. We were inseparable. We spent
every waking moment together, and my parents, who still
didn't realize that anything was wrong, indulged my every
idea. Blue had been heading for a life in the fields—something I didn't fully understand. But because I was fond of
him, because I wanted a playmate, he was spared that. In
time, we found Delilah—or she found us—and Blue fell head
over heels in love with her."

She ran her hand along the inside of his arm. "You're here
and you mentioned seeing Delilah. Where is Blue?"

Heath looked away up the street toward where his imag-
inary Blue had run. He expected to have trouble forming the

word, but it fell from his lips with an ease that shook him. "Dead."

"Dead?" Courtney stopped walking and gripped his arm. "Oh, Heath, I'm so sorry. What happened?"

She hadn't even known Blue, but there was more pain shimmering in her eyes than he'd seen on any of his own family's faces—people who'd known Blue for his entire life. "He was hanged."

"But that's horrible! How did it happen? Who did it?"

This was it, Heath realized. The moment he'd been running from for the past five years. Everything inside him screamed to pull away from Courtney before he answered, to put some distance between them so he wouldn't taint her with his own ugliness. Everything but one tiny piece of his heart that needed to feel something beautiful and alive, something soft and forgiving.

"Blue was in love with Delilah," he said again. "From the time we were fourteen until our twenty-third year. He asked permission to jump the broom with her, but my father wouldn't grant it. And nothing happened on Bonne Chance that my father didn't approve. Blue kept hoping. I even interceded for them, but my father wouldn't hear of it.

"And then one day we learned that my father had sold Delilah, and within an hour she was gone. Just like that. No warning. No regard for Blue's feelings, or hers. No regard for her mother, who had been on Bonne Chance her entire life. Delilah was property, and she was gone."

"What did you do?"

"Nothing. To my eternal regret, I did nothing. Oh, I spoke with my father, but he didn't want to hear what I had to say, and I accepted his verdict. I accepted his refusal to hear me. I accepted his brutality. And I did nothing. Losing her devastated Blue, but I'd never been in love before—not like he was. I didn't understand how deeply it affected him until the night we discovered that he'd run away. He never said anything to me, but I knew he'd run to find Delilah, and I knew that if he was caught, he'd be killed. So when my father put me in charge of the men who were going to track him, I went."

Her face betrayed nothing of what she was thinking, but he wished it would. Was she sickened by him? Disgusted? He might like to stop now, but he couldn't. Not with the story half told.

"We tracked him for three days before we found him. And when we did . . ." The words caught in his throat, and his heart felt as if it might explode. "When we did, I'm the one who talked him into coming back. I thought I was saving him. I thought that my father would reprimand him and everything would be fine. That's what was supposed to happen, but my father had other ideas."

The tears were spent now, and white-hot anger replaced them. "When we returned to Bonne Chance, my father ordered me to finish the job. He ordered *me* to put a noose around Blue's neck. To string up the man who was closer to me than a brother, who cared more about me, who knew me better than my own flesh and blood.

He paused, remembering. Wishing he could turn back time. Wondering if the pain would ever go away, if the hatred he bore his father would ever lessen.

"I refused," he said when he could speak again. "I thought I could save Blue. But my father simply had someone else do it."

Courtney's face was a mask of horror, her skin pale, her eyes dark and luminous. "Oh, Heath. My God."

"I brought him back. That's the part I can't live with. If I hadn't hunted him down and talked him into coming back with me, he'd be alive still."

"You don't know that," Courtney said gently. "If you hadn't found him, someone else would have. Someone else killed him when you wouldn't."

"But I *did* find him. I found him because I knew where to look. I *knew* how he thought. I *knew*, and I was able to corner him. When I had him treed like some animal, I asked him to trust me. And when he did, I took him back to his death."

"But you can't blame yourself for that. You didn't know what your father would do. You thought it would be all right."

"Don't you think I've tried to make myself believe that?

The point is that I *should* have known. If I'd paid the slightest attention to the kind of man my father was becoming, I *would* have known. He was corrupted by money and power, and I was corrupted by the life his money bought for me. And because of that, hundreds of people suffered. Some died. Blue wasn't the first to die on Bonne Chance, and I'm sure he wasn't the last. I couldn't save Delilah. I couldn't save Blue. And I didn't even bother trying to save the others."

"And you believe that it was your responsibility to save them all?"

"Yes, if I had the chance."

"And it's your failure if you couldn't?"

"Yes."

"There's no credit here for trying? No points earned for what you *did* do?" She gripped his hand in both of hers. "You're too hard on yourself. Heath. You ask too much of yourself. No one could live up to that by himself."

"The point is, Courtney, that I didn't try hard enough."

"Really? Then tell me, Heath, what more you could have done. Tell me what you didn't say that would have changed your father's mind. Tell me."

Heath stopped walking and leaned against an empty hitching post. "I could have said something."

"What?" She propped her fists on her hips and waited. "Tell me exactly what you could have said that would have guaranteed a different result." When he didn't immediately answer, she nodded as if his silence had answered for him. "You can't change your father, Heath. You can't change anyone but yourself. And you did that. You left Bonne Chance. You refused to participate in that way of life any longer. You refused to contribute to the wrong. Doesn't that count for something?"

"Not enough to make up for a man's life."

"There's nothing more you could have done," she said again. "And you're being unfair to yourself if you accept responsibility for your father's cruelty."

Heath tried to absorb what she said. He had the feeling that believing as she did would make him feel a whole lot better. But he couldn't. "I understand what you're saying," he told her, "but it's just not that simple." He pushed away from the hitching post and held out his arm. "I only wish it were."

Chapter 13

COURTNEY HAD BEEN sitting on the bed for an hour, but the page in front of her was still blank. Heath had gone into town with Philo and Moonshine, which had left her with a rare quiet moment to gather her thoughts. But a fat lot of good it had done her.

She'd left the door open to let in as much of the afternoon sunlight as possible, and the sweet scent of the apples Moonshine had bought at the Mercantile a few days earlier filled the cabin. She leaned against the wall and sighed contentedly. If anyone had told her when she'd first arrived that she'd feel even one minute of contentment here, she'd have laughed in his face. But the cabin was becoming more comfortable all the time, and since she'd had a bath and Heath had finally opened up about his past, life had grown downright pleasant.

She should be ecstatic now that she had paper and pencil, but she couldn't seem to find anything to sketch. It had only been a few weeks since she'd worked, but it might as well have been years. So much had happened, so much had changed, she wasn't sure how she felt about life or even who she was anymore.

She'd always sketched with a cynical tone, and her edgy

illustrations were what her Denver editor liked and what had caught the attention of the New York publisher she was supposed to meet with. Now, she couldn't seem to draw anything of substance. If she'd been working at home with her room full of supplies, she could have found her way by trial and error. But paper was too precious to waste. She wanted to work out the picture in her head before she committed anything to paper.

So she thought, and she stared at the blank sheet of paper, and she flicked a fingernail against her teeth. She studied her toes and wondered if her feet would ever feel soft again, sat aside the makeshift desk Moonshine had cut for her from some old lumber, and paced the tiny room from one end to the other. When an errant daub of mud on a section of log caught her eye, she stopped everything to scrape it off, then decided that now would be a fine time to get the dirt she'd noticed two days earlier from the corners of the room.

When the images still wouldn't come, she went back to the bed and lay on her back, staring at the ceiling and trying to remain open to a new voice for her work. She hummed one of her favorite Toby Keith songs for a while and tried not to obsess over the fact that she had only two weeks left until her interview in New York. She could feel the job slipping between her fingers, but whenever she tried to panic over it, she couldn't.

Not that she wanted to panic. But three weeks ago she *would* have panicked, like it or not. Now she couldn't even work up a healthy amount of worry. She was changing right in front of her eyes, and that frightened her.

She *could* panic about that.

She was letting herself get too attached. To Heath. To Philo. To Moonshine and Geezer . . . This was the very thing she'd warned herself about over and over and over again. But no matter how logical staying detached might be, putting it into practice wasn't so easy.

Heath wasn't nearly so gruff in the mornings, and he spent a lot more time hanging around the cabin. In three days they'd chatted a whole lot about mundane, everyday things like how much wood Heath needed to chop and how many biscuits Courtney ought to make, but neither of them had brought up that conversation again.

Courtney loved the new easiness between them and she was trying hard to trust it, but trust didn't come easily to her. Especially since she believed more strongly than ever that she'd finally found the key to getting home. She just didn't know how to use it yet.

But one of these days she *would* go home again. She'd open a door and there would be the future, wake up and find herself in her own bed, turn around and find herself talking to Ryan. It had to happen. And what did she think would happen to her heart when it did?

She was setting herself up for heartbreak. She knew it, but she couldn't seem to stop it. She'd get back to her own time and she'd have to face the fact that Heath and the others had been dead for more than a hundred years. Just how did she think she was going to handle that?

And why was she thinking about this, anyway? Wasn't she supposed to be drawing? If she *did* make it home in time for her interview, she'd have a hard time getting the rusty wheels of her creative process working after such a long break.

But again, it was easier to say than to do.

She was still bouncing from one subject to the next when she heard voices outside and realized that more than an hour had passed. Jumping at the excuse to set aside her work again, she rushed to the window and saw Heath, Philo, and Moonshine struggling together to carry a huge wooden half-barrel toward the cabin, with Geezer trotting happily to one side.

The men called directions to each other. A little to the left, which, of course, resulted in one of them veering to the right and nearly bringing them all to their knees. After a bit of growling and a whole lot of snipping, they started walking again.

Courtney bit her bottom lip and grinned. A tub? He'd brought her a tub? It wouldn't be large enough for a soak, but what luxury to have a bath whenever she wanted one. A hundred red roses, champagne, and a cabin filled with candlelight couldn't have been more romantic.

She danced with excitement as they turned into the yard and even giggled—*giggled!*—as they tried to put it down in unison. Courtney never giggled, but she felt like giggling today.

She ran to the door and threw it open just as Heath straightened and turned toward her. And then, because the laughter had worked its way into her heart and because the anticipation on his face was just too much to resist, she flew down the stairs and threw herself into his arms.

He laughed, and oh! how she was starting to love that sound, and wrapped his arms around her. "What's this for?"

"The tub. You couldn't have found anything I'd like better."

Heath pulled her close and kissed her briefly. Too briefly for Courtney, but anything more would have been out of place with the other two as an audience. When he pulled away, his eyes were dancing with merriment. "I like the show of thanks, but what makes you think the tub is for you?"

"Who else would it be for?"

Heath scratched his chin and glanced behind him. "I don't want to say anything aloud. Wouldn't be polite. Might hurt his feelings. But you *did* mention something about poor old Geezer back there."

Courtney folded her arms and tried to look serious. "You brought the dog a tub."

"Exactly."

"I see." She tilted her head and looked beyond him to where Geezer was nipping at something crawling beneath his fur. "And who's going to give the poor thing his bath?"

"You are."

"Oh, no." She nudged his shoulder playfully and turned back toward the cabin. "This is your idea, buddy. You get to do the honors—*and* clean the tub out afterward so I can use it."

Heath chuckled and caught her hand as she stepped away. "You really think I'm going to put that old flea-bitten hound inside that brand-new tub?"

"Yes, I do. The poor old thing probably hasn't had a bath as long as he's been alive. I'm curious to see if he cleans up as nicely as you did."

Heath pulled her close again and scowled down at her. "I'll find a way to clean the dog, but it won't be in *that* tub."

It was so easy to trust when he was here and looking at her like that. She snuggled close and slipped her arms around his waist. "Fair enough." And then, because Philo was watching a little too closely and she could see his mind racing with ideas, she made herself let go of Heath and put some distance between them. But the look in Philo's eyes, the smile on Heath's face, and the pride in Moonshine's expression all combined to touch her heart, and she knew that she'd never forget this moment as long as she lived—no matter where she was.

Later, when Heath and Moonshine were struggling to put Geezer into the small tub of water they'd hauled from the river, Courtney and Philo sat together inside the cabin. Spending time with the old man was becoming more than a habit, and she'd miss him when this was over.

But she didn't want to think about that tonight. She wanted to enjoy the time she had with them—no matter how short it might be. Since Heath was bathing Geezer, she'd agreed to sew a button on his shirt and stitch up a hole he'd gotten working at the livery stable. They'd spent a few precious cents buying a needle and thread at the Mercantile, and now she was embarking on yet another domestic adventure. One she had absolutely no training for unless you counted a long-forgotten seventh-grade home economics course.

Philo watched her struggle to thread the needle for a few minutes, then shook his head and held out his hand. "You want me to show you?"

"You sew, too?"

"Of course I do. I've been on my own most of my life, missy. Who do you *think* sews on my buttons?"

"Sorry. Silly question." She handed over the needle and thread and watched as he trimmed the edge of the thread with his knife and wet it with his tongue. "You've had quite a life, haven't you?"

"S'pose so. But, then, so have you."

Courtney smoothed her hands across Heath's shirt and smiled at the sounds of man versus dog coming from outside. "So what's next, Philo? Have you decided what to do about the Jezebel yet?"

"Not yet."

"Have you heard anything more from Tyree Caine?"

He scowled up at her. "No, and I don't want you worrying about him. He's my problem and I'll figure it out."

"If Tyree Caine is killing people, that makes him everyone's problem."

"We don't know that Tyree killed Verlis," Philo said firmly. "That's just Moonshine jumping to conclusions."

"If you really believe that, why did you abandon the Jezebel and move into town?"

"I didn't abandon her, first off. Second, I'm an old man. Too old to be messin' with trouble. And in the last place, if I'd a' known you were going to start getting worked up about it, I never would a' mentioned it."

"Why? Because it's none of my business, or because I'm a woman?"

"There are some things women just don't need to worry about. Scum like Tyree Caine are one of 'em."

Courtney readjusted the shirt on her lap and crossed her legs. Heath's raised voice drifted in from outside, followed by Moonshine's laugh, a happy bark from Geezer, and a loud splash. "As far as I'm concerned, we're all in this together."

"I'll go along with that," Philo said with a glance toward the door. He handed her back the needle and thread and picked up his knife again. "But that still don't mean you need to worry your pur—"

"If you tell me not to worry my pretty little head," she warned, "I'll jab you with this needle." At his look of round-eyed shock, she tempered the threat with a grin. "Honestly, where do you men come up with that stuff? Do you really think my head is filled with fluff? That I'm not strong enough to handle the truth? That I'm going to faint dead away if something frightens me?"

Philo shook his head and used his knife to pick something from between two back teeth. "You have more spirit than that. You're a strong woman, Courtney. No doubt about it. But that still don't mean I'm gonna talk to you about Tyree Caine and his boys."

"And what if something happens to you?"

"Well, then, I guess it happens."

"What if you're hurt?"

"I'll heal."

"What if you're killed?"

"Then I'll learn to play the harp."

In frustration, Courtney jabbed the needle through three layers of fabric, the holes in the button, and straight into her finger. She swore softly, dropped the needle, and popped her finger into her mouth. "Have you always been this stubborn?"

"To hear my mama tell it."

"Well, it's irritating."

"So she used to say." He studied the fresh piece of wood he'd brought to whittle with as much care as if he actually intended to create something. After a minute he set it aside and leaned forward with his arms on his thighs. "I'm not going to worry you, missy. It makes this old heart glad to see you smile."

"I won't be smiling if you get hurt—especially if it happens because you refuse to take Tyree Caine seriously."

"And what would you have me do? Go up against him? Whack him on the head with this here stick?"

"Report him to the law. Maybe they could do something."

Philo laughed and shook his head in fond exasperation. "The law won't do nothing about Tyree Caine. Hell, we barely *have* any law around here."

"Then at least talk to Heath. If the two of you got together with Moonshine and some of the others, you could defeat Tyree's gang. I know you could."

Philo straightened again and raked his fingers through his hair. "I'm old," he said again. "I'm tired. I don't want to fight. I want to reminisce and wonder about what might have been."

Courtney flushed guiltily. "You're right. I'm sorry."

"No need to apologize, missy. I know your heart's in the right place." He dropped his hands to his lap and ran his gaze across her face. "I never had me no daughters. But if I had one, I do believe I'd want her to be just like you."

His words caught Courtney off-guard. Her heart stretched painfully, and Philo's dear old face swam in front of her eyes. Her throat tightened and burned with emotion, and she blinked rapidly, trying to clear her eyes. "I don't know what to say," she whispered so softly she could barely even hear herself.

Philo smiled gently. "Nothing *to* say, is there? Even if you wouldn't want a scruffy old thing like me around, that don't change how I feel."

Courtney stood quickly and crossed to where he sat. Before he could pull away or she could change her mind, she threw her arms around his neck and hugged him. "You have no idea how you've made me feel, do you?"

He cleared his throat roughly. "Long as you ain't mad at me, I reckon that's okay."

He seemed so uncomfortable with the display of affection, Courtney returned to her own chair. "I've wished for a father my whole life," she said when it seemed that they'd both regained some of their composure. "There were a dozen men who could have taken the responsibility—or the blame—for me. If even one of them had ever come forward and said they wished they were my dad or they wouldn't mind being my dad, I'd have been thrilled." She wrapped her hands around her cup and sipped. "Every time Leslie brought some new man home, I'd pretend as long as I could that he was my long-lost father who'd been searching for me and finally found me." She smiled sheepishly. "But then they'd always turn out to be jerks, and I'd always decide I was glad they *weren't* him."

Philo sent her a crooked grin and picked up his whittling again. "Poor dumb fools. Guess their loss is my gain, isn't it?"

"Or mine." Courtney took her cue from him and pretended to take up her mending. "I'd love to have you fill in if you want. Nobody else seems to want the job."

Philo flicked something from his sleeve with the point of his knife. "You'd have to put up with me givin' my opinion."

"Granted."

"Tellin' you when I think you're making a mistake."

She grinned down at the shirt on her lap. "Agreed. As long as you know that part of my job will be to ignore your advice."

"From a daughter of mine?" Philo chuckled and cocked an ankle across his knee. "I wouldn't have it any other way."

A full hour later Heath carried a dripping Geezer across the yard toward the cabin. His shirt and trousers were nearly as soaked as the dog. His hands smelled like something had died on them. But the dog looked like a new . . . dog.

After all the trouble he and Moonshine had gone through to get the mutt into the water, and the work they'd had to get him out again, Heath wasn't about to let Geezer do something natural and doglike, like roll in the dirt or get mud on his paws. He was going to look and smell clean—if only for one night.

Heath stumbled over a rock and nearly lost his balance. Cursed under his breath and tightened his grip on the dog. He wished that Moonshine had stayed a few minutes longer to help with this part of the job, but the kid had gone back to camp, presumably to change into something dry, and Heath had seen Philo crossing the street a few minutes later.

Which meant that he and Courtney had a rare chance to spend some time alone.

After listening to Moonshine sing the praises of the amazing and lovely Miss Geneva Openshaw, the most beautiful girl in all of Fayette County, Ohio all afternoon, Heath was ready to be through with dogs. He was, in fact, in the mood to take up where he and Courtney had left off. If memory served, she'd been thanking him for the tub they'd carted home on their backs. He wouldn't mind a little more of that brand of gratitude.

It might make up for having to carry a heavy, wet dog around in front of half the men in town and compensate for the friendly shouts of derision they were pelting him with. It might even go a long way toward making him feel better about the glaring lack of respect he expected to put up with after this.

He stumbled up the steps and nearly lost his footing for a second time, kicked the door shut, and finally unloaded the heavy, wet, dripping, squirming bundle of fur. Courtney let out a delighted cry of surprise and tossed aside the shirt she'd been mending for him.

She dropped to her knees on the floor and beamed up at him as if he'd slain a dragon for her. That smile alone might make it worth the trouble he'd been through. "Look at him," she cooed. "He's beautiful." She took Geezer's head in her hands and rubbed his cheeks energetically. "Aren't you beautiful?"

Geezer actually seemed to think so. He preened under her praise and held his head higher as he gazed around the cabin.

"He's still ugly," Heath said as he peeled off his wet shirt.

"He's not, either!" Courtney shot a look at him, but when she saw him standing there without a shirt, her expression changed from annoyed to intrigued without so much as a blink.

Heath tried not to show how much that pleased him, but he did take an extra few minutes finding a fresh shirt and getting himself into it. And even when he had his arms inside the sleeves, he didn't button it right away. "What did you and Philo talk about?"

Courtney's gaze was riveted on his stomach. His chest. His stomach. With agonizing slowness, it traveled up, up, up, and finally locked on his eyes. She took a shaky breath and tried to look unaffected. "The Jezebel. What did you and Moonshine talk about?"

"His sweetheart. Did you know he had one?"

"Moonshine?" Her gaze dipped again, then flew back to his face. "No. I didn't."

Heath's blood began to burn and he took a few steps toward her. He buttoned one sleeve as he walked, but it took a while because he couldn't make himself look away from her eyes. "Well, he does. I have it on good authority that Miss Geneva Openshaw is the most beautiful girl in all of Fayette County, Ohio."

Courtney smiled fondly. "I wonder why he's never mentioned her to me."

"Because you never washed a dog with him. A thing like that can bond two people together."

"I'll have to remember that."

Heath finally conquered one sleeve and moved on to the next. "See that you do." His mouth craved hers. His arms ached to hold her. He was hungry for her. Desperate for her. He wanted to share himself with her, and he wanted her to give herself to him. Making love to her would never be enough. He wanted to share her heart, her mind, and her soul.

Did he love her? Yes, he thought he did. He didn't even care any longer whether she was crazy or from the future, or even from the past. He loved her. And he wanted to show her just how much.

Her eyes darkened and her lips trembled, and her pulse beat in her throat like a butterfly trapped in a net. He finished buttoning his second sleeve and reached for her, cupping her cheek in his hand and urging her to come to him. Her breath caught, then released in a shudder and for the first time in his life, Heath knew what Blue had felt for Delilah. No wonder he'd run away to find her.

What if Courtney really was from the future? What if something happened to take her back again? What would Heath do? Would he defy death to find her? Luckily, that wasn't a question he had to answer, but yes. He would.

Courtney leaned into his touch and closed her eyes. She lifted her face so that if her eyes had been open, she would have been looking at him.

Heath's breathing became ragged and need tightened everything inside of him.

Her eyes fluttered open and her lips curved into a thoughtful scowl. She spoke, but not the words of love and desire he'd been hoping to hear. "I'm worried about Philo," she said. "I think you should talk to him."

Like a song interrupted by a nail on a piece of slate, Heath's thoughts ground to a halt and his mood shifted abruptly. "What?"

"Philo. I'm worried about him. He's giving up the Jezebel because of Tyree Caine, but I don't think that's what he really wants."

Heath struggled to get his thoughts moving in the same direction as hers. "What can I do about that?"

"I think he'd keep the mine if he had a partner."

Heath gaped at her. "You mean *me*?" He laughed uncertainly and tried to figure out how he'd gotten from thinking they were damn close to making love to partnering with an old prospector on a worthless gold mine. "I'm not a miner," he protested. "I wouldn't know the first thing about what to do." He held up a hand to keep her silent. "And before you say it, I don't want to know. Grubbing in the dirt for gold is *not* my cup of tea."

"I'm not suggesting that you actually mine. Just that you . . . how would you say it? That you throw your lot in with his. He's going to lose the Jezebel, Heath, and he has nothing else. Mining has been his whole life. He's given up everything for it. Tyree Caine has already taken his best friend and partner. Now he's going to take the mine, as well."

Heath pulled a corn fritter apart and ate half while he watched the firelight warm her skin. "I don't suppose it matters to you that Philo doesn't want the mine?"

"But he does, Heath. You should have seen his eyes when he was talking about it earlier."

Heath ran one hand across his face and tried to find another way to make her see reason. "Okay. For the sake of argument, let's say you're right. Philo wants the mine. I throw my lot in with his, a bunch of us form our own band of men . . . and then what?"

"Then you stop Tyree Caine and his gang from terrorizing people." Her eyes sparkled and her enthusiasm lit a fire somewhere inside her. She was achingly beautiful, but even more painfully frustrating.

"Just like that?"

"Well, no. Of course not." She fell back in her chair and

scowled. "I'm not saying it would be easy or safe. But what if this is what I'm here for, Heath? What if this is why Fate brought *you* here? I know how you feel about injustice. I saw it in your eyes when we were talking about your past."

He stared at her in stunned disbelief. "You're equating Philo's worthless gold mine with Blue's life?"

"No. But I think Verlis's life was every bit as valuable as Blue's—don't you?"

"You're forgetting one thing. We don't know that Verlis was murdered."

"No, but we do know that Tyree Caine whipped an old man, and we know that he tried to force himself on a woman. So what do we do? Wait until someone else is raped or murdered and hope that we can be absolutely positively certain that Tyree is responsible? Or do we try to stop him before it gets to that point?"

"*We*? What part do you see for yourself in this plan?"

She lifted one shoulder casually. "I don't know yet. But Philo is the first man ever who has thought of me as a daughter, and you're the first man I've ever felt this way about. And Tyree Caine is a horrible, cruel man."

"What happened to all the talk about only being able to change myself? About not being responsible for what other people do?"

She opened and shut her mouth a couple of times while she tried out different arguments in her mind. "It's different when it's someone you care about, isn't it?"

"Just a little."

She laughed uncomfortably. "I don't want anything to happen to Philo. I can't bear to think of anything happening to you. But we can't let these men terrorize people and get away with it. It's not right."

"So you're proposing that we become vigilantes?"

"No. I'm not saying we should start trouble. Just that we should stop it if Tyree Caine does."

Exasperated but out of arguments, Heath pulled her close and kissed her forehead. It was a far cry from what he'd been hoping for, but the mood was gone and he'd take what he could get. "Fine. I'll talk to Philo. If he thinks I can help, I'll try. Will that make you happy?"

She smiled slowly and kissed him thoroughly on the mouth. That and the smile on her face was all the answer he needed.

Chapter 14

"WINTER'S ON THE way," Philo groaned a week later as he came out of the small tent Heath and Moonshine had pitched on the Jezebel. "I can feel it in my bones." He'd pulled on his pants and stepped into his boots, but his suspenders draped at his side and the buttons of his union suit gaped open to show a mat of gray hair on his chest.

Heath looked up from the fire and breathed a sigh of relief that Philo had finally woken up. This was their fifth morning back on the Jezebel, but even with Geezer and half a dozen miners from camp standing guard on the cabin, he was anxious to finish the night's watch and get back to check on Courtney. He just hoped that by establishing a visible presence on the Jezebel, they could draw Tyree's attention to them and away from the women.

He checked the coffeepot to make sure it was still firmly settled on the coals and nodded. The frigid mountain air nipped at his ears and nose, and the warmth from the fire was a welcome one. "I heard someone say yesterday that we could have snow in a month."

Philo scratched his side and yawned loudly. "What's it now? September?" At Heath's murmur of assent, "Well, they're right. Mid-October, we could be under a few inches."

Heath stood and arched his back to work out the kinks he'd picked up from sleeping on the rocky ground all night. "I guess Ellis Bailey wasn't thinking about winter when he built that cabin, or he'd have put glass in the windows."

Philo finished one side, scratched the other, then worked both hands together over his chest. "If you and Courtney plan to ride out a Montana winter in it, you'll need something over them holes."

"Yeah, but importing glass panes from the East costs money." More money than Heath had been able to earn yet, and, until this business with Tyree Caine was settled, more money than he would earn in the foreseeable future. He laughed softly, realized that he'd made a noise, and explained, "Just a month ago I was a loner. I had no ties. No obligations. Very few needs. Now I'm thinking about making repairs to a cabin I don't even own, and I woke up in the night with the idea that I should start a nest egg for unexpected expenses in the future."

Philo snapped his suspenders into place and hunkered down in front of the fire with a groan. "Speakin' of the future, son . . . You mind me askin' what your intentions are toward Courtney?"

Heath looked away out over the landscape. No trees or grass or flowers broke the landscape of dry brown earth. There was nothing pleasing or soft as far as the eye could see. What should have been a beautiful stretch of land, hills covered with grass and sage rolling one after another toward distant mountain peaks, was nothing more than a ravaged mess. And yet there was something about this place that spoke to him. The possibilities, maybe. The dream of what it could be without prospectors swarming over it like ants on a hill. A vision of the future, perhaps.

But the vision was a dream. The reality was this. All this destruction—and all for money.

"I don't mind your asking," he said after a minute. "I just don't know what my answer is."

"Do you love her?"

Heath ran a hand across his face and nodded slowly. "I think I might."

"You *think*?"

"No. I know. I'm not sure how it happened, though."

Philo cast about for something to protect his hand from the heat, then lifted the coffeepot from the coals and filled two cups. "How does it ever happen? A fella's walkin' around in his life thinkin' he's got everything under control, and then God throws him a twist. The question is, what'll you do about it?"

Heath shrugged casually. He couldn't pretend that he hadn't wondered about the future a few times, but with Courtney still believing that she could be whisked away without warning, it was hard to make plans. And to tell the truth, he wasn't sure *he* was ready for things to progress into permanent. "I guess time will tell, won't it?"

Philo snorted and sipped noisily. "Time will tell? What kind of fool answer is that?"

"An honest one. I don't know what will happen with Courtney and me." He lifted his cup, but stopped short of actually drinking. "I don't know what will happen for the rest of today. I don't even know if we'll both make it out of these hills alive. It's kind of hard to make plans when the future is so unpredictable."

Philo wagged his head in disgust. "You sayin' you're going to let Courtney slip through your fingers because you can't guarantee what tomorrow holds?"

Heath lowered his cup again, a little resentful over Philo's attitude. But he had to remember that Courtney considered the old codger a substitute father and apparently Philo was enjoying the role. "I'm saying that I don't think it's right to make promises I might not be able to keep."

"You mean you might run out on her?"

"No." Heath glowered at the old man. "Yes. Maybe. I don't know, Philo. There are too many factors involved. Too many other people who've suddenly become a part of my life. Too many things I need to take care of and old debts I have to pay before I can think about my own future."

Philo let out another snort of disapproval and took another noisy slurp of coffee. "That's just about the sorriest excuse for runnin' scared I ever did hear."

"That's what you think I'm doing?"

"Sure looks that way to me."

Heath growled in frustration and wrapped both hands around his cup for warmth. "You want me to ask Courtney to marry me with Tyree Caine out there, not knowing whether I'll be alive tomorrow. You want me to promise to love her all the days of my life when I have no idea how many days that'll be. You want me—" He broke off, aware that his voice had been rising steadily. He lowered it and made an effort to control his mounting frustration. "It's not all me, Philo. Courtney won't even say how long she'll stay around. She's got some cockamamie idea that she's from the future. Has she told you *that*?"

Philo nodded and let his gaze trail across the dirt to where they'd tethered Mule. "She told me."

"You believe her?"

The old man's gaze flew back to Heath's and he smiled. "I'm old, son, not crazy."

Heath's sudden relief came out in a tight laugh. "Well, I'm glad to hear that."

"Thing is, she ain't crazy, neither."

"No," Heath agreed slowly. "No, she's not. So how do you explain this belief of hers?"

Philo grinned and looked away again. "I don't. But, then, I don't figure I need to. I know she ain't crazy, so I ain't worried. I know she's got a soft spot in her heart for a lonely old man. I know she's smart as a whip and a better person than most. Why do I need to worry myself over some idea of hers that may or may not be true?"

Heath shook his head again. "I wish it were that easy. I really do. I've tried to tell myself a hundred times that it doesn't matter. But it does matter, Philo. I don't want it to, but it does. Not in how I feel about her, but in whether I can commit to a lifetime together."

Philo swirled the coffee in his cup and tossed the rest aside. "And why is that?"

"I don't know." Heath pushed to his feet and took his first mouthful of now-tepid coffee. "I wish I did because then maybe I could get around it."

Philo nodded and stood to face him. "I suppose that if you want to bad enough, you'll find your way. I just hope for both your sakes that you ain't fool enough to let this chance get away from you." He put a hand on Heath's shoulder and smiled sadly. "I did that once. Spent the rest of my life regrettin' it."

Heath knew a thing or two about regrets. He didn't want or need to add to the ones he was already carrying. But try as he might, he couldn't get around the questions he had about Courtney. And he couldn't convince himself to make a lifelong commitment to someone who could turn out to be something other than what she seemed.

Thanks to his father, he'd had enough surprises of that kind to last a lifetime.

Early the next morning Heath stood outside the Parasol in the chill of early morning, blowing on his hands to warm them, and dancing to keep himself warm. It had been two weeks since his last conversation with Delilah, but he couldn't put off another one indefinitely. He couldn't leave his debt to Blue unpaid. He couldn't leave his friendship with Delilah in doubt. If he ever thought of a future with Courtney, he couldn't move toward it until he had the past taken care of.

He was going to talk to Delilah today, no matter what. And he wouldn't give up until she'd heard him out. He'd been waiting nearly half an hour and was just about to give up when she appeared. Instinctively he slipped into the shadow of a recessed doorway while she stood on the threshold of the saloon and studied the street in both directions. Apparently satisfied that Heath wasn't lying in wait for her, she walked away from the saloon quickly, but she checked over her shoulder frequently to make sure that nobody was following her.

Heath felt a pang of guilt over making her worry, but he didn't want to risk an encounter so near the saloon where Will or Olaf might decide to step in if Delilah became agitated. So he lagged behind, keeping to the shadows to make sure she didn't know he was there until the time was right.

She hadn't gone far when a tall man with dark hair stepped into her path. Heath tensed for a heartbeat before he recognized the man as Derry Dennehy. So he'd been right about Derry having feelings for Delilah. And judging from the tilt of her head and the look on her face, she felt something for him as well.

Heath had no idea how he felt about that. He wasn't sure how he was supposed to feel. Loyalty toward Blue made him resent Derry's attention toward Delilah. But she was his friend, too, whether or not she acknowledged that fact. He knew she couldn't spend her life alone. He didn't expect her to. And an honest suitor, which Derry Dennehy seemed to be, was a far cry better than a stable of customers at the Pink Parasol.

He should be happy for her. He wanted to be happy for her. After all, Derry seemed like a good sort.

So he stayed in the shadows and watched while Derry chatted and Delilah pretended not to listen. He smiled when Derry pressed a small bag containing some gift into her hands and nearly laughed when, in spite of the gleam in her eye and the smile tugging at her lips, Delilah pretended not to want it just long enough to slip it into her pocket.

After several minutes Derry bowed low over Delilah's hand and moved away, but he walked straight toward Heath's hiding place which meant that Heath had to duck inside a nearby bakery to avoid being seen.

By the time Derry had passed and his way was clear again, Delilah had disappeared.

But Heath was more determined than ever to get through to her. He followed the trail she'd taken the last time he saw her, zigzagging between buildings and hurrying down side streets until he finally caught a glimpse of her in the distance making her way through a field.

Heath fell in behind her as she made her way into Nevada City, and when he realized that she was moving with unwavering determination, he realized she wasn't out for a stroll in the fresh air and decided not to approach her until he saw where she was going.

At long last Delilah reached a small cabin on the outskirts

of town, checked over her shoulder one last time, and raised
her hand to knock. Before she could, the door squeaked open
and a dark-skinned boy flew outside to wrap his arms around
her legs.

Heath slipped into the shelter of a lean-to and watched.
He was too far away to see the child clearly, but he put the
child at five or six years old. Delilah lifted the boy and
hugged him tightly. She kissed his cheek, laughed at something he said, and then disappeared into the cabin with her
arms full.

When the door shut behind them, Heath leaned against the
wall behind him and tried to process what he'd just seen.
She'd obviously come here to see someone she knew. A
friend. Perhaps the child's mother. Obviously, whoever lived
in that cabin was important to Delilah. Important enough to
visit once a week? It certainly seemed so.

Important enough to be the reason she debased herself by
working at the Parasol in the first place?

Heath leaned forward and studied the cabin again. Yes.
Maybe even that important. Delilah had *some* reason for selling herself. But who could *be* that important to her?

A child's laughter floated out of the cabin, and Heath
glanced up quickly. His heart began to pound even before
he could turn intuition into conscious thought. Before he
could process all the implications of his suspicion.

The child.

He remembered the look on her face as she picked the boy
up and knew without being told that he was right. A child
of her own would be the only person important enough to
make Delilah do something she abhorred. But if the child
was hers, and if Heath hadn't misjudged the boy's age, then
she must have been pregnant when she left Bonne Chance.

His knees buckled and he pressed his head against the wall
behind him as the full implication hit him. There was only
one way she could have been pregnant when she left Bonne
Chance. Everyone had known how Blue and Delilah felt
about each other. Everyone knew that if the master had given
his consent, they'd have jumped the broom a long time be-

fore. So if the boy was Delilah's, that meant he had to be Blue's as well.

By some miracle, part of Blue had survived his father's hatred, and that realization filled Heath's heart with wonder. He blinked back tears and lifted his face to the sky, imagining Blue's dark face above him. He swallowed around the painful lump in his throat and spoke to Blue for the first time since that horrible night.

"What now, friend?" he whispered, barely able to squeeze the words from his throat. "If this boy *is* yours, then what do I do? How do I help him? How do I help Delilah?"

A gust of wind curled slowly in front of him, lifting bits of grit and dirt into the air with it.

"She won't listen to me. She won't talk to me. I don't know why. I don't know how to reach her."

The breeze abated for a heartbeat, then swirled again. But there were no words in the wind, no solutions in the clouds. And when the wind stilled again and the air became calm, he knew that Blue had left him alone to search his heart for answers he wasn't sure he could find.

But the stakes were higher, and Heath wasn't going to lose. He'd get through to Delilah somehow. He didn't care how long it took or how hard he had to fight. He'd do it for her. He'd do it for Blue. And he'd do it for that little boy who'd breathed new life into him with a laugh and who'd given him back a belief in miracles he'd lost a long time ago.

Courtney had been trying to keep herself occupied for days while Heath, Philo, and Moonshine alternated watches on the Jezebel. It was her own fault. She's the one who'd suggested the partnership. She just hadn't expected them to move so quickly or to leave her alone in town while they stood guard at the mine. And knowing that Tyree Caine could strike at any time and from any direction made her edgy.

She couldn't concentrate well enough to draw, so she kept her body moving, first sweeping the loose dirt from the floor and then hauling and heating a bucket full of water, and finally scrubbing the entire floor on her hands and knees. The physical exertion helped, but it didn't work miracles. Her mind still raced and her heart still ached when she thought about one of the men being hurt.

She didn't know how she'd gotten in this deep emotionally. She'd warned herself over and over and over again. Yet here she was, worried sick about Philo and Moonshine and half frantic at the thought of something happening to Heath. If she'd thought for one minute that she could help, she'd have been up there with them.

She was still on her knees mopping up the last of the dirt when Heath came inside. He took one look at the wet floor and froze uncertainly. "Should I go away?"

Courtney sat back on her heels and pushed hair from her eyes with the back of her hand. "No, but you can take off your boots before you come inside."

He turned aside without comment. That in itself was unusual, but the set of his shoulders and the look on his face when he sat on the porch to tug off his boots warned her that something wasn't right.

She gathered her cleaning supplies, then bent to pick up the bucket full of water.

"Let me get that." Heath half-slid across the wet floor in his stockings and took the bucket from her before she could protest. He glanced around once more. "Are you finished?"

"I am." She trailed him to the door, still holding her wet rags and trying to figure out what was different about him. "You're home early," she said in her most casual tone. "Or are you just passing by on your way back to the mine?"

Heath smiled over his shoulder and hucked the wash water out into the dirt. "I plan to stay around this evening—if you don't mind, that is. I can come in handy with the heavy work."

"I don't mind at all." Still trying not to seem petulant and childish, she draped the rags across a rock to dry. "It's your home, too. And I'm through cleaning for the evening. I just scrubbed the floor to keep myself busy." That didn't sound casual. It sounded pathetic. She tried steering the conversation away from herself. "I'd much rather hear about what's happening up on the mine and do something to help."

"That'll be a short conversation." Heath lowered the

bucket to the porch and quirked a smile at her, but Courtney
could tell that his heart wasn't in it. "No sign of Caine around
here?"

"Not that I've seen, but then the guards you posted don't
always tell me everything." His gaze flickered away, but
Courtney knew him well enough by now to know that he
was barely listening to her. She folded her arms and tried to
make eye contact. "What is it, Heath?"

His gaze shot back to hers. "What?"

"You're obviously distracted. You're a million miles
away. What is it?"

"You know me too well," he said with a thin laugh. He
sighed and ran a hand along the back of his neck. "I saw
Delilah this morning."

"Did you? I'm so glad. What did she say?"

"Nothing. I didn't speak to her." His smile became almost
sheepish. "I followed her."

"Oh." Courtney didn't know what to make of that, but she
wasn't going to discourage the open dialogue. "Do you want
to go back inside and talk about it? I could make coffee . . .
or something."

"I'd rather have something stronger, but I'll take the coffee
and be grateful for it." He moved away from the door and
waited for her to step through, then trailed her inside and
shut the door.

With the door closed and Heath standing just inside wearing his socks, the cabin felt warm and homey. She spooned
coffee into the pot and filled it with fresh water from the
bucket. "Where did she go?"

"A cabin on the other side of Nevada City." He laughed
softly and ran his hand across his face. "Worse than this one,
if you can imagine." He let out another heavy breath and
dragged his gaze to hers. "There's a boy living there. A boy
I think is her son. I also think Blue may have been the boy's
father."

Courtney settled the coffeepot on the coals and took her
place across the table from him. "Are you sure?"

"I'm not sure of anything. It's just a feeling I get. But the
boy looks about the right age." He leaned back in his chair

and stared up at the ceiling. "You should have seen him. He's dark like Blue, and he raced out of that cabin and hugged her as if his world revolved around her. He has to be her son."

Courtney tried to read his expression, but the emotions there were too confusing. "What are you going to do now?"

He rolled his head to loosen tight neck muscles. "That's a good question. If the boy *is* Blue's, I have to do something to help him. The question is, what can I do? Delilah didn't want to speak to me before. I don't know what she'll do if she finds out that I followed her."

"But you can't just pretend that you don't know."

He shook his head firmly. "No. And I won't. But I can't barge into the Pink Parasol and announce that I know her secret, either." He let out an exhausted groan and sank low in his chair, stretching his legs out in front of him and curling his toes. "I'm sure I'll figure something out," he said, closing his eyes. "Right now, I'm almost too tired to think."

Courtney's heart did a little flip-flop and warmth curled through her like smoke from a fire. He'd come such a long way in the past month, he seemed like a completely different person, and she couldn't help wondering if she'd changed half as much.

She turned to check on the coffee just as the sounds of a fiddle drifted inside through the window. Courtney had learned to live with the open windows in the past month, but she'd been through enough Montana winters to know that temperatures often dropped to well below zero. She didn't know how they'd get through the winter without something to protect them from the arctic cold. Staying warm was sometimes a chore even with double-glass windows and good insulation.

She glanced back at Heath and found his eyes still closed. Maybe they'd have to share body heat when the winter came. Snuggling next to him under the quilts on that old bed might make the winter nights a whole lot more interesting.

She whispered his name, but he didn't respond, so she walked to the window and looked out at the deepening night. The fiddle music had become louder, and the laughter coming from the camp made her wish that she wasn't stuck inside the cabin. But while she might dare venture to Philo's camp in the middle of the day, she wasn't careless enough to wander around the miners' camps after dark.

Still, the tempo of the music made her body sway, and she hummed lightly as she leaned her elbows on the windowsill and let the rhythm catch her. She heard a sound and turned, just in time to see Heath watching her with one brow arched over a pale blue eye. "I didn't realize you liked music."

She blushed, a little embarrassed at having been caught. "Very much. Doesn't everyone?"

"Not everyone." He glanced toward the window and remained silent for a long moment. When he spoke again, she could barely hear his voice. "Would you like to go?"

Courtney wasn't sure she'd heard him right. "To the miners' camp?"

Heath shrugged. "It sounds like they're having a good time, and you seem interested." He tried to sound casual. Careless, even. Certainly nonchalant. But Courtney could feel tension coiled beneath his words.

She couldn't tell if *he* wanted to go, or if he was just being kind. "I'd go along . . . if you want to go."

Heath laughed and shook his head in disbelief. "Are we going to dance around each other tonight, Courtney? Me trying not to step on your toes and you avoiding mine?"

His smile touched her. She shook her head and grinned. "No. Of course not."

His smile faded, but the expression in his eyes was better than any smile. He touched her cheek, brushing her skin with the backs of his fingers and looking deep into her eyes as he slowly drew his hand toward her chin.

Warm shivers raced up her spine and slow heat began to pulse through her veins. Instinct had her eyes closing so she could luxuriate in the sensation, but she wanted to see his expression as he touched her. In the camp the music switched to a ballad, and Heath began to sway very slightly, but in perfect rhythm. "Have I told you how beautiful I think you are?"

The question stunned her, but she managed an answer.

"No one has ever used that word to describe me before."

The corners of Heath's mouth turned down. Still swaying to the music of the fiddle, he found her hand and slid the other hand around her waist. She began to move with him, as naturally as if they'd done this every night of their lives. He pulled her closer and pressed his face against hers so that when he spoke she could feel the soft brush of lips on her cheek and the warmth of his breath. "Men in the future must be fools."

Tears of gratitude filled her eyes, but she managed to keep them from spilling onto her cheeks and ruining the moment. "I wouldn't know," she said, giving in to the sway of his body. "I haven't known that many of them."

"There hasn't been someone special in your life?"

"My mother has lived with twelve different men since the year I turned seven," Courtney said, pulling back just enough to grin up at him. "Men haven't had all that much appeal." *Until now.*

A pleased smile curved his lips. "That's unfortunate . . . for them."

"And what about you? Have there been any special ladies?"

His smile faded ever so slightly. "There was one. Once. But that was in another lifetime."

"Back on Bonne Chance?"

He nodded without speaking, and Courtney thought for a moment that he'd said all he was going to about her. But he tightened his grip on her waist and swept her past the table, and everything tight and reserved inside of him seemed to melt. "Her name was Felice, and we were going to be married. It wasn't that we were so very much in love, but we *were* suited for each other. Our parents had seen to that. We'd been groomed to marry from the moment she was born."

"What happened?"

Heath shrugged casually. "I thought she loved me, so I rode to her family's plantation the night Blue was killed. I told her that I was leaving, and I asked her to come with me."

Courtney didn't have to ask what her answer had been. If Felice had said yes, she'd have been the one dancing by firelight to the scrape of a prospector's fiddle. "She refused?"

"Pointedly."

"I'm sorry." She thought that might have been the first lie she'd ever told him. She *was* sorry if he'd been hurt, but she wasn't sorry at all at the way things had turned out.

His lips twitched as if he could tell just how sorry she really was. "Don't be. If she'd accepted my offer, I probably wouldn't have been strolling through the streets of Virginia City the night you arrived." He brushed a kiss to her temple, as if it were the most natural thing in the world. "I realize now that her saying no was the best thing she could have done . . . but I can't say I thought so at the time."

Courtney let her fingers splay on his shoulder, enjoying the bunch and release of muscles as he moved. "Some of God's greatest gifts are unanswered prayers."

"Indeed." He kissed her temple again and then stopped moving. He released her hand and slid his other arm around her waist. "Indeed."

Courtney's blood tingled and her heart began to pound against her rib cage. Her breath caught at the expression in his eyes, at the desire she saw burning in their cool depths. Somewhere in the back of her mind all sorts of logical considerations banged up against her conscious mind, but she shoved them away. There would be plenty of time to be practical. But practical was the *last* thing she wanted to be right now.

She leaned into the kiss she knew was coming, so that when their lips met she didn't know which of them had initiated it. Strangely, it didn't matter. For the first time in her life, she was part of something larger than herself. Something that had no boundaries and no edges, and in his arms she felt as if she'd come home.

She gave herself to that feeling, even knowing in the back of her mind that this wasn't her home and never would be. Even knowing that she was beginning something that would have to end, she couldn't pull away. Nor did she want to. For the first time in her life, she felt loved and beautiful. Or if not loved, then at least deeply cared for. Even knowing that this feeling, too, would end wasn't enough to make her turn away from it. If there was a price to pay, she'd pay it . . . later.

Chapter 15

For DAYS COURTNEY had been able to feel Heath's tension growing. It was a palpable thing. It radiated from him in waves and fairly crackled in the air of the cabin. It hovered between them as they ate, and filled the space between bed and floor at night. And she felt completely responsible.

She'd overreacted. She saw that now. No one had seen Tyree Caine or any of his boys for days, and Philo didn't appear to be in any danger. She'd jumped the gun and stirred up something that she couldn't control. Now Heath, Moonshine, and Philo alternated watches on the Jezebel, two at a time, and she spent most of her time alone.

Heath and Moonshine had stayed at the mine last night. Tonight, Philo would relieve Moonshine, and Heath would get the following night off. She'd rather have him here with her all the time.

She'd been here for a month now. Only a month. Yet she was beginning to feel as if she'd lived here forever. Some of her memories of home were as sharp as if she'd been there just yesterday; others were fading so quickly she could hardly recall what it felt like to drive a car or listen to the radio.

She thought often about Ryan, and she wondered whether he ever worried about her and what he thought had happened to her. But days would pass now without her thinking of something she missed from her old life.

She was even becoming more used to sketching this way, and the images were coming more easily all the time. The pictures she'd drawn so far would never be published anywhere, but getting the images that filled her head since embarking on this strange new life onto paper helped her figure things out.

Looking back over what she'd drawn in the past week, she could tell, for instance, just how torn she was on the subject of going back to her own time. She'd done one sketch of Ryan from memory, but every other picture featured someone or something from the past. Life was a little easier there in some ways, but these men here had taken her into their hearts, and leaving them . . . well, she just didn't want to do it. That's all there was to it.

Four weeks ago the only thing she'd wanted was to figure out what she had to do to leave. Now she woke up every morning relieved to find herself in the cabin and fearful that she'd accidentally stumble across the thing that would take her back.

How could she leave now that she'd finally found someone who actually *wanted* to be a father to her? Now that she'd found Moonshine, who'd become more like a little brother than anything and whose lovesick chatter about Miss Geneva Openshaw, the most beautiful girl in all of Fayette County, Ohio, helped pass the lonely days? Now that she'd found Heath, whose past was as painful as her own, and whose heart was still as big as any she'd ever seen?

For the first time in her life, she knew love in all its facets, and she didn't want to give it up now.

The trouble was, she could feel the future out there waiting for her. Stalking her. Growing closer every day. Its threat was every bit as large and maybe even more real than the threat Tyree Caine posed to the miners.

She rubbed her arms and turned away from the window, but a movement on the edge of her vision pulled her back

around. Four men, all wearing tan dusters, moved from her
peripheral vision and made their way along the narrow path
that served as a street inside the camp.

They walked slowly, stopping in front of selected tents
along their way, chatting when they found someone home,
peering inside empty tents when they didn't. They didn't
actually do anything unusual, but she could feel an air of
menace even from a distance. And the furtive looks from the
few other prospectors they passed only reinforced her suspicions.

Her heart began to race and her fingers grew numb. She
knew even without being told that she was looking at Tyree
Caine and his boys, and she also knew that they meant trouble.

If she'd been in her own time, she'd have picked up the
phone and dialed 911. But even if she'd had a way to reach
someone in authority, she had nothing concrete to report.
Nothing but intuition on which to base her suspicions.

Maybe she was overreacting. None of the men had actually
done anything to frighten her. But no matter how hard she
tried, she couldn't shake her uneasiness. Something was
dreadfully wrong.

She argued with herself for several minutes, until a gust
of wind lifted the hem of one man's duster and exposed a
holster. For the first time she wished she'd listened to Heath.
She'd feel a whole lot more powerful and able to deal with
the situation if she knew how to use that shotgun. Heck,
she'd feel better if she even knew where it was.

She stood there, watching in indecision, while they moved
toward Philo's tent. She wanted to do something to help, but
what could she do? She wasn't stupid enough to think that
she could fight them and win, but the only man who'd ever
wanted to be her father was over there alone and unprotected,
and she couldn't stand here like a dolt while they bullied
him—or worse. At the very least, she could stand beside
Philo and let them know he wasn't alone.

Wishing again that she knew where Heath had hidden the
shotgun, she started across the street. Not that she could have
hit anything with it, but it might have convinced them she

meant business. Well, she'd just have to convince them some
other way.

She walked quickly, keeping her head high and trying not
to look frightened in spite of the fact that her heart was gal-
loping like a racehorse and she couldn't feel her fingers. They
were one tent away from Philo's now, and she could see the
old man watching them with a guarded expression on his
face.

One man, a tall ugly brute, stood in front of Philo while
the others formed a semicircle behind him. Courtney was still
too far away to hear what they were saying, but it didn't take
a genius to figure it out. Philo rose to his feet, but he looked
small and old surrounded by the four swaggering bullies. Her
heart constricted painfully, and the numbness spread from
her fingers to her wrists.

The way she saw it, she had two choices: either she could
run into Philo's camp and square off against four pistol-
packing gangsters or she could try to rally some of the other
miners to help. She figured she had a much better chance
with the other miners than she did in a standoff, so she veered
off the path and ran past several tents, looking for someone
who might be willing to help her.

Unfortunately most of the men who lived in this camp
were day laborers for local mining companies and that meant
that most of the tents she passed were empty. And the few
that weren't . . . well, the men she found there didn't look
very promising.

One was every bit as old as Philo, and maybe older. Another was very obviously sleeping off a binge from the night
before. A third flatly refused to get involved with anybody
else's troubles, and the fourth was only interested in what
they could do inside his tent if she would just say yes.

Disheartened, she stopped running and struggled to catch
her breath. She couldn't leave Philo alone forever. Maybe
she should just turn back and take her chances. At least the
two of them might stand a chance if they stood together.

When she could breathe again, she set off at a run toward
Philo's tent. She dodged a miner who'd had too much to
drink, jumped over a pothole in the road, and nearly plowed

into the back end of a mule when she came around a corner too fast. But she was finally back where she'd started—just in time to see Tyree grab Philo by the collar and drag him close.

She couldn't hear what they were saying, but she could see Philo's face growing red with anger, and she began to worry for another reason entirely. She didn't want him to sit back and take Tyree's bullying, but she didn't want him to become belligerent and start trouble, either. And Philo definitly had it in him to become belligerent.

Maybe Tyree would even back off if he knew someone else could see what he was up to. There was always a chance.

Taking a deep breath for courage, she slowed, pasted on the best smile she could work up, and sailed in between two of Tyree's henchmen looking no more concerned than she would have if they'd stopped by for tea. "*There* you are, Philo," she sang out, trying not to look at the grip Tyree still had on the older man's collar. "What on earth is keeping you?"

Tyree glanced over his shoulder, and the look in his eyes reminded her so much of Leslie's Loser Number Five, her breath caught. Very slowly he loosened the grip he had on Philo and a feral smile crept across his lips. "Ma'am."

Courtney pulled air into her shrunken lungs and fought to keep her smile from turning into a grimace of distaste. Number Five had been a particularly ugly and cruc' man who'd found great joy in controlling every aspect of Courtney's behavior in the short time she'd been allowed to stay at home. He'd also been vicious with Leslie at times, and Courtney saw all that and more in Tyree Caine's eyes.

In a heartbeat, she knew that Moonshine was right about him, and she wished desperately that she could remember anything she'd learned in those self-defense classes she'd listened to with only half an ear back in the real world. Anyway, she doubted that anyone had ever addressed the issue of going one-on-four against an armed gang, and if they did, their advice would probably have been to run.

But knowing that Tyree had released Philo gave her hope. She moved closer to Philo, but she tried to keep the other four in the corner of her eye. "Can you still walk with me into town this morning? I don't want to be late."

Philo didn't look happy to see her, but that was no surprise. She hadn't expected him to be.

His brows knit into a tight V over his nose. "Town?" It was only one word, but the single syllable was fairly bursting with disapproval, irritation, and annoyance.

"You promised, remember?"

"Tell you what, little lady." One of Tyree's goons took her arm. He was a short man only an inch or so taller than Courtney, with a wide nose and pocked skin. "Why don't you go back where you came from and wait there for old Philo. He'll be along directly, just as soon as Mr. Caine's through talkin' to him."

Courtney jerked her arm away from him. "I'd rather not."

A second man, tall and squarely built, took up position behind her. "Don't worry about Philo. He'll be all right—as long as he cooperates."

Courtney's senses were all on alert and her nerve-endings felt as if they were on fire. She had no idea whether she should address the threat or simply pretend she hadn't heard it.

Before she could decide, the man behind her made a decision for her. "Why don't you just be a good girl and go on home?" His voice was far too close to her ear, and, unbelievably, a meaty hand settled on her backside.

Acting only on instinct, she turned and brought her knee up straight into his groin. He let out a rush of breath, his eyes bugged out, and he doubled over to clutch himself as he fell over onto his side.

Tyree's other men drew their pistols before Courtney could blink, and she heard the distinctive metallic click of hammers being cocked as they took aim. She stared down the pistol barrel, unable to lift her gaze to look at the man who was going to kill her. She heard Philo saying something, but his voice sounded faraway and dreamlike.

And then, suddenly, she heard laughter, and she was able to look away from the gun's barrel, blinking, to locate the sound. It was coming, unbelievably, from Tyree Caine. He dashed tears of mirth from his eyes and motioned for his henchmen to holster their guns again. "Okay, little lady. You've made your point." He reached down to pull his fallen comrade to his feet and wiped his eyes again with the back of his hand. "You okay, Ethan?"

His miserable friend stayed hunched and protective. "Do I *look* okay?"

Tyree laughed again and motioned for his boys to leave, and Courtney flashed a jubilant glance at Philo. But the old man obviously didn't share her jubilation. And it didn't take long to find out why.

Still laughing, Tyree leaned into the space between two of his men and clapped his hands on their shoulders as they started away from Philo's camp. "Poor old Ethan. His first kid's gonna walk with a limp after that. But we ain't gonna kill the little lady over it, are we, boys?" He looked back over his shoulder and fixed her with a look that made her blood run cold. The smile left his lips and a sneer replaced it. "At least not today."

"Are you *crazy?*" Heath thundered that evening. "You went up against Tyree Caine? What the hell were you thinking?"

"I was thinking about Philo!" Courtney shouted back, but her heart wasn't fully behind her own defense. She'd been foolish and she knew it. She'd taken a terrible chance and guilt had been eating her alive all afternoon, but that didn't stop her from fighting back when Heath attacked. She'd never been good at taking blame in shameful silence, and she'd paid the price for it more than once.

"Philo can take care of himself!" Heath roared. "I just thank God he told me about what happened when he showed up at the mine this afternoon."

"I can take care of myself, too. Ask Ethan if you don't believe me."

"I don't need to ask Ethan. I don't need to ask Philo. What you did this morning was foolhardy, Courtney. You could have gotten yourself killed, and Philo right along with you."

"But I didn't."

"But you could have."

"But I *didn't*."

"Only because Tyree Caine has something else up his sleeve. Can't you see that? He knows about you. He knows that you mean something to Philo. He knows that you mean something to me. That makes you a perfect target to keep the two of us in line. Why in the hell do you think we've been sleeping up on the Jezebel for the past two weeks?" And before she could answer, "Because we're *trying* to divert his attention away from you." He paced from one end of the cabin to the other and back again. "God in heaven, Courtney. What were you thinking?"

"I'm sorry. I didn't mean to put anyone in danger. But you've left me here baking corn fritters while you're all doing something, and it stinks. I couldn't sit here sewing buttons while they threatened Philo. I *won't* do that."

Heath took her by the shoulders and locked his gaze on hers. "Do you know what Tyree could have done to you? Do you know what he *wants* to do?"

Courtney was all ready with an answer, but that last question froze it in her throat. "How do you know what he wants to do?"

The guilty look on his face was all the answer she needed.

"He *told* you? He threatened me and you didn't *tell* me? What in the hell were *you* thinking?"

Heath mopped his face with one hand. "What good would it have done to tell you?"

"Gee, I don't know." She was too angry to stand close to him, so she put some distance between them before she spoke again. "Maybe I could have protected myself. Maybe I'd have thought twice or even three times about what I did this morning. Maybe I'd have learned how to use your stupid shotgun. I thought about taking it with me this morning, but I didn't know where it was."

"You thought about—?" Heath cut himself off and shook his head in wonder. "You don't know how to shoot the damn shotgun. What good would it have done you?"

"It might have made them think twice about messing with me."

"Before or after they took it away from you? You don't

use a firearm so you can look tough, Courtney. If you're going to pull one out, you damn well better be ready to use it."

"I know that."

He started to say something, cut himself off again, and studied her carefully. "What did you say?"

"I said I know that. I've heard that before. Everybody says it. Don't pull out a gun unless you intend to use it. Well, I intend to use it, okay? At least, I want using it to be an option."

Heath's eyes narrowed in suspicion. "Are you serious, or is this some kind of game?"

She sank into her chair and propped her chin in her hand. "I'm serious."

"I thought you hated guns."

"I do." She lifted her gaze to his. "I hate Tyree Caine more."

Heath dragged his chair close to hers, straddled it, and studied her face. When he spoke again, he sounded more worried than angry. "Are you okay?"

She nodded miserably and tore tiny pieces from a corn fritter. "I'm fine. Just . . ." She couldn't make herself admit aloud how much Tyree's threat had frightened her and how shaky it left her knowing that it wasn't his first. "I'm annoyed with myself and furious with Tyree Caine and his men. And I'm seriously peeved with you, too. If you'd been here, I wouldn't have gone running over there in the first place." She sent him a halfhearted grin. "I would have sent you."

He shook his head again, but at least he smiled—sort of. "You're making a joke?"

"At least I'm not crying."

He leaned forward and touched her cheek gently. "Is that what you feel like doing?"

"No. I hate crying." She had ever since Loser Number Two smacked her in the head every time he suspected a tear, and told her to stop being such a baby. "And anyway, there's nothing to cry about. I'm fine. Philo's fine. I just want to make sure we stay that way."

Heath cupped her chin in his hand and looked deep into

her eyes. "It's okay if you cry, Courtney. You don't have to be tough."

His voice was so gentle he was going to *make* her cry. She shook her head firmly and tried to scowl. "I thought you hated crying."

"I do. I hate seeing you hurt more."

That did it. There was *no way* she could hold back tears after that. Her throat tightened and a lump filled it. Heath's face blurred, then swam in front of her face. She tried to blink the tears away, but the events of the past month all came together in a lump and combined with the growing fear that she'd have to leave here one day soon.

Heath stood and drew her to her feet, then held her gently against his chest. She fought the emotion as long as she could, but it was no use. She felt the first tears slip down her cheek and felt the moisture soak into his shirt. She heard the soft whisper of his voice as he promised everything would work out and the brush of his lips against her forehead.

He stroked her back gently, and she lifted her face so she could look into his eyes. But his mouth was waiting for her instead. The kiss held everything she wanted and asked for everything she had to give. She never wanted it to end. Fire swept through her, followed on the heels by a need so fierce she wasn't sure she'd survive it.

His tongue brushed her lips, and she opened her mouth to him willingly, as eager to take their contact onto the next plane as he was. Somewhere deep inside, a whispering voice warned that she would be setting herself up for a lifetime of regret if she gave in to this moment. But the absolute certainty that she'd regret it more if she didn't lingered closer to the surface. She might wake up tomorrow and find herself in the twenty-first century, but at least she'd have something wonderful to remember.

His hands moved across her back, then slowly, slowly, up to her sides. His fingers brushed her breast almost accidentally, and she stopped breathing. She struggled to open the buttons of his shirt, anxious to finally feel the fine hairs on his chest, and the warmth of his skin beneath her hands.

He moaned when she touched him and dragged her even

closer. He slid his hands down her sides again, past her hips, and cupped her bottom so he could pull her closer. She wanted him. She needed him. In this moment, at least, he was like air to her.

Wherever his hands moved, fire followed. Wherever his lips touched, her blood turned to warmed honey. The world could have turned upside-down and she wouldn't have known it. And she wanted desperately to join with him in a way that would link them together forever. In the past. In the future. It didn't matter. She loved him and she wanted to be with him.

She must have spoken aloud because he stopped and pulled back slightly to look at her. "What did you say?"

She shook her head in confusion. "I don't know."

"I thought you said that you love me."

She could hardly breathe and talking was so much harder, so she nodded and grinned at the look in his eyes. "I probably did. I was certainly thinking it."

He smiled slowly and rained soft kisses along her chin and neck. "And I wanted to be the first to say it." He unbuttoned her blouse and slowly pulled the fabric away from her shoulder, following the material with his lips.

Her heart soared, but she couldn't seem to speak. She was too fascinated by the soft sweep of lashes on his cheeks, the expression of gentle caring that softened his features, the sound of his breath, the tiny scar near his mouth, the curve of his ear. He loved her. He loved her.

He loved her.

She could have died a happy woman right then and there. "I don't ever want to leave you, Heath. No matter what happens, I need you to know that."

"Then don't."

"I might not be able to control that."

He pulled back again and ran his gaze across her face. She held her breath, suddenly afraid that she'd made a mistake by bringing up the future. But he took away that fear, too. His lips quirked into a lopsided grin, and he kissed her one more time, a long, lingering, soul-searching kiss that did turn her world on its head. "If you have to go, then I guess the obvious solution is for you to take me with you."

He loved her!

"Take me with you now," she whispered.

"Where?"

She glanced toward the bed and grinned mischievously.

"There?" A smile as slow as everything else he did curved his lips. "Do you think that's wise?"

She nodded solemnly and kissed his chin. "I'm sure it's cold on the floor at night."

"Oh, it is."

She moved to his mouth and nipped at his bottom lip. "And it seems just plain mean and selfish to make you stay there."

"Oh," he said on a shaky breath, "it is."

She smiled and followed his example, trailing soft kisses along his shoulder and moving to his chest. She ran her hands down his sides and rested them on his belt. "And because if we don't, I really am going to cry."

Heath grinned down at her. "You *know* how much I hate tears."

"Yes, I do."

For the first time all evening, he moved quickly, sweeping her into his arms and startling a cry of surprise from her. He carried her across the room in three strides and lowered her to the mattress. "Are you sure?"

In answer, she slithered the rest of the way out of her blouse and held out her arms to him. He came to her and she knew his need was as great as her own, the emptiness in his soul as deep as her own. His hands moved across her with exquisite tenderness, and his lips worked magic on her body and her spirit. There were no words to describe what happened between them. Their connection was so much more than sex, so much greater than love. It was like nothing she'd ever known before, and she knew that if she and Heath were separated, neither of them would ever know anything like it again.

When his hands brushed her skin, she felt his touch in her soul. When his fingers worked magic on her, she responded from somewhere so deep inside she'd never even known it existed before. They came together, two spirits, two hearts, two beings in an ages-old quest to become one in the only way they could. And when she cried out, she felt the answering echo from deep inside him.

When it was over, she lay in his arms and prayed as she'd never prayed before that God wouldn't bring her this far and surround her with so much love, and then take it away again. If he did, it would be the cruelest thing she could imagine.

Chapter 16

FOR FOUR WEDNESDAYS in a row, Delilah had found Mr. Roderick Dennehy waiting for her when she left the Pink Parasol. He always stood in the same spot so she'd be sure to notice him. Sometimes he spoke to her, which she found irritating enough. But sometimes he merely smiled and tipped his hat as she passed, and that only irritated her more.

On days other than Wednesdays, he sat at a table in the corner of the saloon and kept an eye on everything and everyone around her. Delilah wasn't sure how she felt about that, either. She didn't want any man acting as if he owned her, but the confusing thing about Mr. Roderick Dennehy was that he never did that—beyond, of course, the time he'd announced his intention of marrying her.

At the Parasol he made no move to speak to her when she was working, and only rarely made eye contact. He made no effort to discourage the customers or to lay claim to her in any way. When he did look at her, his expression was carefully neutral.

At the end of every night, Delilah told herself that she was glad he kept his distance and relieved that he was showing some common sense. But though she would never admit this aloud—she could barely stand to admit it to herself—her willpower slipped a little more with every one of his smiles, and the more silent he became, the more she began to wish he would say something.

On a cool Wednesday morning toward the end of September, Delilah left the Pink Parasol and scanned the street as she did every week. Sure enough, Mr. Roderick Dennehy was waiting for her, but this time the damn fool was holding a bunch of flowers in his hand. Flowers! In Virginia City where scarcely a blade of grass had been left in the ground.

How far had he traveled to find *flowers*?

In spite of herself, Delilah felt a flash of, if not admiration, then at least a stunned sort of awe that anyone would go to such lengths for anyone—much less for her. But that only brought up a new worry.

He was courting her. Any fool could see that, and Delilah couldn't deny it. She had never been the sort to bend the truth. Letting other people think she was white was a sin of omission, not an outright lie. She had more white blood in her than black, anyway. But most folks didn't see it that way, and if she let Mr. Roderick Dennehy continue on, oblivious to the truth, *that* would be wrong.

She couldn't keep hiding the truth, but she couldn't tell him, either. The smart thing would be to ignore him altogether.

She lifted her chin to walk past him, just as she did every week, but she couldn't make herself walk away from that handful of lupine, wild daisies, and Indian paintbrush. So she told herself that she simply couldn't bear to let them die before Isaac saw them.

To keep Mr. Roderick Dennehy from drawing any unfortunate conclusions, she put on an aggrieved expression, folded her arms high on her chest, and took a long look down her nose. "What do you think you're doing?"

His lips curved into a little boy's smile filled with delight, and she noticed that he'd trimmed his beard. "Nothing but bringing flowers for my lady." He bowed with a flourish and held them out to her.

She rolled her eyes in exasperation and held out her hand with feigned impatience. His fingers brushed hers as she took the bouquet in her hand, and she held the flowers close to breathe in their fragrance, even though she tried very hard to look as if she couldn't even see them.

"I can't imagine why you'd waste time on something so impractical," she said with as much haughtiness as she could muster—which even she had to admit wasn't much at all.

He straightened and grinned jubilantly, as if he could sense her weakening. "I'd ride to the ends of the earth if it meant I could see that glimmer in your eye."

Delilah chided herself for relaxing her guard. "Foolish man. There's no glimmer in my eye, nor will there be. Not today. Not ever." She squared her shoulders and began to walk, but she wasn't a bit surprised that he fell in beside her. And if the truth were told, she wasn't even all that angry.

"Ah, now it's stories you're telling me. I saw the gleam with my own two eyes." He made a show of adjusting the lapels of his jacket and leaned close to whisper, "But don't worry. I'm gentleman enough to pretend I didn't."

A laugh escaped her lips before she could stop it. She bit her bottom lip, but the teasing light in his eyes was hard to resist. "You're no gentleman at all, Mr. Roderick Dennehy. You're a scoundrel if ever there was one." She shifted the flowers to her other hand just in case he decided to ask for them back. "I shouldn't speak to you at all. If I had a brain in my head, I wouldn't."

To her surprise, he threw back his head and laughed. It was, she thought grudgingly, a good laugh. Not one of those affected laughs, or a held-back laugh, or even a tittering one. Not a bit condescending, either. It started somewhere deep inside his chest and exploded into the morning with such honesty she felt another layer of her protective coating being dissolved.

"Perhaps you're right, my fair Delilah," he said as they drew even with the corner. "Perhaps I am a scoundrel. Perhaps I will roast in hell when the end comes, and perhaps I'll rue the day that I gambled a penny at the poker tables or took a dram too much whiskey. But I'll tell you one thing I *won't* regret, and that's courting the fairest maid I've ever set eyes on and trying to make her my own."

"You really are a wicked man," she said, but she couldn't keep the bubbles in her heart from spreading to her lips, and she knew they were reflected in her eyes.

He laughed again and kissed her hand, then started walking backward. "And you weren't going to talk to me. Ah, Delilah, you can't resist me any more than I can resist you. It's talking to me you'll be doin', and a whole lot of it, or I'm not my father's son." And before she could tell him again what a fool he was, he tipped his hat and swaggered off in another direction, leaving Delilah clutching his foolish bouquet of flowers in her hand and staring after him.

Wooden-headed man.

Sniffing in disapproval, she purposely stopped watching the swing of his shoulders and the sway of his jacket. But she lifted the bouquet and took another deep breath of the heady scent of wildflowers. He must have traveled a far way to get them. A far way, indeed. And the fact that he'd done so for her was almost enough to soften her heart.

She scowled at the flowers and tucked them in a very no-nonsense way beneath her arm. It *would* do Isaac good to see something so beautiful—even if Mr. Roderick Dennehy *was* a puddle-headed man.

Trust me.

The words echoed through the swamp in Heath's dream, growing louder with each repetition until they overtook the sound of Blue's heartbeat and drowned out Heath's own voice.

Trust me.

Blue knew. Heath could see in his eyes that he knew it would mean the end, but still he slowly, hesitantly, began his descent from the tree. Heath stood behind himself and a little above, so that he could see his own face and Blue's frightened eyes as his friend jumped to the ground. He tried to shout a warning to his dream self, but no sound came out of his mouth.

Trust me.

The echo was all around him now. The words and the heartbeat, mingling together and then breaking apart. He saw himself take Blue's arm and lead him a little away from the others. He saw himself motion the other trackers to stay back while he explained life as he'd once believed it to be.

The hammering of Blue's heart grew louder. He knew. He *knew*! The other trackers knew. Everyone knew except his foolish dream self who wouldn't listen to the warnings on the wind and who couldn't see the mocking laugher in the trackers' eyes.

Trust me. Me. Me. Me.

"Heath? Dadgumit, you in there?" The rhythmic pulsing of his dream turned into the sound of fists hammering on the door. "Open up. It's Philo and we got us a problem."

Heath shot out of bed half a step ahead of Courtney, stepped into his pants, and motioned her back under the covers. Philo might think of Courtney as a daughter, but Heath still didn't want the old codger to see her disheveled from sleep and more beautiful than a woman had a right to be.

Funny, but even the dream didn't seem so bad when he woke up and found her next to him.

"Heath? Can you hear me boy?"

"I'm coming, Philo. Keep your shirt on." Heath grinned at Courtney, lifted the latch, and slipped outside into the deep chill of a late-autumn morning. He could see his breath, and he regretted not grabbing his coat on the way out, but the look on Philo's face wiped away his smile before he could even get the door shut. "What is it? What's wrong?"

"It's Moonshine. I ain't seen him."

Ah hell. Heath's good mood evaporated completely, and he glanced toward the hills. If the miners had left any trees, they'd have been shimmering with autumn colors by now. "He didn't come back down last night?"

"Nope."

Heath swore again and barely refrained from putting his fist through the wall. "Did he have anyone up there with him?"

"Noah for part of the day. I talked to him already. He left to come back before dark, just like we agreed. Moonshine wanted to stay a while because he could feel a strike comin'."

"And Noah *let* him?"

"You know Noah." Philo shivered and hunched a little further into his coat. "Callin' him dumb as a post would insult the post. I told Moonshine not to take him, but he wanted Noah. The man might have pudding for brains, but he's a damn fine shot."

That he was. Heath cupped his hands in front of his mouth, blew on his fingers to warm them, and tried to think. If anything had happened to Moonshine, he'd never forgive himself for agreeing to let the kid help guard the Jezebel in the first place. He angled a sharp glance at Philo. "Where's Mule?"

"Why?"

"Because one of us has to get up to the mine, and I'm the logical choice."

Philo shook his head firmly. "Oh, no, you don't. I'm goin'. You're stayin' here with Courtney."

"And what if something's happened to Moonshine?"

"Then I'll bring him back. It could be nothin'. Maybe he had a fall. Maybe he found a strike."

"And maybe Tyree Caine has struck again."

"Maybe." Philo squinted in the early morning sun. "And maybe Tyree's just trying to get you away from here so's he can get to Courtney again. You ever think of that?"

Heath glanced toward the door and scowled. "Maybe Tyree's just trying to lure you up to the mine so he can kill you when there's nobody else around. You ever think of that? At least here you'd have the cabin for protection, and you're as good with a shotgun as any man. You can protect Courtney as well as I can."

"Maybe so, but if you're dead, she's not going to forgive either one of us."

"She won't forgive us if *you're* dead, either," Heath pointed out. "Which is why I'll go. You stay. It's the best chance we both have to stay alive."

Philo looked as if he was going to argue further, but something changed his mind. He nodded once and waved a hand toward the camp. "Mule's over there. You know where I keep her."

Heath nodded once and turned back to the cabin. Courtney would argue with him about his decision. He knew that, but he couldn't send an old man up into those hills where anything might happen.

Back inside, he found her waiting, and from the look on her face he knew she'd heard every word. She stood near the fire with her arms wrapped around herself, her face sad and her eyes weary. "Do you have to go?"

"Who else will?"

"Philo." She rolled her eyes as she said the old man's name, and Heath knew she wasn't serious. She worried about the old goat too much. "Or we could all go together. That way nobody would have to be out there alone."

Heath crossed to her and pulled her into his arms. "There are a couple of problems with that idea. The first one is, Mule is our only means of transportation. We can't all ride her, and if Moonshine's in trouble, he could die before we get to him on foot. The second is, if you're there you'll be a distraction. I'll be more worried about keeping you safe than about myself. Call me selfish, but I want to come back in one piece."

"And I want you to."

He kissed her briefly. "Then stay inside until I get back. Philo will stay with you and you'll have Geezer."

She wrapped her arms around his waist and pressed her head against his chest. "You'll be careful, won't you?"

"You have no idea." He finally had something to live for. He wasn't going to let Tyree Caine take it away now.

Half an hour later found him riding Mule through the foothills, passing along the boundaries of claims, dodging everything from rocks hurled by suspicious miners to mildly curious glances. The higher he climbed, the more strongly he sensed autumn in the air. The sun was losing strength and the air was downright frigid at the higher altitudes.

He remained watchful, alert for any sign of Tyree Caine or his cohorts, or for any hint that Moonshine had been through there. He stopped at several mines to ask questions, but if anyone knew anything about Tyree Caine, they weren't talking about him, and that left Heath with a very bad feeling.

For the first time since his arrival he was glad there were no trees or undergrowth left to hide behind. It lessened his chances of riding into an ambush. He wound along the river-bed and finally drew up in front of the handmade sign that marked the Jezebel.

He dismounted quickly and checked the tent, walked the stretch of creek bed that ran the length of Philo's claim and climbed the two short hills to the boundary with the claim behind it marked by a sternly worded but badly misspelled warning to keep out.

But if Moonshine had been there at all, there was no sign of him now. Heath dreaded taking the news back down the hill to Courtney and Philo. They'd both feel guilty for involving Moonshine. Hell, *he* felt guilty and none of this had been his idea.

He just knew that if there was one hair out of place on that boy's head, he'd make Tyree Caine answer for it.

They waited all afternoon for Moonshine to come staggering back into camp. Drunk, hurt, tired, lost—none of them cared how he came back, just as long as he showed up. They waited all evening for some word from Tyree Caine. Some hint of what he wanted or some sign that he was taking responsibility for Moonshine's disappearance.

By midnight Heath was afraid that all the discussion they'd had about what might have happened to Moonshine was just wasted breath. Philo seemed resigned to losing yet another friend and partner. Even Courtney seemed to be losing hope.

By morning, when there was still no sign of the boy, Heath knew that the stakes had risen again. None of them might make it out of this alive. There were a dozen or more unfinished pieces of business in his life. Things he couldn't leave undone if something happened to him. The time for tiptoeing around Delilah was over.

The day had dawned cloudy and gray. Heath had to work hard to shake the feeling that the weather was some kind of omen as he waited down the street from the Pink Parasol. His eyes burned from an accumulated lack of sleep over the past few weeks, and his heart lay heavy with worry.

He waited while Delilah and Derry went through their weekly ritual, then walked up behind her and touched her lightly on the shoulder.

She whipped around, smiling, probably expecting to find that Derry had come back. When she saw Heath standing there, her smile faded. "What are you doing?"

"Waiting for a chance to talk with you."

She glanced up the street, then down. "You were watching me, weren't you? Spying on me."

"I think 'spying' is a little harsh, don't you?" Heath pulled off his hat and worked up a trustworthy sort of smile. "I need to talk to you, Delilah. It's important."

She turned away sharply. "I've already told you, I have nothing to say to you, and I don't want to hear anything you have to say." When he fell into step beside her, she sent him a look that could have cut a lesser man dead in his tracks. "Leave me alone."

"Why?"

"I've told you."

"You've told me nothing. Hell, Delilah, I've known you since we were children, and you won't even give me the time of day. Derry's known you what? A week? Two?"

Delilah's mouth curved in derision and a very ugly fire flamed in her eyes. "Are you jealous, Heath?"

"No! Of course not. You misunderstand what I'm trying to say." And she *had*. Absolutely. "I've never felt that way toward you, Delilah. Not that you aren't a beautiful woman. Because you are. But you were always Blue's girl, and you were my friend. Hell, I thought of you as a sister, almost."

"Almost? *Almost* a sister?" She laughed through her nose and turned her gaze away. "I shouldn't be surprised, should I? It would be asking too much to think you'd feel any other way." Her cultured voice slipped a little. "But don't be thinkin' I'm gone fall all over myself 'cuz you be callin' me friend and tellin' me I'm *almost* like a sister."

Confused and irritated, Heath grabbed her by both shoulders and spun her around to face him. This wasn't the conversation he wanted to have. It wasn't the conversation he *needed* to have. And the stress of standing guard against

Tyree Caine and losing Moonshine ate through his self-control. "I don't mind bearing the weight of my own sins. God knows, I deserve every bit of hatred you send my way for what I've done. But my own sins are heavy enough without adding sins I *didn't* commit onto the pile. And I really hate being blamed for something *I* know nothing about. God in heaven, Delilah, *some* people would be pleased by the idea that someone else in the world cared so much about them."

Her eyes burned and color infused her cheeks. Her cultured voice disappeared completely as the anger took over. "Maybe *some* people didn't grow up listening to their mother cry herself to sleep after *your* daddy came visitin' at night. Maybe *some* people wasn't sold off by they own daddy to a man so mean even his own darkies was tryin' to figure a way to kill him. Maybe they didn't spend the next four years of they lives workin' the fields and gettin' visits of their own at night from the overseer. And maybe they didn't have to buy they own freedom at the cost of they own soul. So don' be talkin' about *some* people to me, Heath Sullivan. I have no use for *some* people, nor for you, neither."

Heath heard every word she said, but his mind refused to process them all at once. His father . . . and *Birdie*? His father and *any* of the slaves? He stood in numb silence while her words replayed again and again, and he tried desperately to hear them differently this time. He knew she was glaring at him, waiting for—and deserving—a response. But honest to God, saying anything was beyond him. She'd flattened him so thoroughly, he was having trouble getting air into his lungs.

One by one, the other words fell away and left one line running relentlessly through his head. Sold off by her own father? She hadn't meant that the way it sounded. Surely. Oh, God. No, surely she hadn't meant that the way it sounded. She couldn't have.

Her lip curled in disgust and she pivoted away. He tried to say something, but his voice still refused to work. He didn't know how to feel, and he wasn't sure why. It had nothing to do with her being a slave, with her mother being a slave, with his father being their *owner*, dammit. It had everything to do with the sheer disgusting brutality and bestiality of it, and with the sickening knowledge that that man's blood ran through Heath's veins.

He knew he should say something, should reassure her that the look of horror and revulsion on his face had nothing to do with her, and everything to do with himself. But he couldn't move and he couldn't speak, and he couldn't even lift a finger to stop her when she strode away.

It wasn't until much later that Heath realized he'd forgotten to warn her about Tyree Caine or mention the boy at all.

Courtney was almost certain that her heart had taken up permanent residence in her throat. From the minute Heath had stepped out of the door the day before until the minute he'd come back with the bad news that Moonshine was missing, she'd paced and worried, inched back the blankets over the windows and watched the street, chewed her nails and eaten too much, and then worried that she wouldn't be able to keep it down.

Philo had tried to reassure her, but he couldn't guarantee that Heath would be back, and they both knew it.

And now this morning she was doing it again. Heath was out looking for Delilah. Courtney was left behind to hold down the fort, or keep an eye on Philo, or whatever excuse you wanted to use. Whatever, the B movie translation was "the girl stays behind."

She wasn't eager for another confrontation with Tyree Caine, but if Heath was going to be out there, she'd like to be with him. Staying behind and being kept in the dark was just too hard.

Only the certain knowledge that she would have been more of a hindrance than a help kept her from giving the Spunky Heroine Speech she'd read in so many books and heard in countless movies. It always started with some adaptation of, "Listen, buddy, this is *my* car," and ended with, "I'm going with you, so get used to it."

Her version had a little less to it. It ran something like, "Listen, buddy, I'm in love with you. If you're going to get yourself killed, I don't want to be left behind." Not the most compelling version she'd ever heard.

With a sharp laugh, she tore a biscuit in half and popped a piece into her mouth. Philo looked at her strangely, but she wasn't ready to talk her feelings out, and he didn't ask. Which only made her love him more.

They'd been sitting that way for an hour or more, Courtney shredding biscuits and eating the edible remains, Philo whittling, and Geezer dozing, when a noise outside brought the dog out of a sound sleep, startling Courtney so much she nearly choked on her biscuit.

Philo was on his feet before she could swallow. He had the shotgun up and aimed at the door, and he motioned for her to stay where she was. She'd thought her heart was in her throat before. Now it was in her mouth.

"What if it's Heath?" she whispered so low she could barely hear her own voice.

But Philo heard. He nodded once to show that he'd be careful and turned his attention back toward the door. Footsteps crunched and popped as someone walked across the tiny bits of gravel lining the walk outside the door. Courtney's hands began to tingle, but she shook them to get the feeling back. She couldn't afford to go numb now.

Scarcely able to breathe, she watched Philo inch toward the window. What if it wasn't Heath? What if something happened to Philo? She wouldn't even be able to defend herself. Why hadn't she let Heath teach her how to use the shotgun? She vowed that if she didn't die this morning, she *would* learn.

After several minutes Philo motioned again and crept soundlessly back to where she sat. "I think they're gone."

"What were they doing here?"

"I don't know, but I aim to find out." He turned toward the door, but Courtney grabbed his arm before he could get away.

"You can't open the door. If anything happens to you, we're both dead."

Philo cocked his head thoughtfully. "You could be right. But we can't just sit here without knowing."

"Then let me look. You can cover me."

"And have something happen to you? Not a chance."

Courtney stood so that she could look him in the eye. "I've been sitting here for two days doing nothing, Philo. I can't stand it anymore. So either you cover me, or I cover you. Take your pick."

He smiled reluctantly. "Yep. You should a' been my daughter, all right." He sobered and jerked his head toward the door. "Be careful. Move slow so if they're still out there they can't hear you. If you hear anything, drop to the ground and take cover. You got that? I'm not gonna be the one to tell Heath that I let you get shot."

"I don't expect you to," she assured him. "So be very, very good at what you do, okay?" Now that she had something to do, she felt better in one way and a whole lot worse in another. Her hands began to tingle again and her feet soon followed. She could hear that same strange buzzing noise she'd heard inside the shed.

No. *No!* She couldn't go back now. Not *now*. Not while Heath was still in danger and Moonshine still missing. Not while Heath's past was still unresolved and she was just finding a way to put her own to rest.

Not now, she begged silently. *Please, not yet.*

She moved toward the window and carefully nudged back the blanket. She craned to see out into the yard, expecting at any moment to hear the volley of shots and feel a bullet rip into her flesh. But nothing happened and the silence gave her courage.

She turned to give Philo a thumbs-up and realized that Geezer had crossed to stand in front of the door. He tilted his head to one side and whined softly in his throat. She and Philo exchanged a glance. He moved to stand beside the bed, then nodded for her to open the door.

Seconds felt like hours as she lifted the latch and pulled the door open, but she saw the inert body in the yard as soon as she could see outside, and it took a heartbeat or less to recognize Moonshine lying facedown in the dirt.

Without thinking, she sprinted into the yard and shouted over her shoulder to Philo, "It's Moonshine. He's hurt." She raced across the yard toward him, praying frantically that he was only hurt and not dead.

She reached him in three strides and hunkered down beside him. But when she realized that Philo hadn't followed her, she realized for the first time that Tyree might have been using Moonshine as bait to lure them outside. Her hands grew clammy and her throat grew dry, but she was here now and she wasn't going back inside without Moonshine.

Thank God he wasn't a large man, so she had no trouble rolling him onto his back so she could check for a pulse more easily. She pressed her ear to his chest and heard the steady beating of his heart, and she felt weak with relief. Thank God. Thank God.

"He's alive," she called to Philo. "I think he's going to be okay."

She glanced back at Philo's dear old face and saw lines formed by concern and guilt. At least none of them had to live with the guilt of putting Moonshine in danger in the first place.

She stood, fully intending to help Moonshine back into the cabin, but her fingers began to tingle again and numbness spread like a wildfire up into her hands. The deep bass electric sound began to pulse in her ears and the edges of her vision were blurred by a strange, bright light.

Her knees gave way and she collapsed into the dirt at Moonshine's side. Almost at once, the light faded and the pulsing sound disappeared. But she knew that next time, it would be stronger. And it was only a matter of time before it wouldn't go away at all.

Chapter 17

COURTNEY FAIRLY JUMPED out of her skin as she and Philo got Moonshine into the cabin and made him comfortable in the bed. She chewed her nails breathlessly while Philo gave him a "look-see" and determined that he'd been roughed up, but his most serious injury appeared to be a broken arm. When Philo mentioned needing help to hold the boy while he set the broken arm, Courtney leaped at the chance to leave the cabin.

She found Noah and another prospector that she recognized by sight and sent them to the cabin, then hurried toward town to look for Heath. Maybe wandering around on her own wasn't the smartest thing she'd ever done, but she didn't think Tyree Caine and his boys would strike again so soon, and she didn't have time to proceed with caution.

She shivered in the early October chill and walked fast in an effort to keep herself warm. Somehow while she wasn't looking, the last of summer had slipped away and autumn had settled in. The date for her appointment in New York had come and gone, and she'd been so busy falling in love with everyone and everything around her, she'd hardly noticed it passing. Now there was a very real threat that she'd be taken away from this life and dropped back into that one, and she couldn't think of anything worse.

She tried to stay focused on what she wanted to do. She wanted to find Heath and tell him, not just about finding Moonshine alive and relatively unhurt, but about . . . just *everything*. About how dear he'd become to her. About how much a part of her he'd become. About things she didn't even know how to put into words. She needed him to truly know how much she loved him just in case she never got the chance to tell him again.

He'd been gone for hours, though, and she had no idea where to look. All she knew was that he'd gone to see Delilah, but she didn't know where Delilah lived or how to find her. She could wander for hours looking for a cabin squatting among the tents on the other side of Nevada City and still never find it.

In desperation, she decided to begin her search at the Pink Parasol. Maybe things had gone badly with Delilah and Heath had gone back there to drown his sorrows. Except Heath rarely drank anymore. Not like he used to, anyway. She rarely caught any hint of alcohol on his breath these days.

But if things had gone well with Delilah, wouldn't he have come back to the cabin already? Yes. He would have. She *knew* he would have—if he could.

She found the Pink Parasol without even looking hard. It was a small two-story saloon constructed of cut timber rather than logs—and fairly recently from the looks of it. Two large windows gave out onto the street. Between them was a set of swinging doors that would have looked right at home in any western movie.

She stood just inside the doors for a minute or two, scanning the crowd and praying that Heath would be there. After six weeks in Virginia City, she was used to the men. The women were a different story entirely. A man she thought was Heath for a fraction of a minute sat on the far side of the saloon nuzzling a chubby woman with a horse face and a set of bright red curls. She wore a revealing concoction of garish purple and black and brayed a laugh that rose above the honky-tonk piano, then buried her face in the man's neck.

Courtney dragged her attention away from them and found

herself captivated instead by the miners at the bar. One by one they noticed her and fell silent. Even the piano player stopped banging on the keys, and the sudden quiet was almost eerie.

Itching with self-consciousness, Courtney did her best to smile as she stepped inside. She'd only taken a couple of steps when a small young man jumped up from his seat and swept off his hat. "Ma'am." Courtney tried to move around him, but he shifted with her. "Begging your pardon, ma'am, but this ain't no place for a lady."

Oh, please. This was not the time to start pushing *that* button. "I appreciate your concern," she said, "but I'm not here to disturb anyone. I'm looking for a man."

Someone in the back of the room roared a suggestion that made her face burn, but the other prospectors shut him up almost before he finished speaking. The poor sods lining the bar looked as stricken as their modern counterparts might if a woman wandered into the men's room. If she hadn't been so edgy and anxious herself, she might even have laughed.

"I'm looking for one man in particular," she corrected herself. "His name is Heath Sullivan. Do any of you know him?"

Nobody admitted to it, but Courtney could tell by the looks on several faces that she'd come to the right place. "It's important that I find him," she pressed. "If you know where he is, please say so."

The young man whose self-assigned job it was to protect her delicate sensibilities kicked at something only he could see, but at least he deigned to answer. "He hasn't been in here all day, ma'am."

"Are you sure?"

The boy lifted his red face and looked her straight in the eye. "Yes, ma'am. 'Cept to . . . take care of business, I haven't moved from that chair since morning."

Courtney couldn't hide her disappointment. "How about the rest of you? Does anyone know where he is?"

Very slowly a man at a poker table in the back of the room stood. He was easily as tall as Heath, and roughly the same age, but he had dark hair and a deep five-o'clock shadow on his cheeks and chin. "If you'll pardon me for sayin', ma'am, I don't think Mr. Sullivan would be happy to see you in here."

"I'm sure you're right, but that's not my biggest concern right now. Is there a manager here? Someone who might be able to tell me where to find one of the girls who works here?"

That caught the redhead's attention. She leaned away from her prospector and fixed Courtney with an unhappy glare. "What girl?"

Too late, Courtney realized that by announcing Heath's interest in Delilah aloud, she could be breaking her promise to keep Delilah's past a secret. "I—I'm not sure. I just—" She didn't lie well. Never had. And she wasn't any good at backpedaling over a mistake, either. Following a flash of instinct, she tried to look jealous and hurt. "He mentioned a woman named Delilah. I'd like to see her."

The redhead stood and jiggled the front of her camisole with one hand so that her breasts would settle properly. "You think Charming's gone looking for her?"

Charming? Courtney glanced at the man beside her and took another long look at the redhead who seemed to know Heath. She wondered . . . shook off the question and told herself firmly that she didn't want to know. As long as they weren't still acquainted, some things were better left alone.

"I think Heath may be trying to see her. Yes." Drawing on her memories of Leslie at her worst, Courtney managed a haughty lift of her chin and a shuddering sigh that she hoped sounded distraught. "I just want him to come home." And then, with a silent apology to Delilah, she curled her lip and went for self-righteous. "Do you know where I could find this . . . *woman?*"

The man at her side touched her elbow gently. "There's a chance I might be able to help. If you don't mind me walking outside with ye."

Courtney was set to refuse again, but the look in his eye changed her mind. With one last glance at the redhead, Courtney pivoted toward the door and hurried onto the boardwalk with her escort a step behind. Instantly, as if someone had sounded an "all clear" whistle, conversations resumed in the saloon and the piano player started banging out a sour rendition of "Dixie."

Once outside, her companion took the lead and moved a little ways away from the door before he spoke. There was something warm and comforting about his smile, but she couldn't put her finger on what it was. "You'll be wondering who I am, no doubt."

"As a matter of fact, I am."

"Roderick Dennehy at your service. And now perhaps you'll do me the honor?"

"Dennehy? Are you serious?" Goose bumps raced across her skin, and Courtney wondered if this man was somehow related to Ryan or if it was some strange coincidence. When she realized that she'd been staring, she gave an embarrassed laugh and held out a hand. "I'm Courtney Moss, and I'm very happy to meet you." He grinned and she had her answer. And somehow knowing that she was with one of Ryan's ancestors took away the last of her nervousness. "I'm sorry. I don't mean to stare. It's just that you remind me of someone. Someone very special to me."

"Do I now?" That grin curved his mouth again, and tears stung Courtney's eyes. "Well, isn't that fine?"

"You have no idea." Courtney forced away the tears and tried to focus on her real reason for being there. "Do you really know where to find Delilah?"

"I do."

"How?"

"The fact is that I intend to marry her some day. From the sound of it, though, I may have competition—and from a man I thought I might call friend."

"You want to marry Delilah?"

A gust of wind lifted the hair away from his forehead. "Honest and proper."

Courtney shivered in the chill blast, but the knowledge that Heath would be thrilled to know that someone loved and wanted to care for Delilah warmed her. "Will you show me where to find her? It's important."

Derry tipped his hat and motioned her forward. "My pleasure. As long as you don't mind me givin' Heath a solid pop in the nose when we find him."

Courtney laughed for the first time in days. "There won't be any need for that. His interest in her is not what you think."

The hope in Derry's eyes touched her heart. She wished that she could set his mind at ease, but she'd already come dangerously close to breaking Heath's confidence. She'd have to let Delilah or Heath tell him the rest of the story.

She wondered if he knew about Delilah's son. She wondered if he knew about Delilah's heritage and whether he would care. But she told herself that if he could be responsible in any way for Ryan—one of the dearest, kindest, sweetest, most generous people alive, in *any* century—Delilah's background wouldn't matter. She hoped so. She hadn't even met Delilah yet, but she liked thinking that Ryan had descended from such a wonderful union.

Derry set a rapid pace in the cool breeze, and Courtney's legs were burning by the time the small cabin on the outskirts of Nevada City came into view. When she saw the squat cabin with its listing walls, her heart sank. By comparison, this place made her cabin look like a palace. Even from a distance she could tell that no one had patched the spaces between the logs, which meant that it must have been freezing in there. Bad enough for adults, but how was the child faring?

She turned to say something to Derry and realized that he'd stopped walking a few feet earlier. She doubled back toward him, scowling in confusion. "Is that it?"

"It is."

"Then why—?"

"Delilah isn't aware that I know about this place, and I don't want her to know."

"But—"

He worked up another Ryan grin and turned aside. "She'll tell me when she's ready."

"But what am *I* supposed to tell her? How do I explain how I found this place?"

"I suppose you'll think of something." He sent a longing

glance toward the cabin and his grin faded. "It's not that I'm leaving you in the lurch. It's just that if I don't let her proceed at her own pace, I'll frighten her away."

Courtney touched his arm gently. She had no idea how much Derry knew about Delilah, but from what Heath had told her, his instincts were right on. Wasn't it funny that she'd had to come into the past to find the kind of men who loved and cared about the women in their lives? The kind of men who kept their promises and lived up to their commitments?

Or maybe they'd always been there but she'd been too blind to see them.

"You're right," she said. "I'll think of something. Go on before she sees you."

She waited until Derry had disappeared, then squared her shoulders and climbed the steep hill that led to Delilah's cabin. But it took all of her courage to knock on the door, and if she hadn't been so frightened of being sucked back into the future without one last chance to see Heath, she probably wouldn't have found the courage at all.

It took a while for the door to open, and when it did Courtney found herself looking at one of the most beautiful women she'd ever seen. A goddess with a Halle Berry face and creamy skin with just the slightest touch of something exotic about her eyes. She took Courtney in with a sweeping glance, and her face set itself into stern, wary lines. "Yes?"

"Delilah?"

The wariness doubled. Tripled. Her eyes rounded and her gaze flicked out to the yard and back again. "Who are you?"

"My name is Courtney Moss. I'm a friend of Heath Sullivan's."

At the mention of Heath's name, Delilah's eyes grew hard. "What do you want?"

"I'm looking for him. I was hoping you might know where I could find him."

Delilah took a step backward and gripped the door with both hands as if she intended to shut it in Courtney's face. "I haven't seen him."

Another gust of wind made Courtney hunch deep into her

shirt, but the thin cotton didn't offer any protection from the cold. "But he came looking for you this morning. You must have seen him. Please. It's important. I'm not here to harm you. I just need to find him."

Delilah shook her head firmly and started again to close the door.

Courtney stepped in front of it and kept it from latching. "Please, Delilah. Please. It might be my last chance to see him. Please don't deny me that."

For a second or two Delilah acted as if she hadn't heard, then slowly her eyes lifted to Courtney's and she nodded once. "I saw him. But that was early this morning. I don't know where he is now."

Courtney sagged against the door frame in frustration. If Heath wasn't here, where *was* he? Her gaze drifted across the tiny room, and she saw the other two people for the first time—an elderly woman with chocolate skin and thick gray hair, and a boy with wide innocent eyes who was watching every move she made.

Courtney smiled at Delilah. "He's a beautiful boy. You must be very proud."

Delilah stiffened and shoved at the door for a third time. "What makes you think he's mine?"

Courtney felt one brief flash of hatred for any woman who would deny her own child. Old anger at Leslie flared through her and everything she'd ever longed to say to her own mother rose to her lips. But when her eyes met Delilah's and she saw the deep fear mirrored there, her anger evaporated before it began.

"I'm sorry. I—" She shook her head in despair and wondered if she'd ever learn to keep her big mouth shut. "I'm sorry. I didn't mean to say the wrong thing. It's just that—" She cut herself off with a wave of her hand and started away from the cabin.

"It's just that what?"

She turned slowly back to face Delilah. "It's just that he's a beautiful boy, Delilah. And you're not in this alone. You have no idea how much Heath cares about you. You have no idea how much he wants to help you and make sure the two of you have what you need."

Delilah shut the door behind her and came closer. "Heath told you all this?"

"Yes. And don't be angry with him for that. He cares so much it's eating him up alive. He had to talk to someone, and he trusted me." She laughed sharply and gestured at herself. "Of course, I've totally blown it now by telling you. He'll probably never trust me again. But you know what? If it helps mend this rift between the two of you, it might just be worth it. I love him and I want to be with him forever, but even more than that I want him to be happy. And he won't be. He *can't* be until you start being his friend again."

Delilah rubbed her arms for warmth and looked toward the hills. Silence stretched between them for so long, Courtney went through half a dozen emotions from hope to frustration to resignation before Delilah sighed and looked back at her again. "He could be down at the river," she said quietly. "The river at Bonne Chance was always his thinking place."

The rush of relief that surged through Courtney was so strong, she could barely catch her breath. "Thank you. Thank you." She started away, then raced back and threw her arms around Delilah. "Thank you. You have no idea how grateful I am."

Delilah still looked cautious, but she did manage a thin smile before she turned away and went back into the cabin. And Courtney held on to that smile, and the fact that Delilah had warmed enough to suggest where to look for Heath, as signs that things might work out between them, after all.

Now, if she could only figure out where to look along the river. . . .

Delilah had been right, of course. She found him along the banks of Alder Creek in the one place along the rocky shoreline where someone might go to think.

It wasn't until she got a good look at his face that it occurred to her to wonder why Delilah had guessed that he might be here. Something was wrong. His mouth was turned down in a deep frown, his brow creased with worry. Sadness and something else she couldn't identify filled his eyes.

He looked up at the sound of her footsteps and made a valiant effort to wipe the worry from his expression. But even with the threat of the future looming over her, she couldn't make herself press for an explanation.

"Courtney?" He'd been a million miles away, and it took a visible effort to pull himself back to the moment. "What are you doing here?"

"I've been looking for you." She moved toward him, uncertain what to say and what not to say. "I thought you'd like to know that we found Moonshine."

He blinked a couple of times as if he was having trouble understanding her. "Is he all right?"

"Philo thinks his arm is broken, and he's been roughed up a little, but he's alive and his heartbeat is strong. I think he'll be fine."

Heath smiled, but the effort seemed to take everything he had. In the face of his distress, Courtney's concerns faded to nothing.

"That's good." His smile flickered and died. "That's real good. I'm glad." He ran a hand across his face and turned partially away.

Courtney's heart raced and curiosity nearly killed her. She moved closer still and touched his hand with her fingertips. "What's wrong, Heath?"

He shook his head as if he couldn't find the words to verbalize it.

"Whatever it is, you can tell me."

"I don't think so." He slid a glance filled with misery at her. "It's not that kind of problem."

She wanted so desperately to help him, but he seemed so shattered she felt helpless to do anything. Yet she felt instinctively that to turn around and walk away would be the wrong thing to do. "What kind of problem is it?"

"Mine."

"Really? There's no one else involved?"

This time the look in his eyes was filled with resentment.

"Solving my problem isn't going to get you back to the future, if that's what you're thinking."

He might as well have slapped her. It couldn't have hurt any more. "That's not why I'm asking. I'm asking because I love you and you're obviously very upset. I thought maybe it would help to talk about it."

"I don't think so."

One half of her heart told her to let him wallow. The other half knew that he was standing on the edge of an emotional chasm and she had to help him find his way across. "It has something to do with Delilah, doesn't it?"

He didn't say a word. He didn't have to. His eyes answered for him.

"You're surprised that I figured it out? Well, don't be. I've already talked to her. How do you think I knew where to find you?"

That got his attention. He looked at her—*really* looked at her for the first time since she'd arrived. "You talked to Delilah?"

"Briefly."

"Then she told you?"

Courtney might have been able to manipulate the answer she wanted by lying, but she wouldn't do that to their relationship. If it was ever to be anything good or strong or right, it had to be based in truth. "No. She only told me that you used to think by the river at Bonne Chance."

That should have brought a dozen angry questions to life, but Heath accepted it and turned away again. She waited, scarcely breathing, for him to talk to her. For him to share this painful moment and allow her all the way into his life. But he remained stiff-shouldered and silent for so long, she nearly gave up hope.

"You might be right," he said after what felt like forever. "Maybe I do need to talk it out. God knows, I can't figure out what to think myself.

"I'll listen." Courtney took two steps closer and slipped her hand into his, but she took care not to pressure him.

He glanced at their joined hands and smiled faintly. "I told you that Delilah was a slave on Bonne Chance. . . ."

"Yes."

"Well, I found out today that she was far more than that."
His lips thinned and his eyes grew cold. "She informed me
this morning, that my father ..." He stopped, swallowed
hard, and looked away.

Courtney had heard stories about life on some plantations,
and two possibilities leapt into her mind immediately. But
she remained carefully quiet and waited for Heath to tell her
on his own.

"I always knew that my father had a fondness for Birdie,
but I thought—" He broke off with a bitter laugh and slanted
a cold glance at her. "You should know that you're holding
the hand of a blind fool who's been so caught up in his own
head for so long, he couldn't even bother to notice the most
obvious things right in front of his eyes. I *thought* that my
mother's animosity toward Birdie was unusual, but I didn't
realize that she hated her because my father snuck out to the
slave quarters, that Birdie was the object of his affection, or
that Delilah—"

He broke off again and rubbed his eyes with his free hand.
"She's my sister, Courtney. My own flesh and blood. She's
my father's *daughter*. As much a part of him as I am. But
he never told me. I'm thirty years old and I never knew that
she was my sister until today."

Courtney's lungs expelled all the air they held and her
stomach knotted in the face of his pain. "But you know
now."

"Yes. I do." Heath swung around in agitation. "I know
now. Now that she's been through hell. Now that she's been
raped by overseers and sold into prostitution. I know now. I
know that my father sold his own daughter like a piece of
furniture. That's what I come from. That's what you're in
love with."

Such wretchedness filled his eyes, Courtney's heart ached.
She tilted her face to the sky and drew in a deep breath. The
scent of wood smoke hovered on the fringes of her consciousness, but she could also detect the crisp scent of river
water and the musty smell of wet earth.

"You're wrong. I'm in love with you, and you are not

him. What he did was wrong. Horribly, unforgivably wrong. But you could never be like him. Not if you tried for a million years. You don't have it in you."

"And what if I do?"

She turned to face him and took his other hand in hers. "You won't allow yourself to be, Heath." When he snorted a brittle laugh, she said again, "*You won't.* If the temptation arises to treat someone unfairly, you won't give in. I've seen you in action, remember? You didn't have to take me to the cabin and give me a home, but you did. You didn't have to muck stables to buy my breakfast, but you did. You didn't have to go to bat for Philo and listen to Moonshine talking about Miss Geneva Openshaw, or give Geezer a bath and let him sleep by the fire. But you *did.* You did all of that in the short time I've known you. There are some people who never do that much good in a lifetime."

"This is different."

"No, it's not. You won't get to a place where you're tempted to make a choice like the one your father made if you don't take little steps along the way to get there. It takes a lot of hard work to desensitize yourself that much. Every day you're alive, a thousand times a day, you'll make little choices that define what kind of person you are. It's the little choices that count the most, Heath. And you make those all the time."

He turned away in disbelief, but Courtney wasn't about to give up now.

"You said yourself that you didn't notice what your father was becoming. Isn't that what you told me?"

He looked back and offered a grudging nod, and she knew that she had his attention.

"Then you know it didn't happen all at once. You don't have to become him, Heath. It's not written in the stars or decreed by Fate. You choose who you want to be. You can't bring Blue back, but you can make life right and good for Delilah and that little boy. And you aren't alone. There's a good man out there who wants to marry her. I'll bet that he'd do everything in his power to make her happy."

"Are you talking about Derry Dennehy?"

"Yes. You know him?"

"We've met."

"He seems like a good man. I think he'd be a good father to your nephew."

He let out a soft laugh tinged with disbelief. "My nephew."

"Your nephew and Blue's son. A little human being who is part of both of you. Isn't that the most incredible miracle ever?"

He looked at her hard and the intense pain shifted subtly. "Just about."

Courtney gave his hand a gentle squeeze. "Don't waste a minute worrying about your father. He has no part of this. *They're* your family, and whether Delilah is ready to admit it or not, they need you. And you need them."

He nodded slowly and trailed his gaze to the tops of the trees. Almost absently he lifted her hand to his lips and pressed a kiss to her fingers. "At least now I know why she's been so angry with me. She thinks I knew all along."

"But you didn't, and I know that if you'll keep trying she'll listen to you. She's not an unreasonable woman. She's just hurt and frightened."

"I hope you're right." He shuddered once and the tension seemed to leave his body. He pulled her to him and wrapped his arms around her. "I hope to God you're right."

She leaned against him, drinking in the sense of him and trying to memorize his scent, the rhythm of his heart, the sound of his voice. She thought about telling him why she'd come looking for him in the first place, but this wasn't the time or the place for that. And besides, she saw no need to worry him with something neither of them could control.

He had far too much on his mind already.

Chapter 18

COURTNEY STOOD ON a chair in front of the window and struggled to peg an extra blanket over the opening. Wind whistled past the walls and dust devils danced across the hillsides. The overcast skies had grown dark and the threat of rain hung over the valley. Gloom pervaded everything.

Heath and Philo had gone out to search for other prospectors who might be willing to stand up against Tyree Caine, leaving Courtney to look after Moonshine. The boy seemed a lot stronger than he had two days earlier, but Courtney still didn't think he was ready to sleep on the cold ground in a tent.

She glanced over her shoulder, caught Moonshine watching her, and smiled. "Are you okay? Do you need anything?"

He blushed and averted his gaze, just like he did every time she made eye contact. "I'm fine."

"Are you warm enough? Heath found some extra quilts in the pine storage box. I can get you one if you want."

The boy's Adam's apple bobbed in his thin neck, and he struggled to slide a glance close to her face. "Thank you, but I'm fine. Really."

"Then how about coffee? That'll help take the chill off."

"Naw. I don't want you to go to any trouble."

Courtney could have pointed out that making coffee wasn't anywhere near the bother that letting him sleep in her bed for two nights had been, but she was pretty sure he wouldn't see the humor. She hopped from the chair to the floor and dusted her hands on the back of her jeans. "You know what? It isn't any trouble at all. I'm making some for myself. I'll just make a little extra."

He slid another glance in her direction, and this one came even closer to touching her face. "You sure Heath doesn't mind you and me being alone like this? I mean it doesn't seem right, you being a lady and all."

Courtney bit her lip to keep from smiling. "And you being a gentleman?"

"That's right." This time, his gaze actually landed on her face for a split second. "I'm not as fancy as some, but I do know what's seemly and what's not."

"I understand all that," she assured him somberly. "But we're out here in the middle of nowhere and you're hurt. And besides, I really don't want to sit out this storm alone. So it seems to me that a few of the rules can fall by the wayside, don't you think?"

Moonshine pondered that for a minute, scratched above his ear with one finger, and shrugged. "I suppose that would be okay—as long as Heath doesn't get the wrong idea."

"I'm sure he understands." Courtney carried the coffeepot to the table and pulled the tin of coffee from the shelf Philo had tacked up a few days earlier. "I've known you almost two months, and I don't think we've ever really talked. Why don't you tell me something about yourself. Like what you're doing in Montana. I don't want to sound rude, but aren't you a little young to be in a place like this?"

Moonshine leaned back against the pillow and did his best to look old and tough. "He—heck *no*." A slow flush crept into his cheeks, but the damage she'd done to his pride was stronger than embarrassment at a near slip. "I'm here to make my fortune, same as everybody else."

Courtney smiled to herself and ladled water into the pot.

"And what will you *do* with your fortune when you make it?"

"I'll marry my sweetheart, that's what."

"Miss Geneva Openshaw from Fayette County, Ohio?"

Moonshine's face burned, but he nodded eagerly.

"She's waiting for you?"

A proud grin split the boy's face, and he leaned up a little on the pillow. "She sure is."

Courtney's heart warmed at the look on his face, and she hoped for his sake that the girl *was* waiting. She put the coffee on the fire, pulled the crock of sourdough starter from the shelf, and measured some into a bowl. "When was the last time you heard from her?"

"Couple of months ago."

In this day and age, that was probably the equivalent of a phone call the day before. "And what does she look like?"

Everything on Moonshine's face grew soft. "She has hair the color of new-plowed soil and eyes as green as spring grass. And she sings like an angel—an angel straight from heaven. Matter of fact, it wouldn't surprise me to find out that's what she really is."

Courtney measured flour into the bowl and worked the mixture through her fingers to make dough. "Well, Miss Geneva Openshaw is one lucky woman," she said after a minute or two. "It's wonderful to know that someone loves you, don't you think?"

Moonshine sighed happily. "I've loved Geneva since I was thirteen and she was eleven. Mama says Geneva should be proud of being a farmer's wife, but Geneva doesn't want that. She watched her own mother work herself to practically nothing, having babies and working in the fields alongside her pa. She doesn't want that kind of life, and I don't want it for her." He smoothed one hand along the front of his shirt and smiled to himself. "I aim to give her the life she deserves."

"And you're here to make your fortune so you can." Courtney smiled at the lovesick boy in front of her. "How does she feel about you being so far away?"

"She don't like it," Moonshine admitted. "But it'll all be worth it. She'll see."

"Has it ever occurred to you that maybe she'd rather have you than money? That maybe she'd rather hold your hand in an evening, even if it meant spending some time on the farm while you saved for another kind of life?"

Moonshine scowled up at her. "There ain't no saving on the farm, ma'am. My pa goes years without seeing more than a few cents' cash. If we start out working the land, that's where we'll end up."

"You haven't said what you want," she pointed out carefully. "Do you want to work the farm?"

Moonshine shook his head slowly. "The only thing I want is to be with Geneva. Long as she's by my side, I could do anything and be happy."

She sighed softly and looked up at him again. "That's lovely, Moonshine, and very romantic." And sweet. How could she have forgotten how sweet young love was?

The boy stirred uncomfortably, but he looked pleased. "It's just how I feel."

"And you've been in love with her for how long?"

"Five years, going on six."

"And you still love her just as much?"

"More."

Courtney shook her head in wonder. She didn't think any of Leslie's relationships had lasted that long, and she'd been an adult—sort of. But here was this gentle boy who'd trekked across a continent to build a life for his sweetheart. Who fought a gang of roughnecks in the morning and wrote love poems at night, and who'd loved the same girl for nearly a third of his life.

Six weeks ago Courtney hadn't believed in love. Now she saw examples of it everywhere she turned. Were these people really so very different? Or had she just learned how to see the love that had always been there?

Gold.

Of all the damn things.

Heath glared at the leather pouch in his hand and scowled

at Philo's retreating figure as he rode Mule up Warren Street toward the turnoff to the cabin.

Gold.

The old codger had done it. He'd found a strike on the Jezebel. In the blink of an eye the old man's fortunes had changed—and Heath's along with them. Judging by the size of the pouch Heath held, there was a great deal of gold on the claim. More than Heath could spend in a year. Hell, probably more than he could spend in five.

A few weeks ago he hadn't even had the price of a meal. Now he could probably buy and sell half the town. The first thing he'd do would be to retrieve poor old, patient Warrior from the livery stable. Then he'd talk to Courtney about a larger house, and a house for Delilah, as well.

Gold.

Damned if Philo hadn't been right all along. By rights, it was Verlis's windfall, but Heath had listened to Philo often enough to know that Verlis would have wanted good people to prosper. Who better than Delilah and her son?

In the mood to celebrate, he pushed into the Pink Parasol, ordered a shot, and slapped a tiny nugget on the bar in front of him before Red Will could ask. He saw the glint of avarice in Will's eye, and he sure didn't miss the interested glances from other miners lined up along the bar. Gold in any form always got noticed, so Heath made sure to keep the rest hidden.

He turned, smiling, and recognized Derry Dennehy eying him from the other end of the bar. "Looks like you've had some good fortune."

Courtney might be excited about Derry's intentions toward Delilah. Heath still wasn't sure. "I guess it might look that way."

Derry laughed good-naturedly and clapped one hand on Heath's shoulder. "That's what I like about you, Sullivan. You're a man who doesn't mince his words." He swallowed a pint or so of beer and wiped his mouth with his sleeve. "It seems that the two of us have some mutual friends. That considered, maybe we should spend some time getting better acquainted."

Heath wasn't in the mood for small-talk, but if Courtney was right about Derry's intentions, he should probably make an effort. He leaned onto the bar, but he made no effort to hide his skepticism. "All right."

Derry grinned. "Nice start. So tell me, Sullivan, you been around here long?"

"Depends on what you consider long." Heath swallowed half a shot and turned his glass in circles on the bar. "I've been here two months."

"In a town like this, that makes you an old-timer, doesn't it?"

There was something open and guileless about the guy. He always seemed to be exactly what he said. But Heath still didn't trust him. Delilah had been through too much already. He wasn't going to let her get hurt again. "Yeah," he said. "I'm practically a founding father."

Derry laughed and signaled to Red Will. "Another drink for my friend and me, if you will sir," he said, flashing a handful of coins.

Will refilled both glasses and retreated to the far end of the bar where Sloe-Eyed Sally was attending to a glassy-eyed miner with a full pouch and Fat Nell's breasts held a young man's eager attention.

When Heath realized that Delilah was watching them from the other end of the room, he smiled to show that everything was all right. But apparently she still wasn't ready to talk to him. He turned to say something to Derry and caught the expression on the other man's face.

"This mutual acquaintance of ours," he said, running his finger along the moisture left by his glass. "I've been told that you have intentions."

"That I do." Derry dragged his gaze away from her reluctantly. "I've been told that you do not."

Heath conceded that point with a stiff nod and turned his back so that Delilah couldn't see him so easily. "Why should she consider you?"

"Ah, now there's a question." Derry turned with him and leaned both elbows on the bar. "Because I would live to make her happy, and I would die to see her sad. But if you'll forgive me my curiosity, why should I answer a question like that for you?"

Heath turned and searched the crowd again until he found her. His heart twisted and all the memories they'd shared played through his head in the time it took to blink. He imagined Blue standing beside him, and he knew that his friend would approve of Derry. And if Blue approved, what right did Heath have to disapprove?

"Because," he said, slinging back one last shot, "she's my sister."

She really shouldn't let Mr. Roderick Dennehy walk with her so far. She really shouldn't.

She shouldn't believe that look he kept giving her, either. Or trust the fact that he hadn't yet touched her beyond a mere brush of the fingers, a kiss on the hand. Real love wasn't possible for women like her. She knew it. She *knew* it. And yet here she was, walking down the street right next to Mr. Roderick Dennehy in broad daylight and acting as if she didn't know a thing.

They walked in silence, as they had taken to doing on Wednesday mornings. She never spoke at all, and he wouldn't speak until they reached the corner where he always parted company with her. He seemed content to just spend time in her company, to be seen in public with her—which in itself was a very fine thing indeed.

Last week he'd even been bold enough to kiss her hand. And even though her heart had thrilled by the very gentlemanliness of it, she hadn't yet made up her mind whether she'd allow a repeat of such brazen behavior.

That in itself made her wonder what was happening to her. Mr. Roderick Dennehy treated her as if she was shiny and new. Unsullied. A lady. When he knew very well who she was and what she did. What was wrong with him?

And then last night he'd been talking to Heath. Only the good Lord knew what had passed between them, but she was nervous as a cat this morning. She watched his eyes closely, worried that Heath had said something about who she really was. There *was* something different about the way Mr. Roderick Dennehy looked at her this morning, all right. She just couldn't figure out what the difference was.

It wasn't disgust, and it wasn't that vacant, faraway, superior look white folks got when they were forced to face a darky. But Delilah couldn't tell what it was for sure, and that meant she'd have to bring up the subject—which she most emphatically did not want to do.

What if *she* said something wrong in the process? What if she gave herself away and jeopardized Isaac's entire future by asking the wrong question? Well, she couldn't let the morning go by without finding out what was on Mr. Roderick Dennehy's mind. It would be a whole week before she'd get another chance to talk with him, and in a week she might go crazy with wondering.

Taking a deep breath for courage, she slid a glance at his strong profile, his fine straight nose, the half-smile playing about his lips, the fine wrinkles in the skin around his eyes— proof in Delilah's mind that he smiled far too much, especially since there was so very little to smile about.

But a man with a ready smile . . . well, there wasn't a finer thing a woman could ask for, really. A man who could make good from bad and laughter from tears. A man who found sunshine in the middle of a downpour—a woman could spend a lifetime with a man like that. It was the sour ones you had to watch out for.

Listen to her rambling on in her head. Thinking that way— as if she could actually have a future with Mr. Roderick Dennehy. As if she *wanted* a future with him, she thought with a sniff. Trouble was, no matter what she told herself or how often she did it, her heart was starting to have a few thoughts of its own.

Squaring her shoulders, she broke the silence before she could change her mind. "I noticed you inside the Pink Parasol last night." As if she didn't notice him *every* night.

His eyes rounded in surprise, but a pleased smile spread under his beard and the skin around his eyes crinkled. "Did you now? And should I be flattered to hear it?"

She wagged a dismissive hand at him. "That's up to you. I noticed you talking with that man. The tall blond one."

Half of Roderick's smile faded, which left him looking hopelessly confused. "Are you talking about Heath?"

"I suppose. Yes. Yes, of course, I'm talking about Heath." She couldn't seem to walk and figure out how much to say at the same time, so she stopped in her tracks and twisted her fingers in the fringe of her shawl. "The two of you seemed to be getting on."

"I think we were." Roderick's face evened itself out again. "Any objections?"

"To you and Heath talking?" *Yes!* "No. Should I have any?"

"I don't know." One hand floated toward her, as if he was thinking about touching her. Just when she started to hope he might, he drew it back and balled it into a fist. "I suppose the two of you have your reasons for what you're doing. And he's a hard fellow not to like. But if I were him . . ." His voice trailed away uncertainly and he wagged his head. "Well, I wouldn't be standing at the bar swilling dust cutter if I were him."

His meaning wasn't at all clear, but Delilah felt compelled to point out one small truth he seemed to be forgetting: "But you *were* standing at the bar swilling dust cutter, and you have been every night for a month or more."

"Only so I can keep an eye on you."

In spite of her confusion, Delilah felt herself smiling. "Then you don't like the foul taste of whiskey? You're merely torturing yourself for me?"

His lips quirked. "Indeed, lass. I suffer in silence night after night, hoping for a smile, a look, a word."

Delilah liked the fact that he could laugh at himself. She needed more laughter in her life. So did Isaac. She liked the musical lilt of his voice, too. "We were talking about Heath," she said sharply, more to keep her own thoughts in line than as a reprimand for Roderick. "You were telling me what the two of you talked about."

"Was I now?" One brow quirked over a fine, clear eye. "And how is it *I* don't remember that's what I was doin'?"

"Too much dust cutter, perhaps."

"Aye." His lips twitched again, but he tried to look serious.

"Perhaps. So you're wanting to know what we talked about, are ye?"

Just as she'd feared. She'd given herself away. She lifted her chin and tried to look unconcerned. "Not particularly. But you've been trailing after me for so long, I thought perhaps a bit of conversation . . ."

Again, that mock-serious expression crossed his face. "Ah. Well and it's kind of you. And I'll be thanking you for your kindness, but I'd hate to bore you with the details of our little chat last night. If it's conversation you're granting me, I choose something far grander. The weather, perhaps—or how beautiful you look this morning."

It took all of Delilah's concentration to keep the frown on her face when she scowled up at him. "Are you teasing me, Mr. Roderick Dennehy?"

"That I am, Miss Delilah."

"Well, I'll thank you to stop it. I have a particular interest in your conversation with Heath Sullivan."

Roderick's smile faded, but only a little. "You're wondering if he told me about you?"

This time Delilah had no trouble frowning. Her heart thumped wildly in her chest, and she forced herself to look away, but she couldn't keep her hands still and she ended up twitching the cuffs of her shirtwaist nervously. "What would there be to tell?"

Roderick took her by the elbow and began walking again. "I'm sure he's a wonderful fellow. There's not a doubt in my mind. And you know that your current occupation causes me only the slightest twitch of concern now and then—and only because I'm concerned for your own safety." He smiled down at her. "I don't need to be your first love, Delilah, but I insist on being your last." He lifted his gaze to the street again and chatted on as if they were having a normal conversation. "The thing I don't understand is how a brother can stand by and watch his sister . . . Well, any normal brother would at least make an *effort* to provide for you. If you were *my* sister, you wouldn't be forced to earn your own keep."

Delilah's heart did a little whirligig as if it was dancing to some silent music. "Brother?"

Roderick's step faltered slightly. "Indeed. Are you after telling me that you *aren't* his sister?"

Delilah shook her head slowly while she tried to make sense of the conversation they were having. "No. Of course not."

"Then he didn't lie?"

"No." But why had he suddenly claimed a family connection after all these years? Why now? Why here? Why—? Her thoughts broke off suddenly as a possible explanation occurred to her for the first time. It seemed impossible. After all, everyone in the slave quarters had been aware of Sebastian Sullivan's activities, and the other white folk at Bonne Chance had condoned every vile thing he'd done. His own wife had known. So how could Heath have been unaware?

It seemed impossible, and yet when she remembered the look on his face the other day, and the things Courtney had said . . .

"I could tell you why Heath hasn't rushed into the Pink Parasol to save me," she said to Derry. "That is, if you want to hear it. It's not a pretty story, and you may change your mind about me when you do."

Derry captured her hand and squeezed it gently. "And what are you going to tell me? That you murdered the last Irishman who wanted to marry you?"

She smiled even though her heart was about to burst from fear. "Not exactly." She looked into his kind eyes and prayed as she'd never prayed before that God would let this gentle man love her after he learned her truth. She focused on her fingers because she couldn't bear to see the light in his eyes die. "I'm going to tell you that until a year ago, I was a slave. I was born on the plantation owned by Heath's father. *I* was owned by Heath's father, and so was my mother. He . . . He . . ." The words caught in her throat, and she struggled to force them out.

But Derry lifted her hand to his lips, and without consciously willing it, she let her gaze meet his again. "You don't have to say it, Delilah. It matters nothing to me."

"I was a slave, Derry. Do you know what that means?"

"Aye. I do. Do you think I care?"

Delilah stared at him, struggling to believe that he might actually be saying what she so desperately wanted to hear. "That's not all. I have a son. Isaac. He's five."

Derry grinned from ear to ear. "Ah, and now I *am* a happy man. And a fortunate one to boot. A son already?" His eyes sparkled mischievously. "And me not having to do any of the work to get him here."

"His skin is dark," she warned.

Derry's smile faded. He captured her other hand and held both against his chest. "Delilah, my love, *do* you think I care about something so trivial as the color of the boy's skin?"

Tears pooled in her eyes and her heart filled with emotion so strong she knew she'd never be able to express it.

"If you insist on having something to worry about," he said, pressing a kiss to one hand, "I'll give it to you." He leaned close enough to kiss her lips but stopped just short of doing so. "*I* come from a long and distinguished line of horse thieves."

In spite of her bursting heart, Delilah managed a surprised laugh. "Are you serious?"

"As the day is long. My sainted mother used the last of her money shipping me to America so I could escape a noose that was waitin' for me." He did kiss her then, the softest and briefest kiss of all time. "But I promise you, Delilah me love, that I've left that long tradition of horse thievery behind me. I'm a respectable gambler now, and I could even be persuaded to change my ways again. So, you see, the question is not whether I'll have you, but whether you'll have me."

Chapter 19

THINGS HAD BEEN different between Courtney and Heath since their talk by the river. Tyree Caine had done another vanishing act, but no one trusted it. Now that Philo had found gold on the Jezebel, they kept a close watch on everything and Courtney jumped at every unexpected sound. Moonshine had moved back to the miners' camp, so her nights with Heath had taken on a special quality, but there were currents below the surface that kept her on edge.

Heath had finally taught her to use the shotgun, and she'd even become a competent shot, but she still hated guns and she prayed every day that she wouldn't have to use it. Add to that the creeping certainty that it was only a matter of time before the future came to claim her, and she was becoming jumpier by the day.

She'd be pegging out laundry when without warning her fingers would begin to tingle. She'd be bent low to pull dinner from the fire and that electrical thrumming would start pulsing in her ear. She'd turn to say something to Heath, and the light would creep into the edges of her vision. She tried desperately to convince herself that there was some natural physical explanation, but in her heart she knew. Two months ago she'd prayed frantically to be taken back to the future.

Now it felt like the one thing that could ruin her life completely.

Heath sensed something, but Courtney hadn't been able to tell him yet. Not with everything else he had to worry about. Still, she caught him watching her at odd times. He'd stop in the middle of oiling a shovel, or with his ax raised and ready to split a rail for firewood, or with his spoon halfway to his mouth, or in the middle of a cup of coffee, and he'd drink in whatever she was doing as if he were instinctively creating memories to savor when she was gone.

She found herself doing the same thing—and not just with Heath. If she had to go back, she wanted to take her new family with her. She wanted to remember the way Philo tilted his head and squinted one eye when he thought. The way Moonshine looked when he talked about Miss Geneva Openshaw. The sound of their voices and the roar of their masculine laughter.

She built special memories of Heath. His face, certainly. His body, definitely. His touch. Oh, yes, his touch. But most of all she wanted to take his sounds back with her. The rush of his sigh when he grew exasperated with her. The thunder in his chest when he laughed. The breath of his whisper. The caress of his voice. She couldn't bear the thought of spending the rest of her life without hearing them, and she found herself listening to everything, not just with her ears but with her heart.

A week after Moonshine's return, Heath and Philo rode together to the mine, leaving Noah and three others to keep an eye on Courtney while they were gone. Now that Philo had actually found gold on the Jezebel, Courtney finally understood why Tyree wanted the mine in the first place. He must have suspected that the gold was there all along.

They'd talked endlessly around the table about the threat Tyree posed. None of them believed that he'd back off now, but both Heath and Philo believed that he'd concentrate his efforts on the Jezebel itself. Courtney had pleaded with them never to ride into the hills alone, but even knowing that they were together, she couldn't relax.

But if she thought about Tyree Caine all day long, she'd

go crazy. Instead, she tried to concentrate on a sketch she'd been working on of the expression on Moonshine's face when he talked about Geneva. She was close, but there was something wrong with his eyes. Some wisp of emotion that eluded her.

In her own time, she had books and old sketches she could reference for ideas. Here, she had nothing but her own memory. Heath might have been able to help. At first, she'd hidden her sketches from him, but it hadn't taken long to find the courage to show him a few.

His reaction had fueled her self-confidence, and she'd been pleasantly surprised to find that he had a skilled eye for detail. He was reluctant to offer suggestions, arguing that she didn't need him botching up a perfectly good sketch, but the few he *had* offered had provided just what the work needed to make it perfect.

This sketch would have to wait, she supposed, until the mess with Tyree Caine was behind them.

She held the sketch to the light, so focused on finding that ethereal quality that she didn't hear the footsteps outside her door until they were almost upon her. She turned, expecting to see Heath or Philo or Moonshine. Instead, she found herself looking into the beady black eyes and cruel smile that belonged to Tyree Caine.

Her blood ran cold at the sight of him, and when three men moved into the doorway behind him, the blood in her veins froze. Where were Noah and the others? Out of commission, obviously. She prayed they weren't dead.

She glanced to the wall beside the bed where she'd left the shotgun. She finally knew how to use it to protect herself, but it wouldn't do her any good on the other side of the cabin.

Tyree stepped inside and took a long, slow look around the cabin. His tongue lashed out, snakelike, and he turned that deliberate stare on her. "Well, look what we have here, boys. A pretty little lady all by herself." He strolled into the room one calculated step at a time and motioned for the others to follow him. "What are you doing here all alone, sweetheart?"

Courtney lowered her sketch to the table and watched him move, acutely aware of every sound the others made, every whisper of wind coming from outside. She kept her chin high, knowing that if she let Tyree think she was afraid of him, she'd be playing right into his hands. "I'm not alone."

Tyree's lips curved into an icy smile and he looked around the cabin with exaggerated surprise. "No? I don't see anybody else. Do *you* see anybody else, boys?"

Three of the men murmured responses. The fourth stepped into the light, and Courtney recognized him as Ethan, obviously still upset about the knee she'd planted in his groin and ready to pay her back. Time seemed to grind to a halt as she looked into his hate-filled eyes. "*I* don't see anybody else, boss."

She knew these men. She'd grown up around men like these. Some a little better. Some worse. Time hadn't changed them, but it had changed her. She'd once let them color her views on life and on love. But she'd learned something since then, and she wasn't about to let Tyree Caine or the others get the best of her.

Tyree took a step closer and raked his gaze over her again. "So what's a pretty little thing like you doing all alone?"

Courtney thought quickly, trying to picture the parts of the cabin she couldn't see and searching for something she could use to protect herself. Her heavy cast-iron skillet hung on the wall behind her, but she'd have a hard time getting to it and she wasn't sure how much damage she could do with the odds stacked four-to-one against her.

She lifted her chin and met his gaze squarely. "I want you out of my house."

Tyree snaked out one hand and grabbed her chin before she even saw him moving. "What if I don't want to leave?"

Instinct got the better of her. She tried to pull out of his grip, but he was too strong. "I got business with your friends, lady. And Ethan here . . . Well, Ethan's got business with you." His fingers pressed into the soft skin beneath her chin, and she could feel new bruises forming with every breath.

"They're not here," she snarled, ignoring for the moment the threat from Ethan. "I don't know when they'll be back."

Tyree's foul stench filled the air between them. What little light there was in his eyes faded, and his gaze became soulless and opaque. He tilted his head to one side and the smile on his lips evaporated. "You got it all wrong, little lady. I don't have any intention of waitin' around here for your men to come back. And I ain't gonna chase all over hell and back tryin' to find them. But Ethan and I figure that if you come pay us a visit, your men'll come to us. Isn't that what we figure, Ethan?"

Ethan grinned and revealed a set of stained, brown teeth. "That's what we figure."

"And maybe you and Ethan can talk about old times while you're there." Tyree tossed a lascivious grin at his buddy. "Isn't that right, Ethan?"

Ethan eyed her with the same gleam Loser Number Three had reserved for beer and other women. Courtney couldn't hold back the shudder of revulsion, but it only earned a laugh from Ethan and the others.

Tyree released her chin with a small shove that sent her stumbling backward. "Bring her along, boys. I'm getting tired. I'm ready for it to be over."

Two of Tyree's men lunged forward and grabbed her arms. She tried to twist away, but they were both much stronger than she could ever hope to be. She lashed out with her feet, trying to kick her way free as the men dragged her toward the door. But Tyree's third man merely caught her feet in both hands and held her.

Should she fight or go limp? Should she scream? Or would that only make things worse? Since she couldn't see how things could *get* much worse, she sucked in a deep breath, screamed at the top of her lungs, and prayed that there was someone left in the camp who'd pay attention.

Almost before the sound left her mouth, a dirty hand clamped over her face and cut her off. Strangely, she could feel the fear in every cell of her body, but her mind remained clear and her awareness of the fear was almost dreamlike. She felt as if she were thinking in slow motion, and yet only a heartbeat or two passed before she realized that she couldn't just *let* them cart her away.

She thrashed violently and managed to break loose one of her feet. Encouraged, she kicked as hard as she could, trying to connect with shins, feet, Tyree's back. She didn't care, as long as she inflicted damage. But the only response was that the third man caught her free foot and lashed her legs together with a length of rope. When her feet were secure, the dirty hand slipped from her mouth and she let out another bloodcurdling scream just before someone stuffed an equally filthy rag into her mouth.

Panic rose like bile in her throat when she realized that she couldn't save herself. Working together, two of the men tossed her across the saddle in front of Tyree Caine. Blood rushed to her head as the horse began to move, and she realized that this was it. She might never see Heath again. She might never spend another night in his arms or another minute at his side. Tears of fury and fear filled her eyes, but she blinked them away.

She couldn't lie here feeling light-headed and wimpy. She couldn't let Tyree Caine and his boys use her to hurt Heath and the others. As long as she was still alive, there was hope and a way out.

She just had to find it.

"I'm tellin' you, he's given up," Philo said for what Heath swore was the hundredth time that day alone. "Now that we got other prospectors standing with us, Tyree Caine *knows* he ain't no match for us."

Heath shook his head—also for the hundredth time— tossed his saddlebags over Warrior's rump and bent to cinch the saddle itself. "Tyree Caine doesn't know anything of the sort. He's biding his time, that's all." He straightened and looked out over the barren hillside. "I just wish I knew why he wants the Jezebel so badly."

Philo snorted a laugh. "You have to ask? The Jezebel's giving up the gold now, son. That's what Tyree wants. But he's smart enough to know he ain't gonna get it."

Heath shook his head again. "There are plenty of other mines around. Some are producing just as much gold. Some are producing more. I don't understand his fixation with *this* mine. What's on this piece of land that he can't get anywhere else?"

Philo tilted his head and squinted thoughtfully. "It ain't dirt. We know that much."

In spite of his mounting concern, Heath managed a laugh. "No. I think we can safely say it ain't dirt." He turned back to the tent and scanned the ground around it to make sure they hadn't left anything. The sky had been growing darker by the hour, and he was anxious to finish up here so they could get back down the mountain. "If it *is* gold he wants, I want to know what it'll take to get him to come after it. I'm tired of waiting for him to make a move."

"Maybe he ain't gonna."

"No, he's gonna. It's just a matter of when." Heath put his foot in the stirrup and swung up into his saddle. "I just hope we didn't make a mistake by leaving Courtney alone."

"She ain't alone," Philo said on a grunt as he pulled himself onto Mule's back. "Noah and the others is watching her, and Moonshine's there if anything goes wrong." He took a minute getting himself settled before adding, "Besides, Courtney's no slouch. She knows how to use the shotgun now, right? She's not gonna let anything happen to herself."

Heath wished he could share the old man's confidence. He prodded Warrior gently and started down the hill with Philo right behind him. Maybe it was the gathering storm or the slate-gray sky, but he couldn't shake the growing feeling that something was wrong. The nerves between his shoulder blades twitched and his hearing seemed more acute. He could hear the sound of his own heartbeat, and the closer they got to the cabin, the louder it became.

They rode into the valley and began their approach to the cabin with Philo still arguing that Heath was imagining things. But as they drew abreast of the first tents in the miners' camp, Heath saw a hunched figure sitting on the side of the road nursing his bloodied head in both hands. The man looked up, and Heath recognized him with a jolt.

He was off Warrior before he even consciously thought of dismounting, and he hunkered down in front of Noah. "What happened?"

"Tyree and his gang." Blood matted Noah's forehead and ran in streaks down the side of his face, but his voice was strong and Heath felt a deep sense of relief. "They rode in here a couple of hours ago. Got the jump on me."

Heath forced himself not to look at Philo. He was too sickened by the sight of another downed man. "You all right?"

Noah grimaced and gingerly touched the back of his head. "Right as rain. Don't know about the others, though."

"We'll find 'em," Philo said, his voice grim.

On the edges of his vision Heath could see how stricken he looked. He recognized the guilt in the old man's eyes, and some of his own anger faded. Philo was an old man who'd lived a long, full life, but not everyone got the chance to stare ruthless cruelty in the eye, and it was hard to see it coming when you didn't recognize it.

He pushed to his feet slowly and held out a hand for Noah.

The other man waved him off. "Forget about me. You don't have any time to waste. They've got two hours on you easy, and with this storm comin', there's no telling how long it'll take you to get there."

The prickly sensation between his shoulder blades grew stronger. "Get where?"

Noah squinted up at him and shot an anxious glance at Philo. "Wherever Tyree and his boys hole up. There's at least five of 'em. That's how many rode in here, so I'd figure double that, at least."

Heath let his gaze travel toward the western hills and wagged his head slowly. "It's a trap. We're not riding into it."

"But you gotta go, Heath." Noah touched his head again and winced at the blood that came away on his fingers. "Who knows what they'll do to her if you don't?"

Heath's gaze flew back to Noah's earnest face. "Her?"

"They took Courtney with 'em. Had her slung over the back of Tyree's horse like a flour sack."

Heath's blood slowed to a crawl and his heart slowed with it. He shot a glance at Philo and saw the matching horror on the old man's face. For the second time in his life, someone he loved was in the hands of a monster—and he felt as powerless to save her as he'd been with Blue.

That feeling lasted less than a minute. In the time it took to get back into the saddle, he knew he couldn't let this end the same way.

He'd bring Courtney back alive . . . or he'd die trying.

Heath hunkered down at the top of a hill and studied the layout of Tyree's camp in the valley below him. It had taken far too long to get here, partly because he'd had to wait while Moonshine babbled directions to Gold Strike Gulch, and partly because Philo had talked sense into him, insisting that they'd never make it back alive if they didn't have some men to back them up.

He'd worked hard at shutting down his emotions as they rode. He'd made the mistake of wearing his emotions on his sleeve when he tried to save Blue. He knew now that only cold, calculated thinking stood a chance against someone like Tyree Caine. He could have done a better job at shutting them down two months ago, but he hadn't had anything at stake back then.

Nothing had meant anything to him. No one had mattered. And he'd been an empty shell of a man. As heartless and unfeeling as Tyree Caine and his followers. Loving someone might make him vulnerable. It might even make him hurt. But it made him human, dammit. It made him human.

He crouched low and tried to count the men milling around the camp. Four sat around a fire in a center ring created by three tents. Two more stood guard near the west end of the camp. Another two near the eastern tip. One near the string of horses. That made nine—and Tyree Caine himself, who Heath figured was inside one of the tents.

He wondered if Courtney was with Tyree, but he forced the questions away. He couldn't let himself think about what was happening to her or it would distract him. He'd be better able to save her if he could stay focused.

Unless Tyree had a handful or more men inside the tents, the odds were fairly even. That was one positive note. Maybe the only one. On the down side, they'd have a hard time getting any closer to the camp without being seen.

He glanced to his left and saw two of his own men taking up positions overlooking the camp. On his right, Philo lay on his belly in the dirt, his rifle already trained on someone or something in the camp.

They could have opened fire from where they were, but Courtney might easily get caught in the crossfire, and Heath wouldn't put her in any more danger than she already was. The object was to rescue Courtney and get her to safety, not to wipe Tyree and his men off the face of the earth—although all things considered, that might have been a nice fringe benefit.

On the ground far below, he could see four more of his men snaking toward the camp using their elbows to pull themselves through the dirt. Men who had come to this country to avoid the war, but who'd jumped into another one because he'd asked for their help. Damn if that didn't beat all.

Focus, he reminded himself sharply. Only two things mattered—finding Courtney, and getting her out of there. There would be plenty of time for reflection later.

He inched closer and tried to discern movement inside the tents. Very soon the sun would drop behind the hills and they'd be forced to light lanterns. That might help him see where Courtney was, but it would make it a whole lot harder to see the enemy.

He heard a breath of a sigh from Philo and glanced at the old man to make sure he was doing all right. He shouldn't have been here. He was too old and tired. But he'd have shouted loud enough to raise the dead if Heath had tried to make him stay behind. And he was a good shot. A damn good shot. Heath hoped it didn't come down to a shoot-out, but if it did, Philo would come in handy.

Focus.

Shadows lengthened across the campsite, and Heath knew they had to make a move soon. He motioned for the others to hold their positions and backtracked to a place he'd noticed earlier where he could get down the hill without too much trouble. They knew—he'd told them all—that he didn't want this rescue to turn into a bloodbath. But *he* knew that the miners were tired of Tyree running roughshod over the rest of them. It wouldn't take much to set off an all-out war.

He moved cautiously, one agonizing step at a time toward Tyree's camp. Every sense was heightened as he strained to see even the slightest movement from one of Tyree's men and to hear the signal his own men were to give if they spotted Courtney. He could feel the air against his skin and taste anger and fear on his tongue.

Step by step. Inch by inch. He dug the sides of his feet into the dirt each time he moved to keep from sliding, and forced himself to be patient. To move slowly. To keep Courtney's safety uppermost in his mind. It was the only thing he cared about. The only thing that mattered.

But God help Tyree if he or any of his men had laid a hand on her. If they'd hurt her in any way, God would have to help them because Heath sure as hell wouldn't.

He scanned the camp again, but he'd dropped low enough now to have lost his vantage point. Someone moved on the edge of his vision and he froze in place, holding his breath as one of Tyree's men stepped into view and back out again.

He tensed, not daring to move but waiting for the shout of alarm. But, miraculously, the man must not have seen him. And then, as he stood there, suspended halfway between the relative safety of the overhang and the precarious edge of Tyree's camp, the cry went up. Not from where Heath stood, but from the other side of the clearing. Before Heath could move, hell broke loose.

A shot rang out, followed immediately by several more. Angry shouts and the sound of running feet split the silence. Dust and dirt flew and the scents of gunpowder and charred wood filled the air.

No longer worried about giving himself away, Heath charged the remaining distance down the hillside. Most of Tyree's men had run to the other side of the clearing, but three were smart enough to anticipate trouble from other directions.

Trying to make himself a smaller target, Heath crouched

as he ran toward the closest tent. His heart hammered in his throat and bits of memory from the night Blue died flashed in front of his eyes.

Focus.

Courtney was here somewhere. Tyree had used her to lure Heath into the open. He couldn't afford to lose his concentration.

While bullets flew past him and shouts pierced the air, Heath checked first one tent, and then another. When he determined that the second tent was empty, he turned toward the third. He told himself to hurry. That Courtney needed him. But his arms and legs moved with almost dreamlike slowness, and the voices around him slowed and dragged so that each word grated, unrecognizable against his ear.

While he struggled to make his feet move, Tyree Caine appeared in the doorway of the third tent. He saw Heath. Smiled. Reached behind him and dragged Courtney into the opening with him. "Is this what you're looking for?"

Something inside Heath urged him to take aim and shoot. To put a bullet between Tyree's eyes and be done with it. But the look in Courtney's eyes stopped him. She knew and loved the best parts of him. She'd helped him to find them again. He couldn't lose them now.

He looked away from her wide, frightened eyes and met Tyree's gloating stare. Somewhere behind him a shot found its mark and a man fell to the ground with a groan. Heath kept his gaze straight ahead. "Let her go, Caine. She's not part of this."

"Oh, I beg to differ." Tyree nudged Courtney out of the tent and drew the muzzle of his pistol along her cheek. "I've made her a part of this. You have what I want. I have what you want." He lifted his shoulders and laughed. "*Whatever* are we to do?"

"What do I have? Whatever it is, take it. You want gold? It's yours. You can have anything I've taken from the Jezebel. Take it and be done with it."

"You think that's enough for me? Your miserable half of the gold on the Jezebel?" Tyree laughed again and shook his head. "You know, the funny thing is, it didn't have to get this far. All I ever wanted was to get those two old men out of my way. They were the only thing standing between me and an empire. I own every piece of land around that stupid mine. Every speck of gold that comes out of those hills is *mine*. Getting those two old fools out of the way should have been easy. It *would* have been easy if you hadn't decided to save them."

"So you killed an old man for his land?"

Tyree shrugged elaborately. "He was old. He would have died soon, anyway."

"And Moonshine?"

"The boy?" Tyree laughed at Heath's concern. "I didn't kill *him*, did I? And I won't, either. As long as he keeps his promise to leave Virginia City and you get that old man off his claim." He craned forward to look at Courtney's face and his smile returned. "And the little lady will be all right, too. Course she'll have to decide which of us she prefers . . . *after*. But that decision shouldn't be too hard to make. I've never known a woman who'd choose poor and weak over rich and powerful—have you?"

Memories of Felice rushed Heath. Of her harsh laughter when he'd asked her to leave with him. Of her cold eyes when she'd told him to get out of her sight. Of her disgust when she'd realized that he'd turned his back on money and power for the sake of integrity. Of her undisguised revulsion over what she'd called his pathetic concern for Blue—someone she hadn't even considered worth his notice.

Had he met the woman who'd make that choice? Yes, he thought he had. He opened his mouth to say so, but something tore through his shoulder before he could speak, and a split second later he heard the second shot just before it ripped through his thigh.

Courtney watched in stunned disbelief as Ethan took aim and fired. He shot Heath twice before she could even shout a warning. Heath's leg buckled and he crumpled to the ground in front of her. She opened her mouth to shout again, but no sound left her mouth, and that's when she noticed the tingling in her fingers and the dull electronic pulsing in her ear.

Maybe she'd just been too frightened to notice it before. Maybe she'd been too busy watching Heath to see the light pulsing at the edge of her vision. Or maybe it was real this time.

The shouts and gunshots around her faded into a stony silence. She tried again to call out to Heath, but if any sound left her lips, the silence swallowed it before it touched the air.

She knew that Tyree Caine still stood beside her, but she couldn't feel his hand clamped around her arm any longer or the cold steel of his pistol against her cheek. She was being taken back into the future. Now. Now, when Heath lay hurt and bleeding at her feet. Now, when Philo was out there fighting to save her.

She watched in horror as the shotgun flew out of Heath's hands and realized that he was completely at Tyree's mercy. If she could have broken free to help him, she would have. But she had no strength. The pulsing light was pulling her away.

There was only one way to save Heath now. She had to give in to the future and let it take her. Maybe if she disappeared right in front of Tyree's eyes, Heath would have a chance. At the very least, she wouldn't be a distraction to him. He might be able to save himself if he didn't have to worry about her.

After allowing herself one last glance at Heath, she closed her eyes and surrendered to the light, to the warmth surrounding her, to the future and the life she'd cheated by coming here in the first place. It would kill her to live without Heath. It would hurt for the rest of her life to be without Philo. But leaving was the only way to save them, and she couldn't stay knowing that they'd sacrificed everything to save her.

Don't surrender.

The unexpected voice brought her eyes open again, but the scene in front of Tyree Caine's tent had disappeared. There was only light. Incredible light and warmth, and the kind face of a dark-skinned man who stood where Heath should have been. The brilliance of his smile rivaled the light that surrounded her and love filled his eyes.

Don't surrender.

His lips didn't move, but she could hear him just the same. And she knew him. Suddenly she wanted Heath to know that Blue was here. That, in fact, Blue had never left him. She looked into Blue's eyes and she knew that death was nothing more than moving through time. No different than what she'd done to come to the past. No more painful or frightening. That the finality of death was the greatest myth of all, and love was the one thing strong enough to transcend it.

Don't surrender.

The words she'd spoken to Heath about choice came rushing back at her. In her own voice. In someone else's. In no voice at all. She could choose life or death. She could choose a life filled with love or one that was heartbreakingly empty. She could choose to stay or to leave. It was up to her. It had always been up to her.

If she left, she'd be safe and Heath would be alive, and they would both be alone. If she stayed, they could stand and fight together. Maybe they would win. Maybe they would lose. They might live, or they might die. There was no guarantee.

But when was there ever?

Chapter 20

Heath DIDN'T KNOW how it happened. He didn't know why it happened. He only knew that one minute Courtney was standing in front of him and the next, she was gone.

Gone.

Into the future? He didn't have time to wonder. She'd disappeared and he knew instinctively that she'd made the choice so he could save himself. He had one split second to use her precious gift before Tyree gathered his wits and finished him off.

Pain pulsed through him with every heartbeat. Fire filled his shoulder and leg. His head swam with it, but he had to keep himself together. He had to use what Courtney had given him. There were others who relied on him—Delilah. Her son. Even Philo and Moonshine to some extent. And Courtney, herself. If she *had* gone back to the future, he didn't want her to read that he'd died today.

Drawing on everything he had left, he dragged himself toward the shotgun that had flown out of his hand only seconds earlier. It seemed like miles, but he knew he had only a few feet to go. The burning in his limbs spread and his good arm shook with the effort. In spite of the chill, sweat poured into his eyes.

From the corner of his eye, he saw Tyree snap to attention, saw the barrel of his gun raise, and he knew this was it. It was over. The heartache, the pain, and the misery would soon be a thing of the past. But so would the joy. The scent of the morning. The soft glow of sunrise and the burnished gold of the sunset.

Time seemed to stand still as he looked down the barrel of Tyree's gun and inched closer to his own weapon. He heard a jubilant shout in the distance, recognized it as Philo's, and heaved a sigh of relief that the others would be safe. At long last his fingers brushed the barrel of the shotgun and time began to move at its usual frantic pace. He heard the click of Tyree's hammer, as he brought the shotgun up to his shoulder and took aim. He squeezed the trigger, knowing that it might be the last thing he ever did.

And then, unbelievably, Courtney was there. In front of Tyree. He watched in horror as the shotgun blast flew toward her and in stunned disbelief as it hit Tyree, somehow impossibly passing right through Courtney on its way.

Tyree took the blast and stumbled backward. A dark red stain spread across his chest, and he collapsed in a heap on the ground. Heath was on his feet before Courtney could move, hobbling toward her in spite of the searing pain, so frantic with worry he hardly noticed it. His leg buckled twice and he nearly didn't make it. She moved toward him, spoke his name, cried out to him. He knew it, but he couldn't hear her. His blood pulsed in his ears so loudly, he couldn't hear a thing.

He heard Philo behind him. Knew numbly that the old man was alive and well and fussing over him. But Heath couldn't be bothered. He needed to get to Courtney. It was the only conscious thought he had.

His arm hung limply at his side and his leg buckled again, this time sending him to his knees. Courtney broke free of whatever held her in its grip and raced to him. She spoke his name over and over while she tried to get him to lie down. He saw Philo standing over Tyree's body and nudging him with the toe of his boot. A dark cloud filled his vision and the pain became so intense, he couldn't think. He tried to tell

Courtney . . . something . . . but his mind wouldn't work well enough to remember what it was.

He'd remember later. When this was all over and he stopped hurting. They'd won. That's all that mattered. They'd won together.

He lay back on the ground and smiled. But when Blue's dark face appeared above him wearing that grin he remembered so well, Heath's smile slipped. The sky faded and he couldn't hear a damn thing. The only thing he *could* see was Blue's great big smile . . . and he knew that his fight had been for nothing.

His last conscious thought was the realization that he must surely be dead.

Heath was surprised that death hurt so damn much. He was even more surprised that it smelled so bad. Like rotgut. The bitter sour smell of rotgut whiskey. The hushed voices of angels . . . voices that weren't actually hushed and that didn't sound like any angels Heath had ever imagined.

"I told you to put the damn fool thing right there," one voice snarled close to his ear. "You listenin' to me or are those ears on your head just to keep your hat from fallin' down over your eyes?"

"If I could use both hands, I would," a slightly higher male voice responded. "And maybe I could *use* both hands if someone knew how to set a broken arm."

"You'll pardon me for saying so," a less familiar voice said from farther away, "but I think if you just let the women . . ." The voice drifted away and Heath sought the blessed oblivion he'd known minutes earlier.

But something prodded painfully into his shoulder, fire roared through his upper half, and Heath nearly bit his tongue in half as he jerked reflexively. He tried to speak, to urge the others to listen. Surely women would have a lighter touch.

He could feel something moist on his face, something cool against his lips. Just as he thought the pain was going to recede, the prod moved in his shoulder again and the pain nearly tore him in two.

His eyes flew open and focused on an unfamiliar face. Its

mouth moved and sounds came out, but Heath couldn't make sense of any of them. He tried to remember how he'd gotten here. He tried to ask if Courtney had survived. Surely an angel could tell him that.

He tried to speak, but his mouth was too dry. His tongue stuck to the roof of his mouth and his lips felt parched and bloodless.

And then a disconnected voice. A voice that belonged to no one, but one that he'd have recognized anywhere. A voice like a summer night on Bonne Chance. "If you keep poking around like that, you'll finish the job those muddle-heads only started. If anything happens to him, you'll have *me* to answer to."

Heath blinked. Focused on the dark cloud swirling overhead. Blinked again and it became a low-beamed ceiling stained with wood smoke. He turned his head slightly and caught a frown edged with concern as Delilah moved to stand beside him.

Maybe he wasn't dead after all.

He had to tell her. Had to let her know what he'd seen. Had to share. He ran his tongue across his lips and managed one word. "Blue—"

Delilah smiled down at him, but the smile evaporated almost immediately. "Oh. So you're alive, are you? Alive and buckin' for attention just like you always did." She looked away and said something to someone Heath couldn't see. "Stay back there, Isaac. There's no reason for you to see this mess."

Isaac? The boy. His nephew. Heath let his head fall back onto the pillow and ran his tongue across his lips again. "Blue?"

She glowered at him, but he could see the affection behind the annoyance. "Of course Blue."

Heath fumbled with whatever they'd thrown over him, wanting to find her hand, needing to make her listen.

She pressed him back against the table and covered his hand again. "You hold still. Make this hard on me, Heath Sullivan, and you'll wish Tyree Caine had done his business instead of sending you back here for me to take care of."

Pain split Heath's head and he closed his eyes against it, but he managed to croak, "Courtney."

"Is fine. Resting. You can see her when I'm through with you."

Resting? Heath's eyes flew open again and he tried to get up onto his elbow. "Where is she?"

"In bed." Delilah shoved him onto his back again, but her eyes were kind. "She's fine, Heath. Whatever she went through up there took a lot out of her, but she's fine. If you want to end up over there in that bed with her, you'd better let me get these bullets out of you."

He lay back willingly this time and clenched his teeth while Delilah worked. He moved in and out of consciousness, remembering the fight, the moment when Courtney vanished, the moment when she reappeared in front of the blast from his shotgun. He remembered Blue. The smile on his face, the peace in his eyes, and he knew that after this the old dream would be gone forever.

After what seemed like days, he felt himself being carted toward the bed and felt the corn husk mattress sag beneath his weight. Courtney was there, pale and wan, but beautiful and alive. Miraculously alive. And just beyond her, huddled in the corner, the solemn face of a small boy who watched Heath with wide dark eyes that he could only have inherited from Blue.

"Isaac," Heath muttered before oblivion claimed him. "My boy."

Courtney watched Heath for a week. Watched every breath he took. Felt every moan in her own body, every sigh in her soul. She waited and paced and listened to his heartbeat. She cleaned his wounds and slept only when he slept. And if he stirred at all, she was instantly awake.

And when she wasn't doing that, she prayed.

Thank God for Delilah, who cooked and cleaned and washed bandages without complaint, who provided a listening ear when Courtney needed one, and who understood Courtney's heartache during Heath's bad times. Thank God for Philo and Moonshine, who hovered almost as close by

as she did, herself. Whose kind faces mirrored a kind of
anxiety Heath would probably find hard to believe. Thank
God for Derry, who looked after Delilah and raced with Isaac
around the yard, and whose laughter could be heard mingling
with Isaac's childish giggle at almost any given moment.

Courtney had come into this world feeling alone, but she'd
accumulated quite a family in the short time she'd been here.
There were families of all kinds, she'd finally realized. The
family she'd been born to had taught her strength and resil-
ience and self-reliance. The family she'd created in her heart
had taught her acceptance and forgiveness and unconditional
love. She was a better person for having learned all the les-
sons that had come her way.

Late in the evening, a full week after the shoot-out on Gold
Strike Gulch, Courtney sat holding Heath's hand until she
couldn't keep her eyes open any longer. Delilah had assured
her repeatedly that Heath was recovering nicely, but Courtney was still a product of her modern upbringing. She'd have
felt a whole lot better if he'd been in a sterile hospital with
tubes and monitors and antibiotics pumping through his
veins.

When she was afraid that she'd fall asleep in her chair,
she gently put Heath's hand on the bed and turned to gather
her blankets from the corner. She spread one on the floor and
stifled a huge yawn, then unfolded a second blanket and
shook it out.

"I'll bet it's cold on the floor this time of year."

At the sound of the unexpected voice behind her, she
dropped the blanket and whipped around to find Heath
watching her. Her heart leapt and tears of gratitude and joy
filled her eyes. "You're awake."

"It seems so." He shifted uncomfortably and touched a cautious hand to the bandage on his shoulder. "And you're alive."

"Yes."

"How did you do that? Up at Gold Strike Gulch? How did
you not get shot? I thought for sure I'd killed you."

She laughed softly and wiped tears away with her fingertips, then sat on the foot of the bed. "I was going back. I
thought it was the only way I could save you."

"To the future."

"Yes. I was coming back again when you pulled the trigger. I must not have been all the way here."

"So it's true?"

"Yes. Do you mind so very much?"

He shook his head and managed a half-smile. "It stopped mattering to me a long time ago. But can you stay?"

"Yes. It's my choice." She pulled her knees up to her chest and rested her chin on them. "I could feel it coming before that day. I was going to tell you about it, but there was always one thing or another to keep me from bothering you. I went looking for you that day by the river so I could tell you, but you'd just found out about Delilah. . . ."

Heath's lips gave a weak quirk. "Did I dream it, or was she really here?"

"She has been every day since you were shot. Philo's pouting about her taking over his physician's duties, but I don't think he really minds. We're all just glad that you're alive."

"And Moonshine?"

"Has sent a letter asking Miss Geneve Openshaw of Fayette County, Ohio, to join him here."

"Lucky boy." He held out his arm and gestured for her to move closer.

Courtney shook her head and stayed where she was. "Are you kidding? I thought I'd lost you. I'm not taking any chances until I know that you're healthy and staying with me for a long, long time."

He tried to scowl, but he was still too weak to look more than mildly perturbed. "Yeah? Well, I thought I'd lost you, too. I was sure I had." He tried to sit up, but fell back against the pillow weakly. "How did you come back?"

"I just wanted to enough, I guess." She wondered whether to tell him the rest or wait until he was stronger, but this time when the silent whisper brushed her ear, she knew where it came from. He deserved to know. He needed to know. "I wanted to," she said again, "and Blue told me not to give in."

His gaze shot to hers. "You saw him, too?"

"Yes. Did you?"

He laughed softly. "Yeah. I did. I thought maybe *I* was crazy."

"You're not." She couldn't resist the urge to lean up and kiss him. A brief kiss. A chaste kiss. One that wouldn't hurt him or strain his wounds or . . .

He captured her with his healthy arm and dragged her onto the bed beside him. He let out a moan when he brushed her up against his thigh, but she scooted away and leaned up on one elbow so she could see his face. "I don't want to hurt you, Heath."

"You won't."

"How can you say that? You've been running a fever for days, and you looked like you wanted to die just now when I touched you."

He grinned weakly, but his expression quickly grew solemn. "The only thing you could do to hurt me is to leave me. Promise me you won't ever do that."

"I won't ever do that."

His grin gained a little strength. "Say you'll marry me."

"I was beginning to wonder when you were going to make an honest woman out of me."

"*Me?* You're the one who said you'd never marry. You made that quite clear the night we met."

"I believe *you're* the one who said you didn't see eye-to-eye with marriage."

"Did I? Are you sure?"

"Positive."

"Well, then, it was a slip of the tongue." He fell back again and tried to look weak, but she could see the laughter in his eyes. "I'm a wounded man, Courtney. You can't be cruel to a wounded man."

"I would never do that."

"Then say you'll marry me and spend the rest of your life with me."

She leaned up and kissed him lightly. "I will marry you, Heath Sullivan. And I will spend the rest of my life with you."

He smiled contentedly, rested a hand on his chest, and looked up at the ceiling. "I wonder what the future will bring."

Courtney grinned and snuggled up against his uninjured shoulder. "Only time will tell, my love. Only time will tell."

Sherry Lewis is a much-lauded and bestselling romance author. She was a *Romantic Times* Award finalist.